To Kill A Common Loon

A Novel by
Mitch Luckett

Media Weavers, *L.L.C.*

First Edition

Published by
Media Weavers, L.L.C.
P.O. Box 86190
Portland, OR 97286-0190

Designed by Donnelleigh S. Mounce, Graphic Design Studio, LLC

Printed in the United States of America

Luckett, Mitch
    To Kill A Common Loon / by Mitch Luckett
    ISBN 0-9647212-4-4
    1. Title   2. Fiction   3. Northwest   4. Mystery

Special thanks goes to Eric Witchey. Had he not headed me off at the pass at an important juncture of my life, I never would have written this book.

Special thanks also to Jim Frey, friend and writing coach. He taught me how to write a "damn good novel."

Acknowledgments

I thank Marlene Howard for her understanding, encouragement and faith in me. I thank Spud Howard for his good eye and kind heart.

Thanks go to members of my long-standing writer's group: Sue Bronson, Bonnie Graham, Linda Lesley, Martha Miller, and Rae Richen. They kept me honest.

Thanks to Jennifer McCord and Judith Massee for the time, energy and intelligence they contributed to LOON.

My thanks go to the Suquamish Tribal Center and Museum, the Jamestown S'Klallam Tribal Center and the Skokomish Tribal Center for affording me the opportunity to walk upon tribal ground, talk to tribal members, study the exhibits and peruse reference materials.

To the staff and volunteers of the Audubon Society of Portland I have been privileged to work with the past decade, thank you for tolerating my chatter, nurturing my talent and forgiving my ignorance.

Thanks to Elizabeth Rose Cauley for believing in me in the beginning, Geri Doran for inspiring much needed explosive energy in the last rewrite, and Phyllis Loper for her abiding tolerance of me during the whole process.

From "Song of Hiawatha:"

From the red deer's flesh Nokomis
Made a banquet to his honor.
All the village came and feasted,
All the guests praised Hiawatha,
Called him Strong-Heart, Soan-ge-taha!
Called him Loon-Heart, Mahn-go-taysee!

Henry Wadsworth Longfellow

My playful guide led me through an underwater snarl of tree roots in the river logjam. I had no trouble keeping up until I came upon some long strands of kelp-like stuff. A faint pink color seeped from the black kelp. My tongue tasted a sweet sanguine saltiness, drifting with the current. A danger signal went off in my brain.

But it was too late. I got hung up in the stuff. That black kelp clung to me like magnetic tape. Insistent, thick, cloying stuff hanging down about three feet, sighing and sashaying in the vigorous current. The kelp was anchored fast in a tangle of olive-green vine maple branches above my head. My ears heard a noise like water whispering secrets. My animal instincts suddenly recoiled. Warning. I needed air anyway, and about bolted to the surface. But I couldn't suppress a certain curiosity.

Parting the dark, strand-matted path in front of me, I ran smack into a blue-brown, naked nose.

I reared back, but not before I beheld the face of an Indian woman, with a pair of stunned, onyx eyes. Those eyes, in the aqueous turbulence, cried buckets of tears. The pink liquid seeped out of a jagged round hole above her right breast. A bullet exit wound. Back shot. My heart fell to the bottom of my malformed feet. I gagged. The long strands of turbid hair closed around me like live octopus tentacles; whispering, squeezing, imploring. A voice spoke in my mind, "Old one, find my killer. Avenge my death."

1

Good Times and Breakdowns

"Faded Love," is a country-bluegrass tune with a soulful melody, and I knew it by heart. I'd played a crowd-clapping rendition a thousand times before on banjo or blues harmonica. I slipped an "A" harmonica into a steel-framed holder and carefully strapped the holder over my scalp scar tissue and bony shoulders. "So," I said to Medusa, my dog riding shotgun, "Dr. Rothenberg thinks he's a music critic. Well I'll show him. I'm gonna coax a decent tune out of this little rascal this morning or die trying."

Medusa, a Tibetan terrier/pit bull mix, coughed a rank, meat-flavored alarm in my direction.

At midnight, I'd left Portland, Oregon, heading north on Interstate 5. Near Tumwater, Washington I turned left and followed the signs for Port Townsend. I was still in that gray zone between dark and dawn traveling on twisty Highway 101, skirting Puget Sound, an inland sea, on the eastern rim of Washington State's Olympic Peninsula. My headlight beams illuminated several fireworks stands as I passed through the Skokomish Indian Reservation. According to hand-scrawled signs attached to the plywood stands, I could get rockets from ILL EAGLE, M-100s from CUTTHROAT and bombs from MADDOG. I speeded up.

Dr. Rothenberg, a Veteran's Administration Psychiatrist, claimed playing harmonica while careening down the road is a reckless and dangerous attitude. "Picking and driving doesn't mix," he said.

What did he know about attitude? I'd been playing music while driving the highway since I ran away from home at age sixteen. It's simple. If I hadn't played music while driving down the road I wouldn't have played much. It's the way I learned. It's the way I lived.

Just middle-of-the-road tunes, though, nothing on the cutting edge. Waltzes like "All The Good Times Are Past And Gone," cause you to lurch down the freeway at fifteen miles-per-hour in three-quarter time. Kick-ass tunes such as "Foggy Mountain Breakdown" vibrated my old, blue VW Bus down the freeway at warp speed threatening to sail asunder any second. Semi-trucks and passenger cars tend to screech their brakes and blare their horns at you, breaking your all-important rhythmic concentration.

Motorists can be so insensitive.

"Faded Love," was a perfect thirty-five miles-per-hour tune for coastal Highway 101. Unfortunately "Faded Love" does have some devilish sharps and flats in it, suggestive of long-legged shore birds chasing willy-nilly the outgoing tide. You been to the sea shore, you've seen them in the sand weaving this way and that.

That spring afternoon I'd received a package from my deceased friend's lawyer. The package revealed an oyster-colored plastic box containing Josh Whittier's ashes, a sealed legal letter and a map to Josh's wilderness property on the Dosanomish River, the final destination for his remains.

The map was in Josh's delicate, ailing hand. I shoved the legal letter in the glove compartment still sealed. Why open it? While still in control of his faculties, Josh told me he'd left me part interest in the forty acres drawn on the map. His ex-wife, from their divorce settlement, owned fifty percent of it, and he split his fifty percent between me and someone else. He didn't say who the other inheritor was and I didn't ask. Josh said that between the two of us, and his ex-wife, we'd have to come to terms on how to split it up. Or, maybe become joint tenants.

Fat chance of that. I wasn't splitting anything with anybody. Or sharing for that matter. What a concept. I'd been a loner all my life. It's how I survived. What did I care about the other owners or about a piece of unimproved forestland in the middle of nowhere? Get in and get out quick. Get some quick cash from a settlement and get a fresh start on my post-traumatized life in another big city. Downtown Seattle had a certain grimy neon allure.

I'd met Josh in the VA outpatient clinic, him with an inoperable brain tumor, me with a severe head injury. We made a deathbed compact: He would give me a roof over my head if I would take care of him as he lay dying. Hey, it was an offer I couldn't refuse. Medusa and I had been living on the mean streets. During the last three months of his life, when he was coherent, Josh spoke of his wilderness property on the Olympic Peninsula in glowing terms. Called it one of the last wild places. In return for a third interest in the property he asked only that I camp out a few days on it. He was a very sick man and I didn't want to hurt his feelings, so I said yes. I intended to do it too. Maybe spend as much as a week far from the madding crowd. Listen to the river, feed the birds, look at the stars, relax, and ponder my new beginning in the big city with the money I'd get from selling my interest in the wilderness. Wilderness? Who needs it? But of course I'd spread Josh's ashes on this Spirit Knoll he'd marked in red on the map. I owed him that much. I was determined to honor Josh's wish for his remains, come hell or high water.

In the course of the next few days, I experienced both.

With hands on the wheel and eyes glued to the unfamiliar rushing road ahead, I blew and I sucked on "Faded Love" 'til my eyeballs hurt, but could coax out only a dissonant noise that squealed like a snared, wounded animal. Medusa buried her snout under her pillow and moaned. Josh's pet rabbit, Merle, a spoiled flop-eared semi-dwarf, thrown into a makeshift cardboard cage for the trip, commenced bleating and thumping.

I knew "Faded Love" by heart. But, since the wrecking bar incident that concussed my cranium, what my heart knew by heart, my head had struck dead.

I had lost the universal beat. I couldn't carry a tune in a paper hat.

2

The Dragon and the Dog

"That wrecking bar scrambled your right and left brains," Dr. Rothenberg told me. "You may never play music with any expertise again." He was a stubby, unnaturally pale man, with white hair and eyebrows, as if he'd been left under black plastic too long. He spoke with a non-aerated, operatic accent. "Get over it," he said. "That's not the worst of your problems. You must stay calm under all circumstances and you must take your medication. If you don't, your world will fall into chaos and torment. You will descend into madness and fantasy. Voices will speak to you. Apparitions will appear."

I had dumped my medication in a trash barrel at a rest stop. Hadn't taken the zombiefying stuff for days anyway. And I was doing just fine, I was. Just fine.

I almost missed the turn-off onto the Dosanomish River Road. I had no sooner turned, when I glanced over the harmonica mask mounted on my face and beheld, in the shadowy light, a menacing gray shape with an upright twitching tail plugging the middle of the river road.

It was too late for any semblance of control; my blue bus swerved, plunging me headlong through a coarse tangle of barbed blackberry canes, down a sharp embankment into the glacially-fed waters of Josh's beloved Dosanomish River.

The impact jolted me into reconsidering the wisdom of seeking to change my vagabond life. But a sinking bus in a sucking bog is no place for any in-depth reverie. I'd made it to the entrance of the Dosanomish River Valley, but far from experiencing the rapture of a new beginning and a release from old haunts, I stared liquid oblivion in the face. Different liquid than the booze bottle I'd climbed out of back in Portland after getting my head bludgeoned; same, I suspected, oblivion.

My blue bus tipped at a forty five degree angle, not in the main channel of the river itself, but in a low-tide mud flat, mired up to its front axle. The impact splash covered my forearm, hanging out the window, with sticky muck, filling my hyperventilating nostrils with the sour smell of dead fish and rotting vegetation. My mouth and rattled teeth had somehow survived demolition from the metal harmonica holder, and I pushed up from the duct tape-covered steering wheel with both arms. Madrone trees, slick orange trunks and thick masses of dark green leaves, hovered above and to the right of me, swaying like out of synch jazz dancers. My chest felt like it had been slammed square with a stout fiddle. Bruised ribs squeezed my lungs, and numbed legs vibrated as if they'd never waltz around the dance floor again.

My blue bus sank a foot more in black ooze. Black ooze surrounded by brown water. Since the age of seven, I had an unnatural fear and loathing of deep water. My Pentecostal Preacher step-dad, confusing hydrology with theology, tossed me into a muddy pool on the Mississippi River, with the old, "if God loves you, you'll swim, if not, you'll sink." God hated me. I sank like a wet brick. I knew I was a goner. Came to rest right on top of a sharp-whiskered, two hundred-pound mud catfish, who, probably terrified as I was, hurled me to the surface. Nearly gave my step-dad a heart attack, Satan interfering with God's work. That mud cat saved my life. Nevertheless, I have since been afraid of water, scornful of fish, and haven't cared a whole lot for Pentecostal Preachers either.

While better than crashing into the river itself, I also knew that tideland mud had pockets of quicksand-like consistency. I had minutes to escape and something had jammed up against my seat belt release latch.

My VW bus was stuffed to the teeth with the detritus of a squandered past recently gotten out of hoc with all but my last twenty dollars. Some of which: banjo case, pool cue, Josh's fiddle, and the box containing Josh's ashes, had ricocheted off my shoulders and head and tumbled to the floorboards.

The sticky mud on my forearm felt like a bad birthmark. My head spasmed. My poor injured noggin sure didn't need any more pounding. I felt a blackout, or worse, a hallucination coming on. I fumbled for my zombie pills in the ashtray, oh no; I'd thrown them out at the last rest stop. I clasped both hands around my head, harmonica holder and all, and squeezed. Crush out those accusing tongues and tormenting images. But it was too late; and I wasn't lucky enough to black out.

Medusa barked in my ear and brought me back to the sinking bog. My apricot-colored dog lunged with all her forty pounds into siege mentality at imaginary haunts. She didn't know what I was conjuring, but whatever it was she was ready to do battle with it. With incisors the size of raptor beaks, she began thunderous, staccato-clacking warning signals on the passenger window, emitting chesty growls in syncopated rhythm, a kind of reggae beat, primitive and loud.

My left hand was coated in mud, head slathered in sweat.

Loosed from his cardboard cage by the crash, Merle boomeranged around the bus, floppy ears sounding like cap pistols, colliding with me and Medusa, making the most pitiful bleats of helplessness known in the existing universe, other than my recent attempts at "Faded Love." Merle projected a tangy smell of fear; the low-on-the-food-chain fear of hunted, trapped prey.

My blood pressure surged. The top of my head buzzed and sizzled like locust hordes flung out of seventeen years of hibernation. I touched the extensive scar tissue around the acrylic plate in my head. Out of the corner of my eye, a black-and-white common loon took awkward flight with a quick disbelieving glare and a fare-thee-well yodel over its satiny shoulder. For a dazed moment, I watched the loon fly doggedly toward the headwaters of the Dosanomish and an uncertain future; its red eye fixing me until it went around a bend in the river.

I struggled to free the seat belt latch and noticed with horror that the black, tide-flat ooze directly in front of my mired bus, was agitating and frothing. Then, like an exploding cyst, a stinking butt-ugly, tavern-green dragon burst forth. Elpenor! I blinked and blinked again. Shit! My calves turned to worm castings and the roots of my hair dissolved. The locust buzz in my head increased by one hundred decibels and began pulsating like a bottomland, Ozark tornado.

"Elpenor! How the hell did you get here?" I said. Notwithstanding a radically different shape than when he appeared to me on my last booze binge back in Portland — as a Seventh Day Adventist with the mocking head of a hyena — it was ol' Elpenor all right. I knew him well. Elpenor was a much too personal, nasty vision. And in Josh's beloved river too.

Monster frolicking in baptismal foam.

Elpenor's booming voice rattled the loose fitting hatch door of the van. "Go back, Harp P. Gravey, this place will destroy you."

My jaws loosened, I knew him well but I still screamed and cringed as I always do at any first new sighting.

Medusa quit gnashing the window and jumped in my lap. My dog's genetic makeup was a paradoxical union, creating, on the one hand, a timid little Tibetan house dog whose sole purpose was to bring merriment and good luck to her master, and, on the other hand, a giant-jawed meat-eater able to crush mastodon bones. Medusa shuddered and, in true passive/aggressive form, as was her confused genetic nature, licked my face around the harmonica holder and simultaneously pissed in my crotch. It gave my seat a hot bath, floated a fine effusive scent of urine to my nostrils, and made my eyes sting and water.

So far as I knew, Medusa couldn't see Elpenor. She could however, smell my sweat and sense my terror. And my terror, triggered by my private demon, was the only thing that scared hell out of Medusa.

Up to my running boards in muck, I found my voice. "Stay away from me," I said. The dragon Elpenor bobbed with the incoming tidal ripples, florid froth hissed around him. Elpenor spoke through big yellow teeth and rubbery lips. "This pastoral place is not what it seems. Here there be dragons. It's unsafe. Dangerous. It will drown you."

His voice, in the low-bass register, snuck up on me and jellied the juices in my glands.

Bracing myself up with one hand on the steering wheel, I hugged Medusa with the other, who, since pissing, quit quaking and looked up at me for guidance, her tepid meat-flavored breath mingling with rank, slough stink. My lap felt warm and sticky. I took a deep breath of the noxious mixture and bellowed back at Elpenor: "I'd rather drown in the Dosanomish than choke to death in a drunken stupor on Third and Burnside in Portland."

"Watch out what you wish for, ol' son," Elpenor said, "it just may come true."

A jet of black ooze squirted up through a gap beside the VW clutch, bathing my ankle with cold mud. The mud on my ankle sent a message to the mud on my arm that made my whole body shiver. I fumbled for the handle and rolled the window up.

"I'm trying to change my life," I said. "You still show up to sabotage me!" It's hard, once initiated, to get out of the blame game. A loser's contest I'd become most adept at winning.

Elpenor, I learned while my head was still in the bottle, was what the VA Shrink called a paranoid delusional manifestation made possible by head trauma. Sitting there, nose-dived in the Dosanomish, I saw him in the shape of a dragon very similar to the one planted in my head from stories told to me by my great grandfather Two-Loons. Grandfather Two-Loons would've called Elpenor a "shape-changing shithead." Grandfather Two-Loons would've concocted a healing poultice for my head wound and driven away Elpenor with ritual dance. Rhythm was the only character trait I was aware I inherited from Grandfather Two-Loons and I didn't have rhythm anymore.

Elpenor's torch-red eyes, deep and dark as the pit of a gold mine, bored into my flesh, stripping away all false bravado and flaying open my soul.

Pointy, grotesque vampirish ears flapped to the blue beat of some unholy boogie. His thick, brackish hide looked to be an unhappy marriage between a diamond-back rattler and an over-heated radiator. A huge honker nose with raveny black-haired nostrils snorted and oinked.

Seeping in through greasy orange rust holes in the floorboard of my van; Elpenor's hot breath, blown my way by a down river gust of wind, smelled like ether, old ravioli cans and stale hangovers; the stench of a low-bottom alkie. I quickly got used to his familiar smell and his new shape incarnation. It's his acidic sewer mouth that, like always, got to me.

"You think this pristine valley," he said, "this back to nature crap, this baptismal water bullshit, this last wild place, piece of wilderness land that Josh stuck you with is going to make one iota of difference? You can't escape. You could go to the top of Mount Olympus, and I would be there waiting with a bottle of Ol' Crow, a basket of resentments, a bucket of excuses, and a one way ticket to a short happy life back to the Third and Burnside bowery of Portland. That's the level of success you've been groomed for since early childhood, Podna. Hell, it's your legitimate birthright. Why keep fighting it? You deserve to be a homeless bum."

I hated Elpenor. I hated his insinuations. I hated his scaly skin and pink nose.

The hate welled up and exploded across my tongue in a rippling scream. Clasping the steering wheel for ballast, I put everything I had behind the hate, months and years of fear and frustration. It tore my throat, fluttered my salt 'n' pepper, wild hair and resonated throughout the bus and valley beyond. Merle jumped out of his hiding place. Medusa whined, buried her nose in my neck. The "A" harmonica, still clamped close to my mouth, wailed in dissonant sympathy. The acrylic plate in my head vibrated like an untuned harpsichord.

Elpenor snorted steam out his nostrils. Sulfuric foam bubbled around his midsection, causing redwing blackbirds nesting in nearby cattails to check their young.

"There, there, Harp ol' Podna," he said, "You need a drink. Help you deal with all this frustration you brought on yourself."

My bus, with a soft sigh, sank in the mud a few more inches. I, Harp P. Gravey, was going not with a loud bang but with a soft slurp.

I had to escape. My fingers once again struggled with the seat belt.

Just as the clasp let go, the bus lurched backwards. My head bounced, paddleball-like, off the steering wheel. Thank the Lord for duct tape padding. Even so, I blacked out for an instant. Saw my great grandfather Two Loons telling me Ozark stories about animals that turned into humans. Or, about humans that turned into animals. One story was about Grandpa Two Loons turning into a blue jay when he was a young man. He spent a whole summer as a blue jay, raiding corncribs, imitating hawk calls, mating with a female blue jay. He told the story with a straight face, like it really happened.

"I had to become a bird," Grandpa Two Loons told me, "in order to become a man." Grandpa Two Loons mating with a blue jay? Cracked me up. Even so, it was my favorite fantasy.

I regained semi-consciousness and saw scenery going by backwards. Huh? My VW bus, always dependable in spite of years of abuse and neglect, was, without benefit of gears and guidance, backing out of a watery grave. My ears heard a Detroit engine over-revving. My eyes saw, in the rearview mirror, a rigid silver chain leading away from my blue bus to disappear into the morning fog.

I vowed at that miraculous moment to write the clever Huns a letter extolling this, heretofore unknown, fail-safe feature of their wondrous machine. I allowed myself a twinge of momentary romantic regret that I wasn't going to give up this mortal coil and float away to El Dorado in a banjo-shaped coffin, a bluegrass band hanging on my hearse wagon.

Elpenor slipped under water with a sour scowl and a warning hoot. "Here there be dragons," he said again. "Turn around. You are damned if you go further."

Medusa growled deep in her chest. Smacked the front windshield with her teeth.

Elpenor left no sign but the bad taste in my mouth and a vitreous smear on the mudflat.

What was I going to have to do to get rid of him? The curse of course, I suspected, was that once you have seen the dragon, the dragon will dog you forever.

3

The Princess and the Duck Turd

The backing bus settled, with a loud clank of metal on metal, on almost level ground. I could see up the river valley. There was a thin crown of orange clouds haloing the snow-covered western mountains, catching the first blinding, spring-morning sun. The nearest mountain had a bad case of clear-cut mange. Huge buff patches of trees had been scalped out of the fabric of the forest, giving the impression the mountain was disturbed and angry. Behind the thin elliptical clouds lurked a dense throng of ripe, plum-colored thunderheads biding their time.

That curious common loon, the one that had given me such a red-eyed look, was flying happy to his home up there with nary a worry in the world. Flying. Oh, my self-pitying mind careened, to be out of this mess and soaring above the clouds in his carefree shoes.

Medusa dashed to the back of the bus and began pounding the hatch door with her reggae voice and teeth. Merle, warm and furry, had lodged himself underneath the back of my twenty five cent sweatshirt I bought at a church rummage sale because it reminded me of my great grand-father Two-Loons.

The lop-eared bunny, in his instinctive frenzy to hide from carnivo-rous calamity by burrowing deeper, gouged little pain-stabbing tear trenches in my skin. Rabbit claws don't slice neat and clean like a cat, they tear, like tiny barbed fishhooks, the tiniest tear taking months to heal and leaving a vermilion scar. I couldn't begin to reach around behind me in the bus, so I flung open the door and did a blind leap out into the shifting fog. Gravity slammed the door shut behind me.

My left foot hit a sinkhole, and I did a header into the tide-flat mud. Soft, sulfuric-smelling sludge absorbed some of the impact but still jammed the harmonica holder against my face and jarred my beleaguered noggin. I had instinct enough to close my eyes, but as usual my mouth was open when it should have been shut. I squirmed up to my knees, spitting shore bird offal and curdled mosquito mishmash. In my nostrils lodged a salamander-sized shard of booger-brown sea kelp, cold, slippery and reeking of fermented skunk cabbage.

I wrestled the steel-and-mud, harmonica mask from my head and slung it down. Then I extracted sea sauerkraut from my nose and, with a surprisingly unmuddied right sweatshirt sleeve, swiped away the sludge from my face.

My eyes cleared. Movement caught them. And there, floating on a dais of silver crystalline scallops through the aquamarine mist came an enchanted water-spirit Indian Princess. Was this another induced vision?

The mud-caked harmonica and holder had landed at her Adidas-enshrined feet. I was entranced. Couldn't budge, the hump of the hiding hare Merle, on my back forgotten. The princess hovered a few feet in front of me and gazed down with mournful eyes. Those transfixing orbs were framed by the high cheekbones of the Northwest Coastal Indians angling down to a narrow, nibbleable chin. The Indian Princess had a full ruby, Cupid's bow mouth with a slightly pouting lower lip and a perfect Anglo-Saxon nose. She had on a green cap with the words Wildlife Care Center, inscribed in yellow letters. I marveled at the detail my mind conjured. Whoever heard of a care center for wildlife?

Heavy gold-plated earrings, in the classic twisted pose of a leaping salmon, pierced ears too ripe and juicy for such a small sprite. For, in stature, small she was, no more than a hundred pounds and five feet tall. A soft leather medicine bag hung between modest breasts under a red plaid, work shirt. Worn denim jeans fit snugly around round mature hips.

Her skin was the rich golden color of wild salmonberry honey and as clear and smooth as untouched fairy-bell blossoms.

A breeze, moist and cool, blowing in off Puget Sound, teased the goddess's long, bluish-black hair, and made it shimmer like the feathers of a Stellar's jay in flight. She smelled of peat moss, salt water and . . . fiddle rosin? . . . the natural ingredients, I surmised, that shape water nymphs.

I knelt, as if in peasant prayer, at the toes of her royal tennis shoes. She was my first up close encounter with either a real or imaginary stranger in a strange land, and I wanted to make a smart initial impression. I involuntarily hacked a regurgitated duck turd at her feet. It left my tongue and mouth, oddly enough, with a sweet river aftertaste.

The princess regally ignored the sacrilege. She nudged the harmonica mask with a cautious foot. "It is either an ill-formed present day Adam," she said, "expelled from the garden for having the worst case of braces I've ever seen in my life, or the hunchback of Notre Dame come to wreak havoc on our humble valley."

The enchantress's words caressed me, washing over my shivering body, further expunging the mud. Her voice clued me that she was flesh and blood. It was too soon to celebrate, but maybe hallucinations were behind me and I was on a reality streak. Every bit of newly exposed skin felt a tremor of irresistible attraction to the woman, aching to be close to her, brush up against her. A wildness deep inside me formed a plan to somehow get to touch her, and by so doing establish a bond between us.

As I scoured my mind for a reasonable explanation of my predicament, an earthy voice in the mist sounded. "You can mock me all you want, Daughter." An Indian man, much older, emerged from the shifting mist behind the princess. "All I said," he said, "was I felt a pop in the dimensional fabric, as if there's been some kind of cosmic cross-over between universes, and then I heard this anguished scream coming from this cursed Dosanomish River."

His flat voice triggered a spark of long-dormant familiarity. I struggled, with light-headed effort, to rise. "Grandpa Two-Loons?" I said.

The old Indian paled. "What's that about loons?"

"No. . . . No. Sorry to alarm y'all," I said. "My name is Harp P. Gravey and I was having an adrenaline hallucination brought on by a head injury and not taking my medication. I saw a monster in the river."

"This damned Dosanomish," he said, "revealed the river demon, *Kaalpekci*, to you?"

I surprised myself. Besides Josh and the pale VA shrink, I had never told anyone else about my draconian companion and have no explanation for the confession except cranial driftiness. "Elpenor to me," I said. "But by any other name he still smells the same." Attempts at levity on your knees in a mud bog don't wash. The old Indian's cracked lips didn't crack a smile. I stood up.

He turned to squint at the nearby forest. Catching his silhouette against the islands in Puget Sound, I noticed something hanging from his nose, a gold ring the size of a quarter attached to the middle cartilage. It added a slight edge to his big-toothed frown. The ring danced a jig when he spoke, skewing his upper lip. Being nearly the same tarnished bronze color as his skin, it could've been mistaken for what we used to call back in the Ozark Mountains, as a harelip.

The old man was about my size, a little below medium height, with a two-foot ponytail and thick, narrow ears, a coarser color than his skin. He smelled of linseed oil and cedar shavings.

Hard not to stare at a middle-aged, ringed-nosed man, Native American or not.

4

Bag balm and Wet Chickens

The princess stared at the pulsing hump on my back. "I'm April Old Wolf," she said, "and that rambling old man there is my father, Malcomb. Stay still Quasimodo, you're evidently in shock. I'll see what I can do about that unsightly growth on your back. And don't encourage my father." April glided, in white tennies, around behind me. I nearly pitched forward as I felt no-nonsense fingertips rasp up my spine. My sweatshirt flew up, and April, the goddess, lifted a trembling weight from my back. "Well look what we have here," she said. "The hump turned into a beast of the forest. I'm not even going to ask how this rabbit got here. Since rabbits are one of your totems, Father, I suppose you're going to make something mystical out of it." She tossed Merle at Malcomb.

Her father snagged the bunny behind the neck with one hardened, bronze hand, held him up for inspection, nuzzled his belly with his ample nose and stuck him in a side pocket of his buckskin jacket. "Not mystical, Daughter," Malcomb said, "practical. Rabbits have strong hind legs, the better to escape hungry predators. Finding a rabbit in the beginning portends a swift journey."

"Journey?" April said. "Whose journey? What journey? I have to be at the wildlife clinic for the morning feeding in two hours. If I'm not back, injured animals will die. You promised I'd be back in time. Just because some nitwit verifies that there's an ancient demon with a blood grudge against our clan — such as it is — dwelling in the Dosanomish,

doesn't mean we're going to get sidetracked on one of your mythical jour-
neys this morning."

Nitwit? Safe to say I hadn't bowled April Old Wolf over with clev-
erness. "Certainly not my journey," I said, "I don't have to hunt for my
demon. He finds me."

Malcomb tickled Merle behind his flop ears. "Well somebody's going
on a journey today," Malcomb said. "This rabbit was put here for a reason. Omens don't lie."

April took a deep breath. "Okay Father," she said, "you have to have
a journey. I'll give you a journey. You were right in the first place. Let's
just say we're on a very practical journey. You could say our search for
Molly Jenkins — the slut — is a journey. By the time we get Harp P.
Gravey here taken care of it'll be time for me to get back to the clinic.
You'll have to continue searching for Molly Jenkins by yourself."

Malcomb tugged on his nose ring. "You do yourself and Molly a dis-
service by calling her a slut," he said. "She's merely searching for love
the best way she knows how." Merle peeked out at me and showed his
buckteeth. My interest perked. Being on the road most of my life I would've
had very little love and companionship were it not for so called loose
women. Some of my best friends have been sluts. "Molly Jenkins," I said,
"who is Molly Jenkins?"

April produced a small, green can from a fanny pouch around her waist.
The label read, Bag Balm Salve. April sniffed the outside of the Bag
Balm can. Wrinkled her nose over the lid at Malcomb. "Last night," she
said, "my father had an urgent dream about Molly Jenkins, a long time
acquaintance, and my brother's some time girl friend, being in trouble.
He wakes me up two in the morning to go look for her. Living with an
old, self-proclaimed shaman who has a very active dream life is about
as much fun as smacking yourself in the head with a wet chicken to wake
up every morning."

"I've never tried that," I said, "but I have set the radio alarm to a right-
wing talk show — "

" — It's not like that bitch Molly," she said, "hasn't run off with some hot-guitar-picking sleazo dozens of times before." April stabbed my shoulder with a finger, expecting agreement, I suppose, on the general dissipation of hot guitar pickers, which, if she'd waited for a reply, I would've provided. Never met one that didn't have the morals of an alley cat.

Finger jab or not, my body responded to her touch. My shoulder burned like a bullet had penetrated it. The wildness in my gut turned acid into honey.

"This time is different," Malcomb said, "I know you don't want to hear it, but I feel something absent from Molly's spirit energy. And don't call her a bitch."

"The only spirit energy Molly's missing," April said, "is a conscience." She ripped the lid off the little green Bag Balm tin with an angry pop. "Take off that muddy rag, Mr. Harp P. Gravey. "

A whiff of the exhilarating odor of camphor cleared my mind. I obeyed April.

How could I not?

Malcomb held out his hand and took the soiled shirt.

Suddenly, the highway noise came closer. A motorcycle and rider had veered off the main road and followed my VW bus path through blackberry canes. It came to a halt beside April and Malcomb's old Ford pickup. The motorcycle's muffler blat, blat, blattered so loud it drowned out the flooding river. The bike was a beaut, one of those fifties Harleys. All spit and polished chrome and a Mediterranean blue paint job. The rider was dressed in leathers and wore no helmet. His thick, black hair bounced on tensed shoulders. One of his eyelids drooped and the other eye gleamed like a hot brand on brown flesh. He turned off the engine, gleamed at April. "What the hell you all wasting time here for?" he said. "You're supposed to be looking for Molly."

April's back stiffened. "Being an authority Loren," she said, "you would know about wasting time. We haven't abandoned our search for your precious Molly. We had to stop and pull Mr. Harp P. Gravey here out of the river."

The biker's mismatched eyes faced me. "You got no business rescuing white meat when your own blood is in trouble."

April put an arm around me. Hip bumped my hip. "I'll rescue," she said, "who the hell I want."

Malcomb, my sweatshirt in hand, sloshed over to the biker, put the other soiled hand on his shoulder. "You shouldn't talk to your sister —"

" — Half-sister," Loren said. "Don't you remember Pop, her mother's that anthro bitch you fucked from Delaware." He twisted away from Malcomb's grip.

"And he's never lets me forget my mother was a white anthropologist," April said. "Especially when he needs money for a bottle."

"If my mother had set me up with a Veterinarian Clinic," Loren said, "I sure as hell wouldn't piss it away on treating wild animals and I probably wouldn't need to drink either."

Malcomb's big hand hung in the air. He held it up. "Stop your bickering you two. We've got work to do. We'll continue searching for Molly, Loren, but in the meantime we're going to pull Mr. Gravey up onto the road. And you watch your manners, Loren. I suspect he's not entirely white. He has some native blood in him too. Certainly not as thick as you, but then who is?"

Loren nodded at me. "Yeah, you may be right," he said. "Another thin mixed blood on the Peninsula. No wonder my sister has got the hots for you."

April shied away from me like a robin from a raven. "I only just met this man," she said. "I definitely do not find him the least bit attractive. Look at him. Under that coat of mud he looks white to me. He's better off being all white or red. Hybrids have the worst of both worlds."

I figured I'd better clear the air. "I only knew my great grandfather Two-Loons as a child — "

Loren kick-started the Harley. He revved it so loud it made my ears ring. Instead of turning the big machine around he raced at me, ignoring tidal mud gunking-up his clean machine. I stood my ground more out of surprise than courage. The front wheel of the bike came to a stop between my legs, blue fender nudging my crotch. The metal felt hard and unyielding. Up close, I noticed a four-inch fresh scar on Loren's tricep. "Great Grandfather, huh?" he said. "Your blood goes too far back, and, from your accent, you're from some clan down south. You'll never fit in here. Go home. You're distracting us from finding Molly." He blatted the bike's engine. A puff of purple carbon dioxide ejected from the rear of the machine. I smelled hot oil fumes mingling with cool river humus, an antagonistic mix.

I waited 'til the rpm's died down. "If there's a poor white-trash Pentecostal tribe," I said, "then that's where I belong. Way I was raised anyway. And I never asked to fit in here or anywhere else for that matter. Get me up on the road and I'll make like the boll-weevil and search for a home." I sidestepped, to get away from that vibrating fender before the Native American Hell's Angel popped the clutch.

Loren beckoned me closer, leaned over, leathers creaking, and, whiskey-breathed, whispered, "Watch out white-trash," he said, "you break my little sister's heart and I'll break you." The scar on his tricep had little scarlet jagged edges, like toxic centipede feet, where the stitches had been. His bicep was knotted with muscle. Then he turned and shouted to Malcomb. "I'm heading for Seattle. See if Molly's over there."

"No," Malcomb said, "Don't go to Seattle. Molly's not there. I can feel it. You'll just get lost yourself."

"Yeah, right," Loren said. "You can feel it? I'm going to believe that? If you had any of the old powers how come I didn't inherit them? They're gone Pop. Give it up. Maybe they never were there in the first place. Just tired stories, rituals and myths made up to tell around the fire on cold winter nights." He reached a hand up and squeezed his father's hand. He averted his eyes, glanced at a raven landing in a madrone tree. The tips of his mouth quivered. He dropped his father's hand. "I'm going to Seattle. Do some research."

He crawled the Harley in a circle and we watched as he climbed through the blackberry vines, then, up on blacktop he tromped it, spewing a tail of chocolate sludge on the windshield of a large RV, puttering along highway 101 like some great, silver slug.

"Molly's not in Seattle," Malcomb muttered to himself, shaking my shirt. He squinted at the shirt's picture.

"By the gods, is this a pair of loons?" He said. He walked over to a clear pool and threw the shirt in to dunk it, sloshed it around, wrung it out.

"Research my fanny," April said to me in a low voice. "Loren's researching the inside of a whiskey bottle. See what's at the bottom of it, what makes it tick. Research!" She watched, shaking her head, as Loren disappeared around the bend. The soft brown skin on April's neck was peppered with light freckles. "Damn him, when's he going to straighten-up?" She squeezed the Bag Balm can so hard grease oozed over the lip onto her hand.

She wiped the excess off on my back. She didn't just dab the salve on the rabbit rips, she dived right into that little green can with both hands and slathered it all over, sorta kneading the tight muscles as she found them, a natural-born masseuse. I wondered, excitement replacing fear and cold, if there is something intrinsically erotic in Bag Balm? And further, could terror be followed so quickly by arousal? Is there a sensory conduit between fear and sex? And one step still further, love? Love on a mud bog? Could April be the one? The one to nourish my soul? The one to end my loneliness?

Perhaps it was as sensuous to be the slatherer as the slatheree.

April's clever hands, so warm and exploratory, belied her general field-marshal attitude. I have always been susceptible to touch. Touch me with care, caress me with tenderness, stroke me with concern, and I will defy heaven and hell as your champion.

Those fingertips transmitted longing signals to the rest of my lonesome body. Every neglected patch of skin, muscle and bone demanded equal attention from those moist, intimate hands. Erogenous zones I had either forgotten about or given up for lost reared up and began shooting spangled rockets at my brain. The primary message being, "This is the stuff of your eternal quest for love and intimacy. It is what you need most and what you have run away from all your life."

The secondary message, hot on the singed heels of the first, being; "You clod, its been two years since you've gotten laid."

5

Beater Guitars and Embracing Mud

The tension, starting with the synthetic plate and scar tissue in my head, flowed out of my body through my feet to dissipate into the magic river mud. The mud, the Dosanomish River mud began to feel . . . well . . . comfortable. It connected me to April, to the Olympic Mountains, to some quiet place; like an old beater guitar bought at a Goodwill Store, already broken in just to your liking, creates a spiritual link with you and the dead donor. The soft black mud pooled around my feet, links of chain, anchoring me fast to the spot.

An irresistible urge to sing overwhelmed me, something I hadn't felt in the months since beginning medication. Strange words popped into my head. I let 'er rip:

> "Olympic Mountain morning
> the bluffs so vast and steep,
> are memories all of you
> that I can hope to keep.
> And if I had just one wish
> To bless me on this dawning
> It's to share with you everyday
> An Olympic Mountain morning."

April never missed a stroke with the Bag Balm. A light aroma of cherry-scented shampoo circled my head, as she whispered in my ear. "You're straining your voice. Reaching too high. Find a key that fits you. That smaltzy song would sound good in a minor key, say B minor. I kind of like it though. Where did it come from, I never heard it before?"

"I never did either," I said, as offhandedly as manageable. "The oddest things just sorta pop into my head these days."

April's stroke slowed. "First you see monsters," she said. "Now you expect me to believe you made that verse up on the spot. You really are quite balmy, aren't you?"

I let her accusation hang there in the damp air. Urge to sing spent, I ached to curl into a fetal position in the embracing mud and sleep the sleep of the innocent with the exotic April cradled by my side soothing my slumbering brow, placing ambrosial kisses on my exposed neck. Naked as Adam and Eve.

Well, maybe not so innocent.

Even in my state of make-believe bliss, my muscle consciousness sensed a difference between April's two hands. Her fingertips on one hand, the left, oh yes, it was most assuredly the left hand fingertips, were rougher than the other. Dare I dream of lovely grooved calluses?

I couldn't resist. I unstuck my mud-cradled feet, spun around, grabbed her left hand and held it up to my eyes for detailed inspection. It was true, there they were; encrusted calluses and caked, microscopic canals, the stuff of rapture.

April backed up a half step but didn't snatch her tiny, brown hand away.

Only one thing I know of causes that kind of abnormalcy. Instrument strings. Steel or catgut. I'm a slow learner, but since the wrecking bar encounter, I've had flashes of intuition that sometimes hit. It came to me: the calluses, the scent of rosin. "You're a fiddler," I said.

April's free hand tugged on a leaping salmon earring. The salmon cavorted with delight at her touch. "Those calluses," she said, "could come from playing any stringed instrument." She still didn't pull her left hand away.

"They could, but they don't. No, I sense a fiddle here."

"Could be violin. The grooves would be the same."

"But it's not. May I kiss your fingertips?"

"You may kiss my Watus — "

"Please. It's an innocent request. Your calluses are so lovely caked with mud."

April searched my eyes for intimations of lewdness, and, I presume, finding none, said, "Help yourself but don't get greedy." That cinched it. Fiddlers are great at making bold, snap decisions. They are also adept at being adored. Fortunately, I was primed for some serious adoring.

I closed my eyes, drew April's left hand to my lips, and pecked each fingertip individually, lingering but a second, enough to allow the tip of my tongue to subtly tickle the grainy surfaces. The grooves were even, hard and precise. The brand of a perfectionist. My tongue divined she was a practitioner of technique, a master of mechanics. I tasted Bag Balm, and blood, and mud, and sweat and rosin; a simmering erotic stew.

My tongue, I fancied, channeled something else too; the saucy, bittersweet pungency of love deprivation. April, like me, was a long ways away from her last good kiss.

"I play banjo," I said, my eyes closed, sniffing her musky fragrance, listening to her breathing become huskier.

"I know," she said, "You have that banjo look."

Banjo look? What the hell is a banjo look, I wondered? I'd seen hundreds of banjo pickers and they all looked different to me. Physically, I certainly didn't resemble a banjo; long-necked with a large round butt, although I'd seen a few banjo pickers that had bottoms the size of an axe handle. At forty three years old and five foot, seven inches inches, I had always had an underfed, on-the-road, look about me. Since being wounded, I was down to a hundred and fifty pounds, ribs glistening through river mud like ripples on a washboard.

They shaved my head for the operation and I hadn't cut my hair since. It grew back as thick and curly as before, only this time a hint of gray bled through the black.

That banjo look? It came to me, all male five-string banjo pickers look alike in a broad general way; I've never seen a handsome one. Banjo pickers are quirky, odd-shaped, eccentric and interesting, but definitely not good looking. Comely guys play guitar, mandolin or fiddle. They steer clear of banjos. I don't know why I never realized it before.

There's one more thing about banjo pickers I never noticed: They have an incipient melancholy about them, which is ironic since the music they play is considered joyful music. Much like clowns whose makeup hides a troubled psyche, banjo pickers' festive music is a cover for a damaged soul.

Perhaps that's why we take up banjo in the first place.

Okay I got it. April's initial impression of me; ugly and fucked up.

Before she'd ever even heard me play a note. And, in the condition my condition was in, she probably never would. With that thought, this five-string banjo picker got a whole lot sadder, which, in turn, probably gave me more of that banjo look.

April, seeing I was tongue-tied, added, "But hey, I gotta tell you, being a banjo picker is not the only thing wrong with you. For starters, you could work on your entrances."

She tugged her hand away from my lips.

I was reluctant to let go of her warm fingers. My tongue loosened. "You inspire me," I said.

"You're kinda cute," she said, "but you're such a liar and much too needy for me." She took her hand back. "Doesn't take a degree in psychology to recognize a loser when you see one. I've had enough of flaky relationships. Besides you're probably just passing through and I'll never see you again."

Did she say cute? I've never been accused of being cute before. What happened to that banjo look? "Hey give me a break," I said. "I've had a run of bad luck. And I'm not just passing through. I plan to stick around a while."

Well, well, so long Seattle. Where did that come from? April's touch told me tales I hadn't heard in years. Maybe never.

"Don't stick around because of me," she said. "You haven't a chance." Her eyes had an intense glow around them.

"I've inherited some land up the Dosanomish a ways," I said. "I'm going to build a cabin on it." One lie leads to another.

A thickening morning fog closed in behind her, hiding the mountains and upper Dosanomish. She grabbed a handful of her blue-black hair and squeezed it. "Oh great, just what we need, another absentee property owner in the valley who'll be opposed to Native Tribes' fishing treaty rights. Probably want to put a basalt mine on the Dosanomish, too. I'm sorry now we pulled you out of the bog. " She punched my collar with the flat of her right hand. Didn't hurt me physically but jarred something loose in my psyche. She sniffed the handful of hair, her neck arched and she looked away toward Puget Sound.

I tottered. Twenty feet across the swampy water stood a thatch of cattails claimed by a pair of noisy, red-winged blackbirds. Newborn birds chirped, and yellow beaks bobbed skyward in a nest. The main channel of the river was to the south through a thicket of red alders and cottonwoods. The engorged river brought the clean smell of melted snow past the mud flat

A cold breeze blew through the cattails. The sun's rays baked the mud on my legs and pinched my skin. I shook. Chunks rolled off my skin leaving my flesh exposed to the wind. Goose bumps covered my calves.

All hope with April, my princess, gone. Worst thing of all, she was right. I was a loser. I had absolutely nothing to offer a woman of April's caliber. Hell, truth be told, I had nothing to offer a woman, period.

The mud clasping my ankles tugged at the truth. I saw it all clearly: I had been blaming it on my head injury, when, in fact, for years, long before the wrecking-bar incident, since my failed love affair with a sassy bass player named Susan Conroy, I had been on a slow, downward path to wisdom.

It took a passionate encounter with a beautiful woman like April to shatter my disguise. Perhaps the Dosanomish River, pounding in my ears with its rhythm of relentless clarity, guided me to port in a terrible storm. But what to do now? Where to go? I may have been in port but I wanted to sink to the bottom of the sea and drown. Below the revelatory roar of the river, I thought I heard a whisper, *"Enough of this self-pity. You need to get on the road again. The road is your life. The road is your love. The road is your home. You need to get on the road again."*

Elpenor! I recognized Elpenor slinking around the dead booze cells coagulated on my consciousness. Trust him to prey on my weaknesses. "Elpenor," I said out loud, "I know when I'm not wanted. You don't have to tell me."

April's eyes widened. "You're balmy as a Chinook wind in December."

Sometimes, Elpenor is right. It was time to go. Get out of April's disgusted sight. I needed to get my lucky — well maybe not so lucky — sweatshirt back from Malcomb and do whatever it took to get on down the line. Move over Loren. Seattle, here I come. Maybe I could circle back and see April once I got myself together. Give her another chance. Impress her with my success.

No. Knowing my old habits, I knew when I got in the neon glare of Seattle I would never be back. I would be forever lost in a concrete wasteland.

6

Binder Twine and Duct Tape

A big cat screamed. I jumped a foot in the air. My feet popped out of the mud with a stout thwock. I came back down, landing heavy and sinking deeper.

"Jumpy, too," April said. "Take it easy. It's just an immature kitty in the back of our pickup."

Sure enough, the scream came from the red pickup. Malcomb had my sweatshirt draped over the fender of their fifties era, dirty, red Ford pickup truck. Its dented body looked as if it had been through an Ozark hailstorm or a sledgehammer initiation party. Contrasting that, it had a dense, shinny winch with lots of chunky iron teeth bolted to its reinforced, front bumper. A stout silver chain connected it to the back bumper of my beat up bus, which dripped mud and looked sorrier than usual. Would my bus run? Roll me into Seattle today? I was eager to get started, get out of April's contemptuous sight.

Through the cab of the red pickup, between slits in a gun rack holding a short, fat gun case, I spotted, imprisoned in a cage, a pair of maddened, lemon-yellow eyes scouring my bus. They were fixed on Medusa, who I realized had remained uncustomarily quiet for a spell. I now knew why. She had scrambled through the moving debris to the back of the bus to lock eye-horns with the lemon eyes. Medusa's fur bristled. Her bone-crushing teeth bared in a silent growl. Her cat-killing stance. Her target, a caged mountain lion.

Why not? It seemed natural that April — hadn't Loren implied she was a veterinarian — and her father would have a cougar caged in their truck. To show my level of wilderness sophistication I decided not to ask about it. I prayed the cage was secure. I also prayed Medusa didn't push too hard on the hatchback door of my bus. The latch was broken, and I had it tied shut with binder twine.

Thank God for duct tape and binder twine, twin tools of the broke, broken and homeless, holding a life together by a sinew.

Sometimes a twine, for a time, is all it takes. Sometimes it breaks.

Malcomb quit fawning over my sweatshirt. He looked up into the gray sky and down into the deep river and out across the wide sea and back at me. Then he looked again at the front of my sweatshirt. His lips began to move; old man talking to himself.

I lifted my heavy foot with a loud gaack, intending to go over and ask Malcomb to pull my car all the way out of the bog, just as he loped back to us. "Before you two consummate in the mud, I want — "

"Father! What an asinine thing to say, I only just — "

Malcomb ignored her. "Old Iron Loins here hasn't looked at another man since that dingy pedal-steel player went to Nashville. You're the first one she's given the time of day to in two years."

April's face turned a deep copper. Her hands made fists. "In this permissive day and age, most caring fathers would be proud of a daughter that embraced celibacy, but not yo — "

"Oh be quiet Daughter and look at this." Malcomb held up my raggedy sweatshirt for viewing. There wasn't a trace of mud left; and, strangely enough, it looked cleaner than it had ever looked before. Though faded, you could see the two loons shine through.

It was as if I was seeing it for the first time. It was a black and white silk-screen silhouette of two common loons in the foreground, necklaced necks draped together suggesting a lovers embrace. One had soft red eyes filled with mystery and adoration, sharp beak closed, head bowed. The other looked out with an angry blood-engorged eye, stiletto beak poised, neck cocked and head tilted as if bugling a battle cry. One was a lover, the other a warrior. A loon warrior. What a concept.

Fading in, as part of the backdrop, yet overshadowing the loons, hovered a sepulchral face, part human, part bird; part man, part beast; luminous eyes, fierce dagger nose, and a melancholy mouth that looked on the verge of moving, giving utterance. Written underneath the loons in miniature calligraphy were the words, voice of the wilderness.

I'd pulled it out from underneath a pile of fire-damaged hymnal books and bought it for twenty-five cents at the Southeast Portland Saved From Perdition Sulfur Lick Baptist Church rummage sale. "I bought it because it reminded me of my great grandfather Two-Loons."

"Oh no, Father," April said, "I know where this is leading. It's the hat isn't it?"

Malcomb flipped the shirt around to get a better view. "Yes, the image on this sweatshirt is the one I see when I don the sacred hat handed —"

"Mangy pile of dead hair with faded feathers," April said. Her hands clenched into fists, then dropped to hang limp at her side.

"Show some respect child," Malcomb said. "That ceremonial headdress was handed down through many generations —"

" — Of deadbeats and drunks." April finished for him.

"Of storytellers and shamans," Malcomb said. "Your blood, your ancestors which you show no respect for. And yes this —"

"They lost our fucking clan, for Chrissakes!"

Malcomb shook the sweatshirt, splattering me with cold spray. " — is the Two Loons of my recurring dream. I think the loon in my dream is a *Tamánamis* — the ghost of an old one — and is trying to tell us something important about the spirit world and our traditional connection to our home place."

Although only a few feet away, April shouted at me, her warm breath drying my mustache. "Through several generations of alcoholism and government off-site education, our ancestors forgot or misplaced the exact location of our primary sacred ceremonial grounds. Mr. Slipshod Shaman here has been searching for it all his adult life and has got as far as a diseased headdress and this Dosanomish valley. Now, a demented banjo picker shows up with a moth-eaten sweatshirt design of two lovesick loons with some kind of demon face watching over them. Talk about grasping at spiritual straws."

A demented banjo picker? I'd been called worse. But never by anyone with such wondrous fingertips.

"Here," Malcomb handed me the sweatshirt. "Put this back on. I want to try something." He turned and did a surprising sprightly lope back to the red pick-up.

"You're in for it now," April said out of the side of her mouth. "He's going to want you to try on that ridiculous ancient headdress. Claims he sometimes has bursts of revelations when wearing it and keeps trying to find other crazies who do too." She poked me with a callused fingertip. "You qualify."

In spite of my resolve to leave, I thrilled at her rough touch.

Malcomb retrieved something from behind the seat of the pickup. From a distance, it looked like a massive stack of black snakes. Oh great, I thought, we got mountain lions, why not reptiles too?

April leaned close to my ear. "Might as well humor him," she whispered, "we'll get out of here quicker. And don't worry about catching any cooties, I flea-dipped that frowzy, damn thing this morning. Soaked it good."

As Malcomb brought the headpiece nearer, it appeared to be thickly layered coils of lackluster, black human hair, conically fashioned and cleverly topped by two dull black 'n' white feathers stuck in a wooden spindle. The feathers bobbed and swayed rhythmically, making a little metronome click that timed the old Indian's gait. Malcomb shoved it in front of my face. It smelled of must, mold and flea dip.

Malcomb adjusted the feathers to stand straight up. "These two feathers came from the sacred loon. There was a time when loons were as plentiful in this land as The People — our ancestors. The hair is from ancestral medicine shamans of my clan. I would consider it an honor if you would try it on."

I slipped the cold, wet sweatshirt over my head. "I'll try on the hat if you'll pull me back on the highway so's I can get the hell out of here."

"My daughter will be disappointed," Malcomb said, "but I'll agree."

"Your daughter," his daughter said, "is going to feed you, piece by piece, wagging tongue first, to the gulls, when we get home."

Hey, what harm could it do? I would've preferred the long, flowing, colorful, eagle feather headdresses — the kind the plains Indians wore on television — but it didn't fit into my mud ensemble. After all, that fateful morning, I had already been bathed in dog piss and dipped in shore bird shit. I could hardly be judgmental about a mangy headdress. Once dipped in dung, it's difficult to maintain a sincere stance of sterility. Besides, it would only take a second. Then I'm gone, gone, gone, like the old country tune says.

I did, for the old Indian's sake, seek to conjure some majesty for the moment. I bowed my head slightly, perhaps mixing eastern and western cultural metaphors, and stuck out both hands, soiled palms up, to receive the royal crown of dead hair. As Malcomb placed it in my arms, Merle, peeking out of Malcomb's leather coat pocket, laid his ears flat, flexed his buckteeth and bleated an alarm.

Decades of dead hair doesn't weigh much. It was light as a feather — well, two feathers, which, revolving on their spindle, went click, click. Close-up, I imagined I saw little mites crawling in and out of the hairy labyrinth. Though unsanitary and repulsive, it exuded a certain comforting arcane glow and an affable tingle registered on my fingertips. It began to buzz. A syncopated beckoning buzz. A buzz with rhythm. I couldn't stop a song from pouring out of me.

> "Well I'll keep on traveling that lonesome highway,
> searching for that home I've never found,
> make me a pallet in your byway,
> and I'll settle down in Puget Sound."

April's eyes widened. I guess I showed her. Perfect pitch.

Malcomb's big ears wagged. He licked his nose ring. Scratched his butt.

All doubts dissolved and I plunked the hair hat on my head, nestled it down, avoiding the acrylic plate and scar tissue. Damned thing had a near-perfect fit.

I'd made some righteous mistakes in my time to get me to the pitiful level of existence I was in, but that hat, without a doubt, was the biggest mistake I ever made.

The universe shifted an inch to the right.

Time slowed. I saw April's wonderful onyx eyes widen further, like some nocturnal owl caught in a high headlight beam.

I attempted a smile at an attentive, lip-dancing Malcomb.

Then a fire axe whacked me in the general location of my unhealed head wounds. My tongue spasmed. Nose gushed blood over my lips and chin. Mud oozed around my feet, grasped my ankles like leg-irons and lugged me down in the inky clay. I heard an anguished moan — I think it was me — followed by a pop in Malcomb's dimensional fabric of the universe. April reached a Lilliputian hand out for me but I was gone, gone gone. Malcomb's friendly split grin evaporated and I spiraled-up into a thin-aired, splintered reality.

7

The Bald Eagle and The Hairy Encounter

I soared due west toward the high Olympic Mountain, above the swirling storm clouds, the pain in my head gone, serene. Unlike swimming, I'd always secretly dreamed of flying, admiring the fierce grace of prairie falcons, the powerful majesty of red-tailed hawks, the nocturnal acrobatics of great-horned owls. There I was, Harp P. Gravey, sharing the sky with those noble predators, my black and white wing feathers bending — .

Wait! Wait! Wait just a damn minute! Wing? Feathers? Who. . . . What was I?

My mind careened. What dreamlike madness ensnared me? I broke aerial rhythm to arch my ringed neck around and view my avian body.

No doubt about it, I was some kind of awkward bird all right. But . . . oh no! I was no multi-colored noble predator proudly dominating the sky, not even an irresponsibly reprehensible raven exuding dark mystery. I had the clumsy black-and-white checkered body of a damned, defenseless loon — a silly, clownish, insane-sounding common loon.

I cried out in anguish, which, by the time it escaped my newly acquired pointed, black bill, corrupted into the forsaken wilderness laugh of some transformational maniac. It resonated from the mountain peaks, filling the sky with wild, demented wailing, peaking in a high-pitched tremolo yodel. The echo glanced off my feathered cranium, piling ridicule onto scorn.

I thought about a grand gesture of contempt for the folly of blind fate, a suicidal dive bomb to smash my metamorphasized body into the indifferent earth. If it was a dream, I would wake up; if not, go out in an explosion of flattened flesh and matted feathers.

Bad habits transcend species. Even in my dream spirit animal, I maintained a marvelously addictive self-pity. Powerful medicine.

Suddenly, some undefined contraction of creature exhilaration seeped through my besotted anthropomorphic brain.

Oh Mama! Mama! Feel that clean air swoosh through my alabaster and obsidian breast plumage. And look, over there, snow-covered sawtooth mountain peaks poke out of angry red clouds smooched by a lustrous sun as big as Montana. And there, might that be the Space Needle in Seattle on the eastern horizon? Could be perched on the top of it in an hour. What eyes I have. What a schnoz I have. What fun this is. Blessed Felicity has visitated my floundering fledgling soul.

I'm flying! I'm flying! Point me towards Seattle and get out of my way.

All earthbound reservations forgotten, I decided at least to give soaring a try. How could I not? Three thousand feet up in the sky, it's either fly or die.

Even in a vivid dream, which I was sure I was in, how many humans get such an opportunity?

Though timid and awkward, I attempted to exercise flight control. First, I did what any rational human being would do: Take over. Take stock. Stomp on the brakes.

I dropped like a sack of wet rocks. Control be damned. Almost ripped my rib cage apart straining to level out. Struggling for steady flight, I found myself in clouds, turbulent and tortured, flying blind through deafening thunder and exploding yellow lightning flashes, made all the more amplified and eerie because I had no sense of smell whatsoever.

Thinking like a rational human being obviously had limited application in loon life.

Suddenly fearful of heights, I really didn't care to see how far down the ground lay. I flapped upwards, chest constricted, cussing my sloppy uncoordinated wings, out of the opaque cloud cover into the steamy morning sunshine. As if in reward for effort, above me a couple thousand feet, soared one of God's noblest creatures, a mature bald eagle.

What a sight, resplendent in glistening satiny black and white; never been that close to the American national bird in the wild before. Easy to see why the eagle was chosen for greatness over Ben Franklin's ignoble turkey. A dedicated birder, such as my late friend Josh Whittier, would give his eye teeth to view the noble bald eagle soaring up close in the sky, its natural habitat. Too bad I didn't have Josh's binoculars. On second thought, wouldn't have done me much good.

Nothing to keep me from taking a closer look. I began chugging toward the big fellow. Ask his expert advice about this frustrating flying business, possibly make friends, compare notes, find common ground. . . . Hmmm . . . let's see, what could we talk about? If I remembered my birding class notes right, the classes I went to, to humor Josh, the bald eagle is the dominant top-of-the-food-chain predator in the North American skies, and I was. . . .

Hey, what do you know, he was heading toward me and covering the distance between us with the clip of a greased arrow. No doubt he recognized my plight and hastened to a mercy mission. Lend a hand . . . ah, wing to the new kid on the block. Nice of him to offer. What was that old cliché: birds of a feather stick together. We were almost of a feather, both black and white.

I was genuinely humbled by his magnificent acceleration. I cursed my own tedious, frumpy flight. How mesmerizing, he was. The sun reflected, in little golden flashes, off his yellow, riveting unblinking eyes. And those claws! Would you look at those claws! As Eagle barreled toward me, I became hypnotized by those grandiose, imposing, upturned talons, aimed straight for the fractured collar on my exposed throat.

In the split second before impact, it came clear to me that, I, a lame-looking loon out of water, as it were, was the imperial eagle's natural prey.

I panicked. No way I could out fly that meteoric fool. No way, in view of his natural armor and weaponry, I could stand and fight — not with my toy beak and waddley toes. No way. I was in his sky with his rules and my unprotected bungling butt. Last-ditch thoughts; *get out of this dream fast!*

Didn't work.

I tried the Homo sapien solution to aerial survival; I locked brakes, frozen with fright!

Even as I dead weight dived, I felt stinging talons rake across the top of my head. Pain seared my brain. Motor nerves driving the rest of my body broke down. Like a head shot goose, I plunged down, down, down, faster and faster, through the electrical storm clouds, at once thankful for the cover from that treacherous eagle, but knowing unless I found the strength to pull out, it really made no difference.

I was a dead duck.

Why didn't I wake up? Falling from great heights always catapulted me out of nightmares before.

With every fiber of my feathered being, I willed my body to function. Sensation trickled in. Then, in a jolt of energy, I regained partial steering. But by that time, I had probably reached terminal velocity for a dead-weight falling bird. Could I still pull up?

I tried flapping my wings and felt my breast bone rend: Exquisite torment, side-splitting, wing-wresting, life-giving torture! By the time I managed to slow and finally check my speed, I felt as if I had split in half, that I'd become — dare I say it — two loons.

I had little time to revel. As I dropped through the cloud cover, further terrified at how close the ground loomed, Eagle waited. I spotted him, diving too, breaking through the clouds just a few yards away and overshooting me.

I had foiled the scurvy avian hell-bird only momentarily. Low-life scavenger that he was, he probably expected to scrape my broken body off the ground. I couldn't suppress a deranged, triumphant yodel, which only served as a location beacon for Mr. Master Predator.

Damn. Even as a dream-spirit, my big yap got me in trouble.

Eagle arched in aerial elegance. He spotted me with those yellow, unforgiving eyes and zeroed in for another pass. No hurry. Why strain yourself for a crippled, easy kill?

Why indeed? My chest felt like a mad butcher had diced it with a stainless steel meat cleaver. One eye was out of commission, soaked with dripping blood from the first attack. I blinked back blood and I began to hate that arrogant, peacocky, son-of-a-bald-bitch.

Anatomy is, indeed, destiny.

It was at that exact moment human reasoning ceased and the wild creature in me took over. I knew, in the way defenseless prey has known for millions of years, the only thing that could save me was cover. A loon's only cover is water. Harp P. Gravey's unnatural fear of water be damned. We're talking survival here.

I instinctively grasped that the thick foliage below and about a mile to the south hid the upper Dosanomish. A ribbon of brown floodwater occasionally shown through the green vegetation. The sky may be eagle's element, but water is loon's. I felt a surge of species pride, sixty million years of it. My ancestral voice gave utterance: "For I am Loon; deep diver, breath holder, brother to swimmer, swamp singer, bringer of mud to naked humans." I wailed out a cacphonous song of boastful defiance. I hadn't felt so alive in years.

Rattled, Eagle backed off, gave me a second to think. The song felt grand, but the fact remained, I still had some hard traveling to do. If I didn't get a move on, it would be my swan song.

But how to get to the river? I couldn't brake again. My chest was so damaged I'd never be able to pull out. I could only flap laboriously and glide in excruciating, blimp-like slow-motion.

Glide? Gliding!

I ceased flapping my inordinately small wings, banked sharply downward. I gathered speed and maneuverability. Unfortunately, Eagle, carrion-eating, cock-sucker that he was, sensed my feeble strategy and renewed his comet attack. In an instant, he was on my feathered tail.

I swerved, I dipped, I corkscrewed, losing height but gaining some small ground in the direction of the Dosanomish. If I didn't log some level flight time, I would surely crash into a tree before I reached the water. If I did level out, I would feel murderous talons rip into my back. Even when I reached the water, I would have to slow down for a vulnerable landing. How long could I maintain momentum, every muscle in my body craved surcease.

Eagle's massive air-displacement twisted and tugged at my tail feathers, drawing me backwards. Flaps of his wings sounded like claps of syncopated thunder; fucker was his own bottom-end rhythm section.

My mind raced. I had to skew the odds. I'd seen a thousand chase scenes in the movies and on TV where-in the hero escapes by cleverly inserting some immovable object, such as a train or eighteen wheeler, between themselves and their superiorly equipped pursuer. Not much chance of happening on a locomotive or semi-truck up here in the sky.

How about a parade? Where's the hell's a parade when you need one.

Endless, empty, gray sky surrounded me. Embraced me. Mocked me.

From the corner of my clear eye, way down to the right, I spotted a nest. The nest was a massive concoction of sticks and canes perched on the very top of a lightning-damaged, old-growth fir.

Josh once told me most birds were highly territorial and protective of their nesting area. I gyrated toward the nest. I prayed it wasn't the murderous Eagle's home. If so, I was gonna be right on time for dinner. I have no explanation for it, but the thought of being Eagle's main course so terrified me that I managed a burst of speed.

When I got within a few hundred feet of the nest, I leveled off and coasted straight for it. Eagle screeched a few inches behind my floating body, coming in for the kill. Two white fuzz balls greeted me with baleful eyes and gigantic, gaping mouths as I pulled up in time to skim their beaks.

From out of nowhere, I caught a lick of supersonic motion behind me. I hunched my long, vulnerable neck and closed my one good eye, expecting talons in my back. The air vibrated with a shattering winged whump and a beak-shriek of surprise and rage. And I sailed on. I banked left to see two jumbled bodies tumbling in a flurry of ruffled feathers and rumpled pride.

It worked! It worked! An adult thunderbird had blind-sided Eagle. I couldn't resist a quick loop-de-loop, though my body protested in agony. I had thwarted the mightiest winged predator of the Pacific Northwest.

Thunderbird, known to humans as an osprey, by far the smaller of the two raptors, rode the back of the bigger bird wild bronco style. The winged, raptor-rodeo broke apart, and Thunderbird, beak foaming with feathers, shrieking an ancient war-cry, enraged with parental righteousness, attacked again head-on.

Eagle, minus a frothing of feathers, did not seem so much injured as he did surprised. No doubt about it, getting knocked out of orbit wasn't something that happened to him every day. He had a shocked look in his yellow eyes, as if to say, "Who dared attack his royal highness! And foil an easy meal too?"

While Eagle's pride smarted, the plucky, though seemingly suicidal, Thunderbird kept at it. My painful sightseeing loop completed, I crippled on. I saw no more of the sky-borne cock-fight. I had my own feathered buns to bolster. Weakened, I fought blackout. I felt pops of pain as more muscles tore in my chest. Blood whipped into my good eye. Tree tops shaved my exposed belly, threatening to eviscerate me from withers to rump. Fir boughs swished and tugged at my gangly good-for-nothing legs.

Dizzy, losing control, I was quickly calculating the minus survival stats of a crash-landing when I heard a distant dream voice speak, *"You can make it. So much depends on you. You must come back."*

Come back! Come back where? It made no sense. Yet I vaguely recognized the voice.

Without warning, Thunderbird pulled up beside me, looking none the worse for wear, and *Cheer-eeked*, puffing clouds of eagle feathers. I took it as an all clear signal — no eagles on the horizon. It was all up to me.

"No way I can make it," I radioed, "I'm going down in the bush."

The voice — was it Thunderbird or was it a ghost *Tamánamis* transmitting through the plucky fish hawk — began singing in my ear.

> *"Olympic Mountain Morning,*
> *beautiful, rare and high,*
> *loving you was high as I*
> *could ever hope to fly,*
> *and if I haunt these lonesome hills*
> *and think of you all day,*
> *will the ancient gods of love and dreams*
> *direct your soul to stay?"*

Singing, for God's sake. Added another verse to my recently coined song. How could that be? And at a time like this. What possible good could singing do? And in a B minor key too! April's suggestion. It made me furious! In the time it took to listen to that vapid verse, I could've been plotting a way to escape from my tormented dream.

I passed over a derelict lodge-type dwelling, practically smacking its tall, oversized chimney, and then over a rocky bluff. Below me appeared the bountiful Dosanomish. Yes! Muddy water never looked so beautiful.

All recrimination against the disembodied singer forgotten, I made a beeline for the river. I realized that the oddly familiar voice had tricked me, coaxed a few more life-giving yards out of my waning strength.

As I neared the surface, my inefficient feet came alive like I'd punched some kind of automatic landing gear button. But, there was no getting around it, I was speeding in too fast and hard for a gear-down water landing. I back pedaled. My wings flapped at random, wind-blown sheets on a clothes line. I heard snapping sounds in my chest like chicken bones twisting apart at the joints. I hit hard, flip-flopped and commenced cartwheeling down the middle of the channel until finally crashing against a log. I came to rest upside down, head in a root-wad, back against crusty bark, feet flailing and butt exposed to a nippy canyon breeze.

Bad enough viewing a strange world through the eyes of a different species, try it standing on your head. Upside-down trees seemed to root in the gray sky across the river. A turbid spring runoff, thick with roiled sediment, lapped at my head. I clung to a protruding overhanging root with a tangled, webbed foot. A green branch from a nearby submerged log bounced in and out of the churning water, showering me with cold spray and making a bongo thwocking noise in my left ear.

The pain in my chest was in the muscles that nurtured flight. My wings were useless. I wouldn't be airborne again for a long spell, if ever. Grounded and stranded in a strange, hostile land.

But of course, it was all just a bad dream, I thought. Now is a perfect time to rouse from this nightmare, to clip this chimera in the bud, to bestir and bedamn this vivid vision, perchance at some future date to share this quaint fantasy with a new-found friend and marvel at it's perilous reality.

No dice. The raging water clued me; maybe, just maybe, I was not in a dream.

I looked down into brown water two inches below my black beak. My long neck stretched down and I took a sip. Tasted of peat and leaf mold. I spit it out. Up in the sky with Eagle hounding my tail, I saw the river as my savior. Now, I changed my mind. What was it Elpenor had warned me about, "Watch out for what you ask for." Catfish fear seized me, seeped into my feathers. What monsters lurked under this river's surface, ready to gobble up a defenseless loon? My hold slipped an inch. What if my damaged wings failed me in water as they did in air? Had I escaped the mightiest winged predator in North America only to drown like a hound in the Dosanomish? I thought about trying to right myself and climb the logjam but what was I going to climb with and, supposing I succeeded, what then? My experience had already proved I was a sorry flyer and my instincts told me I was a worse walker. I wouldn't get ten feet. No wonder either, as I peered up at my stick-like gray legs they seemed to be growing right out of my asshole. What a rotten configuration. In order to move on land, I'd have to push my body forward like a tub of guts. Me thinking I could perch on top of the Space Needle was ridiculous. Those webbed feet weren't made for perching. What the hell were they good for anyway? And how did loons survive for sixty million years?

There was no getting around it. I had to take the plunge. Once again, it was sink or swim. I had to trust the Dosanomish to keep me afloat, help me survive long enough until I figured out how to once again get my mind back into my human body.

Speaking of human body, I had no idea what happened to it . . . me . . . Harp. Did Harp P. Gravey — the human — have a stroke, heart attack, or worse, exchange mental faculties with the loon whose body I now possessed and abused? Was there a Homo sapien running around on the mud flat varooming and yodeling at Malcomb and April? April thought Harp was nuts before the transformation. What must she think now?

With all Harp's failings and problems, I would have gladly traded my present loonness to be in his dissipated body at that moment.

8

The Awesome Unknown and the Purple Hat

I stretched my long neck down again, took a deep breath, closed my eyes and let go. Head first I plunged into the murky gloom.

The quick current grabbed me like the jaws of some rough beast, shook me and sucked me under. My wings fluttered for control, convulsed and seized-up. Useless. I tumbled over and over, scraping bottom. Suddenly, my body righted itself and began slicing through the water like a greased torpedo. I opened my eyes, turned my head and witnessed a miracle; those stick legs and dangly toes of mine performed like an Irish Ceili Dancer.

What a much-welcomed thrill. Something excelled on this alien bird body. My legs went from useless drumsticks in the air to talented and powerful pistons in water. I decided not to throw them away after all. My toes sprinted for the surface.

Polar water cooled the stinging from my head wound and washed the blood from my red eyes. The ripping pain in my chest subsided into a dull throb.

I broke the surface and floated. My red eyes glanced around. I'd crash-landed in a deep brown pool formed by a massive logjam, bordered on the south side by a tall green fir forest sloping up foothills to the Olympics. The fir tops were shrouded in frozen pewter-colored clouds. To the north, a sheer bluff rose perhaps sixty feet high. There was a toothless gap in the bluff that corresponded to massive boulders in the river. Looked like a section of the bluff had collapsed into the Dosanomish, causing the logjam.

Overhead, the storm cloud I'd dropped through now extended from the mountains to the west down to the eastern horizon. Lightning flares flashed in the clouds. I looked down the river channel toward Puget Sound. How far from the Sound mud bar had I flown? Five — ten miles? Whatever the distance, I suspected the only chance I had to reverse the metamorphoses was to follow the river to its mouth and then what? Merge with Harp's body by some transformational magic. What I wanted to do, if and when I found him, before any exchange of bodies, minds or souls, was to give him a good peck for general blockheadedness in trying on that hair hat.

First though, I needed to spend a few minutes resting, healing, getting acquainted with this avian body.

I was not alone. I had flesh and blood, feathers and fur for company. A dipper, a robin-sized sooty-gray bird, bobbed to the beat of inner drums on a knobby branch in the logjam. The inner drummer missed a beat and the dipper froze. Then flew, hugging the water, up stream.

Down the river a black bear and two curious coal-tinted cubs wandered out of a thicket of cottonwoods and began frolicking in a shallow tributary. The mother suddenly stood on hind legs, sniffed the air, snorted, then dropped down on all fours and fled back into the forest; her frightened cubs blundering behind her.

My feathers agitated, webbed toes curled. Well, well, all kinds of things with big teeth and claws prowling around out here in the wilderness looking for dinner. Whatever the pitfalls and dangers of living on the mean streets in the big city, being eaten wasn't one of them.

A couple of charcoal-colored, river otters dashed in and out of dark tunnels in roots underneath the canopy of an old-growth, western red cedar along the southern river bank. Spying me, the otters quit their antics and stood on their hind feet. We had ourselves a staring contest. They turned to each other and had a chatting conferee. Then, one of the otters did the strangest thing; it clawed over the logjam, came to a vine maple tree trunk sticking up, stopped and pointed its snout down, looked up at me, barked, pointed down again, barked at the tangle.

I knew river otters were playful creatures, and guessed it wanted to engage me in some kind of hide-'n-seek game. I had no time for otters. I was in no shape or mood for games. Besides, I didn't know whether otters were omnivores or not. Eagle had taught me to exercise caution over curiosity.

I was a long way from the safe city. The place was teeming with wildlife. While the animals I could see were no immediate threat, what about the ones I couldn't see, bandit-faced raccoons for example, agile swimmers and deadly predators. Coyotes, even mountain lions that lurked in the dense forest and preyed on defenseless birds. I sensed my ability to evade predators depended upon my strength as a swimmer and diver. I knew there were no two hundred pound catfish in the chilly water but what else lurked below?

I had to chance it. I dived, gliding at first, trying to get some rhythm in my kicking, and realized I no longer was afraid of the water. More than that, I liked it. Who would've guessed, me, Harp P. Gravey liking water?

As a loon, I sensed water meant safety and security. A haven against the hungry predators of the world. Unfettered about attacks from above by dive-bombing hell birds.

There was something in the mountain water that inspired a burst of bravado. No longer able to contain myself, I did an underwater pirouette of salvation giddiness, a childish somersault of — whether loon, man or lunatic — joyous celebration at cheating the minions of death. I drank of the magic waters of the Dosanomish to the point of intoxication, let it get inside of me, fill me with rhythm, burst me with song. I swam in a song. Water song. Bird song. Love song. The waves of music caressed my feathers, soothed my worries and seduced my soul. I dived. I bubbled. I laughed. I was, for better or worse, alive! To honor the occasion, I composed a little impromptu nonsense limerick of triumph:

"Oh lazy eagle come play with me
and I'll tell you no false lies,
follow me into the briny sea
and I'll peck out your flinty eyes,
Surprise, surprise, surprise surprise!"

I mumbled on. "Ho, ho, ho. Put me on the Olympic team, please. Show me an athlete that can do the kind of water acrobatics I can. Take a gold medal without a doubt. 'My, what big legs you have Mr. Common Loon.' 'The better to kick you in the shins my sharp-toothed friend.' 'Ain't nothing common about you, Podna'."

It was the closest to intoxication I'd felt since climbing out of a bottle. Intoxication while alert and clear-headed. I had no idea such a notion existed.

A fingerling trout swimming by broke my ecstatic mumblings. I, without so much as a twinge of revulsion or conscience, snaked out and swallowed the fellow whole. Slid down my long slippery throat with a satisfying wiggle. YEECK! What was I thinking? I, Harp P. Gravey hated, whether baked, fried, broiled or fricasseed, fish with a passion. Here, I ate one fella raw.

You know what? Never tasted anything so delicious in my life. I was so hungry I could've eaten a giant mud cat. And the waters were full of food. My keen eyes spotted fish everywhere. Big ones, small ones, colored ones, dull ones; Medusa and I never needed to go hungry again. A veritable moveable feast floated before my ruddy watchful eyes.

Predation is in the beak of the beholder.

Hey, I spied another little silvery, red and purple-banded trout, throat sized. They don't come any fresher. The finny fellow was on to me though. It knew I was top predator in that puddle. For a few seconds anyway, I thought I was top predator until a whiskered mouth full of small sharp teeth, swallowed the trout. Visions of a cold water, cat fish terrified me and I turned to dive but before I could get kick-started, a black blur blocked my path. Narrow, mammal eyes stared into mine from a distance of six inches.

A red tongue flicked out of whiskered lips.

I surprised myself. I had an immediate and deadly reaction: I cocked my neck and stabbed at one of those beady little eyes with my dagger beak. I hit thin air . . . ah, thin water. And if the beast had wanted to, it could've severed my exposed throat then and there.

In a swirl of water that suggested underwater agility to equal mine, the eyes loomed again in front of me, blocking movement. This time I looked at the face closer. The way it had swallowed that fish, it was definitely a meat eater, but the face was that of an imp, not a loon killer. I recognized the otter that had been playing on the logjam.

It had not given up on me as a playmate. Those intense otter eyes suggested it wouldn't take no for an answer. I must follow. I decided to humor it. Then I'd slip away down river to a dubious rendezvous with Harp at the first opportunity.

On the water's surface, I must have drifted with the current, down past a pile of landslide boulders. We swam around them and I noticed etchings in the stone. A face, with a long, wavy beard and some kind of thorned crown or hat, glared through yellow lichen at me. The hairs . . . ah, feathers on the back of my neck stood straight up. My legs were weak but I managed to give myself an extra kick-thrust past that stone face.

More hallucinations? Being in the body of a bird does not give you a firm grasp on reality. Maybe I caught a glimpse of the great *Kaalpekci*, Malcomb's water devil.

My playful guide led me through an underwater snarl of tree roots in the river logjam. I had no trouble keeping up until I came upon some long strands of kelp-like stuff. A faint pink color seeped from the black kelp. My tongue tasted a sweet sanguine saltiness, drifting with the current. A danger signal went off in my brain.

But it was too late. I hung up in the stuff. That black kelp clung to me like magnetic tape. Insistent, thick, cloying stuff hanging down about three feet, sighing and sashaying in the vigorous current. The kelp was anchored fast in a tangle of olive-green vine maple branches above my head. My ears heard a noise like water whispering secrets. My animal instincts suddenly recoiled. Warning. I needed air anyway, and about bolted to the surface. But I couldn't suppress a certain curiosity.

Parting the dark, strand-matted path in front of me, I ran smack into a blue-brown, naked nose.

I reared back, but not before I beheld the face of an Indian woman, with a pair of stunned, onyx eyes. Those eyes, in the aqueous turbulence, cried buckets of tears. The pink liquid seeped out of a jagged round hole above her right breast. A bullet exit wound. Back shot. My heart fell to the bottom of my malformed feet. I gagged. The long strands of turbid hair closed around me like live octopus tentacles; whispering, squeezing, imploring. A voice spoke in my mind, *"Old one, find my killer. Avenge my death."*

I shuddered, suffocating. My body broke free of the tentacles and plowed to the surface to inhale huge gasps of free oxygen. My lungs swelled to the size of softballs and stretched my sore breastplate. A cold breeze buffeted my head, carrying tailings of a wild animal shriek of pain that came echoing down the canyon.

A rack of fatigue shook my body. Creeping throughout my torso, from webbed feet to dagger beak, came a debilitating numbness. My head lolled. Loon life in the avian fast lane was catching up with me. I knew, in the way of wild animals, I had only minutes before total physical meltdown.

I dived, wanted one more look at the crying woman before collapsing.

The woman's body was wedged tight in the snarl of various kinds of roots. The chaotic roots resembled skinless tree bones, polished clean by the swift current.

A fingerling cutthroat darted in for a nibble of torn flesh around the bullet wound.

The bullet could have gone in her back most anywhere, ricocheted off several rib bones, destroying cartilage, muscle, ripping through her heart before exiting.

The fingerling trout saw me and skittered away. Needn't have been afraid. I was too weak of body and sick of soul to eat the finny fellow.

Half way between her naval and thin black pubic hair, a tattoo swayed with the water. Closer, I made out a tiny tomahawk imbedded in a wild, red rhododendron. Very original artistry. Not your typical commercial tattoo.

One arm hung down straight out from her body, fingers splayed as if reaching out for a helping hand. I let the hand rest on my back for a second. Her other arm was hung up in some branches.

I felt horror and sadness and a tiny bit of gladness and guilt, thank-God-it-wasn't-me-I'm-still-alive-and-kicking sort of thing. Oh, how I'm kicking. Considering that alternative, being a common loon wasn't so bad.

I had to see her pleading eyes again, her only link with the living. Who knew when her body would be discovered by humans and given a proper burial? I took my saber-like beak and tugged at her eyelids. Wouldn't close. Those pleading, disbelieving eyes followed my every move. Don't know why her opened eyes bothered me, but it didn't seem right to let her head out into the awesome unknown like that. I scoured the river bottom and found a couple of flat roundish rocks, about the size of a quarter and wedged them in her eye sockets. I mentally said a remembered Pentecostal, graveside prayer and sang, in my head, a few bars of Amazing Grace.

Satisfied, I started for the surface, but I spotted a glint of gold cupped in her left hand hung up in branches. My initial reaction was to let it be, forget it; but then some perverse curiosity took hold of me. Maybe it was a clue to her identity. I still couldn't see it clearly but I could tell it was part of a stick pin. Fortunately I had a handy, built-in spearing tool at my disposal and I plucked the gold pin free from her hand to take a closer look up above. My head got pinched between two vine maple branches and I left some feathers when pulling loose. It's what happens when you stick your neck out into places it doesn't fit.

Gumming my golden treasure, I surfaced.

Overwhelming fatigue and numbness took control. The eagle gash on my head oozed blood. Blood-scent attracts predators. My pinched neck, where I lost some feathers, felt naked and exposed. I had to find safe cover for myself and a hiding place for the hard kernel of metal in my beak.

Ah yes, the logjam. I spotted an oblong hole in a big-leaf maple limb. Swam, my strength ebbing, toward it. Suddenly, my feathers froze. I had developed a prey's sensitivity to danger.

I shook the blood off my head. It scattered in circular scarlet beads in the brackish water around me. There, across the river, on a tiny ledge underneath the looming bluff, a man sighted me in with binoculars. I never moved a pin-feather. My short tail tucked. Instinctively, I knew that coyotes, raccoons and cougars are dangerous, but man is, by far, my worst enemy.

First thing I focused on, strapped to his back, a high-powered rifle. Boy was I ever a target! On display! Talk about ducks in a shooting gallery. I hadn't a chance. If he took that gun off his back I'd have to attempt another dive. Doubtful success.

Across the wide river, I could make out his full red beard, red suspenders, loose jeans cut off at the bottom and a purple cowboy hat with flamboyant plumage stuck in it. Strange, don't see many loggers wearing a purple cowboy hat adorned with ostentatious feathers.

He dropped the binocs and, with a shrug of a muscular shoulder, unslung the rifle.

No time for further observation, it was now or never. I dived. And flopped. The numbness had spread to my legs rendering them useless as wilted straw, couldn't kick a cormorant. I hung my head and willed my broken body to sink.

Wonder of wonders, it did. My loon body did sink! Through some kind of decompression process, I sank below the surface, a submarine with engines cut. This loon body was full of survival surprises.

I stopped about a foot below the surface and peered up through running water at dark corduroy clouds, see if any bullets splayed the water.

I waited. And waited. An underwater ripple, coming from the direction of purple hat, fluffed my feathers. Some large object thrown in the river. I couldn't swim, so I stuck my head barely out of the water and glanced at the far bank and beheld the rifle leaning against a cedar snag, the purple cowboy hat cocked jauntily on top. Had the flamboyant logger fallen into the frigid waters of the Dosanomish? A heart attack, possibly?

Or had he dived? What possible reason could he have for that? Hold on, doesn't the murderer always return to the scene of the crime? Possibly to retrieve something, such as a gold pin lost in the melee.

I remembered the hard little gold pin in my bill; rolled it around, bit and gnawed at it. Who did it belong too? Bad enough, I had transported into some Kafkaesque metamorphosis, I had also bungled and botched my way into the middle of a murder.

I tried once more to reach the logjam and hide the murder clue.

Without warning the water exploded into spray not two feet behind me.

Disoriented, I instinctively attempted to fly, but pain stabbed my chest and I couldn't raise my wings. The spray settled, I turned and stared, on eye level, with a red beard, rheumy eyes, chiseled forehead and bald pate. I was transfixed, couldn't move. The murderer had me at his mercy.

A red-knuckled hand with deep ridges, snaked out and nabbed me by the neck. Blacksmith's wrought-iron grip. I choked. Purple Hat stuffed my body underneath his hairy arm pit. My mind spun. Delirious. Why is he doing this? Why didn't he just shoot me and get it over with?

Something caught in my throat. I felt my consciousness evaporating. Not wanting to strangle while comatose, I had time for one stout swallow. My throat tore as the obstacle passed. Oh no! Me and my big beak, I'd eaten, most likely, a major clue to a murder. After being captured by a logger with a purple cowboy hat, destined quite possibly for the stewpot, facing, if not boiled, fried or fricasseed loon breast, then agonizing death by coagulated colon, my last thought before losing consciousness, was, "Oh shit."

9

The Vision and The Totem

"The smelling salts did it; he's coming round," I heard April say. I came crawling out of a mystic fog, sniffing a tart fruity perfume, mixed with the green walnut aroma of body sweat. Cradled in April's capable arms, my head resting on her cinnamon medicine bag which, in turn, hung between her warm rising breasts. Though spacey, I knew I was back in human form. Real form. Harp form. Hugging April's human form.

And damn glad of it. What a powerful dream! A terrifying nightmare. It harkened me back to the nightmares I had while first hospitalized with my head wound. I tried to brush the eagle and dead body off as just another schizoid experience; an imagined, unreal, preposterous vision: loons, eagles, thunderbirds, dead bodies, water devils, killers wearing purple hats. What poppycock. What kind of macabre tricks was my wounded mind playing on me in Josh's last God-forsaken wilderness?

But if it was just a dream, why did I have a big lump of sadness in my chest for the murdered woman. Her crying eyes reached out to me, across the chasm of reality.

And what about that damn bird. It was downright ridiculous but I felt the figmented, fictional loon was part of me. I must admit, his ultimate evisceration at the hands of the purple hatted murderer — dream murderer — left me with a dryness in my throat. My short, stumpy throat.

I was getting to kinda like the loon. He had some admirable traits, unlike some actual Homo sapiens I'm all too familiar with but won't mention.

What was it the pale Veteran's Administration shrink had said to me? "Unless you take your medication, I suspect your mind, much like a true schizophrenic's, will not split so much as splinter, bombarded by delusions and hallucinations, which will seem sensorially real to you. You'll be unable to concentrate for long, or distinguish imagination from reality."

"What does that mean in layman terms?" I asked.

He held a white-skinned hand up to his pasty face and peered through slits between his fingers. He spoke into his palm. "Ever read anything about demonic possession?" He laughed, high baritone, imitating the Phantom of the Opera.

"Don't squeeze him so tight, Daughter," I heard Malcomb say, "He needs air. Give him some air."

"No air! No air!" I said, mind your own damn business Malcomb. What irony. Two years without so much as seeing, touching or sniffing the lusty perfume of a woman's neck and now to have a water nymph princess shove my nose in her throat. Being human had its moments. I needed suckling time to consider the ramifications of a squandered life.

I snuggled deeper. Sucking aromatic air in great gulps. A nurturing respite from an indifferent world.

The rhythmic flow of the Dosanomish lulled me, cradled me with womb-like comfort and care. The swoosh of a speeding car on nearby Highway 101 punctuated the regular flow of the river like an intermittent pulse. April's heart-beat drummed a sacred cadence in my ear. I heard redwing blackbirds discussing the dietary needs of their young.

Her callused fingers stroked my hair. "I've never seen anybody have such a fit in my life," she said. "What kind of tricks are you playing on him with that damn wretched headdress? I should've sold it at my garage sale last year."

Aha, April, my love, had relented her rejection of me. She did care for me. No woman could hold a man the way she cuddled me and not care. Perhaps I still had a chance with her. Seattle could wait.

Malcomb held the ratty headdress like rare glass. "I don't know," he said. "I hoped he'd have a mild reaction, maybe get a glimmer of a message from the spirit world. See if he had any gift whatsoever. Ninety-nine percent of the people that try it on don't even get that. Only Crazy Wilma Eats-Raw-Fish — "

April quit stroking my hair. "Father! Crazy Wilma's a diagnosed paranoid schizophrenic who never stays on her medication more than two days in a row. You didn't try that headdress on her, did you?"

I perked up. "What was that you said about eating raw fish?"

Malcomb hung his silver head. "Crazy Wilma went nuts over raw fish when she had the ancient headdress on. No one, not even Crazy Wilma, has ever gone into a catatonic trance and then seizures before. No one except for vague stories handed down by the elders about ancient medicine men. And then there's what happened to your Great Grandfather."

April grabbed a fistful of my hair. "What about my Gre ..? Never mind your tall tales now. Let's get Mr. Harp P. Gravey out of here. Take him to the Wildlife Care Clinic where I can examine him. See if he needs medical help. Looks like some scar tissue broke open from the convulsions and he's bleeding. Look! He's got a synthetic plate in his head. He could've done a header and died."

My signal to fess up. I moved, steeling for stress to my head but not for the needles of pain that shot through my chest. Surely, I reasoned, after catching my breath, any transference of impairment from one species, in dreams or delusions, to another, is purely psychosomatic. "I'm okay," I gasped. "You were right, Malcomb, about dreams sometimes seeming more real than everyday life. I just had a doozy. You can take that wretched headdress and stick it where the sun never shines. I don't want anything to do with it ever again." I wrapped my arms around April for support, clasping the gentle curve of her hips, stroking the slenderness of her waist, burrowing into the haven of her coppery cleavage.

A fellow, escaped from the nether world of demonic possession, can't get too much motherly comforting.

I peeked out at Malcomb. He'd captured the accursed headdress, held it at arms length, staring at it, a devotional, reverent look on his face, as if he'd had a revelation. He transferred the look to me and, trance-like, spoke, "I thought the gift had been lost. Tell me, did you, as the old stories tell, detect a hint of an animal spirit?" His heavy salt 'n' pepper brows spread wide with pleading. The wrinkles around his eyes were nests of writhing curiosity. I could make his day. Could also make me look like a damn fool to April. Correction, more of a damn fool.

Oh, what the hell. No one, least of all a fiddler, expected rationality from a banjo picker mired in a mud-bog. Might as well spread the ooze and let it stick. "I've been told that I have delusions," I said. "Sometimes they involve a shape changing dragon like the before mentioned Elpenor. But no, I didn't get a hint of a spirit animal."

Malcomb's mouth slanted down. He almost let the headdress slip out of his grasp.

"Well," said April, "now that that's settled, we — "

I continued. "I had a vision I'd actually become a common loon. You know, flying, swimming, diving and almost dying; the whole ball of wax. That hat is downright dangerous. Had my way, it'd be in the river floating to kingdom come right now."

April's body became rigid, drawing away from me. Malcomb almost dropped the headdress. His nose ring went quiet, his lower lip slack, cheeks ashen. I felt like I'd switched to a minor key in the middle of a tune while everyone else still played in the major.

"I hope you're satisfied," April said to me with a hoarse whisper, reaching behind and unclasping my hands from around her waist. "Telling my poor deluded father a bald-faced fabrication like that. It was the absolute worse thing you could've said. The common loon is the ancient totem for our disbanded clan. Where did you come from anyway? Did you come here just to torment me? I think I could very easily hate your guts."

Tears tumbled down Malcomb's creased leathery cheek, and he sniffled — nose ring dancing — hairy nostrils palpitating. His thick ears wiggled and waved.

Feeling abandoned, I stood up. I blew it. What had I said to set them off so?

"A, by-the-gods, common loon," said Malcomb. "Gavia immer. At long last. I have found you. You've. . . ." sniff, sniff, "made me so goddamn happy." He let go of the hair hat with his right hand and hooked a finger through his gold nose ring. Ripped it off his face. Blood dripped over his lips, down his chin. He flung himself on me in a bear hug and sobbed.

Over Malcomb's shoulder, April shook her head at me, black hair flying, leaping salmon earrings scaling mighty waterfalls, and made the age-old gesture with her muscled fiddler's hands of wringing a fowl's neck.

My short throat spasmed, swallowing a phantom chunk of coal.

10

The Hired Gun and
The Drugged Cougar

Car brakes screeched on highway 101, shattering my already shaky nerves. Over Malcomb's shoulder, I saw a crimson-red, brand-spanking-new Jeep Grand Cherokee with monster wheels and a rack of quad-lamps sparkling in the morning dew. Compared with the oxidized blue paint on my VW and the flaking rust finish on the Old Wolf's Ford, the Cherokee shone like a Gibson Mastertone Banjo in a pile of tambourines.

April straightened. "Oh-oh, Gabe's Goons."

She sidled close and elbowed me in the ribs. "Listen Mr. *Birdman,* we'll just say you got hurt in the crash. They'll see the bleeding and they'll also see you're not right in the head." April drifted away from me.

Malcomb released me. I stumbled. "Who are Gabe's Goons?" I said.

April put her hands on her hips. "The local militia up in arms over Native American claims to shell fishing rights on Puget Sound beaches. Financed mostly by Gabe Moody, head of a family that's made its fortune by raping and plundering this land. Although we're not on the beach, technically we're on Gabe's shellfish beds now."

Malcomb hugged the hair hat to his chest. "One of them's Big Steve. I never seen the other one before. I don't like his looks. Watch your mouth April. You let me do the talking." His voice sounded far away. Merle, in his coat pocket, jiggled his bunny nose at me.

They didn't call him Big Steve for nothing. He was dressed in tight camouflage fatigues, one-size-too small, except for his hat, which appeared to be one size too big. He stood well over six feet and, with long, powerful legs and rugged, black, pillow stomping military boots, high-stepped easily over barbed blackberry vines. He had narrow hips and broad shoulders, and if there was any justice in the world, he should've been ugly. But, of course, as we all know, the capricious gods of anatomy are strangers to justice. He had the thick, blonde curls and high, Aryan cheeks of an Adonis.

It was only as he drew closer that I noticed a flaw in his rugged good looks: his blue eyes had a flat surface sheen as if the irises were painted on with milky watercolors. He had a pistol strapped to his waist. Probably, by the looks of the exposed grip, a Colt forty-five.

Big Steve stopped three feet away, towering over us. "These are private shellfish beds and you people are trespassing." His booming baritone was made all the more manly, I suspected, by the pistol at his side. It's been my experience that gun-toting adds projection to a mediocre voice, like an invisible, though cheap, microphone.

April brushed my arm, alerting body hairs to rise to attention, stepped in front of me and marched right up to the overgrown militia man. Her long blue-black hair shimmered with morning shadows, the back of her brown neck arching as graceful as a blue heron. The bill of her Wildlife Care Center cap came up to Big Steve's barrel chest. "What the hell do you mean 'you people' Big Steve Loper," she said. "You played four years of high school football with my brother Loren. Seems to me just last month you brought in an injured cormorant to Old Wolf Wildlife Care Clinic for me to operate on. Who you calling 'you people,' and what are you doing in that stupid get-up?" Her cap bill pecked him in the ribs.

Big Steve, momentarily confused, hesitated, then puffed up with pride. "I know the uniform's a little too small for me, April," he said, "but I'm now a Sergeant in the Port Gamble Militia. Lieutenant LeRoy Peck, that's him over there inspecting your kitty, says we have to address all foreigners politely before we shoot em. Ha, ha. That's a little joke he makes to all new recruits." Big Steve's laugh sounded like it came from the bottom of a sour pickle barrel. He tilted backwards at the waist. He caught his cap as it tried to slide off his military haircut head.

April dug her feet deeper into the mud as if she expected them to take root. "Shooting people different than you is not funny," she said. She pressed forward. "And just what are you doing out here?"

Big Steve glanced sideways at Lt. LeRoy, who seemed to have an unnatural, fascination for the caged cougar. Lt. LeRoy managed to get a stout stick poked through the cougar cage. The cat, with a drugged listlessness, swatted at the probe.

The big man backed away from April, then bent forward until his lips hovered near her leaping-salmon earring. He lowered his voice. "Hey, give me a break April. We're searching for Billy Moody. He's been gone more'n a week. His older brother promised us a bonus if we found him. You ain't seen him, have you?"

April leaned to look around Big Steve at the cougar-prodding lieutenant. "No, I haven't seen Billy and don't care to. So, Gabe's got himself a hired gun?"

Big Steve snorted. "A professional soldier. Which reminds me, I better obey orders. April, what are you doing out here on Major Gabriel's property. You know how property owners are up in arms over this whole shellfish mess. The Major says that until the appeals run out, he owns the property and we're not to let anyone trespass. Let alone Inj . . . Native Americans."

"What the hell does it look like we're doing here, Big Steve?" April said. "We were searching for Molly Jenkins when we stopped to pull this man out of the river."

Big Steve scratched behind his right ear. "Molly's sure changed since we were in that Tomahawk Club back in high school," he said. "You don't suppose her and Billy ran off together?"

They looked at each other. "Naaaawww!" they said in unison.

"Gotta be just a coincidence," Big Steve said.

"Gotta be," April agreed. Both were adamant, as if the thought of Billy and Molly being together defied some unbreakable social register.

Lt. LeRoy tore himself away from jabbing the big cat, and strutted our way through barbed blackberry canes, as well as anyone could while protecting polished snake skin boots.

I was looking at him with the sun at his back; but even so I could see the man was as chilling and gray as the mud bog mist. Slope-shouldered and razorback-hog-gristled, he had a long, stony face connected to a wiry neck, perched on top of a stringy body. He reminded me of a turkey vulture condemned to dine only on opossum innards and secretly relishing it. Even chewing gum, he had an immobile, thin upper lip and a tuck and swivel lower jaw. His practically non-existent bottom lip appeared to disappear anew with each chaw as if he were eating himself. His eyes were glittery, his teeth crowded, little and sharp.

Big Steve began nervous introductions, "Lt. LeRoy Peck I'd like to —"

Lt. LeRoy held up is hand. "Save it sergeant. Have you read these mud people their rights," he said, his voice like a sharpened saw blade. He wedged his clothes hanger body in between Big Steve and April. Close quarters for all three. Big Steve took a hurried step back.

The lieutenant wore tailored fatigues, officers' garb I presumed, ordered from a prestigious mail-order house back east. The jacket had padded shoulders and lots of hidden peckerwood pockets to conceal things like knives, guns and grenades.

He broke military dress code with his boots and hat. His boots were Texas goat stompers, orange and black rattlesnake skin so shined and unabashedly gaudy and glaring that it wouldn't surprise you a bit if they jumped up and spit venom of their own volition. His skin was the color of wet cement under the smoky, yellow fluorescent lighting in old time pool halls, and he wore a brand-spanking-new, olive-green, partially camouflaged cap that broadcast, *"I'm a Legend in My Own Mind."*

April screwed her feet into a more firm footing in the river mud. I wasn't happy with her rigid demeanor. I'd spent four years in the service and recognized a born believer when I saw one. Born believers, like Lt. LeRoy have a way of staying alive while getting everyone around them killed.

"No need to read these folks their rights, Lieutenant," Big Steve said, "I know these people. They weren't stealing oysters. They were helping this man." Big Steve's voice took on a subservient timbre. His handsome, pink face flushed with the responsibility of a messenger with a rotten message and he wiped his forehead with a meaty palm. I noticed a tattoo on his tricep but couldn't make out any details.

Lt. LeRoy's face was inches away from April, blasting her with bubble gum breath. "They're trespassing, aren't they," he said. "Remember your training, soldier. You know our orders. Make a citizen's arrest. If they resist, shoot em." He had a smirk on his thin face, the result of too many sessions of peering down a sight at defenseless targets that don't shoot back. Standing so close to April, he couldn't hold her unflinching stare. His little, glittery eyes darted back and forth between the three of us. In a deliberate threatening gesture, he rested one hand on the chrome-plated handle of a nine-mm Sig Sauer semi-automatic. He hooked the thumb of his other hand in his bulging ammunition belt.

"No call for trouble. We were getting ready to leave," said Malcomb. His voice was non-threatening, like the way you'd talk to a vicious dog. "This man is injured from the accident. We're taking him to the clinic."

I could understand why the lieutenant called me mud people. I still looked like I'd rolled in the dirt. April, where she'd succored me, had traces. And Malcomb, still holding the drab headdress as if it were going to light up with divine energy any moment, was not exactly a shining example of cleanliness but, mud people?

"Don't look injured to me," Lt. LeRoy said, "just looks filthy. Fits right in with you mud people. We'll just stop off at the jail first. The good sheriff in these parts is in our squadron. I figure he can help us out with some charges."

I shivered. Stone-gray clouds blocked the sun, throwing us all under a thick, dark cast-iron skillet of sky. Redwing blackbirds, busy nesting in nearby cattails, ceased singing. Irate, their babies hungry chirping became strident. A west wind whipped down through the valley, bringing a whiff of burning meat. Thunder rumbled in the distance. Blood vessels in my forehead throbbed. My piss-stained jeans, sticky and damp, felt glued to my crotch.

"You tin soldier, buzzard-faced phony," April said. "If you're going to arrest us we might as well make it more interesting than trespassing." She slapped him. Hard and vicious. Sounded like a spatula whacking a small, empty tin kettle.

I thought his glittery eyes were going to rumba out of his head. Took him so much by surprise that he fell backwards into Big Steve's giant arms. Gotta hand it to him. He bounced back like a new bungee cord and pulled his chrome-plated nine-mm Sig Sauer with a smooth, practiced motion.

He had my undivided attention. A gun in the hand of a militant racist is a volatile mix. Seemed to me a low profile was called for.

Elpenor strayed around the periphery of my consciousness. *"This is a good time to practice keeping your mouth shut, ol' podna'. That pushy woman done gone and got herself into a peck of trouble, but it ain't no concern of yours,"* Elpenor whispered.

"Put that damned thing away, you nincompoop," April smacked the lieutenant again. This time, I swear I heard acorns rolling around in a tin can.

Overhead, a gull quarreled with a raven over a piece of stringy crab.

Lt. LeRoy, not caught by surprise a second time, absorbed the blow, sidestepped, whipped the gun up, quick-draw fashion, pointed it past April's ear and squeezed the silvery, steel trigger. The report, in the quiet morning, barked like a hound from Hades. Everyone, especially Big Steve, jumped. The big man's handsome face cracked like a ceramic pot. I think until that moment nobody expected such extremist reaction to what was, at worst, a debatable minor legal infraction.

The redwing blackbird's nest in the cattails exploded. Twigs and feathers scattered, baby birds, never again to chirp and gulp, burst into bloody meat morsels. Adult birds, in their confused anguish, cried out *check, check, check,* followed by a high, *slurred tee-err, slurred tee-err.* Brilliant wing patterns of crimson, bled against a backdrop of swampy despair as the parents swooped and dipped trying to put the mutilation right. The warm, gutty smell of abrupt evisceration mingled with cordite smoke.

The gull and the raven, nature's stoics, unruffled, ceased bickering and waited for an unchaperoned, easy meal to float by.

April, hands clasped over her ears, sat down with a squishy plop, her dark hair dragging mud, making a chocolate swirl. Malcomb, juggled the headpiece, nabbed fistfuls of dead hair, and tucked it out of harm's way under his arm, careful not to bend the two top-knot loon feathers.

Big Steve's cap flipped backwards off his head. He grunted, face sallow as a cake of cheap bird suet. He lifted his big feet and, took a gargantuan sticky step backwards onto the errant cap.

I crouched, ears ringing, waiting, responding more to some long-ago military training than a plan.

Lt. LeRoy, smoking gun still erect and pointed at the bog, took in our reactions with his darting, gloating eyes, swinging the weapon around to stick it under April's nose. "I could execute you right now for striking an officer, and only bleeding-heart liberals would blame me. As it is, you mud people need to be taught a lesson." He cocked his free arm around to backhand her.

My ears rang free and from out of nowhere came a not-to-be-denied voice, "FREEZE SOLDIER!"

11

Leaping Lions and Killing Genius

Overhead, the white gull and black raven were startled out of their glutinous vigil. Lt. LeRoy's cocked arm froze, twitching with unquenched bloodthirstiness.

I glanced around, searching for the whereabouts of the man who'd brayed the command. Wouldn't want to be in his shoes when the gun-toting mercenary collected his wits. Clever fellow. Shouting a military command. Wise too, hiding in the trees somewhere out of harm's way. Lt. LeRoy swung the gun around and it came to a stop pointing at me.

My chest clogged, breath came in shallow bursts.

"Who the hell are you to give me orders?" He spat a jumbo, flesh-pink wad of gum into the nesting debris floating by.

I swallowed. "That voice came from somewhere else, most likely hiding in the trees there." I pointed at the orange, dancing madrones. No cause for alarm. A clear case of mistaken identity. I would get the others to verify it.

Malcomb's old eyes were unfathomable slits. Big Steve's dimpled chin rested on his chest. April turned slightly where she sat and tilted her pretty face at me, eyes reading incredulity. All stared at me as if I'd popped the head of my banjo. I realized I had one more delusion to deal with: I not only had voices coming in, I had voices going out. And it wasn't Elpenor.

Lt. LeRoy leaped around April, shying away from her, like a horse coming on barbed-wire. "Smartass, huh?" he said, "If you were in my company, you know what I'd do to you?" The slapped side of his sallow cheek glowing scarlet, his gun hand twitching, he stuck the still smoking weapon under my nose. Had the feeling he was much more comfortable dealing with men than women. "You'd do jumping jacks for two hours with three M-1s strapped together, then down on your scurvy back to make like a dead cockroach for another two hours. Then I'd strip you necked, wash you down with a fire hose and have your fellow soldiers scrub your filthy body with hog bristles." He plied my nose with the gun barrel.

I sniffed the acrid odor of gunpowder. The gull and raven raced, squawking and cackling, for Lt. LeRoy's wad of gum, floating pink and shiny with spit, on a branch barge. The raven won.

My feet were heavy as anvils. Been a long time since I'd looked down the barrel of a gun, and I resolved to handle it like a mature adult, which is to say, blab the first thing that comes into my head. "That cougar's for sale, you know."

Lt. LeRoy gave a chew, even though his gum was missing, for good measure. A wonder he didn't pull a jaw muscle. "Don't try to talk your way out of this," he said. "What do I want with a big cat?"

"Be good to train young hounds with," I said. "Get them blooded before the first hunt. Cull the wimps."

"Training's important," Lt LeRoy said, chewing empty space, lowering the gun to point at my congested chest.

On a roll, I said, "Course you'd have to negotiate with April and Malcomb here. The cougar's their captive. I'm just passing through. I'm sure they'd be more 'n' happy to negotiate with you."

"That's impossible," April said, "and illegal. We can't sell what isn't ours."

Malcomb strolled toward the red pick-up. His feet plopping heavy in the mud. "Cougar'd make a fine training animal." He looked at me and nodded his head sagely as if to say, "I'll play along with your master plan."

Excellent! I knew all along the old Indian could be counted on to back me up in a tough spot. Only one small problem, I didn't have a master plan. I didn't even have a servant plan, that is, beyond getting that gun pointed at some other place besides my chest.

"Department of Fish and Wildlife now owns that cat," April said.

"Damn Fish and Wildlife!" the wiry lieutenant said. "Just another branch of Big Gov'ment. We got our own legal constitution. We don't have to pay any attention to them." He wagged the gun barrel in my face to discourage disagreement.

Convinced me. "Fish and Wildlife'll never know," I said. "Course, you probably don't have that kind of money. Pretty expensive cat." I figured to bring in the grease power of a capitalist challenge. Learned that giving music lessons. Give them for free and students lose interest. Turn that around, and the more you charge, the quicker students learn. Capitalist grease.

I stalled for time to figure out a real plan.

Lt. LeRoy turned to Malcomb, bringing the pointing gun with him. "How much you asking, Chief? I better warn you I ain't in the mood to dicker much with mud people."

As if on cue, the young cougar screamed. Lt. LeRoy involuntarily jumped. His *"Legend in My Own Mind"* cap lifted an inch off his head. His gun hand jerked.

Malcomb waited for the spooked lieutenant to settle down. "I don't negotiate with guns present."

Lt. LeRoy hesitated, glanced, eyes glittering like cheap crystal, at me and then at April, muttered under his breath, "Bitch, I owe you one." Having marked an unsettled score, he holstered the weapon. "That satisfy you?"

I heard a huge sigh of relief from Big Steve.

April glared at me as if I'd lost my mind. Little did she know. Elpenor settled down, though I could still feel him tuning strings in my head.

My classic military diversion tactic worked. All I had to do now was create another diversion to save us from my previous diversion.

"No," said Malcomb, folding his arms across his powerful chest in a ritualistic gesture. "My clan has a tradition of refusing to bargain unless all weapons are out of sight."

I sidled over to April, whispered, "That's an admirable tradition."

April, her face hard as limestone, whispered back, "Our clan disbanded seventy-five years ago. We have about as much tradition as you do. That's bullshit you nitwit."

Medusa growled, clacked the rear window with her teeth. The hatchback door clattered. I remembered it was tied shut with binder twine. If Medusa did knock loose, I could take little comfort that the cat was still caged.

"Well, you're just gonna have to break tradition, Chief," Lt. LeRoy said. "Be within my rights to confiscate that cat and not pay you one red cent. I ain't about to get rid of my weapon in hostile territory." You could see his greedy eyes wandering, drawn to that oversized kitty. Mind already working away at elaborate sadistic training possibilities.

Malcomb shrugged, "Sometimes it works, sometimes it doesn't. Let's get to it then." He unfolded his arms and plodded over to the pickup.

Lt. LeRoy smirked, gave us all a lingering hard look, intending to let us know he still had the power, was in charge here. "I'll take care of you two," he said, "if these negotiations don't pan out to my liking." He strutted after Malcomb. To Big Steve, who was slapping mud off his cap, the lieutenant barked, "Come on Sergeant. We got us some amusement for this afternoon."

"I've got to do something," I whispered to April. "Malcomb's not really going to sell that cougar is he? I never intended it to go this far."

"I don't know whether to kiss you or cold-cock you," April said. "But we just got one more thing on our side."

"What's that?" Had my druthers, I'd go for the kiss.

"Father hates to be called Chief."

"What can an old man do against a trained mercenary?"

"Last guy that called him Chief cut a toe off with a chain-saw the very next day," April said. "Guy before that's shrimp boat capsized and he almost drowned. Course, they both claimed it was an accident. But they never called Father Chief again either. Not to his face."

Big Steve edged closer to April. "April, you know you shouldn't of slapped Lt. LeRoy. He gets real mean. And after today, comes a showdown, I have to take his side." He put his cap on his chiseled head and I caught a flash of his tattoo on his triceps. The big man lumbered after his lieutenant.

I watched the negotiators leaning, arms folded, on the bed of the pickup. Lt. LeRoy reached down and grabbed the stout stick he'd prodded the cat with before. He began teasing the cougar through the cage bars. The feline slapped at the stick and hissed at the militia man. Those claws didn't belong to no kitty.

Having been reared on an intractable red clay and limestone farm in Missouri, I knew what Lt. LeRoy would do with the cat. As a child, I witnessed my born-again preacher, lunatic step-dad starve and then cripple (a well placed bullet to the lower spine) an old boar raccoon and, when he thought it was too weak and pain-delirious to fight back, sic a half dozen hungry red-bone hounds on him. The old boar still sent a couple of those dogs howling hallelujah to the gate before the seasoned alpha-male snapped his neck.

I couldn't let that happen to the mountain lion. My feet, however, felt stuck in place. "Me and my big mouth," I said. "I got the cougar into this fix. It's up to me to put a stop to it." I started toward the pickup, sinking deeper in muck with each step and making a conspicuous sucking sound with each raised foot.

"Not so fast." April caught up with me and grabbed my arm. "See what Father is up to. Follow his lead."

"I'll give it a try," I said, but I wasn't much encouraged when I watched Lt. LeRoy hand Malcomb some money. The old man was actually selling the young cougar to an almost certain torture and death. What kind of shaman was he?

Shaman or no shaman, I had to put a stop to the slaughter. As I approached, Malcomb, stuffing bills in his hand-tooled leather wallet, met me, and winked. "Help me up on this pickup Harp, and we'll hand over this kitty to her new owner."

I bit my lip and gave him a boost then jumped up myself. The old pickup issued a metallic groan. The cat paced in circles. Every pass, his yellow, round eyes locked on Lt. LeRoy. His black-tipped, hooked tail raked the bars, sounding a series of rapid thuds, like the firing of a muffled semi-automatic rifle.

Malcomb stood on the left side of the cage and motioned me to the right. The young cougar gave off a fetid, tangy, caged smell. Malcomb stooped down, and the cat stopped pacing. The cougar pressed his head against the bars, and Malcomb scratched his tawny ears and whispered to him. I could hear some of what he said through the cage. The words seemed to be coming out of the cat's tail, which was sticking in my face: *"quickness and muscle, troubles and tussle, freedom is cheap, with one mighty leap."*

Didn't make sense. Chanting in riddles. I figured it was a mystic, Indian death prayer. The cougar's inner motor started up, and he purred like a big little kitten. The pickup's loose frame rattled. I felt the cat's vibration humming in the bottoms of my feet. One hell of a fine-tuned engine.

Purred like a house cat. It came to me; the darned thing was almost tame. Letting Malcomb scratch him like that. How could Malcomb possibly betray him, sell him down the river? Partly my fault, too. I'd given the old Indian the idea. My thoughts scattered: I let this happen, might as well forget about ever having a beautiful, sensitive romantic involvement with April. I stand here dumbstruck, and I might as well forget too, ever jumping on her succulent bones.

"Hey Chief," Lt. LeRoy commanded, "hand that cage down here. Let's go. Let's go. Damn civilians. Slow as molasses." His face flushed, chewing like crazy — somehow he'd managed to stuff another fat wad of gum in his skinny mouth. Him and Big Steve, face chalky as an unwiped blackboard after a fourth grade fractions class, stood at the foot of the pickup, waiting.

Malcomb straightened up. "You positive you want this cat?"

The cougar turned around, sniffed my muddy pants leg and then pressed his head against the bars like he'd done with Malcomb. I, too, scratched him, tawny fur like thick straw matting. He continued purring, tickling my fingertips, a tune trying to enter through extremities.

"Course I want 'em I paid for 'em, didn't I?" he said. Sensing civilian contrariness, he hooked his trigger finger on his gun.

I didn't like that at all. I saw how fast he'd pulled that gun, showed hours of quick draw practice.

Malcomb had a faint smile on his face. There was a dabble of blood on his upper lip. His head swayed steady, a slow, blues rhythm. I had another flash: Malcomb's plan was to let the cat loose. Insane idea! Old man gone bonkers. I had to stop him. The professional soldier would shoot the domesticated cat in the wink of an eye. And when bullets fly, there's always the danger of someone besides the target being hit, like April, for example. Couldn't let that happen. I straightened, determined to thwart Malcomb's diabolical dumb plan.

"Did I tell you that I hand-carved the cedar wood frame of this cage," Malcomb said. "Its totems are designed to let whatever temporarily caged animal it holds communicate with its cap..."

"Damn talking about the cage," Lt. LeRoy hollered, "let's have that cat."

I glared disapproval at the daft old Indian. Shit! There was that wink again. And, shielding his hand, he pointed at the wooden peg next to his waist holding the cage shut. I had a peg on my side too. No way, I thought. When the time comes, all I have to do is not pull the pin. Crazy old Indian needs my help to make it work.

Malcomb reached through the slats and scratched the cat's rump. "I'm glad you feel that way, cause — " He pointed beyond the two militia men, where April was washing her hands and arms in the river, "you can take a shower when you get home April. Put your dress back on."

The two well-trained soldiers snapped their necks around so fast I could hear cartilage creak.

Malcomb pulled the wooden peg on his side and signaled me, with a nod of his big silver head, to do the same. Asking me, Harp P. Gravey, world's most dedicated skeptic, to trust a man I'd met only hours before.

"I didn't sell you the cage," Malcomb continued in the same monotone voice, "I just sold you the cat. When you get done with him check back with me. I might have more for you by then."

I realized I had about a one-hundredth of a second to make up my mind before the timing would be blown. And as any musician knows, timing is everything. I pulled my pin. The cage creaked open, in agonizing slow motion, from the top down.

What happened next is sort of a movie-reel blur. The tame, purring, almost friendly kitty didn't even let the door open all the way. He pounced on the unfolding top edge of it, and, in another bound he soared. The recoil shoved the cage against the cab. The heavy door slammed, with a tremendous metal on metal BOOM, down on the truck bed.

"What are you pulling, Chief . . ." Lt. LeRoy managed to say before turning, and staring gape-jawed straight into the dense, lemony eyes, from about the length of a short-necked banjo, of pure killing genius.

I wonder if admiration flashed through his mercenary mind. I will say this for the quick-draw master, he did get his gun out of its holster. Shows you the importance of a lifetime of dedicated practice and training. The dazzling arc the unfired gun made when it went flying ass over teakettle into the Dosanomish was truly a sight to behold. It plopped in the middle of the cattail marsh, where, a bullet from its barrel had only minutes before shattered the red-winged blackbird's home.

Malcomb leaned over the cage and beamed a bloody-lipped grin at me. "I saw that trick in a movie once, done with a greenhorn and a grizzly."

The sleek cat landed with all four paws on Lt. LeRoy's sloped shoulders, hesitated a second, head down as if he were licking the back of the lieutenant's neck. They teetered, the nattily dressed military man with the head of a lion — sort of a modern-day, upside-down, backwards Sphinx — then the cat launched again, springing off the lieutenant's shoulders with a ripping sound, his mouth full of something, a mighty leap to land on top of my bus — infuriating Medusa who smacked the rear hatch with renewed vigor — then up to a limb on a big-leaf maple. Firmly perched, he stopped, looked around, twitched his magnificent tawny tail, put down the object in his mouth, which I recognized as the camouflage hat with the insignia *"I'm A Legend In My Own Mind,"* and let out a short, flat shriek. The shriek was followed by a deep growl that caterwauled into a metallic scream rising to a near-perfect, high-tenor falsetto. A signal designed no doubt to hamstring the courage of nervous prey; the hunt was on.

Malcomb's jacket pocket, with Merle inside, vibrated so hard it's a wonder the stitching didn't give way.

The rabbit scratches on my back felt like cracks in arctic ice.

Warning done, the cougar, with what appeared to be some pride, picked up the cap by the bill, shook his head back and forth, as if displaying a trophy, then disappeared into the rainy north woods.

12

Lost Dog and Elusive Rabbit

Funny about Big Steve. You'd think, with his imposing size and all, he'd be a hard man to lose. But he simply vanished. A magician's act. Now you see him now you don't. All that remained of the considerable space Big Steve formerly occupied was his military-issue camouflage cap, which seemed to rear up and hover in the thick damp air before collapsing beside two deep furrows in the mud leading under the pickup.

Malcomb stood with arms folded, silver head bowed, a ghost of a smile playing about his wrinkled lips.

April stood knee deep in the imperturbable Dosanomish, poised to dive if the unpredictable cat had leaped toward her. Then, a look of alarm crossed her water-nymph face and she began wading toward the attacked lieutenant.

The militia officer wobbled but still stood, unrecognizable though as the same tough hombre he'd been a few minutes before. His face looked pinched and flattened. Without the self-validating cap, his head looked about half its previous size. Small, in fact, and naked. Bald as an eagle came to my mind. Although I knew, from first-hand experience, bald eagles weren't really bald.

"Clack, clack", Medusa's fangs hammered the hatch window.

The shoulder pads on Lt. LeRoy's fancy officer's camouflage jacket looked as if they'd passed through a paper shredder. The cocky lieutenant staggered, hands clasped to his wire-thin throat, one ear lobe spurting dark red blood, long face turning blue. His restless eyeballs rolled back in his head, and he fell over backwards, making a splat in the mud. A sticky, sanguine smell hovered in the air.

It was at that exact moment Medusa busted open the hatchback door on my bus, leaped out — barking like no tomorrow all the way down — to land square atop Lt. LeRoy's camouflaged chest. If you think that might of hurt, I'm here to witness it didn't faze Medusa a bit. She did a somersault in the mud, paws plowing air on the upswing, and hit the ground in full, furious pursuit of the cougar. She, too, disappeared, growling and mud-flinging, with nary a glance backwards, hot on the trail of the cap carrying cat, into the rainy north woods.

My heart soared out of my body and sailed after Medusa. I calculated, *if she catches that cat she'll be too driven to back off. Ripped apart. A city dog not understanding the new rules out in the wild.*

I leaped out of the bed of the pick-up on legs like rubber bands. Sweat poured down my neck and chest. I smelled like shredded skunk cabbage and tasted copper in my mouth. Medusa's baying, already far in the distance, got weaker and weaker and trailed away, a fade-away, done-gone dog-song. I never should've brought my city mutt out to this godforsaken place.

Malcomb climbed out of the pick-up behind me.

"I have to go after Medusa," I said. My feet tried to take a step. One knee gave. Malcomb held me up. "Best thing you can do for your dog," he said, "is not get lost yourself, which is what'll happen if you go out into the deep woods alone. You're unprepared. You're too weak. You need to rest up for your journey." The old Indian's hand felt rough and safe.

I glanced at the tall trees and thick undergrowth. Up-valley a chain saw growled to life. My stomach growled a response. "Medusa? What will happen to her?"

"I haven't the foggiest," Malcomb said. "Let's hope she doesn't catch up with Clancy."

"Who the hell's Clancy?" I said.

"The cougar, of course." Malcomb said.

"How do you know a cougar's name?"

"He told me. It was a great honor. Cougar's don't reveal their name to just anybody."

My head felt airy. "I don't know why not." I said. "I should think it's quite common."

Malcomb ignored my feeble sarcasm. "Clancy told me he likes hats and also likes your dog. Although I can't tell whether Clancy means for food or friendship. There's a translation barrier."

"So you . . . ah . . . speak to animals, do you?" I said.

"I do," he said. "but, mostly I listen. When we get home we'll pray to the earth spirits to look after your dog. If she's a good dog, she'll find you."

Now there's a thought. Suddenly, I realized why I felt so warm and comfortable around Malcomb; he was as bonkers as me. If I left the tidal-flat, how could Medusa possibly find me? How could I find her? Hell I had trouble hitting my own butt with both hands. It's a cinch though, I wasn't going to Seattle until I got my dog back.

Nonetheless, Malcomb was right about resting up. Way I felt, I wouldn't last two hours out in the deep forest. I needed to eat something and get a couple hours of sleep. Then I'd search for Medusa.

Big Steve, having slithered out from under the pickup, his olive camouflage outfit painted with a coat of gray mud plaster, was busy rushing around trying to capture Merle. The bunny had somehow slipped out of Malcomb's coat pocket. Merle hippety-hopped, ears flopping, around the mud flat, leading the big man on a merry chase. The bunny wasn't about to get caught by a militia man nor dash into that forest after the cougar and the dog.

Big Steve passed close to me and I noticed that tattoo again with some red coloring on the underside of his forearm. I made out a tiny tomahawk. It sparked an association of sorts in my subconscious but my mind refused to go there. Instead, my mind spotted Big Steve's mud caked gun lying under the red pickup. Probably lost it during his cougar-inspired exodus.

Lt. LeRoy sat up, April sponged his oyster-colored face and frayed ear with a torn piece from her flannel shirt.

"Sergeant . . . Sergeant . . ." he said, "oh, whatever the hell your name is!" Lt. LeRoy had gotten his voice back. "Shoot these dirty mud people for attacking an officer." He staggered, with April's help, to his feet, then slapped her hands away. Mud flew like pig flop hit by a fan. "Get over here and assist me," he said. "I can't stand to be touched by her filthy hands." He, very unmilitary-like, babbled and almost collapsed. April caught him and held him up until Big Steve arrived.

In the midst of chaos, I could still appreciate the irony of the militia officer calling us mud people. He should look at himself in a mirror. In fact, all of us, except for Malcomb, looked as if we'd just crawled out of a crawfish hole. The little mud flat had surreal body swirls — like snow angels and devils — and blotches everywhere, overlaid with tiny rabbit tracks, as if we'd conspired to design a mythic mural.

"Shoot them! Shoot them!" the lieutenant ranted as Big Steve guided him through the barbed blackberries to the scarlet Jeep Grand Cherokee.

"I lost my gun sir," said Big Steve, looking over his shoulder at me. I nodded to him, ducked under the bumper and retrieved his forty-five.

"Lost your weapon? Lost your weapon? That's a court martial offense, soldier."

"You lost your weapon too, sir."

"That's different. I'm an officer. I don't have to abide by —" Big Steve shoved him in the Cherokee and slammed the door. The lieutenant's voice faded to indistinct rumblings.

Big Steve came high-stepping back. "April, Malcomb, I sorta helped you out this time, but don't expect me to again. Now I'm a sergeant. I get respect. Nobody ever gave me that before."

I handed his weapon to him.

April said, "We did, especially Loren, in high school."

"That was a long time ago," Big Steve said. He holstered the gun, mud and all, turned and high-stepped back to the Grand Cherokee. He started the sleek automobile — it purred like a contented cat — and headed for Port Townsend. The passenger side window rolled down, and Lt. LeRoy stuck a wiry arm out as they drove away. He shook his fist at us. "You'll pay! I'll get you all!"

If I never saw him again, it'd be too soon; although I had my suspicions that, like a childhood trauma, the gummy lieutenant turned up where you least expected him.

13

Shamans and Pentecosts

Malcomb reached in his back pocket, pulled out his billfold. "Speaking of paying. That's the easiest two hundred dollars I ever made." He extracted a bill and handed it to me.

"What's this?" I said.

He pinched his nose where his gold ring used to be. He winced. "It's one hundred dollars. Your cut. It was, after all, your plan. Damned clever one, I might add."

"Plan? My plan?" I said. "That was an insane plan. What if the cat had attacked your daughter? What if Lt. LeRoy had pulled his gun in time?" I fingered the hundred dollar bill. It was five times more than what I had hidden in my bus.

Malcomb said, "I knew you'd never let that happen. Hear that April? We got us a reluctant, modest shaman on our hands." Malcomb chuckled, ambled over to a blackberry thicket, reached down and plucked Merle out of hiding. I hadn't even seen the bunny.

"Shaman? You got to be kidding?" I said. "I'm no shaman. A Pentecost can't be a shaman. It's against nature. It's against God. I refuse. It's unfair."

April backed me up. "Madman is more like it," she said. "Father, it's beginning to rain. We haven't even got a good start looking for Molly Jenkins."

"We will hunt for her," Malcomb said, "after we get Harp settled in our house."

April looked down at her Adidas. "What makes you think I'm going to allow him in my home?"

"Please don't argue with me on this child," Malcomb said. "Look at him. He's a mess. He needs looking after and I need time to determine what ceremonies will be best to heal him while still cultivating his spiritual powers. You take Harp in the truck. I'll follow in his bus."

April rolled her eyes at me. "Hocus Pocus nonsense."

Nevertheless, she took my arm and, for a second, it was a toss up whether she meant to rip it out of its socket, or support my tottering bulk.

"You know how to drive one of these things?" I mumbled to Malcomb as he closed the VW hatch door. It wouldn't latch, but the spring hinges kept it closed enough for things that didn't ram it, like my long gone dog.

I had the impulse to retrieve my banjo from my bus and take it with me, but resisted. I trusted it and the VW to Malcomb. Seemed like a suitable tradeoff to get to ride in close quarters with April. Both her and me looked like we'd dipped in the same pig waller.

I disengaged myself from April and retrieved Big Steve's camouflage hat from a thicket of vines. Flapped the mud off.

April said, "Leave it. It was too big for his head anyway."

"We should get this back to Big Steve," I said. "We sorta owe him a favor."

"I don't want to touch it," said April, "Throw it in the back of the pick-up. The overgrown dummy. Big Steve was always looking for acceptance. Strange, isn't it, I remember Molly and him and Loren being in that silly tomahawk club together in high school. As I remember it, the full name was 'The Tomahawk 'n' Rhododendron' club. That was back when Indians and whites around here got along together much better."

Stopped me dead in my tracks. "Wait a minute," I said. "Did the club members all have the same tattoos?"

"Yeah, that's one reason I wouldn't join," April said. "You had to mutilate your body by getting one of those silly tattoos as an initiation."

"Was the tattoo a tomahawk buried in the trunk of a rhododendron bush?" I said. "Blood was coming out of the wound and the handle of the tomahawk had little black and white feathers on it?"

Malcomb stopped by the blue bus. April's neck twitched and she kneaded her left cheek with her knuckles. "How would you know about the tattoos?" she said.

Rain beat down in sharp cold pellets. Dark clouds skulked across the heavens. Thunder echoed off the mountains. Both April and Malcomb waited for my answer.

My voice a whisper, I said, "I saw the tattoo on Big Steve's arm. I've seen it before. I think I might know where Molly Jenkins is."

"Did you spot her somewhere on the way up . . . Shelton?" April said.

"You saw her in your vision didn't you?" Malcomb said.

"Yes, I saw her in my dream," I said. "At least I hope it was a dream. But there's no way I could've known about those identical tattoos. There was a dead woman in my dream. She had a tattoo like Big Steve's. I think maybe it was Molly Jenkins." Nobody hurried to get out of the rain. A sharp wind from the east buffeted us, turning bog scum into runny dun paste.

"It wasn't a dream," Malcomb said "That's why her life force has been missing."

"I think you're both full of shit," April said. "If she's dead, where's the body?"

"I don't know, exactly," I said, "I think it's somewhere up the Dosanomish, stuck under a massive logjam." I shivered, the hard rain beginning to feel like shards of glass on my exposed head. I needed a protective hat.

"Do you remember any landmarks?" Malcomb said.

"Well there was a thunderb . . . osprey's nest close by," I said. "An old lodge with the roof caving in, a steep bluff, with a gap, like a canine tooth missing, to the north.

"Kaalpekci Peak," said Malcomb. "We know of it. Full of bad luck. Come, the tide's rising, let's get out of here before we get stuck in the mud again. I'll figure out how to contact the authorities."

"You sure you never been here before?" April said.

"Never," I said, "but there is one more thing you should know. Molly Jenkins was murdered."

Malcomb and April cast a glance at each other. A faint rasping noise came from the old Indian's lips. A seal bark carried in on an ocean breeze smelling of crab flesh.

"Father," said April, "let's wait until there's an actual body found before we tell Loren. If it's true, this'll put him over the edge."

Malcomb cupped his face with a worn palm. "It just might do that," he said, "if he doesn't have a good alibi." He tilted his long-eared head toward me. As he climbed into my bus his movements slowed, like he'd just gained twenty pounds of ugly fat "And you say you're no shaman," he said.

"What I said was," I said "I don't want to be a shaman."

Before I got in the old red pickup, I took a deep breath, put my hand to my forehead as a shield to the rain and took a last look around. I had spent what, maybe two hours on the mud bog but it seemed like a lifetime. Hard raindrops were already beating the swirled-and-gouged mud stage back into shape, erasing our presence. Red-wing blackbirds, in the khaki-colored cattails, had settled down, perhaps assessing how to carry-on after their babies had been exterminated, home decimated. Heavy clouds, sluggish as cold serpents, slithered overhead, hiding the sun.

The greedy raven, as I watched, disgorged Lt. LeRoy's wad of gum. The opportunist gray gull pounced on it. One beast's failure is another's opportunity.

I glanced up the river valley, alive with spring sap, toward the mountains. Did I hear a distant baying? I had let my faithful dog get lost up there in that wilderness. Poor girl. Now we both were really alone. No warm body to snuggle up to at night. No foul breath to wake up to. Worst of all, no bark of protest if I attempted to take a drink of booze. If I go to Seattle, I said to myself, without Medusa, I might as well jump into the molten crater of Mt. St. Helens. End it hot and quick.

No, no Seattle today. I am stuck in this Godforsaken wilderness until I find my best friend.

My inherited land was up there waiting for Josh's ashes. Maybe a temporary home for me? Nah, more like a black, moist hole, an anvil hanging around my neck. A muscle over my heart twitched. If my dream wasn't a dream, Molly Jenkins's body lay up there in the river too. I remembered her staring eyes, beseeching me to find her killer and avenge her. I suspected, although not clear how, Molly's destinies and mine were intertwined. I was stuck on the Dosanomish until I found Molly Jenkins's murderer.

The Dosanomish continued to sing to me its rhythmic song with relentless, inexorable clarity.

We pulled out on Highway 101. I fought fatigue and tried to rest my sore head in April's soft lap. She pushed me away. "Unless I believe that spirit animal crap," she said, "there's only one other way you, Mr. Harp P. Gravey, could know about Molly Jenkins. And what the hell does the P stand for?"

I scrunched up in the far corner. "Pearl."

"Pearl? Did you say Pearl?"

"I said Pearl."

"No wonder you're such a wreck," she said, "going through life with a name like Harp Pearl Gravey."

She whispered under her breath, "Thank God, of all the losers I've fallen for in the past, he won't be one of them. He's too cute to be much of a banjo picker anyway."

I slept. Slept deeper than I had slept since before my life became a tuneless bruise.

14

Out of a Vision World and Into a Dream Land

Lying in a bed in some kind of wood artifact storage room I floated, feverish, in and out of dreams. I could hear a fiddle playing, pigs grunting, dogs barking, people singing, hornets buzzing, drums, laughter, crying. No banjos though. Why weren't there any banjos? Banjos should be issued at birth.

I saw my human self inside a video game, the way I was before and after my cranium got crushed.

Before, I had been a maintenance drunk able to minimally function, keeping up a little rented house in the Errol Heights (known to the locals as Poverty Flats — to the cops as Felony Flats) section of Portland, Oregon. My last lover, a base player named Susan Conroy, had abandoned me two years previous. Susan packed her big, upright base fiddle and went to Nashville with dozens of our jointly written songs. Only thing she left behind was one broken heart.

I went into a two-year tail spin. By my erratic behavior, I pretty much soured my chances of ever playing with any legitimate local bluegrass band in Portland. I was eking out a living doing one-man-band type solo performances — mingling storytelling with music — and hustling sucker fish on neighborhood pool tables around town. Only two things I'd ever been good at was playing music and shooting pool, neither of which I could do any longer.

Portland, while well on the way to becoming a big city, is still, in many ways a small town. The music community is small, and unfortunately so is the play-for-money pool shooting community. I pulled one hustle too many. And with the wrong fish.

Pool betrayed me. The part I can't figure out is why did I do it? Had the fish cold but overplayed my hand. Rubbed it in. I knew the danger but couldn't stop myself. It was like I was hard-wired to forget all the tenants of successful hustling.

Hint; never tell the leader of the Gypsy Jokers motorcycle gang you've just hustled out of a thousand dollars, he shoots pool like pigeons fuck.

His goons caught me out in the parking lot. Took a number ten wrecking bar to my skull.

I first met Elpenor in the Intensive Care Unit of the Adventist Hospital. He was posing as a doctor. Elpenor sorta gave himself away as a fraud when he blew fire out of his nostrils and ridiculed my penis. I put up with him for four weeks and a blur of operations, and then, fleeing Elpenor, snuck out of intensive care, and went on a diehard booze binge. Worse thing I could've done. Elpenor thrived on alcohol. He gave new meaning to the term demon rum. New meaning also to the art of shape changing.

It took two stinking months, after I climbed into a bottle, to lose my rented house and hock my instruments and pool cue. I began living out of my VW bus on the mean streets. Elpenor took to the street like a slug on gull guts. The dragon became a constant companion and persecutor, on a diabolical mission to destroy me from within as I was destroying myself from without. Somehow, the weaker I became, the stronger he got. The law of inverse proportion run amuck. My booze elevator, with Elpenor as trickster attendant, hit bottom with a boom. Well, not really a boom; the bottom sounds more like the cry of a naked child abandoned on a toneless ice flow. Worse than being abandoned, I had Elpenor.

While on that dehumanizing ice flow, I rolled over in the back of my bus one morning and there was Medusa, stinking of street garbage and rat fur, snuggled up against me; giving of her warmth, her strength, her unselfish and uncritical love. She licked my runny nose. I swooned from her foul breath. She licked harder, thriving on mine. The ice flow formed a bridge to the desolate tundra.

I found out Medusa's name from some of the local bowery boys. She'd been around for months, terrorizing the locals, living off scraps. I don't know where Medusa came from or why she picked me for a pack pal.

I owe her more than just loyalty. She saved my life. I managed, with Medusa by my side, to steer my way off the alcoholic ice-flow to shore. And into the psychiatric outpatient care unit of the VA hospital.

That's where I met Josh Lawrence. Josh was diagnosed as paranoid schizophrenic. It was a money-saving, quickie diagnosis and dead wrong. Josh had a brain tumor and, by the time they discovered their faulty diagnosis, it was too late for any life-saving treatment. Josh became my savior, not so much because he gave me a temporary home and introduced me to recovery, which he did, but because, as much as I needed him at the time, he also needed me. I nursed him as he lay dying.

Somebody needed me. Me. Harp Pearl Gravey.

Josh, even though he knew I couldn't play them anymore, was upset at me pawning my instruments. He said he believed I would someday be able to play music again. He insisted I get them out of hoc and gave me the cash to retrieve them. He called it hospice wages.

I called it death dues.

Suddenly, my reminiscent video game was pre-empted by a video game of Great Grandfather Two Loons telling me tales. Drum and mouth-harp music beat in the background. Grandfather said, "*You chose to sing to me while covered in my mud in order to become cleansed. Now you have recognized me, you must pray to me. You have come home. You have become linked to me as I am linked with one of the ancient gifted ones. If you pray to me — ask for guidance — I will send a Tamánamis to give you advice.*

For my favor, you must do this thing; I have been violated, insulted. My banks are filled with evil spirits. You have found the body of one of my daughters, Molly Jenkins. She was brutally murdered. Her death must be avenged, her killer brought to justice. You must join forces with your animal spirit helper Qo-oo-la. Then swa'da power will find you.

I replied in my cocky, nomad voice, "Hey forget that home crap. I learned a long time ago I ain't got no home in this world anymore. And no offense, but having a common loon named Qo-oo-la as a partner to search for a cold-blooded killer doesn't exactly fill me with courage and confidence."

"Qo-oo-la is a brave spirit warrior. Perhaps his loon power will rub off on you and you will be so lucky as to become loon-hearted yourself. Cherish your spiritual connection to the earth; without Qo-oo-la you will not survive in this strange land. If you and Qo-oo-la succeed then harmony will find you and you will once again permit music and love to enter your impoverished soul."

Grandpa Two Loons' spirit image flashed a brilliant phosphorescent white, and floated backwards faster and faster down an ever-narrowing dark tunnel until disappearing. I smelled peat moss soaked in vinegar and tasted sour salmon spawn on the back of my tongue.

15

Of Bees and Yellow Jackets

"Scrape away the mud, dung and dog piss and he's not a half-bad look-ing man for a has-been banjo picker and all around lunatic." April's musi-cal voice rippled over me. She stood with hands on huggable hips, peering down at me as I lay caccooning under soft covers. I shook my head to clear it. As my eyesight refocused, I saw her long, thick hair coiled in a bun on her head with a stick stuck through it. She had on light green hospital scrubs with the words Old Wolf Wildlife Care Clinic stitched over her left breast. Dozens of small yellow and black feathers stuck to her shoulders and arms. There were also little dabs of orangeish dis-gorgement and pink smears of blood on the dull green smock. I sniffed a faint aroma of intestines and turpentine.

I had never laid eyes on anyone so fetching.

Malcomb stood by his daughter's side wearing a charcoal apron, an ugly, unfinished wooden mask, the size of a garbage can lid, snugged to his chest with one arm, a wooden mallet in his right hand. Curly shav-ings of bright wood clung to his silver hair and faded denim shirt. The air around him gleamed with an expectant rosy glow.

The bed had April's clean, fruity fragrance, like tree-ripened cherries popped open after a crisp summer's storm. I gathered the rainbow-col-ored, velvety quilt around my neck, feeling the sumptuous grain of the fabric, a breath of warm air tingling my skin. The quilt had the same leaping salmon, blue and purple, pattern print that was on the earrings April wore at the mud-flat.

I hadn't lain in such a fine bed in years. I wanted to dive into it, immerse myself, never come up for air, like — what was the loon's name the spirit voice used in my dream, Qo-oo-la? — did in water. What kind of name was Qo-oo-la, anyway?

"Qo-oo-la?" I said out loud. Didn't sound half-bad, really, once you got your breath into it.

"What was that?" April said. "He's talking gibberish but at least he's coming out of it."

"Qo-oo-la," repeated Malcomb, rolling the word around on his tongue. "It is not gibberish. It is close, in tribal language, to the word for insane-sounding singer. How could he know that unless he had some kind of vision?" He lay the mallet down on the foot of my bed and shifted the ugly mask. It had a long, vicious nose. I took an instant dislike to that appendage.

"Easy," April said. "It's just the nonsensical mumbling of the tail-end of his delirium traumas. For Christ's sake, after he put on your precious hat, the man had a grand mal seizure Father, and has been in 'n' out of a coma for two days. Hey, he didn't have many arrows in his quiver to start with, I expect he's got less now." She put a cool hand on my hot forehead. With her other hand she fluffed-up my pillow.

"What's *Tamánamis*?" I said. "What happened? How did I get here?" My mouth was dry and my tongue was as rough and poisonous as a newt's orange underbelly. Then, like the eagle's scurrilous dive, it all came back to me: the lion, the leap, the done-gone dog, the eagle, the osprey, the gold pin, the purple hat and Molly Jenkins, the dead woman with imploring eyes. And, of course, the loon, Qo-oo-la.

"Ha!" said Malcomb. "I suppose *Tamánamis* was gibberish, too. Very few people know that word. I'm telling you April, that hat is magic. The old ones have been in contact with him."

April snorted. Feathers flew. "If your old ones have contacted Mr. Harp P. Gravey here," she said, "then I'd say they've waited centuries to commit a terrible case of poor judgement or mistaken identity."

"That's not for us to say," said Malcomb. "Look, his mind is clearing. We're being rude. Let's let him talk. I want to hear him talk."

"You're not going to believe the dream . . . dreams I had," I said. "But wait. Let's deal with the reality first. The mud flat? Medusa? Did she come back?" I rambled but couldn't seem to help it. I had a vague recollection of taking a shower and crawling into bed in a room with dozens of wooden statutes. I looked around. They were still there, surrounding me, watching. Wooden animals flocked together, reeking of oil and cedar pitch and burnt charcoal. One black bear statue winked at me. An otter stuck out a red tongue. A large fish, possibly a catfish, grinned with a mouth full of big, sharp teeth.

I glanced out of the window at a gray morning fog creeping into a work yard of more wooden carvings. Some carvings were huge, totem poles. Gulls stood sentinel on the roof of an open-faced shop building with a red metal roof. A raven landed in their midst. The guarding gulls separated to give the black bird plenty of room. Beyond the red-roofed building, shore birds ran in tight flock formation along the tan beach. Beyond the shore birds, lights flickered in dwellings on islands across the Salish Sea, an ancient name for Puget Sound that just popped into my head. It was either dusk or dawn. Or, it was so dark from low-hanging black clouds that people left their lights on.

April patted her coiled hair. "We've put out the word on your dog up and down the valley," she said, "and haven't heard a peep. It's been two days now. If I was you I'd give up on her. The chances of a lone city dog surviving out there in that wilderness are nil. Especially if she catches up with Clancy — that hungry cougar."

My brain felt coated with mold. For some reason I was schooched down toward the foot of the bed. I attempted to slide up toward the head and ran into an irresistible obstacle. "Oh shit, that's right," I said. "That cougar has a name. I've got to go after my dog." I tried to rise and was knocked back by a burst of cranial dizziness.

April arched an eyebrow at Malcomb. "Clancy has a name," she said, "cause that's what was on his collar when we found him in Jeremy Jones' garage eating his Doberman watch dog."

Malcomb hooked his chin into his chest. "Clancy is not his real name," he said. "He told me his real name while in my cage but made me promise not to tell anyone."

April drew her upper lip back, showed pearly white teeth to her father. "Can it with that talking-to-animals crap, Father," she said. "Clancy was undoubtedly raised in captivity, hopelessly *imprinted* with humans. He got too big and someone kicked him out on the highway. April hesitated, her eyes focused above my forehead. "Interesting, that cougar showing up the same morning you did."

Malcomb nodded. "There's that pair of ospreys nesting up river too. They're the first ones seen on the Dosanomish in my lifetime. I believe our ancestors had a hand in killing the last osprey many years ago because of the misguided belief it stole fish away from our tribe. We couldn't do anything then about the real fish thieves so we took it out on other animals."

"Bad *Tamánamis*, huh, Father?" April said.

"Ha!" Malcomb said. "You mock me but there's that word again April, and from your lips. But you're right, for seventy five years, a powerful bad *Tamánamis.*"

"An osprey?" I said. "I saw . . . wait and minute. A Doberman? That cougar killed one of the most vicious breeds of dog there is?" I was having trouble keeping up.

April clenched her fiddler's hands in tight knots, concealing the attractive callused fingertips. Her lips, between clipped words, formed a seamless line. Her chin and cheeks were paler than the rest of her face, like she'd been dusted in mauve chalk. "Actually, Clancy killed two trained attack dogs. But he only ate one, and then only the juiciest organs, you know; heart, liver, kidneys. Easiest prey he could find probably."

My lungs strained against my ribs. My kidneys heavy as six-volt batteries. Heart thumping like a bunny on a coyote path with no exit. I struggled again to crawl out of bed, rescue my precious mutt from having her organs non-surgically removed. My head resisted. It felt lumpish and heavy, like it weighed two tons.

It did weigh two tons! There was some kind of turban attached to the top of my skull. Stuck tight, I punched and pulled at it to no avail. "What's the hell's this thing on my head?"

"Father's idea," April said. "I couldn't talk him out of it. It came to him during one of his prehistoric healer power dances."

"I had no choice," Malcolm said. "You kept talking about yellow jackets in your delirium. Pigs too. Curious combination."

"After my head operation," I said, "I spent some time in VA rehab. They had video games. My favorite — you gotta realize I was not thinking too clearly — had pigs and yellow jackets chasing the hero. If the hero took a misstep a large metal object dropped on his head."

April waved her hand in dismissal of my explanation. "Night before last, my father stayed up 'til dawn, dancing and singing and worrying that skunk cabbage root, sow thistle seeds and hornet's nest poultice. Says his healing spirit tells him it will subdue the demon that's in possession of your mind. I doubt you'll be chasing through the woods after a dog with that coned carbuncle."

"It doesn't look all that bad," Malcomb said. "Actually it makes a distinctive hat. I haven't been that inspired since Eola Gibbons asked me to treat her gout."

April marched over to a small desk, scattered through the clutter, found the object she was looking for, blew a cloud of wood shaving dust off it, wiped it with her elbow, and brought it to me.

I stared into a small wood-framed mirror at an ashen face, with sunken hazel eyes, flat cheeks and a stubbled beard. As if that wasn't enough to frighten me, grafted onto my cranium, obliterating my wild, salt and pepper hair, was a hoary looking hornet's nest. The gray of the nest so matched the pallor of my skin it was difficult to tell where the insect abode left off and the humanoid forehead began. The nest extended my head by a foot.

I squeezed the nest with both hands and it wheezed like a roll-your-own smokers' lungs, causing the enclosed section of my skull to pressurize and contract. The tiny synthetic plate in my head swelled and pinched. I rubbed my fingertips along the surface of the hornet hat and felt the rough texture of fine sandpaper. An odor of mildewed paper and insect feces drifted down to my nose and mouth. I pried the hefty hive from side to side and it threatened, if dislodged, to take skin and flesh and plate with it. The turban didn't budge. There for the duration.

Damnation! Elpenor would have one more thing to ridicule me for.

"Did you?" I asked Malcomb.

"Did I what?"

"Cure that lady's gout?"

"You betcha."

April gave a dry laugh. "It's debatable. He cured Eola Gibbons's gout all right. So much so that she took up long-distance swimming. She was last seen eight months ago by the lookout on a Russian fishing boat. She was three miles out to sea chugging away towards Orcas Island. Watch out for Father's cures. They maybe heal the ailment but kill the patient."

Malcomb clinched his jaw. "Eola will turn up," he said. "She's just went for a rather long constitutional."

Hold it! I cocked my head. Did I hear something up there above me in that papyrus fortress? A distant nattering, a flock of nut hatches gone bananas? I pointed to the nest.

"A hatching," April said, the seam in her lips parting with a dry click. She took a step backwards.

Malcolm nodded in agreement. "Probably some left-over pupae — in a separate compartment away from your noggin of course — to draw out the poison. The hatched infants will die before they have the strength enough to eat through the compartment walls."

"I say," April said, "imprisoned like that, those nasty yellow jackets are probably pretty pissed off."

I laid my top-heavy head back down. The nattering settled down into a droning. Yellow jackets! Why did it have to be yellow jackets? I loath yellow jackets. Let me tell you about yellow jackets. They are not bees. Bees buzz about, plump and serene, spreading good cheer and kissing blue lobelia and red clover. Bees bring the golden gift of honey, without prejudice, to the world. Bees harbor no species anger or racial vengeance against humans. Bees are benevolent.

Their distant feuding cousin yellow jackets, however, would rather sting a horse than kiss a hyacinth, would rather shatter a picnic than scatter yellow pollen and would rather steal a chunk of red melon than stew a batch of gold honey. Yellow jackets! Why did it have to be yellow jackets?

To make matters worse, I was allergic to hornets. At least the Missouri kind. If stung, I could go into anaphylactic shock and die in five minutes if I didn't get an antidote. I hadn't carried epinephrine, the antidote, in years. Just another reason I'd lived in a city the last twenty years. Fewer hornets. The wilderness and I were incompatible on several levels.

16

Wackos and Blown Kisses

"I'm allergic to hornet stings," I said.

"Relax," Malcomb said, "I've reinforced the hive compartments with a leather lining. If any of the pupae do live, the only way they could possibly escape is when I take the nest off. And we'll be ready for them then."

April stepped forward and leaned over me, listening to the hornet hat. I got a clearer picture of the orangest of the gull-gut disgorgement on the chest of her light green hospital smock. It sparked another memory in my muddled mind. A mangled exit hole.

I saw across the room, superimposed over the wooden bear's snout, the pleading dead eyes and blue cheeks of the woman in the river. Murdered! Of course, that's the murder the dream voice told me to solve.

I drew away from April, pressed back into the pillow. "Oh God, the body! What happened with the body? Did you find the lady with the tomahawk tattoo?"

April smiled, stepped forward and patted my forehead. "Relax. There is no body, no tattoo. It was all a hallucination, a nightmare.

You know you have this one long curl sticking out from under Father's poultice."

"All the same," said Malcomb, "I'm going to go finish your mask. I suspect you'll be needing it. Besides they're still searching up there on the Dosanomish." Hugging the hefty mask, he left.

By rolling my eyes, I saw April take the curl and roll it between thumb and forefinger, tightening a fiddle bow. "But it was so real," I said. "Did you look in the right place? The logjam with an osprey's nest close by?"

"I personally didn't look any place," April said. "I called Sheriff Gloeckler and made a report two days ago. That's all you talked — ranted — about on the ride from the mud flat to here. They're a little slow to mobilize an underwater search party around here in frigid, flood waters for someone like Molly, a Native American with a history of erratic behavior. Specially reported by a stranger. But the word is, some divers are up on the Dosanomish right now."

I wasn't satisfied. "What did you tell this Sheriff Gloeckler? How you knew about the body?"

"I told him a partial truth," she said. "Said I had talked to a wacko — that's the truest part — who reported spotting a body in the Dosanomish. Father is very upset with me. He thought I should have called it in anonymously. But then he bought in to your cockamamie story." She wrapped my escaped curl around her finger and tugged. A flake of gray nest chipped off and shimmied down my nose and caught in my mustache.

April leaned down and blew the flake away. Her breath fluffed the hairs of my mustache and funneled up my nostrils. I drank of it with my lungs. It was hot and had a flavor like wild horseradish and alpine mint. Her lips were inches from mine. She wet them with a pink tongue.

I had the strange sensation April was coming onto me. How could that be when she'd rejected me so decisively on the mud flat? I must be imagining it. Besides, now there was another woman in my life. Molly's eyes, through a muddied, memory film, pleaded with me. "The tattoo," I said. "What about knowing about Molly's belly tattoo?"

April drew back, brushed a strand of hair out of her eyes that had escaped the rock hard bun, and snorted. "Easy. Easy to explain. You could've met Molly any number of places, a tavern, a street corner. You could've had sexual relations with her. She was quite promiscuous. So that takes care of that." April gave my shoulder a not-so-playful punch, forgiving me for indiscretions I committed before I knew her.

My shoulder absorbed the punch and sent a minor shock wave down to my toes. I suspected I did not deserve to be forgiven. "When could I have met her?" Even as I said it I knew the answer: I had blacked-out for four blank days after Josh's death.

"Molly's had that tattoo since high school," April said. "You two wandering souls could've run across each other any time in the last fifteen years. Give it up Harp P. Gravey. You're innocent . . . I mean, hardly that, but you only had a very vivid dream." April drew a finger across her moist lips, testing them. "Now, I'd rather talk about that land you inherited up the Dosanomish. We could use a land owner around here on the side of Indians."

The phone on the bedside table rang. April executed such a sharp intake of breath, the stick-spear in her hair bun dislodged. She shook her head as if recovering from a dizzying clout on the temple, her bunned hair, without its backbone, cascaded down her back. "Damn. I'm expecting a call from the WSU lab about a potential rabid bat. I'll take it in my office. After I take care of that I'll see about getting you some chicken soup. You do eat meat don't you?"

"You don't happen to have any fresh fish," I said. Just popped out. First time in my life I ever asked for fish.

"Fresh fish?" April said. "Funny, you never impressed me as a fish eater, but I'll see what I can do." She opened the door to leave, turned, gave me a careful scrutiny, then blew me a kiss, and closed the door.

First kiss, whether remote or up close, I'd had thrown my way in two years. I lifted my hands, curled them into catcher's mitts, caught it and pressed it to my mouth. Probed it with the tip of my tongue. It had a passionate, melancholy taste.

It did not last long. I sniffed the air, searching. The kiss was gone. Evaporated. Only thing that remained was the scent of lip balm and my racing pulse. Perhaps April was merely shy. Maybe I had a chance with her after all. Why not? Stranger things had already happened to me. I spread my fingers and clasped them over my chest, contemplating making love with the reluctant fiddler.

The other woman would not evaporate though. I could not get Molly Jenkins's underwater eyes out of my mind; eyes with flat stones covering them. April's reaction to Molly was somewhat puzzling too. She had more of a stake in this than she admitted. Probably cared more for Molly Jenkins than she let on.

Molly Jenkins alive? I tried to find some cheer in the possibility, but my heart would not hear of it. Who was Molly? I felt a great need to find out more about her. From April's insinuations, Molly was another desperate, lonely soul looking for love in lousy places. Secretly searching for security. Was that what I was doing too?

Molly Jenkins and I had more in common than was comfortable.

17

Flying Feathers and Howling Coyotes

April's fragile kiss had a short life. She stormed through the door. "After a few direction miscalculations, they found Molly's body. It was right where you said it was in your dream or vision. If it was a dream or vision."

My heavy head got heavier. "Must have been," I said. "No way I could have known otherwise."

April, with a twist of her pretty mouth, fiffed a curly yellow feather off the shoulder of her light green hospital smock. The other feathers, miniature sailing vessels, rocked with her body movement. "You big city folks must think we're pretty dumb out here," she said. "Could be lying through your teeth. But, I must admit you're pretty clever although you don't look it. The way you picked up on my father's gullibleness with that smelly headdress." April stood beside my bed with hands at her side rolled into tight fists. She took two steps backwards. Putting distance between us.

I had to raise my voice to carry to her. My scalp pinched. "Closer, please? I want to smell . . . I mean tell you. What possible reason would I have to lie to you and your father?"

April took another step back. "I think I should wait 'til Sheriff Gloeckler gets here before we delve into that."

I punched my headdress. "Why is this sheriff Gloeckler coming here? Shouldn't he be out looking for a murderer? What do you want him to delve into here?"

She heaved her shoulders. Feathers flew. "I must tell you, I also called a psychologist friend of mine. He says I should be careful around you. You could have multiple personalities. Psychotic tendencies. Right hand not knowing what the left hand is doing. That's why I'm backing away from you." April pulled at her ear but the low-hanging leaping salmon earrings were gone, replaced by howling coyotes. They recoiled at her touch.

"Just how good a friend is this psychologist?" I saw green, detecting competition for April's affections, little as they were at the moment.

"What possible difference does my professional friendship with David. . . . Oh, oh, I see. Don't think because I blew you a kiss before I knew about Molly that it has any significance now. David is a respected therapist. I went to see him a couple of years ago when I was having some love, ah, life passages problems. My private life is none of your business." April's face was flushed and her back was pressed to the wall, a hands distance from the door leading outside.

A wooden shark mounted on the wall over April's head, bared its fangs at me. I bared mine, though less impressive, back. "Why would you call the sheriff on me? "

"Why are you snarling at me?" she said. "Sheriff Gloeckler has issued a warrant for my brother Loren's arrest. He obviously thinks Loren killed Molly in a jealous rage. She was killed by a twenty-two pistol. It's known that Loren has a twenty-two pistol. Ah . . . what did you do with yours?"

"I'm not snarling at you," I said. "I'm snarling at the fish above you. What did I do with my what?"

"Your gun? Your pistol? I figure being on the road as much as you are, you have something for protection of your instruments. Those are really fine instruments — especially the fiddle — to be knocking about in the back of a beat-up bus. How did you get them?" April cocked her head, blew a wisp of hair off her forehead, and checked out the shark above her. It, true to its cunning nature, reverted to inertness.

"You're going pretty fast here but I'll try and keep up," I said. "Those instruments are the only consistent things in my life. No matter what,

I've always kept them safe." I didn't tell her about my recent lapse. Would've lost my beautiful banjo, guitar and harmonicas to a pawn shop had it not been for Josh. "The fiddle is . . . was Josh's. He made me promise to give it to someone who would love and appreciate it.

Let's see, what else? Oh, yes, as a matter of fact I do — did — have a twenty-two pistol." I made it sound casual.

"Aha! Where'd you stash it? It's not in your bus and — "

"It was stolen months ago." I said, lying with alcoholic ease. I had it hidden very cleverly in my harmonica case. To cover up my lie, I attacked. "You searched my bus? You violated my space without my permission?" I feigned outrage but was, in fact, embarrassed. My bus was a nice old bus but to anyone with one iota of anal retentiveness, it could've passed for a mini garbage dump. Much like my mind, I hadn't cleaned my bus in two years.

"Fumigated it is more like it," April said. "Washed it out with bleach and a pressure hose. Someone had to take care of your instruments. I threw most everything else — except some legal papers from the glove compartment — in the trash. Smelled like wet fur, rat piss and booze. I had to search your car. For my brother's sake."

"I still don't understand," I said, "what you're saying about the sheriff. "

April put her small hand on the doorknob. "You're either slow or very clever. What I'm saying is the other way you could've known about Molly's body being there is you could be her killer." Her eyes watered. "And not even know it yourself."

The calves of my legs fused with the sheet. The storeroom filled with shadows. A hollow plumbing noise gurgled in the wall behind me, then hissed, a faulty valve ready to blow. What an insane thought, to be a killer and not know it. In the rehab center, I'd heard horror stories about alcoholic blackouts. People coming off a drunk to find out they'd killed their whole family, then going to the gas chamber convinced of their own innocence.

What did I do those missing four days after Josh died? Drive up here, get involved with Molly, put a bullet in her, and go back to Portland and regain reality in Josh's apartment?

Poor April, no wonder she backed away; considered me a possible murderer. The wooden raven and gull nodded their heads in agreement so hard I could hear wood scraping. The bear shook its head "No." Glad to have some support even though it was no more than sympathetic sap. "A nice theory but easy to disprove," I said, "I have never been to the Olympic Peninsula before."

"So you say," April said. "Where were you a week ago?"

"Down in Portland."

"Can you prove it?"

"Of course I can prove it."

"So give me some names of friends who can verify your whereabouts."

Oh, oh. Throwing those tough ones at me. Asking for friends. After Josh died, I remember having dealings with the funeral parlor director and a few other people but could name no one to call. Josh's ex-wife and computer nerd husband hadn't shown up at the memorial. Probably wouldn't have vouched for me if they did. I certainly had no verifying telephone numbers.

I took a different tact. "What possible motive could I have for killing Molly Jenkins. I don't know her, never seen her before we met in that logjam." I shuddered with the memory of clinging tendrils of hair. The involuntary movement caused flakes of papyrus to float down from my turban.

A pounding began in the red-roofed building. A Stellar's jay picked up the beat and screeched outside my window.

"You say," April said. "I say you could've been one of her lovers. She went for flakes, ne'er-do-wells and banjo pickers." She spit "banjo pickers" like most people say rectal exam.

I looked at April's tense body and black eyes and saw pure stubbornness. She could say all she wanted to about me, but I felt I had a duty to strike a blow for my banjo picking brethren. "The banjo is a very lyrical instrument. It takes real talent to play it well."

"How come so many men butcher it?"

"Most people butcher fiddle too. It just doesn't sound as loud or protest quite as much. It's the difference between tickling a hog and a hornet."

April took a step forward "The fiddle is the most lyrical of all instruments," she said. She kicked a bedpost. I caught a glimpse of a well-defined Achilles tendon.

My groin felt congested. "A fiddle is a piece of wood, strings and horse hair," I said. "It's the fool playing the fiddle that makes it sing. Same as banjo or any other instrument."

April took another step closer. She chewed on her fingertip calluses. "I'd have to be a fool alright, to believe anything you said."

I could see the subtle curve of her neck where it disappeared behind black hair. My skin itched every place the cover touched me. Behind her rain commenced pecking on the window and low clouds smothered the islands in the Salish Sea. I smelled the sweet aroma of shampooed hair. The congestion in my groin tightened. "Well do you want it or not?" I said.

April cocked her head, surveyed the length of my body, large hair rustling. "Want what?"

"Josh's fiddle. I have no need of it."

Her black eyes glinted. "It's stolen, isn't it?"

"No, I guarantee it's not stolen. The same guy who gave me the property gave me his fiddle."

Her cheeks glowed like whipped sherbet. "I've never played an instrument of that quality. How much do you want for it?" Her eyes glanced at the instrument case; fingers stretching. She must have taken it out of its case and inspected it while I lay sleeping. Fiddle hooked her good.

My left hand fingers stroked an imaginary fret board. "Don't want anything for it," I said. "It's yours for the playing of it."

April folded her arms across her chest and hugged herself. "You can't just give away a fiddle of that quality," she said. "My God, the bow alone is worth at least fifteen hundred dollars. You're broke. You could sell it."

My arms were jealous of hers. "I have one hundred dollars from the sale of the cougar," I said. "Plenty enough to buy gas and crackers and peanut butter. No I can't sell his fiddle. Josh instructed me to give it to someone worthy." I wanted to retract my last statement the instant it left my lips. I could start a new life with fifteen hundred dollars.

She rubbed her shoulders with opposite hands. "How do you know that's me? I'm worthy?" she said. "And besides, I just accused you of murder. You can't turn around and give me an expensive fiddle like that. . . . Aha!" She raised her arms to the ceiling. "That's it. You're trying to bribe me, aren't you? You don't miss a trick, do you? Well you're not getting away with it."

"Bribe you? Trick? What are you talking about?" I'd been found out. April was on to me. Knew I wanted to smother her in kisses.

Her left hand gestured toward the maligned instrument and hung in space. "You want me to suppress my suspicions about you and Molly. You think you're so clever. I wouldn't take that fiddle if it was the last one on earth." Her trained fingers did a mid-air arpeggio.

Too late. April was caught. I sensed real passion in her denial, opposing the passion in her fingers. Hope rekindled in me. Where there's passion of one kind there's the possibility for passion of another kind. "Do you know a tune called 'Bill Cheatum?'" I said.

"Every fiddler knows 'Bill Cheatum.' It's part of a fiddler's initiation ritual." She did something with her lips that indicated she knew how to smile.

"That exquisite instrument needs playing," I said. "It hasn't been played in months. It's downright cruel to deny its great need. For the sake of the fiddle god, why don't you give it a try?" More trickery, I knew there wasn't a fiddle god. Unlike, say, the true and only banjo god, a tricky god requiring much sacrifice.

April held her breath and closed her eyes for a moment, dancing hand still extended, fingertips quivering. Then dropped her hand and marched over to the fiddle case. Black hair dancing in her wake.

"For the fiddle's sake," she said, "I'll give it a quick cuddle. Be a sacrilege not to. But I'm promising nothing. I just want to tune it up. Hear its tone." April took the fiddle out of its case and held it in front of her like a baby. She took the index finger of her left hand and traced, taking her time, around the instrument, stroking extra in the half-moon valleys. Her pink tongue traced, in time with her finger, around her moist lips. Tongue finished with its tour, she brought the fiddle to her face and rubbed her cheek against its ancient wood. Her skin and the wood finish fused. She sniffed it all over like one animal might sniff another engaging in sexual foreplay. She held it away from her face and turned it over and inspected the mother-of-pearl inlays on the back. The inlays depicted a connected circle of doves around a bright star. She turned the fiddle back around and tucked it under her cinnamon chin, doves resting on her shoulder.

Oh to be a white dove snuggling on her brown shoulder, tasting her skin, breathing her fresh shampooed hair, cooing love sonatas in her ear.

Keeping the fiddle in place, April picked up the bow, tightened the horse hairs to the right tension, found some rosin and rosined the bow. As she tuned the strings, she glanced over the fiddle at me and smiled. Her face lit up like the inlay star on the back of the fiddle.

My mouth responded. I grinned so hard my lips hurt.

April played. She played "Bill Cheatum." At first stiff and hesitant, then, as she warmed up to the fiddle, sweet and sure. Her face glowed like churned butter. A scent of sweaty rosin filled the storage room.

I could see in my mind's eye, how to fit my banjo picking in with every note and phrase she played. It would be so right, it would be so wonderful. Together, we would capture the essence of lyricism and rhythm.

Wooden animals sprang to life. The black bear cavorted with the catfish. The raven and gull howled and danced a jig. The fox and otter touched noses, bowed and do-se-doed.

I ached to crawl out of that bed and tune up my banjo. Closed my eyes in mental preparation for an attempt. Yes! Yes! I would give it another try. It was time. I saw April and myself playing music together and afterwards, we'd lay our instruments aside, April swooning in my arms saying, "I've always wanted to make love to a turban-headed murderer."

18

Mutants and Baby Pictures

I opened my eyes for an instant and saw the wooden catfish and black bear back at their stations, shivering, as a haunt took shape in front of them. The apparition emerged fully into the body of a coyote and head and beak of the bald eagle that attacked Qo-oo-la. By the murderous look in the eagle's eyes, he would like nothing better than to settle old scores by ripping a chunk out of my April's neck.

"Get away from here!" I screamed. April, starting to own "Bill Cheatum," froze. An A-minor note, jagged and mournful, hung in the air. I realized, too late, the beast was Elpenor. Malcomb's poultice didn't work. Wretch was back, enraged and in the guise of a mutant. Ol' adrenaline surfing opportunist that he was, come to pay me a visit and let me know it was not safe to court love again.

I can think of nothing more certain — not politics, not golf, not baby pictures of somebody else's grand kids you'd never seen in real life — to swamp a musical or amorous surge. The thought of having to face Elpenor every time I thought about making love filled me with profound flacidity.

April, fiddle bow cocked at the ready, a rock amongst quivering wood carvings, said. "You don't like my playing, you just tell me. You don't have to shout."

"No, no, I love your playing," I said, "it's Elpenor; I think he's jealous of you. Look; he's right there." I pointed and jabbed the air.

"Yes, yes, I do see!" April yelled back and swung Josh's fiddle down to her side, her facial coloring, going from copper to a light shade of lavender.

"You do?" I said. "My God, you do see Elpenor? At long last, I am vindicated."

"No," she said, "I don't see your sick hallucination. What I do see though is I can't take a broken-down, banjo picking, madman, maybe even murderer, seriously."

"Ex-banjo picker," I said by way of correction.

April put the fiddle back in the case, slammed the lid shut. "Well Mr. EX banjo picker," she said, "I'm going to AXE this deal before it gets started. As far as I'm concerned, this Elpenor can have your worthless hide. I've out done myself this time. I've fallen for some losers in my life but you're shaping up to be the pre-eminent, first-rate loser of all times."

"Thank you," I said. I spotted a diamond in the rough. There was a compliment in there somewhere. I just knew it. Hold on, did my burning ears hear right? She intimated she had fallen for me? Oh miraculous. . . ?

"And let go of your crotch," she said. "You're embarrassing. You needn't worry, your precious privates are certainly safe from me."

I felt like the emperor that threw all his strength behind protecting the vault door to his family heirlooms, even as the walls to the castle were crumbling. I threw Elpenor a fierce look.

The dragon changed tactics. He leered at April — Okay, I know an eagle can't leer as such, but this one did — like a pervert in a peep show and then the look turned to pure hatred. The eagle's head spoke, with a thin papery voice, like wind blowing across a clear-cut. *This mud people woman is no good for you. She wants to consume your vital juices. Even now she is making plans to sell you out, sap your soul and then abandon you like all the rest. I will help you to destroy her.*

I sat up. "Don't call her names," I said. "and you keep away from her." Normally, I fear for myself in Elpenor's presence, for the first time I feared for someone else. Why did he hate April so? And what could he do to harm her? I resolved at that moment to protect April from the jealous shape changer.

I needed a clever scheme to thwart Elpenor's intentions. Some shrewd and canny plan just to show him that I had the power, that I was master of my fate, that he was just a puny subservient hallucination. I had it! I would never imagine April again in an erotic manner. Never fall totally and blissfully and blindly in love with her. Never lick her exquisite callused fingertips again. Taste her talent on my tongue. Eschew lust, and, now that my involuntary celibacy seemed ancient history, embrace voluntary celibacy.

Ha! That'd show Elpenor who was the crackerjack mind in control of his destiny.

Elpenor raised a huge taloned paw and swiped at April's back. Ghost claws the size of daggers passed through her slumped shoulders. A mistral whipped across my face and a smacking sound, like when my Pentecostal step-dad sucked the brains out of a squirrel skull, pierced my ears. I screamed in pain.

April, trembling, put the fiddle case with the other instruments. "You're getting crazier by the minute. I'm getting out of here. I'm going back to surgery where it's safe."

Elpenor's massive beak hissed at me. *"You can never have her. I won't allow it."*

April opened the side door, a cold wind rushed in, bringing with it the cackle of gulls. "You really do need professional help. I'll call my friend David. I think I can persuade him to give you a free evaluation. He's a very successful, compassionate, sane man." Rain pounded her face. She swiped at the rain. She slammed the door behind her.

I hated this David. I resolved, if and when we ever met, I would peck his lights out. I meant, of course, punch his lights out. Well, I didn't know what I meant. For every step forward I made with April, I took two steps back. I didn't really hate this David character. It wasn't his fault he didn't have a lifelong addiction to failure. Why wouldn't an attractive professional like April have an equally attractive, professional boy friend. What chance did I have against those odds?

I needed to forget about April. Elpenor had pretty much insured I would never, if the chance ever arose, consummate my love for her anyway. I would see this David character and treat him with kindness and respect. Thereby gain April's friendship. Friendship? Yes, that's what I would seek with April.

However I had no chance of being friends with her unless I could convince her I wasn't a murderer.

19

The Gun and the Banjo Brooch

I was alone and so cold. The hornet's nest felt like one giant goose-bump. Maybe if I shivered enough the nest would dislodge.

No such luck. The hive's residents buzzed and thudded, running into reinforced walls.

I should have told April the truth about the pistol. Lying, which came so easily while boozing, lingered in sobriety. I had found the pistol last winter in Old Town Portland. It was lying in plain sight on the side-walk in front of my bus. By that time, I lived out of my bus and worried, with good reason, about my instruments getting ripped off. I shouldn't have, I eventually hocked them anyway. I had a secret compartment in my heavy harmonica case where I hid the twenty-two. I hadn't looked at the gun since I hid it. I remembered it had almost a full cylinder. One bullet was missing, five remained.

I stared at the ceiling, pulled the covers up to my neck and listened to the hive hum and the storm blow outside. I tried to make the hum and the blow into a rhythmic pattern. They wouldn't meld. The harder I tried, the more disjointed and arrhythmic the sounds got. An out-of-synch scraping came from the roof. A squirrel barked off-key. The wooden animals, back at their stations, sulked in an unmelodious manner. Nature was out of whack.

My stomach growled. I nodded my head — no mean feat — and raised the cover, to look at my shrinking gut. I'd never had consistent dining habits, but I'd not had a decent meal in recent memory. On a nightstand next to a dial-type phone was an empty bowl with a red ring. I sniffed it. Tomato soup. Behind the bowl sat a packet of crackers. I tore it apart and stuffed both crackers in my mouth at once. They were so dry and salty I had trouble swallowing. Hit my empty gut with a clunk. Churned and burned like salt in an open wound.

I lay back down, tried to fold my hands behind my oversized head, failed, settled for a chest fold, corpse style, and thought about Medusa and murder and love and loons and sex.

Could I have possibly, in some kind of blackout, driven up here a week ago and killed Molly Jenkins? It was all so ridiculous. Too many unanswered questions. Where was the motive? What possible reason would I have to kill Molly? I squirmed. Knew that when drunks get to the point of having blackouts they don't need a motive, even for murder. It seemed almost ridiculous but all I had to do was check my weapon. Get rid of any possibility it had been fired since I found it. I spotted my harmonica case across the room, a modified suitcase large enough to accommodate three dozen harmonicas, three steel harmonica holders and assorted performance paraphernalia. It weighed as much as a car battery.

I couldn't sit up so I sorta did a roll 'n' tuck out of bed. Landed on my hands and knees, cone head banged the floor. Tried standing but was top heavy. Required too much effort. I crawled across the room. Lay the harmonica case on its side and opened it. The top came up with a sticky smack. Smelled of tin and dried spit. I admired my lovely mouth harps, lying secure and sparkling, each in its own cut-out cradle of foam rubber. Oh, oh, my backup B-flat was missing. It was there the last time I looked, which had been, admittedly, some months ago.

My memory was shot.

I pinched a piece of the spongy tan material on both sides and lifted the whole six inch thick pad out. My breathing stopped. There was the perfect imprint in the foam rubber I'd cut out for the gun, but the gun was gone. Play me a god-damned done-gone, gun song. Play it as a companion to the done-gone, dog song.

I was right after all. The gun had been stolen. But when? And by whom? If not April when she fumigated my bus, who?

I had another secret compartment in my handy case. There was a slit in the lining of the lid and I slid a finger in to retrieve my one and only vest pin, a trophy from a contest I'd won years ago. It was imprinted with a miniature banjo. I wiggled my finger all around. It too was gone.

Could I, as Qo-oo-la, have managed to swallow my own banjo brooch without recognizing it? The answer was yes. Qo-oo-la, intent on survival at the time, had not been concerned with imprints.

I swallowed. My throat felt clogged. I jiggled the foam pad back in place, closed the case. I watched my hands, my long, broken fingernails, fold the latches shut. My arms clutched the nearby black bear around its neck for support. I held on for a few minutes listening to my heavy breathing, each inhalation ending with a strange little eek in the bottom of my larynx, like a bat locked in a dark attic. That squeak was the only sound in the room. Outside a limb could suffer the rain and wind no longer, and crashed to the forest floor. A piece of tin roofing ripped loose and commenced whumping.

My teeth, taking their cue from the metal roof, chattered. I thanked the black bear for its compassion and crawled back to bed, pulled the covers as tight as I could around my elongated noggin and curled into the fetal position. I resisted an urge to stick my finger down my throat and induce vomiting.

My mind wouldn't stop spinning: I, Harp Pearl Gravey, could be Molly's killer. No wonder her eyes accused me. I had plenty of time — four days, I had the weapon, my one vest pin was missing, and I had the motive; irrational, schizoid behavior. If April didn't find the gun and vest pin, who did? Did I stash them somewhere? I'd been in this room two days. Anybody could've walked in here and stolen them. Who else had access?

I tried to find some evidence, besides my total ignorance of doing the foul deed, why I couldn't possibly have murdered Molly Jenkins. The answer was so simple it appealed to my irrationality. Qo-oo-la! No Great Spirit worth His or Her salt, would allow a murderer to transform into so innocent and splendid a creature as Qo-oo-la. There, I'd said it. Not only did I admit it wasn't a dream when I found Molly Jenkins's body, I had admired and accepted the brotherhood of a common loon. I conceded I was a freak of nature.

I stretched out. Removed the covers from around my skull and top-knot. Took a deep breath to clear my throat and sat up. I swayed, but by grabbing the mattress on either side of me, I managed to stay seated. I had to clear my name with April. Remove my own self-doubt. And that meant, find Molly's murderer.

20

Warriors and Lovers

I had to find Malcomb. Get his opinion on how to find out who killed Molly. Loren, his own son was a suspect so he was bound to have some thoughts.

I placed my feet squarely on the floor and lunged toward the door. I staggered forward and conked my headdress on the wall, caught the doorknob before ricocheting backwards. Hung on and hugged that door like a kid with a tuba. The thin hospital slacks didn't protect the skin on my knees. I steadied a minute, glanced behind me. All the wooden animals were encouraging me to succeed, except for the coyote, catfish and raven. Those three were in a huddle, plotting.

I edged open the door, felt the rush of cold air and rain pecking my bare feet. The water, for some unexplainable reason, was exhilarating. My feet felt light, like wings. I forged out into the storm, high stepping, stomach tucked, cone head pointing into a thirty mph wind. I headed in the general direction of the red-roofed machine shop. I glanced off totems, stumbled over wooden animals, buffeted this way and that by an unrelenting wind, until I was thoroughly confused and lost. The sea roared in my ears. I felt sand under my feet. Waves caressed my ankles, beckoning me. Somehow I'd missed the machine shop and was on the beach. I turned around and around and around. With each turn I waded into deeper water. I was terrified but unable to stop.

Suddenly, a firm hand grabbed my arm and led me out of the surf, over a gravel pathway and into the machine shed. Malcomb. He led me into a warm dry room. A fire from an old forge blazed. He handed me a towel and draped a change of clothes over an anvil next to the fire. I stripped off the soaked slacks and toweled down. As I was climbing into a set of overalls, Malcomb spread a mat and blankets down beside the fire. "Lay down here." He pointed to the makeshift bed. "I'll be right back."

"I have to find Molly's killer." I said through chattering teeth.

"I was hoping you'd feel that way. Get comfortable. I'll be right back." He went out a door into the shop area.

I watched the fire dance and jump. Malcomb banged back through an outside door, letting a salt-water breeze fluff the quilt. The old Indian filled the doorway, loaded down like a packhorse. He shuffled in, the strap of a large leather bag over one shoulder, my two-loons sweatshirt draped over the other, and spoke as if we were in the middle of a conversation. "I've been thinking about the area where Molly was murdered. It's always been bad medicine." Malcomb smelled of cedar. Corkscrew, cylindrical shavings splattered his charcoal work apron. He packed the large, wooden mask — finished, I presumed — under one arm and the dreaded hair headdress in the other. "Everyone that's come in contact with that place has had bad luck. I think one of our ancestors did a terrible thing there."

I noticed right away something was different about his face. It was the nose ring. The damn nose ring was back. No, a different ring. More gold-colored. Once again, his upper lip looked split. Old Healer full of surprises.

Malcomb took the mask and hat and set them on a small table. He pinned the two-loons sweatshirt above them on the plywood wall. He then stepped aside and said, "How's that for a shrine?"

"It's ridiculous," said April, entering the tack room behind Malcomb. "And what are you doing out of bed?" She said to me. She had changed into an ankle length, yellow and black skirt, white blouse and round earrings. Her black hair flowed loosely behind her as she paced in front of the fire. She didn't meet my eyes.

"How did your surgery go?" I said. Feeling top heavy, I struggled to keep from listing to one side.

"The patient, a cormorant, died," she said. Her chin jutting out, she walked over to a cobweb-covered window and looked at the totem yard, her back as rigid as a piano bench.

"What do you think Harp?" Malcomb said, spreading his arms before the icons.

"It's ridiculous," said April. "I don't like this one bit. Father what are you planning? Father?"

"I didn't ask you," Malcomb said. "I know what you think."

"It's fine," I said. "Just fine." It was some altar all right. Was I supposed to pray to that? On one level I felt like April, it was ridiculous; a slack-feathered, flea-infested hair hat, a moth-eaten sweatshirt depicting two love-sick loons with a shadowy apparition surrounding them, and the god-awful loon mask that was scarier than a bass player's amp.

I heard a Stellar's jay, *ccrrrtt, ssrrrtt, cccrrrrttt,* scream a territorial warning outside the tack room window. A rival jay, in the distance, answered the challenge.

On another level the mask filled me with fascination. And dread. The mask, upon closer examination, with its black dagger beak and burning eyes, did not represent a docile, subservient spirit. It was a mask of defiance, of stealth, a mask to be worn by a warrior. It definitely represented a loon and more than that, I divined, in that shadowy combative visage, my loon, my partner, my Qo-oo-la. How had Malcomb done that? I felt a phantom feather boogying up and down my spine again.

April swiveled around and picked wet warbler feathers off my topknot, wadded them up and tossed them in the fire. She looked straight at me. "Before Father gets too carried away, I think we should hear this vision tale. This should be good. Try not to lie or fabricate too much. My Father is a very needful man."

"Yes," said Malcomb, "I need to know, to the slightest detail, so I can design your journey ceremony as accurately as possible. Leave out nothing."

"Journey? What. . . . Whose? What journey?"

Malcomb pulled up a hand carved chair. "You said you have to find Molly's killer. Tell me about your vision and I will tell you of the journey you must take to do that. And soon."

"I foresee a journey in your future, all right," said April, sitting on the arm of the chair and crossing her legs.

"So do I," I said, thinking of neon lights. So, avoiding as much as possible staring at the spiritual altar or April's exposed ankle, I told them about the flight into becoming Qo-oo-la. I told them about the dive-bombing eagle. I told them about finding Molly Jenkins and I told them about plucking the gold pin out of Molly's cold, dead fingers. I told them about the man in the purple hat. And, with embarrassment, I told them about swallowing the gold pin before I could see what it represented.

April stopped pacing. She stood in front of the loon shrine, hands on hips, head cocked, staring. "I must admit; the level of detail is extraordinary. What was that name, Qu-yuola?"

Malcomb said, "This purple hat guy sounds like one of those Vietnam Vets been up there in those mountains for years, squatting on a gold mining claim."

April reached out and touched the black beak of the loon mask. "How appropriate," she said. "The deranged being found by the deluded."

Malcomb's thick eyebrows jiggled like horizontal cocoons readying to pop open. "Your journey began before you had gathered your power, and yet you survived. Made you weak and sick as hell but that is as it's always been. Your loon power must be very strong."

"Strong!" I said. "You're kidding, right? My loon power, ain't for shit. Everything out there is better equipped at surviving than a loon for God's sake."

April stroked the long loon nose, gave it a squeeze, held it, then released it and looked at the palm of her hand. She shook her head and hurried over to pick up the phone and punch in a number. While waiting for the other end to answer, she said to me, "I run a rehabilitation center for injured native wildlife. We get all kinds of injured animals, mostly birds. I have three dozen volunteers helping me. The newer volunteers answer the log-in phones."

April spoke into the phone. "Judy, check the phone log for all of Tuesday and Wednesday. See if there's anything remotely pertaining to loons?"

"Yes, that's right. I said loons, as in common."

April addressed me again. "This is absurd. I don't even know why I'm doing it. Yes, I do know why I'm doing it. I'm going to prove to Father you're a delusional nut case."

Malcomb said, "It proves nothing. If there's no report of an injured loon it merely means this purple guy didn't call it in. "

The phone glued to her ear, April's mouth pursed as if she'd bitten down on a sour lemon. "You're sure? Okay. Okay. I'll be damned." She wrote down a number on a pad on the nightstand. "Thanks." Pushed the disconnect button and redialed in a fiddle-fingering blur.

While the phone dialed, she tilted her head up and explained to the ceiling, "Night before last, at the Wildlife Care Clinic, a caller inquired about an injured loon with a bad head wound. The call-in log was signed by Lisa Wheitcamp, one of our first time volunteers. Naturally Lisa didn't get a name, an address or phone number. That's typical; half the people that call refuse to leave a name or address.

I'm calling Lisa right now to see if she might have forgotten to write it down."

"Maybe the caller didn't have a post office address?" Malcomb gave my foot a hopeful squeeze. "Maybe it's your loon, Qo-oo-la?" The loon's name flowed easy from his lips.

"What happened to the loon?" I asked April's back. My back, along the rabbit scratches, began to itch and burn.

"Don't be ridiculous Father. This call-in is just a coincidence. We get several injured loons a year."

"How many with a head wound?" Malcomb said. "Our ancestors understood that coincidence, if examined in depth, is the stark manifestation of inevitability." Malcomb, sitting solid in his hand-carved chair, nodded his head as if keeping the beat to a fast waltz.

The back of April's neck began to get dark red splotches. "Don't give me that wise ancestors crap, Father. I'll have this whole thing cleared up in a few minutes."

April talked into the phone. "Deke, this is April Old Wolf from the Wildlife Care Clinic. I need to ask Lisa some questions about a call-in on a loon the other night. She's gone to the outdoor market in Port Townsend? Well thank you, I'll see if I can catch her there." April started to hang up, then jammed the phone in her ear. "What did Lisa tell you about it? Are you sure? Okay, thank you Deke." April hung-up the phone in slow motion, exhaling in synch, her breath sounding like a deflating balloon. Her skin was waxy and tight. There were gray hollows under her chin and the flesh in her cheeks was rust-red. Her shoulders sagged.

Malcomb said, "More coincidence?"

April backed-up and plopped down on the cot, oblivious to her spread legs and me sitting on the floor. Her voice came from way down in her chest. "Did you say this Purple Hat had binoculars?"

"Yes." My leg was at an awkward angle, cutting off sensation to my foot, but I dared not move it, destroy April's momentum.

"Could he possibly see the gold pin in your mouth . . . ah, beak?"

"Couldn't miss it," I said. "Why, what did this Deke say? Spit it out."

"I suspect my daughter is having difficulty eating crow," Malcomb said.

April threw her father a dark look. "Lisa told her husband, Deke, that this caller wanted to know that if a loon swallowed a solid object would it pass it in its droppings?"

The room fell silent except for a slight wheeze from Malcomb's nose-ringed nostrils. Outside, a boat horn blew from across the water, a heavy, mournful sound. I made an attempt to flex my numb knee but it felt like a lump of lead. Light, from a corner lamp, reflected metallic off April's black hair. Her shoulders shrugged. She shook her torso — grinding her calf against wood frame — struggling to regain the fragile comfort of sanity.

April said, "My God, if all of this makes any sense, it's just possible Lisa talked to the loon-napper, who may be the murderer too." April glanced at me. Let me know how liberal-minded she was, admitting other suspects.

"Yes," said Malcomb, "we have another suspect. That makes two. Loren and Purple Hat."

"Three, counting Mr. Harp Pearl Gravey here," said April. "I'll go in and catch Lisa at the market. See if she might have gotten a name or address and forgot to write it down. Or can remember something that'll give us a clue to who the caller was." She marched toward the door.

"Wait," I managed to holler. My topknot gave a protest buzz.

She pivoted, brushed a strand of hair from her face.

I said, "He does, doesn't he?"

"Who? What?"

"Qo-oo-la that's who. Shit . . . ahh, pass the pin."

"Lets hope for your . . . Qu-rolla's sake, Lisa didn't know what she was talking about and told him what most people assume; that the loon will poop the pin. Not so. Loons have a gizzard." April slowed down. Realized she was talking to an anatomy moron. "It has a big hole going in and a very small hole going out." She demonstrated with her hands. "The gizzard literally grinds," she gnashed the knuckles of her fists together, "things up. Even metal or plastic over a period of time."

I asked a question I didn't want to know the answer to. "Even if we locate Qo-oo-la then, how can we ever retrieve the gold pin?"

"We can't, without cutting out the gizzard."

"Oh Lord," I said, "I don't suppose there's any way you can do that without kill . . . hey, wait. Do you really believe this loon vision stuff or are you putting me on?"

April rubbed hers eyes with the palms of her hands. The lobes of her dainty ears seemed swollen and crimson from too heavy coyote earrings.

"I'm going to play like I do for a while. After all, you've presented another suspect besides you and my brother. As for your other question, either way your loon's dead. We don't as yet have organ transplants for water-fowls. We better find it fast or our clue to Molly's murderer will be ground to dust." She considered a second. "And if Lisa told the caller what I just told you, Qu-mula — where did you get such an unpronounceable name — is probably already dead. Let's hope Lisa — a raw recruit — told the caller that your loon would poop the pin. Would, in effect, lay a golden egg. Purple Hat may let him live long enough for that. After all, he has no idea we're on to him. That a loon I. D'd him." She marched through the door, with nary a glance behind her, her thick, black hair bouncing to the beat of a professional with a purpose.

I rubbed my knee. My numbed leg felt unattached, separated at the thigh. My innocent Qo-oo-la. Probably minding his own business, en route for a rendezvous with a lady loon, make a little whoopy, build a home and then raise a family. Now, he's most likely dead and dissected. All because of me. Even if we were lucky enough to find Qo-oo-la alive and rescue him, we'd have to dissect him if we wanted the murder clue. A murder clue that April believed could incriminate me.

Self-pity settled in around my unharmonious heart with a familiar gloomy zest.

The warrior loon mask, hanging on the wall, closed and opened and focused its eyes, searching the room. Those red eyes found me and stopped. I felt light, as if, like my mom used to say, a ghost had walked over my grave.

April stuck her head back through the door. "I just thought of some-thing else. There's a remote possibility it would work." She chewed her cheek, thinking.

My knee twitched. "For God's sake, say it."

April flattened her ear against the door frame. "We can try x-raying Qu-smoola's gizzard," she said. "Might still be able to make out the inscrip-tion? Or image. That is, if the pin is cast with two different materials so we can get a three dimensional impression. We must also find the bird in time. His gizzard is in a frenzy." Once again she did the gnashing of the knuckles thing. "Grinding to get rid of the foreign elements in his body. Reject the intruder."

"Surely," I said, "it'll take weeks before the pin is ground to passable poop?" That ghost was not just walking but stomping in two-four time, on my grave. The mask's crimson eyes glared at me. X-raying my liver.

April squeezed her eyes shut, thinking. "I doubt it," she said. "But I don't really know. It's been two days already. I have the phone numbers of some internal medicine animal experts in my office computer. I'll stop by the clinic and make a few calls. Get their opinions."

Zip, she was gone; bang, back again. "And you don't really believe, if Purple Hat is waiting for Qo-how-la to lay a golden egg, he's going to wait for weeks. Once Purple Hat realizes that's not going to happen, it'll be off with a loon head." April demonstrated with thumbnail and neck.

"Father," she said, "you get Harp back into the bedroom and let him get some rest. I don't like his color. And get that damn turban off his head. He looks like a cone head after forty miles of bad road."

Gone again. She left a faint smell of clove in her wake.

I hollered after her. "I'm beginning to take to this hat."

Not true, but for some reason I was angry. Not at April or Malcomb or even Elpenor. Qo-oo-la! That's who I was pissed off at. That damn loon. Swallowing a chunk of metal. Why didn't he leave it be? I'd be on the road again if he did. Gizzard grinding the pin to metal shavings. My fingers probed my stomach, see if I could locate where a gizzard might be if I had one. Pushed at my gallbladder. Made me dizzy. Dizziness made me realize I blamed Qo-oo-la for my problems. Good to know I hadn't lost my touch; blame anyone else for my problems but myself.

Here a murder in which I was implicated was crying to be solved on a number of fronts and I was assigning blame rather than trying to solve it. On my ass too weak to do anything about it. My dog was lost and I didn't know when I'd even be able to search for her.

I had to stop passing the buck. Quit feeling sorry for myself and own up to some of this mess myself.

21

Transformers and Transformees

Malcomb led me back into the animal statue bedroom, tucked the covers around me. He went back outside and moments later was back lugging the mask, headdress and sweatshirt. "Don't let April's gruffness put you off," he said. "She was partially raised by her mother, a spirited, hyperactive anthropologist, in Wilmington Delaware. That's where she gets that east coast accent and energy. My daughter believes in science. I'm amazed she gives your vision any credence whatsoever. And don't give up on Qo-oo-la either, he's not dead yet."

"How do you know?" I said. Some other time, I resolved to ask Malcomb details about fathering a child with an anthropologist from Wilmington, Delaware, and also ask about the nose rings.

Malcomb propped the mask up against the wall on the back of a wooden bear. Hung the sweatshirt on the mask's nose . . . beak. Sat the hair hat on the nightstand beside my bed. "In my morning power trance," he said, "I sensed Qo-oo-la still had consciousness. His spirit is still with us."

I scooted to the other side of the bed. "What about my Medusa, my dog?"

"Sorry, I didn't get any canine consciousness," Malcomb said, "but there could be several reasons for that. I don't do domestic animals." Malcomb began setting wooden animals against the wall. I was amazed he couldn't feel the loon mask's power. Malcolm was gentle and careful. The animals, recognizing the touch of their creator, purred and preened. As he petted a river otter, he said, "In a few hours, it'll be dark. Time grows short. You'll want to get there with some daylight to spare. We don't have time for a proper sweat lodge ceremony. I'll have to prepare this room for transmigration now."

I didn't like the sound of that. "Ahh . . . prepare what for what?"

"You want to find Molly's murderer, right?"

"When I get my strength back, right."

"And find your soul mate, Qo-oo-la."

"Loons have a soul?

"All living things have a soul. Qo-oo-la now has a piece of your soul and you have a piece of his. You are spiritually united. You probably won't believe this but the physical transformation you went through may be the easiest part. You must surrender to the soul's transformation too, however terrifying it might be. There is no turning back now. You can help each other survive." Malcomb took the leather bag, the size of a watermelon from around his shoulder and peered into it.

"Yeah right," I said. "A common loon's going to help me survive."

Malcomb produced a chunk of bark and began tearing off pieces with his teeth and spitting them around the fire. "Ah yes, anthropocentric arrogance." Chomp, spit. "I suspect it will be the downfall of our species." Chomp, spit. "I won't bore you with metaphysical hocus pocus or insult your intelligence with a lot of Native American, earth-spirituality excess." Chomp, spit, spit. "But, be it known; something beautiful and terrifying happened to you. It was not a dream. Don't be so quick to scoff at things you don't understand. Qo-oo-la is more likely to help you survive than vice-versa." Chomp spit, spit and spit.

"What are you up to?" I pulled the blanket up around my neck for protection. Spidery legs crept up my calves. My nostrils sniffed decayed wood and denture adhesive.

"Don't be afraid. You must learn to pray for guidance. There are spirits around to help you if you only know how to ask. Look." Malcomb swept his arm at the animal shrine leaning against the wall.

The mask's insane red eyes still summoned me. I was fascinated and appalled. "What happens if a spirit speaks to you and you don't like what it says?"

The gnawed chunk of wood finished, Malcomb pulled out a ball of flower petals wrapped in rubber bands. He began peeling the petal ball like an onion. Malcomb ignored my blasphemous remark. "I was hoping we could wait a while, give you time to get your strength back and give me time to prepare you properly, but it looks like now is it."

"Hey, I'm too weak," I said. "Don't I have something to say about this? You can't send me off to kingdom-come without my permission, can you?"

Malcolm opened his soft leather pouch and handed me a sandwich wrapped in tinfoil. "No I can't. You must not resist too much. Here eat this. It'll give you strength."

"What is it?"

"It is a rabbit leg sandwich on fried bread with a marsh marigold and witches butter — a mushroom — baste. It'll give you escape strength.

I need something of yours. What's in your banjo case that smells so powerful?"

I smelled wild mustard. "Well pardon me a moment while my taste buds fly off the scale. Did you say 'witches butter?' This rabbit isn't . . . ah . . . Merle, is it?" Nevertheless, I took the offering. It was fat and crisp. My hollow stomach rumbled and pitched. I sniffed the greasy, mustardy smell. Saliva flooded my dry lips. A thin line of diaphanous orange edged the crisp bread; I assumed it was the witches butter spilling out.

Without permission, Malcomb opened my banjo case. "No, of course not," he said. "I've taken a personal liking to Merle. He's out back in a new cage. This rabbit came into the Wildlife Care Center injured from a gunshot wound. April couldn't save it. I asked it if I could use its strength and speed before it died and it said yes. I'm giving its strength and speed to you."

"Yeah well, as long as you asked." Screwy ol' man. I was leery but I nibbled. It was pasty but edible. Malcomb found my finger pick bag, sniffed it and smiled. Pulled apart the leather ties and the bag flopped open. He reached in, dumped the silver finger picks on the floor and spread a pinch of quarter-of-a-century lint, dust and sweat in a horse-shoe circle around my body.

At that time, I had by no means acquiesced to putting on the mask or the hat again, let alone contemplate another spiritual journey. The one hand part of me wondered what I had to lose. Maybe I could clear myself of murder. On the other hand, I might confirm my guilt.

I chewed the sandwich and resolved to stall for April's return. She would put a stop to Malcomb's song and dance shenanigans.

The loon mask, hair hat and two-loons sweatshirt had a blue, beck-oning aura. I felt a vague twinge of anxiety and urgency. Then a voice spoke in my ear, *"You must take the journey. Give up resistance. Qo-oo-la needs you."* I looked at Malcomb. "How'd you do that?"

"Do what?" Malcomb quit spreading transformational debris and scratched his oversized, hairy ear.

"I heard a voice." I said.

From his bottomless medicine bag he produced vials of paint. "Sit up. According to legends these Olympic Mountains, called Ho-had-hun, were once people and the rivers were their blood. They were made into mountains by The Great Changer. Some call him the Transformer. He made man and all the animals. He also has the power to change a man into an animal. It is said to be a sign of great medicine to hear the voice of The Great Changer. It is also said to be reckless and stupid to not heed the voice."

I sat up straighter. I finished the sandwich and then licked the witches butter baste off my fingers. Tasted redolent with wild spores. My stomach quit complaining. "It was the same voice as in my dream. The one that told me to unite with Qo-oo-la to find Molly Jenkins's murderer. Doesn't expect much does he?"

Malcomb either didn't get sarcasm or was immune to it. He stuck an index finger in the red paint vial and made a gash across my forehead. Then two others down my cheek. He hesitated, leaned back and looked at his artwork. Shook his head. "No, we'd better put on your Two-Loons sweatshirt first." Malcomb retrieved the sweatshirt from the mask's beak. He motioned for me to sit up straighter and slipped the sweatshirt over the hornets nest, tugged and wiggled it down through my upraised arms, scraping and binding.

I said, "I had no idea, when I bought this sweatshirt at that Baptist rummage sale, that it might get me killed."

"That's why I made the mask," he said. "If you put it on before you put on the headdress, it will ease your transition to the spirit world and help you when you get there." He made it sound like a logic exercise for slow learners.

"How about getting this damned glued-on yellow jacket nest off my head," I said. "It weighs a ton. Hey, maybe the hat's power won't work with this turban on." I gave it another thump for good measure; see if it loosened its iron grip on my head. Papyrus flakes fluttered about. It hummed louder and things moved about inside it.

Malcomb slashed down my nose with white paint and across my stubbly chin with black. "Give it up. That nest won't come off until it's finished doing its healing work. Should be any time now. I don't believe it'll matter to the power of the loon hat. Might even help." Malcomb beamed at me. He had convenient answers for everything. Malcomb scrutinized my painted face; touched up the end of my nose with a sure finger. For such a ridged and knotty finger he had a light touch.

"Help?" I said. "Help get me killed."

"You don't know how happy you've made me," Malcomb said. "Gave me hope and purpose. You got delusions coming in and spirits going out." He chuckled. "You're every minor shaman's godsend, you're a real by-god transformee."

"Me, a transformee? Why me?" I said, "If you're right, why did this transformer god choose me, a homeless, schizoid trauma case and recovering alcoholic? I am a wreck; the least person capable of carrying out whatever mysterious mission this transformer god has in mind. I have a smidgen of Indian blood in me from my great grandfather, but was raised working-class white. I don't even know what tribe. Why didn't this god choose some full-blooded Indian with years of spirituality credentials? Like you for instance? I've never done anything spiritual in my life." I refrained, in deference to his glee, from saying, "Why am I burdened so?" Vagabond irresponsibility was beginning to look more safe and secure all the time.

Malcomb sat down on a wooden fox's back, stroked the rough chisel grooves in its head with one hand and with the other slashed his forehead and cheeks with war paint. He used red and white paint. Fox grinned a toothy grin. "The white man has been here for over four hundred years. He arrived horny. There could be more remote mixed bloods like you than pure bloods. As for my spirituality, I'm satisfied with what small talents I've been given. Except, perhaps, I would like to know what it's like to metamorphosize into rabbit, my spirit animal. To run with those powerful rabbit legs must be exhilarating; can you imagine? Hmmm, maybe you can."

"I can, and let me tell you, exhilaration plays second fiddle to fear. And I'd prefer not to be that terrified ever again."

The old man tickled the fox under its chin. "But the Changer God chooses whom he wishes; he does not care what color your skin is, your class, sex, nationality or your clan or tribe. All blood is red and pure. Does the Buddha bother with such trivia when choosing a corporal vessel? We are all cousins under the skin, descended from the same womb." He put the tubes of paint back in his bag. "Nor what kind of life you've led up until the moment The Changer God chooses to communicate with you, the instance of profound awakening. Perhaps the simplest answer to your question is, you were there at the right time, in the right place to ignite the magic. You were desperately in need and were sorely needed. You got the call and it is you, Harp P. Gravey, who must answer."

I coughed, my topknot wheezed and prickled. "Me, in desperate need of help from some kind of ancient god? I may have got the call but it was the wrong number. As if I ain't got enough troubles? As if I can't take care of myself? As if. . . . You're joking, right?"

"It's no joke," Malcomb said. "My son Loren, according to the police radio, is a prime suspect in Molly Jenkins's murder. He's disappeared and so has his arch rival Billy Moody. My poor misguided daughter April suspects you. Your loon Qo-oo-la, holds the key to unravel this mess."

He held up the mask. "It's time for you to put this on, my son."

Why did he have to say my son? Could he possibly know I'd searched a lifetime to find a father figure? One I could look up to and one who wouldn't abandon me when times got tough? Old man was a scam artist. I fall for that my son hustle I might as well throw away what reason I have left. "Hold it just a damn minute," I said. "I need some more recuperation time. I'm not ready yet. And besides that damn pin in Qo-oo-la's gizzard isn't going anywhere. Another day won't matter."

Malcomb stood and stretched. His old bones popped. "We have to do it now. I believe my daughter called the sheriff. We can't do it in jail, or the mental health lockup. Purple Hat has already had your spirit brother two days. It'll be dark in an hour and Qo-oo-la may not last the night." Before I could counter, Malcomb went into a medicine-gathering dance frenzy. "A yaya a a ye ye hee." He chanted and thumped around me and the fire, kicking up bark chips and flower petals and whatever else he'd scattered into a potent mishmash. Every third pass he would divert over in front of the animal altar and shout and stomp with added enthusiasm. The mask seemed to glow blue, gathering energy.

I still had my doubts. I needed more rest. I needed to think about it. I needed. . . .

The phone rang. Perhaps it was April to the rescue. Malcomb was indisposed so I answered. "Thank God it's you April. Malcomb wants me to —"

"I've got bad news," April interrupted. "I called an avian vet friend of mine in Portland and also the animal forensics lab down in Ashland, Oregon. They refuse to be exact but they concur. It looks like we've got about three to five days — two of which are already gone — before the loon's gizzard sandpaper's the pin smooth. Smooth as a baby's butt."

I sat up. Too quick. My head bobbed from the weight of my turban topknot, adjusting like a rusty spring. "Just three days? That's ridiculous. The pin is metal it'll resist any — "

"Pewter, otherwise known as pop metal, probably for its propensity to snap under pressure. Soft. Softer than sand, softer than stone. And let's hope it's two different materials, otherwise any impression won't show up on the x-ray even if we do get to it in time."

I grasped at straws like bantam hens in a hog waller. "But a gizzard is just flesh and fiber, how can it wear down metal?"

"Gizzards are incredible organs. Qo-oo-la's gizzard has got a thick, rough, leathery membrane on the inside grinding around the clock to expunge foreign objects. So that means we haven't got much time. Much time to find, capture and x-ray that . . . your loon. You better get your strength back fast."

I didn't like the implications of that last remark. April was my reserve, my backup for rationally refusing to indulge Malcomb in another trans-formational fantasy. "What do you mean?"

"I should think it's obvious. I also did some checking on Purple Hat. He is a Vietnam Vet, name's Nat Buntler. Word is he saw a lot of pretty gruesome action in Vietnam. Hates people. We don't know how he feels about animals, except that he did call the care clinic about your loon's head wound as well as its bowel function.

He's staked a gold claim in the National Forest on the Dosanomish somewhere up in the mountains. Nobody knows exactly where it is. Could take days to find his place on foot. I know a helicopter logger up in Port Angeles that owes me a favor. I've left him a message to call me. But the fastest way to get to Purple Hat and your loon is through a spiritual linkup. I never thought I would say something like this — it goes against every scientific precept I've ever been taught — but you've got to take the plunge; put on the headdress, mask and Two-Loons T-shirt. But don't try anything until I get there. Who knows what kind of shock that has on your system. The last time on the Dosanomish mud flat you appeared to have a grand mal seizure. At least if your heart stops or a vital organ ruptures or you go into respiratory arrest, I can administer emergency procedures."

"Well that's certainly a comfort to know," I said. "You've cheered me up considerably. Does this mean you no longer think I'm the murderer? I mean, if you believe I found the woman's body as Qo-oo-la, then you couldn't possibly think I could of put the body there as me, right? So you can call the sheriff off now. And your psychologist friend." I was elated. My skin felt fresh scrubbed with new soap.

I heard horrible squawks in the background at her end. If I was back on the farm I'd say someone was plucking a live chicken. April said, "In your dreams, Gravey. Hey that was pretty funny. Get It. I said, 'in your dreams' . . . never mind. Don't jump to conclusions. Could be a guilty conscience returning to the scene of the crime. Maybe, the loon doesn't know what the loony does. I'll call and leave another message for the sheriff.

Listen, I've got to go. Another emergency surgery; a goshawk ran into a electric line. I'll be home in a couple of hours. You rest. Get some strength back. Don't you dare do anything until I get there." She hung up.

April didn't say what she was going to say in the message to the sheriff.

Malcomb held the mask out in front of me. "Lean forward, I'll help you get this thing over the nest."

"Your daughter says to wait 'til she gets here."

"My daughter is a fine veterinarian but, in these matters, as in matters of the heart, she's way out of her league. If you want to save Qo-oo-la and find Molly Jenkins's killer, sit up."

"April says she can get a helicopter pilot to hunt for Qo-oo-la."

"By that time it'll be too late. Besides, this is your journey. During my dance I received a message to help you take this journey, to find Molly Jenkins's murderer, to fulfill your destiny. You must take it. You can't wait for the physical props. You must take the spiritual path. Lean forward my son."

Damn! When Malcomb talked like that it made the fine hairs on my arms sing. Me, Harp Pearl Gravey with some kind of divine destiny.

Destiny? Who would've thought it? Expecting me, a has-been banjo picker and ex pool hustler, a failure at love and family, to reconfigure my molecules into the body of a six pound bird. Destiny, he calls it. Find Molly's killer he calls it. I calls it insane. Scary as hell, is what it is. Still in spite of being weak of body, my mind felt an overpowering need to join with Qo-oo-la, see what was on the other side.

My rabbit-charged gut growled, feet thumped the mattress.

I leaned forward. Malcomb slipped the mask over the hornet's nest, strapped it in. The disturbance caused the nest to buzz with more intensity.

Malcomb then placed the hat of dead hair on my overextended head. I couldn't help but think how ridiculous I must have looked; A hair hat topped by two centuries old loon feathers, crowning a gray, yellow jacket's nest, giving way to a wooden loon mask the size of a truck tire, merging into my two-loons sweatshirt. I was pinioned. The whole transformational ensemble weighed so much I couldn't have moved if I wanted to.

I braced myself for the mind-jarring jolt of fractured reality like before on the mudflat. Nothing happened. I peered at Malcomb through peepholes in my mask, my nostrils pungent with the heady smell of fresh-carved cedar. The old Indian resumed dancing and chanting.

"Maybe last time was a fluke Malcomb?" I spoke behind the mask. The sound resonated and tickled my upper lip and tongue. I reached up to scratch but...ha, ha..my mistake; I struck a wood beak. So I scratched the beak and, lo and behold, the itching stopped. I touched the tip of my tongue against the tool grooves on the mask. Tasted of green, uncured wood and raw anticipation.

Suddenly a light went off and I smelled flesh burning. A hurricane force wind lifted my body like a feather and shoved me through a black pinhole, gathering speed and direction; a benign arrow searching for a target. I felt apprehension and fear but strangely I knew I had some,

136

however small, control over my destiny. For the briefest of instances, I might even have been able to turn back, had I willed it hard enough.

Then it was too late. There was no turning back. I was there. Problem was, there was no *there*, there.

22

Purple Nat and Gold Nuggets

Blackness. Wind blowing in trees. Damp air. Mouth dry as tar paper. I sensed slow running water beneath me, cramped, not deep enough for my legs to propel. No wonder it was dark, I had my eyes clamped shut, a by-product of terror. I hesitated, reluctant to open them. I gathered courage and snapped my eyelids up. I was stuck in a blue-green kiddie's cheap plastic play pool about the size of a sheet of plywood. At one end a green hose trickled fresh water. The play pool lay on the ground in some kind of rusty wire cage, possibly a dog run, hooked at one end to a small wooden shelter. In effect, I was imprisoned. Trapped. Before I could do anything else, I had to break out of jail.

To do that, I needed to study the lay of the land. Overhead, through more wire, I spied a canopy of pale green maple and darker green alder leaves, affording little sunshine, creating a damp shadowy environment. From a secure wooden gate, there curved a path through the undergrowth leading to a building whose contour I could barely make out. I could hear country music blaring and the clang of a big metal hammer on metal. It almost drowned-out the sound of a river close by. Somehow I knew the river was the Dosanomish. Comforting that.

I took stock, making sure I hadn't turned into a mallard, a mule or a toad. I was getting used to the concept of loondom. Took a deep breath and twisted my neck to look at my body. Wings, tail, legs, black and white feathers, checkered pattern — sure enough I was all there and I was indisputably a common loon. Bigger than I remembered. Well, well, it worked again. Nice to know there was some consistency and continuity in the spirit world, unlike some worlds of which I won't mention.

I chanced flapping my silly little wings but oh, oh, my breast muscles screamed at the suggestion, reducing them to blithering spasms. There'd be no flying for a while, if ever. I may have done permanent damage when I came out of that tailspin fleeing from Eagle.

Here's where one of many paradoxes between man and bird arose. As a human, it bothered me immeasurably that I couldn't fly. I felt weak and vulnerable. I assumed wings were the answer to escaping all earthbound predators. Believed once you had wings you merely kept a wary eye out and took to the air every time you felt threatened. Bye-bye landlubber, good-by.

Not so. As a common loon, Qo-oo-la — hey that sounds good and proper for a name — could not have cared less. As Qo-oo-la, I was more concerned about getting through the fence and down to the river than I was taking flight. Probably because, besides being injured, unlike most birds, I knew I could not take off from land. In fact, though the process was unclear to me, unless I was able to launch off of a long stretch of water, I couldn't get up in the air. Had to do with my wimpy wings and my awkward, I suspected, malformed legs.

I was getting the flight before the escape anyway. First I had to get out of that steel wire pen. To do that, I needed all the physical help I could get.

I continued my quick body parts check. Stuck one of my legs out of the shallow pool and took a look at the dusky crude appendage. Twisted it around. Ummm, not so bad. A stout gray stick, reverse knee and a tough, webbed, three-toed foot. Maybe I could kick a hole in the wire mesh?

Fence kicking requires training. I tried a tentative karate kick at the side of the pool, *frack!* Whoa! Malcomb wasn't kidding. A loon chop packs a potent punch. Could punt a football fifty yards through the goalposts with that hoof. Split a brick. Just call me The Karate Loon. Lovely wilderness sound, a webbed foot kicking cheap plastic.

I wormed my way up and down the plastic pool smacking the sides with one leg, turned and used the other leg. Exhilarating. Good exercise, good move, good to move, felt my sore body responding.

Speaking of body, I became aware of something else too: I was big for a bird, I mean bigger than I imagined a loon to be, two, three times as large as a duck; as big as a goose and heavy too, maybe six-seven pounds. Bad news about my size, I had to shape a bigger hole in the fence.

My training regimen must've created quiet a commotion.

"I'll be damned. What's got into my good luck bird?" It was Purple Hat standing at the gate. I stopped kung fu-ing, paddled to the far end of the pool and leveled my red eyes at him. His cowboy hat was purple all right and it did have clumps of much-abused feathers sticking up. Close up I could see several brightly-colored fly-fishing hooks attached to the brim, and food-labels stuck on that read Chiquita bananas, Organics, and Braeburn apple. The busy hat was tipped back revealing the beginning of a bald pate. A non-filtered cigarette, from the inexact taper on the end I'd say it was a roll-your-own, dangled out the side of his hidden lips. His full red beard covered his mouth. His mustache curved inward down to his mouth suggesting he chewed on it while eating or maybe gnawed on it searching for the bits of food imbedded in it. There were black marks where the fire from his roll-your-own had cut a scorch groove in the hair of his beard. He appeared unconcerned about any asymmetry to his face the groove caused. Got the feeling he didn't care a whole lot what people thought of him. Why should he? When you're the baddest guy in the valley.

His gray eyes squinted behind thick glasses. He undid the latch and opened the gate, strode to the pool, took off his hat and hung it on an errant wire. Good thing no sunshine seeped in down there, I would've been blinded by the billiard ball polish on his bald head. "Let's see if you left me any treasure this afternoon." He bent his bald head to where his glasses were only inches over the water. Duck walked sideways around the pool like that. I edged away from him. Whatever possessed me to nab that vest pin from Molly's hand? Why didn't I leave it be?

What had April said his name was? Fred...Ned...Nat? That was it. Purple Nat spied something — my droppings I blush to admit — poked his finger in the water and touched the black globule on the bottom, dithered it, brought his finger out, sniffed, grimaced, then sloshed it around in the water. He looked up and his mustache dipped at me. His slate eyes probed me, hooks trolling to snag lost treasure. He had a couple of teeth missing and the rest were crooked and stained puce. "Pretty birds have always been good luck for me and I knew you were a find the minute I spotted you with my binoculars with that gold tooth in your mouth. I'll give you one more day me precious, but if you don't shit that nugget of gold by tomorrow morning, its..." he made a throat-cutting motion with his hooked thumb, "the gangplank for you. Har. Har. Har."

Well what-do-you-know. Any friend of Long John Silver's and Gollum's is a friend of mine. I looked into Nat's dreadnought gray eyes and was reminded that Long John had spent his whole adult life disemboweling innocent hostages.

I gagged and deep swallowed. My long, loon throat was still bruised from ingesting the pin. So Nat figured he'd found the goose that was going to lay the golden egg. Not so according to April, he'd have to cut me open to get at it. That meant I had to escape tonight. Get through the fence and down to the river. Fat chance of doing that, I had all the survival skills in this situation of a mouse in a rain barrel.

I wanted April's warm bed with the leaping salmon quilt.

He scratched his butt. "I don't suppose you'd taste worth a damn, too fishy. But I'll make a pot of stew with you anyway."

Somewhere in the small valley coyotes yipped, announcing the evening hunt was on. As Harp, I would have felt lucky to hear the coyotes' call; as Qo-oo-la, the prey, or huntee, it made my feathers fluff.

"Hear that," Purple Nat said, "Or how's this, instead of stew, I feed you to the coyotes or raccoons. There's a lot of them hungry beasts around here'd like nothing better'n to dine on fishy loon meat."

Well thanks a lot, I thought, you don't look like you'd taste all that good either; too crusty. And besides that you look like you'd be hard as hell to clean, so there. "Yodel-y-oled-y-o" in spite of myself I let out a nervous loon laugh. Oh shit, it hurt my chest.

The coyote noise cut off in mid-bark.

Surprised the hell out of Purple Nat too. He toppled back on his ample butt. "Boy, ain't nothing wrong with your vocal chords is there? That was one loud cackle. Spooky too. It's almost as if you understood wha . . . nah, you been out in the boonies too long Nat. Starting to think a damn bird can reason." Talking to himself. I knew the feeling.

So Purple Nat you think that was spooky, get a load of this: Looking straight at him I sang out another yodel, and another. Hey, wanna hear some Jimmy Rodgers? Or how about Eddie Arnold? Nat scrambled to his feet, backed up against the wire. I realized I had a tool, however untapped, for survival — my voice, my song.

"You keep that up," Nat said, "I might have to slice you open this evening instead of waiting another night." He bit at his untrimmed mustache.

I shut my beak. So much for that nifty survival revelation. Liable to get me prematurely axed. I remembered enough about being a veteran pool hustler I should've realized, never tip your hand by overplaying a slight advantage. That's why I ended up in intensive care with a concussion. Can't make too many of those costly mistakes in my present circumstances. Give myself a chance to mull over the possibilities of what my voice can and can't do before I decide to go public. A whole new stage. A singer has to be so mindful of audience perception these days.

Sure did show those yammering coyotes a thing or two about singing to the stars. Hmmm, also gave them a fix on my general location and if they, being seasoned hunters, could read vulnerableness in my voice, they would no doubt be around to alleviate my fears. To paraphrase my favorite Missourian, Mark Twain: "Better to keep your beak closed and be thought a lounge lizard than to open it and have your gizzard removed." Kinda skews the meaning but were Mr. Twain in my perilous circumstances I feel sure he would appreciate my poetic license.

Nat hunched his shoulders, scratched his beard causing black crumbs to fall. "That's more like it," he said. "You know I could get to like you. Like to keep you around longer — someone to talk at in these lonesome mountains — but you're going to have to cooperate." He stepped out of the cage, grabbed a pale blue plastic two-gallon bucket and dumped its contents in my play pool. Little blue and red streaked fishes darted about. "Thought you might enjoy some live food. Now eat hardy and poop me a gold nugget. I find gold in the Dosanomish I won't have to write those damn Soldier of Fortune books anymore. Hey here's an idea, maybe I could train you to dive for gold, har, har, har. Oh that's a good one Nat, train a common loon to dive for gold. You're such a character." Purple Nat stopped. Turned around. Plucked his purple hat off its hook and put it on. "Get to shitting or I'll get to picking — your feathers. Show me some gold by tomorrow morning or I'll have your liver for lunch."

He left, congratulating himself on his erudition. Slammed the gate behind him. It had one of those automatic spring/hook latches. Made a tight metallic sound. Quivered the water in my pool. Not a chance of pushing the gate open and the latch was too high for a belly crawler to reach. No reach. No prehensile paw. No nifty prying tool. No escape through the gate.

I swam in fast circles around the pool, wanting to dive, terrified and with a kind of nervous anger. I hate it when humans do that. Take us animals for granted. What's so all-fired ridiculous about loon, deep diver, diving for gold? Or for anything else for that matter. I could be one rich loon, assuming there's any gold in the Dosanomish. Why confine myself to a river? A loon of my many talents could find sunken treasure in the ocean. Course I might have a little trouble spending it. What makes old Purple Nat think I'd be his lackey? I'd be my own loon. Hold on, I forgot. Purple Nat had no idea whatsoever his captured bird is Harp P. Gravey on a search and rescue spy mission. A mission, the purpose of which, was to deliver a murder clue down river, and, incidentally, save myself.

I kept circling the pool. Stalling. Delaying. My mind grasping at anything rather than the dauntless task at hand.

Purple Nat's idea held real water. The possibilities of using my diving ability to make a living and exploring underwater were limitless. Harp P. Gravey, a man terrified of water, making a living as a diver? Talk about career changes.

I figured if I got out of this cage, which seemed unlikely, the one thing to use my diving ability for was to get another look at those boulders in the river near the murder scene. Felt something very strange while swimming through them. Like the stones were trying to talk to me, warn me.

Definitely been hanging out with Malcomb too long. Talking stones. How long had I been in this deranged mess? What was it, all of three long days now? Malcomb grows on you. Seemed like forever.

I stopped circling. Enough idle speculation. Unless I got the hell out of Dodge I was going to wind up a floater in a sea of boiling vegetables. Or worse yet, coyote fodder. It's a cinch I wasn't going to shit gold.

Instead of succumbing to a weird avian panic, I should be formulating an escape plan. I peddled around the pool looking for a weak spot in the fence. Hmmm, there did seem to be one spot where the fence was bowed outwards and a couple strands of wire pulled loose. Some large animal had been at work.

I stretched my neck for a closer look. I plopped out of the pool and pushed over to the opening. Could just get my head and neck through. Grabbed a wire strand with my beak and pulled. Then pushed. Then bent, trying to use my beak like a pair of pliers. Not a chance. I spit out rust. Beaks weren't made for shaping wire.

And what about that large animal out there that had jaws strong enough to bite and bend metal? Where, oh where did it go? Waiting for me to stick my skinny neck through the hole. Chomp it off.

Time to try my secret weapon. I positioned myself for a karate kick.

I heard something. I stopped positioning and listened. A grinding sound, like the workings in a flour mill, off in the distance. Coming closer. Still closer. Right underneath me! Suddenly I realized it came from within me. How could that be? I've had indigestion before, my stomach growling like a barrel of baby grizzlies, but I'd never heard this noise like pebbles gnashing against each other. Pebbles wasn't exactly right, more like rough stone rubbed against metal.

I had it! It was the metal vest pin. My gizzard was trying to granulate the murder clue. And, if I listened close, was doing a pretty good job of it.

I was spawning pewter shavings. As I began to absorb the omnipresent sound, I wondered how long it would take my efficient gizzard to sand it smooth, wiping clean any writing or symbol, destroying evidence that might be a pointer to the murderer that wore it before it ended up in Molly Jenkins's death grip?

Could it be my own lost banjo pin?

I sensed eyes upon me and quickly searched the thick underbrush outside the fence. I heard a rustle and a snap. Something was out there and it was big enough to break branches. It was already getting dark under the alder and maple leaf canopy. A bat, surfing the dusky air for mosquitoes, swerved at the last second, missing my chain-linked fence. A pileated woodpecker screaming through the woods *kik, kik, kik, kik, kik, kikkkkk!* gave a high-pitched homecoming cry, heading for its nest safe against nocturnal predators. I had no such safe nest.

I pushed back to the play pool.

An Oregon grape shrub, slick green and spiny leafed, twitched and out from behind it emerged the masked face of a raccoon. It headed, light-footedly, for the hole in the fence. No hurry either, paused, raised up on its hind paws and looked around. It had the celebrated cute baby face of a masked bandit. My gizzard quit grinding. The metal pin a lump of lead in my chest. I had no illusions about raccoons. The masked bandit sought to steal my life.

23

The Beast and the Bandits

Pound for pound, a raccoon is one of the most unrelenting and lethal predators in the forest. Also one of the smartest. They have little fear of humans, thus enabling them to penetrate and plunder domestic crops and stock right under the nose of irate farmers. On my boyhood farm in the Ozarks we lost many chickens, geese and pigs to raccoons. And many's the night I sat up with a twelve-gauge shotgun, guarding the barn and chicken house.

Perhaps this was karma. I, in my callow youth, had killed quite a few of the beasts.

Pay back time.

The baby-faced bandit, with four-fingered, prehensile paws, clasped the intractable wire. Was he ever in for a surprise. I tried that buddy. If I couldn't break out, you can't break in. The wire's too tough. Give it up. Go back to peeling crawdads. Go back to. . . . Oh shit. Very deliberately the raccoon bent back the jagged edges of the ripped fence. I watched fascinated as the hole grew. What strength. What talented paws. What trouble my ass was in. My beak made a clumsy clacking noise. If baby face got through that fence I was a goner. Best chance, maybe only chance, I had was to waylay him as he squeezed through the hole.

I heaved my ponderous body over the edge of the pool again and landed on my neck and chest. I righted myself and checked out raccoon's reaction to my tactic. He had stopped arranging the wire and watched me.

He tilted his head, curious. This was not your normal behavior of prey that should've been petrified with fear.

It slowed him down for a moment and then he went back to work, pausing occasionally to glance at me and let out a low quivering growl, more of a hiss with deep-throat vibrato.

"Oh I'm so scared. Please Mr. Bandit, don't growl at me," I yodeled. Pushing with my awkward legs, I scooted on my belly toward the beast. "I am clumsy and vulnerable, Mr. Bandit. Please don't eat me. I'm sure my meat is tough and stringy. My feathers would choke you. My gizzard is full of metal, Mr. Bandit." I could see his sharp teeth behind hissing lips. "What big teeth you have, Mr. Bandit."

Oh, I was being one cool loon, slouching towards my imminent death with controlled calculated adrenaline. Not exactly the way I felt. My head, probably where Eagle had raked me with his talons, throbbed and burned. The inside of my beak was stuffed with cotton. I was taking some action in my own defense but that didn't mean I wasn't giddy with fear.

An alder branch above the raccoon began to shake and rustle. One, two, and then three familiar furry bodies dropped down beside raccoon. Oh shit, he'd brought his whole family. "Come on down here Hortense and bring the kids, we got us a sitting loon, yum, yum."

The raccoon family had themselves a confer, perhaps divvying up the dinner portions, drumstick to junior, wishbone to sister, breast to mama, neck bone to papa — sorry folks, no white meat — while I waddled within arms length of the hole. I sat on my stomach, feeling as unstable as a harmonica player at a harpsichord recital, and waited. No doubt about it, just one of them gets through that hole I'm a goner.

Their strategy decided, junior peeled off from the group and loped to the entrance. Chosen probably because he was smaller than the old boar that had styled the hole and could slip through easier, distract me while the clan popped through and then gang fanged me. The other three lined up at the fence and gave me that hissy growl, meant, I imagine, to cause catatonic terror in my victim body.

"I'm just some poor, dumb duck," I said, "frozen with fear. Be a sport and move on." For their entertainment I faked a violent body quivering and flopped my wing as if broken. Saw killdeers do that when I was a kid. The raccoons seemed to view that as encouraging and mama coaxed junior to hurry the operation. A proper mother sees that her family dines on time. Junior stuck his cute face through the hole. I flopped closer. Could taste fear in my beak like liquid aluminum. Not having any real plan and then, out of the blue, I remembered the warrior loon mask. I waited for that precise moment when Junior's paws were wedged tightly and then I cocked my long necklaced neck and struck. It may not have been adept at bending metal but my bill was one hell of a spear. My rapier beak penetrated juniors nose about one-half inch before it struck something solid. Thunked loud, like a knife hitting bone. The sound hung in the dark air. Hissing ceased.

Junior's cute little bandit eyes blinked incredulity for a split second before he screamed with pain. Blood squirted and splattered all over my checkered black and white feathers and junior propelled backwards out of the hole like a recoiled canon. I know I wasn't supposed to have any sense of smell but I swear I smelled a coppery odor in his blood. My beak, smeared red, tasted salty — could the sea be near — and bitter, like rancid burgundy.

Like some wilderness Mafia family, the raccoons circled around junior.

Through breaks in the leafy canopy I could see stars shining and, if not full, a robust moon glowing through the trees. Deep inside Qo-oo-la, I sensed the moon as my friend. The broken ring around my neck caught the lunar light and lit-up like a luminescent hangman's noose.

It was a good night for cheating death.

The raccoon family huddled over a simpering junior. Papa raccoon broke off and approached the hole, examined it, examined me. Most likely never seen an attack loon before. Who had? I felt great, heart thumping like a rabbit's hind foot, my attack body rocking back and forth, a cradle cloaking a hungry crocodile. Must of been Malcomb's warrior mask making me so damn frisky and reckless.

Could hear Josh's remonstrance, "Don't feed the raccoons. The worst thing that can happen to a wild animal is for humans to become *imprinted* in their minds. Lessens their chance of survival. " He'd be proud of me, I definitely had no intention of feeding the raccoons and thereby impinging their survival abilities. Didn't want to become *imprinted* in their minds or *ingested* in their bellies.

Adrenaline squirting, I wanted a piece of that crusty old boar. "Stick your head in that hole if you feel cocky you old codger, if you can spare the loss of an eye," for I could not afford to merely warn the bandit king. Even in my warrior's bravado I knew I was no match for him if he got in the cage. I had to strike a near mortal blow. Go for the brain via the eye.

The bandit leader snarled at me, his sharp fangs caught a shaft of moonlight. My neck jerked, imagining those bone gray flesh hooks imbedded in my flesh. He pranced to the hole, gave it close scrutiny, and, unlike junior who plunged in negligently head first, stuck his skillful paws in ahead of his snout. Deflector shields guarding against my rapier bill. He wedged in at the shoulders, still only had limited use of his paws.

I cocked my neck and struck again. Hit his paws protecting his eyes. He knew what I was up to. I struck again and again, drawing blood from his paws but causing no stoppage damage. Old boy protecting those eyes, smart fellow, on to me. His shoulders squeezed through, a matter of seconds before the rest of his body followed.

My next strike he swatted away and a pain shot through a major neck muscle. My sparing days were over for a while. I swear he grinned, knew he'd hurt me. Pissed me off. Time for my secret weapon. I flopped over on my side, playing like I was hurt more than I actually was.

The old boar thought he had me, let down his defenses, started using his claws in the dirt to pull himself forward. I think I can safely say I then instituted the first ever karate kick from a loon against a raccoon. I whapped the old boy right between the masked eyes. It sounded like a dropped drum on a plywood stage. I put my weight into it. It jarred my whole body, causing my injured neck muscle to convulse.

Raccoon was stunned or shocked, take your pick. Something wrong with the natural order of things here. He covered his smarting eyes with his paws leaving his nose exposed. I smacked the tender proboscis, felt flesh breaking through skin, blood spurted. I christen you the king of smacked noses! He covered his nose, I whapped him between the eyes again. Bloody and temporarily blinded, he backed out.

Good Lord, had I won? Beaten the plucky predators to a standstill? Written a whole new chapter in the relationship between predator and prey?

I peered at the moon now higher in the trees and yelled a victorious cry. A silhouette of a flying great horned owl crossed in front of it, heard my cry, banked and headed my way. I heard leaves swish and the creak of a limb above me in the maple as the large nocturnal predator landed. Get in line buddy. Owl was probably looking for an easy meal too, which brought me back to reality. Gotta learn to shut up. Secret to good harmony is knowing when to come in. Swing, damnit, swing! Gotta get that swing. Or I ain't gonna have a thing.

If I outlasted Rocky raccoon and his bandit family I still had to get through that hole in the fence and down to the river before morning, scooting on my belly. At that moment it seemed impossible.

To add emphasis to that thought, mama raccoon danced over to the hole. They weren't about to give up, plan being to wear me down. Mama had a nasty nurturing look in her eyes; the Mafia mama. I had beat up on her family and she was going to put a stop to it. Show them how it's done.

"Hey that's no fair," I said, "There's four of you and one of me and I left my teeth at home." Mama raccoon had neither a sense of fair play or humor. My neck drooped. Sore and tired. My head bobbed and when I tried to cock my chin a pain shot down my spine. A moonbeam broke through the rustling foliage overhead and lit-up my little stronghold.

I remembered the comforting voice in my dream. It inferred I was in this fix because I inadvertently gave unconditional respect to the river god. I concocted a quick prayer to the moon god — what could it hurt?

Deathbed conversion is better than no conversion at all. "Oh gracious moon please spare me and I will try to live my life in such a manner as to do you honor. I will sing to you every night and let my children frolic in your moonbeams." The great horned owl shifted on the limb above and hooted, "What children?" with derision. The moon hid behind a leaf cluster, winked yellow at me.

Was that a snap behind the little shed? Predators at the gate, talons above and jaws beyond? It's a jungle out there. How the hell does any prey survive the night? More to the point: How the hell am I going to survive the next few minutes?

Mama, smaller than the old boar, was able to get her paws, snout and shoulders through the hole in one quick shove. Her bandit eyes, close-up, bent on revenge. Her thin lips drawn back, teeth bared in a guttural growl.

I knew my only slim chance was to remain plucky and defiant. Never give up. Show them I'm more than a quick kill and a meal. Fight those clever buggers 'til the end. But a strange thing began to happen to my little loon body: Incipient fear got a mortal grip on it. It started shutting down. A great numbness saturated me as if I had been dipped in novocaine. Wave after wave of lavender dizziness assaulted my skull. My beak tasted bitter saliva, like regurgitated pasta, and my legs clabbered.

Pa, and the kids crowded the fence and stood on their hind legs; front row seats to the coming gory main feature. Mama squeezed, hissing and sputtering. I cast a warbled kick at her defending paws. She shook the feeble blow off. Kept inching forward. I kicked again and again, tossing a lariat at a charging Brahma bull. I was losing ground fast, stubborn beast took my on-the-ropes punches and kept on coming.

Cursed pin burning my craw. I was heavy and bloated with terror, uncoordinated. Futile effort. I had to quit kicking. Considered where to make my last stand. I slogged toward the playpool. Maybe I'd be able to maneuver to some advantage in the shallow water? No alternative really.

Then, just as the old sow squeezed her hind hips through, a funny thing happened on the way to supper. She yelped and, like my cagey bus in the mudflat, began sliding backwards, her claws scratching tears in the dirt. Her eyes, seconds before bent on revenge, crossed with pain and surprise. She hissed and clicked, could feel and see her steamy breath shoot out all the way across the enclosure.

I rolled over, waddled upright. Some feeling came back to my body. A great beast, most likely one of the before heard coyote, had a jaw lock on mama's tail, ripping her out of the hole much quicker than she went in. Mama was rendered helpless by the tight fit and the beast lunged for the nape of her neck, going for the kill.

A moonbeam filtered through the forest overstory and I got a better look at the beast. I was shocked. I had been saved by the ugliest, most hideous, gnarly excuse for a coyote I'd ever laid eyes on. In the ghost light, it was clumsy and awkward. What self-respecting coyote would attack a family of raccoons unless it was ravenous, or loco? One other possibility occurred to me, it wasn't a coyote at all but a starved, feral dog, attacking anything that moves. I caught a glimpse of a familiar cocked tail.

Delayed recognition flooded me. It was my own lost mutt, my cougar-chasing cur, my Medusa. Changed considerably in three short days. The perspective of a common loon, a foot off the ground, is very different than that of a common man way up there.

River fog rolled in, greasy and moist, snagging moonlight and transposing it into waxen orange globules. It surrounded us like a low budget movie set.

Raccoons attacked Medusa in unison. The ghostly orange air erupted into five simultaneous explosive growls followed by the *chomp* and *chink* of teeth clamping down on flesh and tearing through to cartilage. The noise was brutal. Shrub trunks and limbs snapped like bones. There were hisses, whimpers and drunken brawl sounds. It raged sideways, it raged forwards, back again, sideways, spinning and gyrating. I could taste the battle. It had a dank, hot flavor, filleted meat from a fresh kill.

From above, the owl hoot, hoot hooted, and shook its creaky perch.

Raccoons attacked on four fronts — they hadn't the slightest idea about what to do with a battling loon but with the bigger predator, they seemed to have a cohesive battle plan — and they were like gigantic warts on different parts of Medusa's body, grunting, snarling and ripping.

Medusa, in way over her head, was going down, needed help. But what could I do, hurt and on the other side of a fence from the fray. Wait! The old boar had a jaw lock on Medusa's hind haunch, butt wedged against the fence. Maybe my beak had one more campaign in it. I felt light-headed, charged and stabbed the old boar right in his next generation. My stiletto proboscis penetrated the sac and impaled a hard marble-like object. I tasted stale semen and tart urine. A new noise erupted through the din, a primordial shriek. And suddenly, as if choreographed by some woodland director, the characters in the battle act froze. Some universal signal had been sounded.

A mutually agreed screeched truce. Papa clawed over Medusa's back and crashed, bow-legged into the thick forest. His bandit family followed suit.

I could hear Medusa's breath coming in quick loud gasps, could see it mingle with the oily fog, pink and purple mist. Her body quivering with tension. I couldn't resist a soft thank you yodel.

Medusa turned to look at me. Her dark silhouette revealed a strong jaw line, torn ear, tufts of fur sticking out all over her skinny body. Smelled of gums and saliva. Took a beating. I heard a pained whimper.

I cooed with joy. My debilitating numbness evaporated and I flopped toward the hole. Gonna give her a big juicy smooch. I darted my head through the hole and suffered such a pain in my injured neck muscle that I immediately drew it back.

Saved my life.

Medusa, of the bone crushing jaws, lunged for my long naive neck and bit thin air. Teeth snacked together. I somersaulted backwards as she leaped after me through the opening. Could only get her head and part of her shoulders in. Flat-eared and fangs bared, tail tucked, she growled and snarled and snapped at me, crazed with hunger, spittle flew.

Medusa didn't save me because I'm me, Harp P. Gravey, her master, her alpha figure, her pack leader; she saved me because I'm the main course for dinner.

My life saved but heart broken. I sulked well away from those foam-flecked slavering jaws. The irony not lost on me. Could've been eaten by my own hound.

I have met the meal and it is me.

Sadness engulfed me and I stuck my head underwater for comfort. Vowed to become an ostrich in next incarnation. Hide from the ugliness and dangers of the world.

Or better yet, live underwater. Everything I needed lay below the surface. Eschew the open air. An unlucky trout swam by and I lashed out in frustration and nabbed the unfortunate fellow. Hurt my neck but what did I care? I was a goner anyway. How could I make it down to the river by morning? I hadn't even broke out of prison yet. Had my very own hellhound guarding the gate.

How much time did I have anyway? Trout in beak I looked to the heavens for an answer. The moon hung directly overhead, illuminating a dog that in the space of three days had gone feral. The great horned owl, in the maple branches, realizing that the available food was spoken for, ventured *Hoo!, hu-hu-hu, Hoo! Hoo!,* and flapped off to hunt elsewhere. The draft from its wings blew gaps in the overhead alder leaves revealing stars surreal in their luminosity and size. Don't see stars like that in the smog-shrouded city.

What I wouldn't give for a smelly old safe city right then. I tried swallowing the fish but couldn't do it. No appetite. Not exactly my choice of a last supper. I was going to spit it out but happened to follow a moonbeam down to where it shined on Medusa, watching me with those deep, red eyes. The moon gave me an idea.

I crab walked to just out of range of Medusa, tossed the fish up and caught it by the tail and offered it head first to her. I didn't know if she liked fresh trout or not. We, meaning Harp and Medusa, never ate fish. Reason being, Harp hated it. Medusa grabbed the offering and wolfed it down. One starved canine. Settles that. Medusa definitely liked fish. Good. I went to the pool and speared another. And another. After the eighth one she quit wolfing. Started chewing, watching me with not such a predator's eye. Confused allegiances, used to being fed by her master. Still it was a look that I'd never been on the receiving end of before. That hungry, I-can-crush-you-with-one-bite-of-my-mighty-mouth, look.

I felt small and juicy.

24

Taming Songs and Tick Bites

Medusa didn't look like she was going anywhere for a while and, the fact remained, she hadn't a clue I really was Harp P. Gravey, her one and true master. It's a cinch I couldn't move until Medusa recognized me. How could I convince her? Aha! Does not song tame the savage beast? Ignoring the silent coyotes out there, I lined three fish up in front of her and, while she ate, began yodeling the chorus to her favorite song: "Quit Kicking My Dog Around."

> "Every time I go to town,
> boys keep kicking my dog around,
> Makes no difference if she's a hound,
> you gotta quit kicking my dog around."

It was tough going, and I had no idea what key I was in, but I gave it my best shot. Medusa stopped chewing and whimpered. I'd sang the song to her a hundred times before. She always was a tough critic; if I changed the melody or rhythm she'd bark at me. If only I had my banjo to accompany me, she'd recognize the tune better. As it was, she didn't know what the hell to make of me. Couldn't blame her, a loon chorusing a song about a downtrodden dog, had all the potential of being the weirdest supper serenade ever. Since the head-injury accident, musically speaking, I just hadn't been myself.

Medusa began chewing again, slower, watching me, accepting my presence yet shy of total recognition. I had her confused and thinking though. I continued to ululate the melody to her favorite song. She left the third fish uneaten, finally full. Belched, blasting me with fish breath, gave a contented *woof* and lay her weary head down on her paws and rested. Her eyes flickered, the hunger flame extinguished. She slept, tail tucked between her legs.

I thought of something else to possibly clue her. I waited until she breathed in deep sleep, then inched over to her side. A few months ago Medusa had gotten a tic on her back. Few things are nastier. I got the tic off okay but for weeks the bite chafed and ulcerated. Josh and I took her to a vet and got it lanced. It healed into a hard itchy wart, out of rasp reach of her jaws or paws. Drove her nuts. She liked nothing better than for me to scratch it.

My head throbbed and my throat pained as I reached out with my beak and found the hard little knot and began gently massaging it. My probe also determined she needed a bath bad. Medusa moaned and garrumphed in her sleep. I increased pressure. Had to be careful, I press too hard could stab her with my dagger beak. Which could, in turn, incite her to take a chomp out of my drumstick . . . ah . . . thigh. Gotta quit thinking like a human.

Medusa gave a pleasurable, back-throated growl. Her eyes twitched. I tensed. The moment of reckoning was close at hand. Her eyelids opened, looked at me, had a momentary flash of wild-eyed disorientation, realized she was getting her favorite back scratch, eyes changed to undiluted adoration. She cocked her head to within one-quarter inch from my exposed thigh, opened her saber-lined mouth and grinned. I loved that familiar Pleistocene smile, all teeth and curdled lips. I'd never seen her give it to anyone but me. Her pink tongue flicked out and she began licking my leg. Her tail sprang up, tossing wet moldy leaves in the air and wagged so hard I could hear it sucking wind. I was dumbfounded and so delighted I almost broke massage rhythm and dinged her skin.

We stayed like that for a while, getting used to each other. She tasted of composted fir needles and swamp gas and raccoon musk. Touching her, I can't remember ever feeling any living thing — 'cept perhaps my mother's bosom when I was a suckling child — that gave me so much comfort or contentment. Touch, the rudiments of communication.

Medusa must of felt it too. She fell asleep again with her formidable snout — considerably bigger than I remembered — resting on my webbed foot. Her fish flavored breath easy and regular. Settled in like she used to do lying beside me wherever I landed for the night. I draped my long neck over her furry shoulders. Pals once more. Together again. Some comfort at least to know I didn't have to spend my last night on earth alone.

25

The Shot and the Leap

I too was exhausted. Been a short but hard night. Wondered how much of it was left, how much time I had before Purple Nat decided to operate on my gizzard. The moon had traveled across the sky and was now getting ready to disappear behind the western Olympic mountains. Pockets of shadows shimmied in a light breeze wafting up from the river. Probably around two am. Could I afford to take a short snooze before I somehow attempted the dash to the river? Dash, ha, ha my feathered ass. My dashing days were over. More like scoot. Do the ol' *"boot scooting boogie."* Maybe, if it was downhill enough I could curl in a bundle and roll. Or here's another desperate thought, get Medusa to carry me to the river. Make her into a retriever. Say fetch in loon talk. Fetch me to the river. My over-stimulated mind grasped at straws.

Now that Medusa recognized me, trick was, how do I communicate with her? Get her to respond to my loon voice? Help each other get out of Josh's best last wild place? I ever get back to some kind of semblance of sane civilization I may just dump Josh's ashes down the toilet and flee. Sacred knoll be damned! I ruffled my feathers to rid my head of resentful thoughts. Didn't need anything else to slow me down.

Medusa breathed ragged. Whined. Having doggy dreams. Poor girl, probably gotten pretty scary and lonely out there all alone in the wilderness. Wondered if she ever caught up with Clancy, the cougar? Not likely. If Medusa did she'd be buzzard meat by now. Unsettling, knowing the mountain lion was out there somewhere. Probably just as hungry as Medusa. My feathers fluffed again, black & white checkerboard back rippled.

One thing about it, I had tamed Medusa. She was my responsibility. I had to take care of her, get her home. But whose, I pondered, responsibility is it, Harp P. Gravey's or Qo-oo-la's? Both? And of what home do we speak?

The raccoon attack had taken its toll on my body. All that jousting and kicking wore me out mentally and physically. Whether I wanted it or not I dozed. I dreamed the man in the moon, dressed in a loincloth, orange snakeskin boots and a purple cowboy hat, tossed brass necklaces around my neck. He peeled the golden rings off from around the circumference of the moon and flipped them, Frisbee style, down to earth where I had my neck stuck out way too far as a goal post. The man in the moon spoke to me, *"Communicating with Medusa may be simpler than you think. Don't be a dope, figure it out. Your life and Medusa's depends on it."*

He tossed another brass ring — good eye! — and, when it landed, jarred me awake. Good Lord it was getting light. How long had I slept? And why was I still in animal spirit form? Could there be method to this whole madness? Either Qo-oo-la had to die or escape before whatever forces are at work lets me transform back to Harp? Someday, if I survived and things calmed down, be nice to give some thought to how this spirit animal stuff really works.

No time for that kind of speculation, I had to get us out of there. And fast. Purple Nat had all the earmarks of being an early riser.

I scratched Medusa behind the ears as I did every morning for a wake up call. She sighed and opened her eyes, began licking my leg again. Good. It wasn't just a fluke that she accepted me. Now what the hell do I do?

I scooted around in front of her, stuck my breast against her snout, "my you have big teeth," and, cooing gently to her, pushed. She backed out of the hole, stood up and shook her massive body. Moldy leaves and dirt filled the air. A ruffed grouse, off in the forest, drummed an early morning mating call. Good to hear somebody's looking forward to an arousing future. Country music started to twang from the house. I quickly plunged into the hole. I didn't realize how big my body was. I wedged tight, stuck. My webbed feet spun in the dirt but I couldn't move. I nearly panicked. Duck soup! Finished!

Medusa sniffed at me, cocked her head at my grunting, attempting as always to understand and please. Unfortunately I had no command in loon language for "pull-the-fat-bird-out-of-the-hole."

A door slammed.

Some communication, it came to me, even between animals of different species, need not involve the spoken language. I picked up a small stout maple branch and poked it at Medusa. She grabbed it. Played this game before. I jerked it away from her. Although we had no command for pull, this was a game of tug of war we'd played since day one of our partnership. Medusa grabbed it again, growled mock menacingly and hauled backwards. I held tight — what a good stout beak this is! — and paddled with my powerful legs for all I was worth.

In a flurry of black and white feathers, I popped free. Hallelujah! Surprised us both. I almost jammed the stick down Medusa's throat. I let go lest she think I meant to do her harm. No hint of that. She considered it all part of the game.

I had no time for stick games. I had to get to that river before Nat decided to check on me. Oh. Oh. Too late, beefy footsteps on the path. I ducked, as fast as any loon can out of water, into the forest. Medusa, still engaged in her own private party, pranced around me teasing with the stick, growling, making enough noise to wake a well fed anaconda.

I discovered an animal trail leading down to the river and, I swear I tasted the clean, cool flavor of the Dosanomish. Perfume to my senses. The roar of rushing water traveled up the forest path. I pushed and shoved but lordy, I was slow as a slug on a swing!

Behind me I heard Purple Nat shout, "What's going on here?" A pause. "A damn coyote's got my gold nugget. I'm getting my gun." His running footsteps faded toward the house.

"Run Medusa, run!" I yodeled, "Save yourself." Medusa, of course, upon hearing my loon jabber, stopped frisking, stood in front of me as stock still as a stork at sundown. Oh great! Do exactly the opposite of what I say. Dumb dog. Gonna get yourself shot you don't flee. Too late for me. I'll never make it.

Medusa, stick still clamped in her mouth, shoved it at me. Pain and certain death coming through the rye and she wants to play stick games. She poked me again with that damn maple branch. Blocked my access, futile as it was, to the animal trail. I opened my beak once more to warn her and Medusa shoved the stick right down my throat. Tasted like solid syrup. I choked, and the answer, which was right under my nose, came to me. I grabbed the stick firmly in my beak and locked eyes with Medusa. Message delivered. She held the other end and bolted. Off and running.

We headed straight down the animal path toward the sound of running water. I hung on for dear life. Imagined myself to be an alligator snapping turtle. Stubbornest damn creature alive. Don't need a hook to snag one, just a string and a piece of rancid bacon. Bull turtle clamps down on that bacon and won't let go. "Don't let go, don't let go, don't you ever let go," I coached my beak. I knew if I could hang on to the stick, I had a chance.

Easier said than done.

If I needed any convincing though it came fast and quick in the form of a bullet plowing the underbrush beside me, followed closely by the report of a high-powered rifle. Purple Nat not wanting his gold nugget to get away.

Sharp branches beat me about my head and wings. I sailed over downed logs, waist-high sword ferns, spiny-leafed salaal, and jagged rocks, and landed hard on my rubbed-raw belly. Foliage sliced by in a green and brown blur, rifle reports behind, bullets chewing up dead leaves around us.

I never had such a hitch in my life.

Medusa skidded to an abrupt halt. It took a second for me to get my bearings. We were on a brushy cliff over the river. I released my death grip on the stick — my jaws felt charley-horsed — and peered over the bluff and saw churning, white-water, river rapids down about fifty feet, feeding into a treacherous narrowing funnel. Be suicidal to go over that bluff.

But hey, it's not like I had a whole lot of choices. Through the bush, Nat with his high-powered rifle stomped toward us. Only question was, what was I going to do with Medusa? Sacrifice her to save myself? Not a chance. She still had the stick in her iron jaws. Grasping at straws, I grabbed it, pulled with all the strength I had left, to the edge, looked backwards once more to see Purple Nat burst through the evergreens, bald head resembled the round top on a bass fiddle — I had this ridiculous observation that he looked meaner without his purple hat — and leaped.

And dangled. This time I held on hoping to drag Medusa with me. Big baby. I peered up into Medusa's frightened eyes and sent her a mental entreaty, "Come on Sundance, the posse is upon us." Suddenly my brave canine yowled, simultaneous with a gunshot and the unforgettable sound of a fast metal object hitting slow, brittle bone. Medusa spit out the vine maple branch and leaped over me. Warm blood spattered my head. We tumbled down, down, down and I prayed all the way Medusa was not mortally wounded.

I smacked the water on my scraped-raw breast and gasped for control as I tumbled in the rushing undercurrent. I tried to catch sight of Medusa but before I could get my bearings I felt consciousness slipping away; felt Qo-oo-la losing his transmigrational grip; felt the pull of Harp P. Gravey. "No!" I cried. "No, not now, not yet. I can't leave Medusa now. She'll drown for sure." I fought the shape change but to no avail, I careened out of Qo-oo-la's gyrating body and pitched and plunged through that wind tunnel again. Then I floated and drifted in clouds like cotton mushrooms.

I heard a voice from far away. I drifted closer, "He's back," April said, "from the dead from the looks of him."

26

River Rudders and Canine CPR

"A natural metabolic reaction to transmigration," Malcomb said. "You should have let him choose his own path, let him come back naturally of his own accord. Qo-oo-la may have unfinished business."

"I think you're full of crap," April said. "What makes you think he could do that?. And what kind of unfinished business could a common loon have for Chrissake? Yodeling at the moon? And don't think I've forgotten your part in this fiasco. You were supposed to take care of —"

"He's okay," Malcomb said. "You're upset cause you're sweet on him."

"I'm upset," April said, "because I'm a doctor who understands that you can't stress a body beyond endurance."

I smelled blood & guts. A natural by-product of one world overlapping into another? My eyes opened. April shut up. Her face was the color of old feathers on a taxidermied red bird. An inch long pink smear of gore stuck to the collar of her light green surgical outfit, like she had just come from another all night emergency surgery. Gray curlicue feathers clung to her beautiful blue-black hair, which was a mess; wild, tangled strands fell over her face and a thick damp wad hung down between her sweaty breasts. So unlike her. A faint whiff of bleach saturated the air around her.

As exhausted as I felt, April still looked beautiful to me. She held her weary head upright with her right hand on her forehead. With her left hand, she clutched the warrior mask to her breast. The hair hat sat shimmering on the nightstand. Malcomb hovered beside it.

I knew what I had to do. I grabbed the beak of the mask. It pulsed electric. My dry lips clicked when I opened them to speak. "You must put the mask and hat back on me. Medusa's been shot. She may be drowning. I have to save her. Hurry."

April held firm to the mask. "You're speaking nonsense. Where'd Medusa come from? You're obviously delirious. Forget it. I'm not about to let go of this ugly mask."

"No time to explain. Do it! Do it now!" I was acting by pure instinct, not thinking what I was saying. Could see, in my minds eye, my doomed doggy shoving that stupid stick down my throat to save my life. I looked at Malcomb with, what I hoped, was pleading in my eyes. I couldn't do it on my own. April was too strong.

Malcomb understood. "Maybe Harp's loon power is to the point where he doesn't need conditions to be perfect." He walked around April and pushed the hair hat within my reach. With my other hand I touched it.

A jolt shook my chest, lifted my shoulders up off the bed and my feet under April's quilt caused the fish pattern to fibrillate. I saw the terror in April's eyes and Malcomb's lips moving as if in prayer, as I bucked and hurtled off into the unknown. There was no dark tunnel to shimmy through this time and no pain. The hat and mask worked their magic and I didn't even have to wear them. Just connect them.

What had changed?

I had no time for rhetorical ramblings, I was submerged in a treacherous undercurrent, my breast bouncing off the river bottom, and I had in my beleaguered beak, by some miracle, a canine by the tail; unconscious and trailing a brilliant red streak of blood which didn't help my navigational eyesight any. We headed for a narrow water chute between the two bluffs. The river raged and roared like a maddened bull as we plunged through, but I managed to be some kind of subsurface rudder and kept us caroming off rocks rather than smacking them dead center. As involved as I was in guiding Medusa's unconscious body through the aquatic gauntlet and as damaged as my body felt, I marveled at how strong a swimmer I'd become . . . or rather Qo-oo-la was.

Speaking of myself, Qo-oo-la, for one brief instance I wondered how I had gotten from falling off a cliff to hooking onto Medusa's tail? Without Harp's help? Could it be that there was some overlap of consciousness and empathy between species?

I have no idea how long we were in the chute, but figured if Medusa wasn't dead from the gunshot she had to of drowned. We burst out into a calm pool. I hauled her body over to some shallows and latched onto her ear and lifted her head above water. My neck and breast were slathered in blood. Medusa was bleeding to death. No matter, she wasn't breathing. Had to address that one first.

How does a common loon administer mouth-to-mouth resuscitation to an uncommon canine? I don't believe that was covered in my military blue book. First I had to get her head permanently out of water. I propped her muzzle up over a Y branch of a sunken log, darted back about ten feet then charged. At the last second I averted my head and neck and slammed into her chest with my breast. Jesus that hurt. Medusa however remained unmoved. I did it again and again until I could hardly kick with my legs. "Cough you bloody canine. Come on. Spit it out. Don't die on me." My ribs, already damaged by defying terminal velocity, felt like pulverized pumice.

Medusa's face was frozen in a death mask. White eyes rolled up in their cavernous sockets. Water around us red as tomato soup. Nose breath holes like nesting cavities. Wait a second. Breath? I had a handy funnel that fit perfectly into one of those nose holes. I stuck my beak as far down her nostril as possible and blew. Man! Was that yucky! Nevertheless, I pulled my beak out one nostril, took a deep breath, and jammed it down the other one. Blew like the east wind singing down the Columbia River gorge. Then I backed off and slammed her chest again. Huffed and puffed 'til my lungs felt like Jell-O. I alternated back and forth between chest and nostrils until my beak was coated with bloody phlegm.

I strangled. Had to stop. Hacked and spit. I had failed. I had lost her. I threw my damaged wings around her broken body, blood gushed between us, and hugged her as hard as I could. I cried out a death dirge in a minor key to the indifferent forest. I bore down and wailed my deepest sorrow.

The indifferent forest snorted a response. Without warning, Medusa's chest heaved and she up-chucked masticated fish and bilge water in my face. She gave a soft growl. Felt her tail wag underwater, a limp rudder. She grinned, weak as a noodle. Medusa lived! Oh birdsong of joy in the morning!

And was bleeding to death. I grabbed her firmly by one flaccid ear and led her further up the bank out of the water. Her out, me in the water where I could maneuver. When she hit land one front leg dangled. She stood on three legs shaking, in shock, blood oozing from her shoulder. Her sad head hung between her legs almost touching her sadder tail. Her body vibrated. I scooped-up some mud and weeds in my handy-dandy beak and packed it against her shoulder, pressed firmly. A hollow croaking sound erupted from Medusa's chest and she toppled over on her side. Better. The mudpack stayed put by itself and I paddled over and ripped some more from the river bank. Applied it, patted it down and the bleeding stopped. Healing properties, that river mud. Potent stuff. Magic. Somehow, in part, responsible for getting me into this mess.

A thin low fog covered the little sandy beach where we'd landed, and shielded us. Purple Nat could be up there on the bluffs with his high-powered rifle looking for us. Eagle, bent on revenge, could be soaring overhead in the sky on the lookout for me. Land predators, on the early morning breakfast prowl.

Medusa lost consciousness. Her breathing weak but regular. Some kind of miracle she was alive. On the river bank several feet away, white Indian-plum blooms hung on thin stalks and lavender wood violets hugged the ground.

What was I saying, it's a miracle either one of us were alive. I felt impelled to give thanks to the river god.

"Oh mighty river thank you for sparing my true and faithful dog." Strange how natural, as an animal, it felt to worship the life giving elements of the earth. What was that Malcomb had said about the river being the blood of the mountains? And about getting ghost *Tamánamis* power? As Harp P. Gravey, a human, I seemed to have lost touch with that kind of awe and respect. Wouldn't think of shouting a spontaneous prayer of thanks to anything.

That's what I did, yell. Started to anyway, but quickly amended it to a soft loon croon of gratitude. While sacred, those waters could quickly turn troubled.

27

Gray Hunters and Golden Ghosts

As if to verify that, I spotted a creeping movement through the thin fog on the riverbank. I finished the prayer quickly. The mist parted at the seams, responding to some bilious turbulence, long enough for me to catch a glimpse of a dark shape approaching through the undergrowth. Given my track record as a bottom-of-the-food-chain bird, it did not bode well. Life in the avian fast-food lane was fraught with danger.

The morning mist was fast burning off and I caught another glimpse of the shape approaching. No, two shapes. Gray and sleek, built for stealth, with eyes a satin white, a pair of coyotes. The shoreline began weaving, bank mud slid into the water with a hiss, tree limbs dipped down and uncoiled like watchful snakes at a Pentecostal prayer meeting. My salvation supplication was premature.

I cursed the hunters. "Go to hell! I won't let you have Medusa!"

Ten feet away from Medusa's comatose body, the pair noticed me, hesitated. The lead coyote's fur glistened with a healthy brown and black color. He reminded me of a gang leader, cocky and confident, in total control of his street corner. The smaller female sniffed the air and darted glances in all directions, tongue licking lower lip, mistrustful of their good fortune to find such easy prey. Something made her nervous. Maybe Purple Nat had a quick way across the river and was approaching?

Medusa, red blood already drawing green-bellied bloat flies, lay with powerful jaws slack and pink tongue lolling. Her weak breath blew tiny eddies of sand in the beach. Helpless and oblivious. Down for the count. Could only hope for a quick merciful kill.

Although not oblivious, for all practical purposes, I too was helpless. But wait! I dragged Medusa on shore, why couldn't I drag her back in the water? Perhaps I could keep her from drowning or bleeding to death while I outfoxed the coyotes in deep water? Fat chance but what choice did I have? I'd seen the way coyotes kill helpless creatures. They go for the belly first. Eviscerate the victim while still alive.

I clamped onto Medusa's good front leg and tugged. The coyotes observed my canine maneuvering for a moment, then looked at each other, puzzled, as if to say, *"I can't believe my eyes; either that loon is trying to eat that wounded dog or trying to save it from us. If we're quick enough we'll invite them both for lunch."* Then, the casual reconnoitering changed; the big male attacked. Quick as a bullet.

My instincts took over and I, being in shallow water, let go of Medusa's paw, started to turn and dive. Seeing it was too late, prepared to greet forty pounds of jaws and teeth with a beak and a lark. As coyote leaped over Medusa, with one last ounce of strength, Medusa growled, raised her weary head and nipped the big fellow's back paw. Coyote yipped and sliced trajectory, plunged into the water, missing me by a buzzard's waddle.

I escaped to deep water.

Once again Medusa had saved me. But that didn't help her. The big coyote crawled out of the water and limped to his partner's side. Shook off the pure water of the Dosanomish as if it was contaminated. Coyotes took stock once again. No doubt about it, the dog was dead meat.

They moved toward Medusa in unison.

I had only one move left. My beak raised and I wailed a song of deliverance and/or death dirge to my faithful canine friend. I poured it on, put my mother's Irish voice behind it, all her anger and frustration at my drunken dad. Added Grandfather Two-loons' voice of hope and redemption to it. Bounced it off the Ho-had-hun mountains and old growth, ancient trees, known to Qo-oo-la as *The Standing*

People, squeezed it through dense undergrowth and let it soar out over the soothing waters of the Salish Sea. A call for help. Please! Anyone out there? Please!

Let Purple Nat hear or some hunter; anything was better than death by coyote.

Medusa heard, her back leg twitched and she stumbled upright, growled and faced her assassins, listing to the left. Her bottom jaw dragged the sand; ears flat, waterlogged tail drooping. Oh but what a heart. I never saw a more courageous sorry sight in my life.

My song and Medusa's last-ditch bluff had bought her another minute of life but we didn't fool those savvy coyotes. They circled my crippled canine, scanning for the kill. Only Medusa's eyes followed them, her body threatening to disintegrate any second. The mudpack fell off her bullet wound and blood began oozing, exciting the coyotes to attack.

The smaller coyote locked onto Medusa's tail and, as the dog turned, the large one went for her exposed throat.

My heart was a lump of coal, my gizzard a wad of blistering sand, I couldn't watch the carnage. I attempted to dive but suddenly there appeared, from out of nowhere, a golden ghost. A golden ghost that had mastered the art of invisibility; one minute nothing, the next a blur of motion. It was large and it was tawny and it was Clancy, lion of the mountain. The mountain lion broadsided the largest coyote, millimeters away from Medusa's exposed throat. Lion and coyote tumbled and both landed on their feet, snouts inches away from each other. Clancy arched his back, his black-tipped tail stood up and weaved like a cobra and he *phissed* so loud the auditory waves made ripples in coyote's rich neck fur. Coyote, grunted and growled, teeth bared, ears flat, he stood his ground but his center of gravity was leaning backwards, toward the safety of the forest.

Medusa fell over as the smaller coyote let go of her tail. To its credit, the courageous smaller coyote came to the aid of her mate and attacked

Clancy's hind haunch. Clancy wheeled to fend off the flank attack and swatted empty air. Both coyotes lit out, tails between their legs, for high country. The golden ghost watched them disappear through the cottonwoods, into the morning fog, his tail twitching.

28

Murderous Claws and Your Mother

I couldn't restrain myself; I hooted a victory cry and erupted out of the water, flapping my sore wings, webbed feet pumping so hard that I danced, hydroplane style, on water. I propelled in circles, churning vast amounts of water, splashing on Medusa and Clancy.

Clancy, licked his left shoulder, shook the spray off and ambled over to Medusa who lay still, fresh blood pooling on sand. I stopped dancing. Good Lord, Clancy was not the slow-witted, drugged, humiliated beast that Lt. LeRoy taunted. This animal moved with stealth, confidence and authority. Though still thin, tawny fur stretched over a lustrous backbone, shoulder and chest muscles bulging. Freedom became him. That cat was the supreme land predator, without a gun, on the Olympic Peninsula.

And Medusa, brave hound, was a piece of bloody, red meat.

My heart dropped down to my webbed feet. Mouth full of sand and sorrow, some constriction kept me from swallowing. Medusa, my lovely, ugly dog, lying immobile, hardly breathing, didn't deserve to die so defenseless. Clancy opened his fanged mouth over Medusa's exposed neck to deliver the mortal chomp.

I wracked my run-away brain thinking of what I could do and then I remembered a classic diversion tactic. I reared up on my hind legs and, surprising myself, flapped my damaged wings as hard as I could without fainting from the pain, screamed bloody murder and ran across the water and attacked the lion of the mountain.

Well, attack is not exactly the right word. Even a battle-maddened, warrior loon is not dumb enough to attack head-on a mountain lion. I played like I was attacking the beast, the clever plan being to divert Clancy from his canine meal, then I would, at the last moment, feign injury and lead him astray. Theory being, an imprinted cougar knows a plump loon tastes better than a mangy dog. As per usual I got caught up and over-estimated my slack, overplayed my hand; I went too far. Didn't realize how much propelling passion lived in the heart of a common loon.

Clancy stepped over Medusa and, quicker than a pneumatic punch, swatted my chest with one of his pistoned paws. I had seen those mur-derous claws up close back on the mudflat in Malcomb's cage. Surprised me, how painless filleted breast meat felt.

I jettisoned airborne, tumbling; river, sky and forest joined in a whirlpool of interconnected seamless blues and grays and browns and greens. I steeled myself to smack the water but it didn't happen. I didn't stop. I watched my bloodless avian body, amidst separating feathers, plunge into the river but I — my spirit self — continued to twirl and gyrate. I yell-yodeled idiotically to the big cat standing over Medusa, *"Surrender! We have your mother!"* I caught dizzying glimpses of Clancy slurping Medusa's blood and tried another yowl of apology to my faithful dog for failing her in her time of great need but could manage only a tuneless croak, much like my butchered rendition of "Faded Love."

The shape shift came, a hard needle of light in the whirling void. The restless murmur of the river faded. My stomach catapulted and bile threat-ened to explode from my beak.

29

Of Pigs and Pain

This time April was waiting and this time she came prepared.

I ran my hands over my chest, neck and stomach. No shredded flesh or severed arteries. My mind caught up with my body and I whispered, "I'm not ready. Clancy's got Medusa. Qo-oo-la's breast is ripped open. I must go back." The walls had a watery film on them, as I looked around for the hat and mask.

"They'll just have to get along without you," April said. "Your space-rangering days are over for a while fly-boy." She whispered under her breath to Malcomb. "He's delirious. Where the hell did Medusa and Clancy come from?"

"Doomed, without me they're doomed," I said. My voice seemed to come from a great distance.

Malcomb, his face the color and texture of overcooked meatloaf, looked over April's shoulder. "April's right this time," he said. "You can't survive another transmigration right now. But don't give up hope. Remember, while still caged, Clancy told me he liked Medusa."

"Yeah, for breakfast," I said as I felt a needle prick my skin. I had just enough time to say a prayer for cats and birds and dogs and false pride before I slept.

I dreamed of pigs and wasps, chasing me in an enclosed, self-sustained environment with no exit. The sky was a flattened sheet of opaque glass.

Smudges appeared in the glass, oil slicks in the sky. We were trapped in a video arcade. The pig and wasp armada attacked me from below and above. I sensed you had to know the rules to survive, and I didn't have a clue.

30

Spears and Mirrors

I woke up. Alone. A cold draft hit me as if someone had just closed the outside door. Footsteps, going away, crunched on gravel. I sensed the mask, hat and shirt were gone from the room, stashed somewhere way out of my reach, like Qo-oo-la and Medusa. Chilly air crept underneath my blanket and nestled against my body. I could feel my skin shrink. Living by myself most of my life, I have never felt so alone.

Had I caused the horrible death of both my best friend and my spirit brother? One by teeth, two by claw?

My ears heard weeping and chattering. I sat up and moaned. The papyrus turban still weighed heavy on my head. Head burdened down with hornets and sorrow. Sorrow stings.

Across a room full of sad-faced wooden animals, tears flowed from the ligneous eyes of a river otter. Perhaps a cousin to the otter that got me tangled in Molly's hair. Outside my window a Douglas squirrel perched on a branch, scolding, its tail in a frenzy of jerks. The squirrel eyed some food left on my nightstand; another witch's butter sandwich and a glass of water. The thought of food churned my stomach, yet I had to eat. Get some strength back. Only two ways to get to Medusa and Qo-oo-la. And I had already failed at one. Didn't April say something about a helicopter? I grabbed for the telephone, find the clinic number. My hand fell on the wooden-framed mirror on the end table. I picked it up and looked at my face to see if it was the face of a killer or just a blundering fool. Broken blood vessels on my cheeks seemed more damaged than usual; transmigration flight is not conducive to rosy cheeks. The paint slashes Malcomb put on had dried and already faded, as if its job was over. I grabbed a napkin off the end table, doused it with water, closed my eyes and scrubbed my face clean. The water felt cool and soothing.

When I opened my eyes I did not see my face staring back at me in the mirror. Fog clouded the glass. I gave it a shake. Mumbled an incantation.

> "Mirror, mirror, in my hand
> let me view this cursed land.
> Mirror, mirror, tell me true
> is Medusa dead and Qo-oo-la too?

The fog broke and there was the lion and Medusa on the sandy beach. Clancy still licking the blood from the dog's bullet wound. I was transfixed. Couldn't let go of the mirror. What kind of unholy vision was this? Was I going to have to watch my beloved Medusa be lion lunch? I almost threw the mirror down.

Instead, my mental camera zoomed in for a closer look. Telescoped to the big cat's nail-puller mouth. So close I could see the rough burrs on his tongue, a tongue red with Medusa's blood.

But wait. The cougar tongue did not seem to be doing a bloodthirsty licking. It was more a licking like a mother cat cleaning a kitten. Not quite that either. It was like a kitten licking its mother. Glory be!

I know it was rude but I'm afraid I stared. Never knew how big and pink a cougar's nose was. Overshadowed the small closed mouth. His whiskers were black at the base turning into white further out. He had a white goatee tipped in red, possibly Medusa's blood. The ears, tiny antennas twitched and swiveled slightly of their own accord, constantly listening for signals. His lower cheeks were splotched satin black and everything else was a rich burnished gold color.

The eyes dominated that face, amber and unslitted, almost round and human-like in repose, topped by sparse white eyebrows. Those round eyes glanced up, as if he knew he was being watched, and looked straight into mine. So startled me, I dropped the mirror. The glass shattered. Shit! Should've looked around for Qo-oo-la. See if he was still bobbing in the current.

But what was I saying? Had I become so desperate I pulled cat faces out of mirrors, my bludgeoned brain clinging to a shred of hope for Medusa? And why, since I was pulling hope out of a mirror didn't I see Qo-oo-la?

Still, if Clancy had spared Medusa, might he have done the same for Qo-oo-la?

It was all too confusing. I needed to get out of that room. Get some fresh air. I found clean jeans, underclothes and a denim shirt folded on the table. Not mine but they fit. I dressed and stepped outside. Ocean breezes rustled big-leaf maple leaves, bringing smells of fruit blooms and salt water. The Salish Sea, to the east past some outbuildings, was placid and slick.

Shrubs near the back door were swelled with tight, spring buds. Each shrub's new growth was a different shade of green, camouflaging the brittle stalks and spikes of older growth. Pink petals shook loose from a crab apple tree and floated down to cover a large mustard-brown banana slug crossing on the cobblestone path in front of me. The pink petals contrasted with the slug's slimy black blotches as if the scavenger was a carrier for a deadly pox. I high-stepped around the gastropod.

My feet danced a few stumbling steps. Medusa and Qo-oo-la might be alive! Took a few minutes to soak in. Sure, it was a hallucination in that mirror but nevertheless, in my heart, I embraced hope.

I took a deep breath. The air was saturated with a sticky suggestion of new pollen, sperm for another season. My legs had a mind of their own, though wobbly, they wouldn't quit skipping.

Ten feet away from the house, I boogied through a wooden gateway into Malcomb's totem work yard. A five-stall totem pole barn, at the far end, blocked my view of the Salish Sea. Cedar carvings and totems stood or lay all around in various states of progress. An overpowering scent of cedar filled the work yard. Wood chips lay in auburn piles everywhere. I spotted an ancient totem lying on some blocks. I felt drawn to it.

Before I could get close to the reclined totem, I heard a footstep behind me and caught a whiff of mold and methane. I turned and a stone spear point pinned me to an upright, uncarved pole. I grabbed the shaft of the weapon with both hands. Held tight. The long stone point was a thing of ancient beauty and modern death. The spear's elaborately carved shaft — I think the image inlays were rabbits in various bodily contortions — was attached to an Indian man. "You have stolen my birthright white-eyes," the spear holder said. "I should kill you."

"Whoa here fella, you can have your birthright back. I don't want it." You'd think, with all the accusations flying about, that I'd set out on a reprehensible mission to burgle birthrights.

I shoved the spear back at a broad shouldered, big headed man. I'd seen him somewhere before. He had a long plains Indian, eagle feather headdress on, which appeared to have been folded, spindled and mutilated, as did the man's denim and dirty street clothes. The street clothes were a drunk's dead giveaway, a skid-row uniform. It's the same everywhere.

Underneath the feathered hat, twisted strands of dirty black hair hung over his forehead, through which eyes, like chunks of onyx gravestones, glared at me. One eyelid was lazy and drooped, the other eye compensated by opening too wide. His lips were chaffed and he kept moistening them with his tongue. A tongue as opaque and swollen as a slab of bacon fat. I recognized Loren, April's brother, gone way downhill since I last saw him heading for Seattle on his blue Harley. Number one suspect for Molly's murder. And if he killed once, he could kill again.

However, rather than thirsting to impale me with the spear, Loren appeared to hold on to the shaft in a desperate need to keep from falling over. He wobbled and the shaft began circling faster and faster and wider and wider at his end as if I was stirring an overbalanced sticky fruitcake with a six foot swizzle stick. I let the shaft rotate in the palms of my hands, keeping my fingers well away from the jagged stone point; my musician's protective instinct still there even though musical ability was trashed.

The spear holder's wide eye circled too, caught in the vortex of the agitating pole. He moaned, let go of the weapon, stumbled and sat down on the tail feathers of his headdress, causing it to tip sideways on his head. Brittle quill cartilage crunched. "God, with that hornet hat on — one of Father's healing concoctions I bet — and my toad sticker pointing at your chest, you should've seen how screwed-up you looked." He laughed and coughed and spit a piss-yellow wad of phlegm into a recent downpour puddle.

From atop the red roof of the totem shop, a watchful raven flew down and fished the phlegm out of the puddle, gulped it down and flew back to its perch. Yuck!

Loren's head was bowed in resentment and self-pity. Where was the macho biker of only a few days before? A combination of booze and bad news had done him in. Bad news? When did a drunk ever need bad news to drink? Did he even know about Molly?

"How long have you been around here?" I said. "What have you heard?"

"I heard enough," he said. He fingered a feather and snapped it, like a toothpick. "I been around a couple days. I heard Father and April talking. I crashed in the tack room and found my old childhood spear and headdress. And well, I had a stash of Nighttrain there too." He stared at the eagle feathers he sat on as if he couldn't figure out what it was; what it had to do with him.

"Did you hear them talking about the murder?" I squatted beside him, careful to balance my hornet hat. Occurred to me, Loran and I made quite a couple; his dusty headdress, my flaky hat.

"Nah," he said, "I just heard them talking about searching for a loon. What a family, huh? Should be looking for my Molly and they're looking for some damn bird."

"They found Molly Jenkins," I said. "It's her that was murdered." I watched Loren's face. He had Malcomb's nose and long ears. He swiveled his head toward me, shook it as if a cockroach had crawled in his ear.

"Molly? Molly's been murdered? Molly's dead? No! Not my Molly!"

"They found her body in the Dosanomish," I said.

Loren grabbed a big fistful of feathers. The knife scar on his arm puffed up. I could see tiny red lines running perpendicular to the main gash, like escaping centipede legs. He buried his face in soft, swollen hands. His big shoulders bunched. I put my hand on his collar. His shirt was grimy and smelled like the men's bathroom at a busy bus stop. "The police are gonna want to know where were you last Saturday night," I said.

Loren raised up. "Why would they . . . oh no, they don't think I could've killed her. I've loved Molly since we were in first grade together. I could never kill Molly."

His shoulder muscles were as tight as old growth bark. "You better have an alibi," I said.

Loren brushed my hand off his shoulder. "Alibi? Hell, I can't remember one day or night from the next. What do I know about an alibi? I need a drink, not an alibi."

"Do you have blackouts?"

"I've been having blackouts since high school. I been on this binge since I found out Billy Moody was sleeping with Molly. Look what Billy, the dirty bastard, did to me." He displayed his scarred forearm, the crooked scar tightened against his clenched muscle. As he turned his arm I saw his rhododendron and tomahawk tattoo, a match with Molly's.

"He's been missing for over a week too," I said.

"He doesn't . . . didn't want Molly. Just wanted to run her down and humiliate me. Hey, I bet Billy killed her. Then took off. With Molly dead, I don't care what happens to me anymore. I'll find Billy and take care of him once and for all."

Loren grabbed my arm, I grabbed the trunk of a totem pole, and together we staggered up. Old eagle feathers in the lower half of the headdress rasped and shattered.

Something heavy and metallic clunked to the ground behind Loren. "Shit," he said. I caught a flash of black underneath the busted feathers. Loren let go of me, reached down and picked up a gun.

It looked familiar. "Where did you get that pistol?"

He pointed it at me. His hand shook. Over his shoulder, I noticed a rain squall out on the sea. Cool air blew off it, whistled around totems and whipped up wood shavings in Malcomb's workshop. I felt like I had one of those wood shavings caught in my throat crossways, dry and grainy, couldn't swallow. The wind brought the faint smell of fecal matter and the sound of seals yapping and gulls scolding.

Loren waved the gun in the gulls' direction. "None of your business," he said, "where I got this pistol." He brought the tip back pointing at my chest.

First Lt. LeRoy and now Loren wanting to shoot me. Me, this time, without a caged cougar to sell. Where is there a mountain lion when you need one? "The gun's mine, isn't it?" I said. "You stole it." An idea came to me. "You got into my harmonica case and stole my B-flat harp and my trophy pin too."

"Don't know nothing about a harmonica or a pin," he said. Loren had a stubborn jut to his jaw like April. His eyes looked away. The transparent lie of a drunk. "My gun was stolen so I stole yours. It's only fair." His eyes watched a movement out to sea.

My turn to lunge. I grabbed his weapon wrist. He swung at me with his other fist. I caught that wrist too. Faces inches away from each other, we grunted and groaned, pushed and shoved, trampling on the tip of the eagle headdress until it came off his head. Loren's breath had a hot hog fat smell to it.

He had forty pounds on me and was ten years younger, and, though plastered, a lot stronger. My hold slipped. Time for me to summon my secret weapon, my loon karate kick. We were too close though, and, while pushing away for position, my feet got tangled in the headdress. I went down. Losing my grip on Loren. Once again, looking into the small, round hole of a pistol point.

My forehead burned. Wait a minute; my topknot began playing a musical melody. A by-god bluegrass melody. On chimes no less.

A bloody bluegrass melody on chimes; I knew it had to be an auditory hallucination.

But, Loren heard it too. "Listen, it's the doorbell ringing in the house."

Loren stumbled over to peer through a grove of orange-trunked madrone trees. He could see the front door of the building from there. "Oh shit! It's Sheriff Gloeckler at the door and he's got that dope-sniffing beast, Barbie Jane with him. She'll sniff me out. I can't hide around here anymore."

The chimes rang again. Took me a second to recognize the melody of a standard banjo/fiddle piece called "Billy in the Low Ground." Bluegrass on doorbells; it was either a sign that the music had hit the mainstream or the impending technological dark ages.

I said, "Why don't you give me the gun and turn yourself in to the sheriff."

"Not a chance," Loren said and steadied the gun at me. I could hardly see the deadly twenty-two caliber hole in the center of the barrel. "I need some money for the Winston Ferry. Gimme your billfold."

I pulled my wallet out to show Loren it was empty — I kept my last twenty hidden in the glove compartment of my bus — and, too late remembered the one hundred dollar bill given to me by Malcomb for selling the mountain lion to Lt. LeRoy.

Quick as a toad's tongue, Loren snatched the bill from my wallet. "Just right. I'll take that as a down payment for stealing my birthright Mr. Shaman, laman." Loren's thick tongue licked his dry lips. He backed away — as if a half dead man with a hornets nest on his head is going to try and stop him — stuck the gun behind his back.

I figured I'd give it one more shot. "Look, I really need that pin," I said. "It's the only thing I ever won. They're gonna get you sooner or later. If you give yourself up now you're more likely to live through the ordeal of being tracked down like a dog."

"I don't have your damn banjo pin," he said. "You better worry about yourself. Leave me be." Loren's one good eye was already drifting east. He turned, loped off and disappeared around the corner of the totem shop, heading in the general direction of Seattle. His once magnificent headdress lay broken and trampled on the ground.

Did I tell him my pin was a banjo pin?

Well, well. That didn't work worth a shit. Not only did I not get Loren to give himself up, he threatened me with my own gun. I knew he stole my banjo trophy pin too. Why wouldn't Loren give it back to me? I could clear my name. Well, not necessarily. But I could clear up any nagging doubts I had about my own guilt. Wasn't doing Loren any good anyway. Oh yeah, he's a practicing alcoholic. He doesn't need a rational reason, certainly not for returning stolen keepsakes, maybe not for murder.

My legs, being unsteady, sure weren't going to run from the sheriff. My whole body felt like it had been wracked by a one hundred five fever for a couple days. Best I talk to the law and get it over with. What can he know? Should I tell him I transformed into a loon and contaminated a murder scene by stealing a clue? Perhaps the only clue? I was sure to get a warm reaction to that confession. Go over like an out-of-tune twelve-string guitar in a bluegrass jam. Liable to throw me in jail for impersonating a sane person.

Omigosh! I paused. What would they do if they did believe me? Hunt Qo-oo-la down and shoot him. Cut him open like a factory chicken and rip out his gizzard? I couldn't take the chance. Give me a few hours of rest and I'd have strength enough to hunt for Qo-oo-la myself.

What if I find him? Boy, that's a concept. What happens when you come face-to-face with your spirit animal? Is it even possible?

I had to stall. Come up with a reason why I knew about Molly's body, other than being the murderer and, other than discovering her as a loon. Problem being, there were no other ways.

I still had my empty wallet out, poor once more.

Buzz, buzz, buzz insisted the hornets nest, getting louder, vibrating the shell. Also heavier. I sensed something was near at hand. Could Malcomb's fail-safe system be faulty? Would the marauding yellow jackets break through the membrane barrier and commence gnawing on my noggin? Would the damn thing explode? What? Where was the owner's manual on this thing? I needed to lie down again; the harsh, human world took some getting used to.

As did the animal world.

Neither of which I was very fit for.

I dragged my feet around the banana slug whose slimy body was dotted pink with spring blossoms, now near the end of his laborious sidewalk journey.

Lucky fellow.

31

Stings and Fits

I stumbled inside, took my clothes off and got back into bed to await Sheriff Gloeckler. I shifted the pillows around, making a nest for my elongated head and thought about Molly's murderer. So far there were three suspects: Purple Nat and Loren Old Wolf and me. Course the police didn't know about Purple Nat. Come to think about it, other than seeing him as Qo-oo-la, what did I really know about him? A character dressed like him would stand out like a sore thumb in this small community. Unless he was sequestered and reclusive. Could he be, like Malcomb said, a Vietnam Vet turned survivalist? Holed up in the mountains with an arsenal the size of a Winnebago, could blow the top off Mount Olympus?

Where was that sheriff? And where was April? Out on another emergency animal rescue?

While waiting, I snoozed, dreaming of that damn video game again.

I awoke to a mouth breathing warm air in my ear. AAhh, April had returned and, bowing to the inevitable, planted a smooch on my neglected lobe. I turned, threw an arm around her, grabbed onto a bristly back and ran smack into, snout to snout, a pink humongous whiffer. "Yech!" I hollered and pressed backwards into the pillow. My video game dream had crossed-over into ugly reality.

"Gump, gump, gump," sayeth the snout and waddled in reverse, peering at me with beady eyes, hidden in layers of fat. Floppy ears flat with recoil. Not the first time I've had my kisses criticized.

We stared at each other, pig and I. "Where's your bazooka," I yelled. In my nightmare pigs attacked me with every conceivable weapon and all I had to defend myself was a blacksmith's hammer and bellows.

Up close and personal, in the daylight, the pig was one of those pot-bellied pigs, emphasis on the potbelly, which obscenely dragged the floor, constituting a fifth leg. Didn't even smell like a pig. Pigs, to me, always had that exuberant potent barnyard aroma, the familiar earthy odors of sour mash, alfalfa hay, damp straw and assorted excrement. This porker had an artificial coconut scent mingled with talcum powder. She had a red bow ribbon tied to her corkscrew tail, and, hanging around her five-chins neck, was a rhinestone collar and a silver plated badge which read, "Deputy Barbie Jane". Barbie Jane's hooves — 'scuse me — manicured nails were painted a thick lacquered pool table green.

Now I'm a pushover for pigs. Pigs, as a rule, are a delight. Of all the farm animals I grew up with on a limestone and red clay farm in southern Missouri, I liked hogs the best. My favorite fairy tale as a kid was the Three Little Pigs, saw Charlotte's Web dozens of times, already seen the movie Babe, three times. But ever now and then a pig comes down the pike that sure puckers my poultice. Barbie Jane was no fairy tale pig full of innocence and naivete. She came out of my scrambled brain and damaged psyche. Probably taking over where Elpenor left off. Not to be trusted. I took a distinct dislike to this one. Yes, this one had a lived-amongst-humans-too-long look. Barbie Jane's essence of porcineness, had been compromised. That's when I realized I was looking at a real flesh 'n' blood creature. Not some foul beast out of my own hallucinations.

Barbie Jane, real pig, did not think much of me either. She snorted and grunted and made pawing gouges in the soft wood floor with her front hooves, glancing at the door, no doubt expecting the sheriff, any minute.

"That's right," I said. "That's what we'll do. You stay over there and I'll stay here and we'll wait for your boss to come in."

Barbie Jane waddled closer, causing her rolled flesh to quiver and the wood floor to sway. Lard layered eyes were like black insect larvae hatching. Yellow, stringy mucus slid out of one plump pink nostril. Breath smelled like perfumed kerosene.

I hunched forward. Most everything in the milky-way galaxy scared me these days but, be damned if I — a farm boy long gone from a farm — was going to let an overweight, housebroken hog intimidate me. Deputy Pig and I had ourselves an Ozark Stare-Off. Neither willing to blink when, of a sudden, Malcomb's hefty turban toppled off my head and plunked right down on pigs snuffling schnoz.

"Eeiiiiiiooic! Eeiiioooic! Eeiiiooinc!" squealed Deputy Pig. Sounded like a real pig! You never heard such carryings-on in your life. You'd a thought I'd taken a splitting maul to its ornery carcass, although, by the lightness my head felt upon the hornets nest hat's removal, the bewitching bandage weighed as much as a gym class medicine ball. Helium bubbles floated in front of my eyes. I grabbed hold of the bedstead to keep from drifting away.

After thumping the pigs nose, the papyrus cone rolled against the wooden raven. Raven played dead.

"Buzz, buzz, buzz," went the detached nest.

Deputy Pig squealed and squealed and lurched around the room scraping and bucking, toppling wooden animals like bowling pins, tromping the medicinal hat into shredded gray flakes and backed into a corner. The wall and attached fish mask shuddered.

I heard more buzzing. Louder. An unfocused drone. The plate in my head vibrated. I pressed my index finger against the plate to stop the tickle sensation. I thought at first the buzzing came from within me. Wouldn't be the first time I heard noises since I beat my head against a wrecking bar. Not so though, the source of the sound came from without.

It came from the shattered hornet's nest. The poultice hat appeared to be reassembling itself, rising, in a dark, roiling cloud.

I pressed down harder on my vibrating plate with four fingers, scratched around the edges with my thumbnail. My whole hand and wrist tingled.

Deputy Pig, taking a break from squealing, watched the nest hum to life. No mammal moved. The crushed nest gave off a sterile, antiseptic odor. I calculated the mad-dash distance to the door or window. If stung, would I go into anaphylactic shock?

I do not know if Barbie Jane knew or sensed the significance of the humming and swirling insect dance in front of her nose, for, at that very moment, the fish mask fell off the wall onto the porker's tenderized behind. Poor Deputy Pig, attacked from the front and the rear, did a flat-footed leap and landed, *kablam,* atop the insect swirl with her gargantuan belly. More woodcarvings toppled over.

The fish mask soared through the air and plunked down on my banjo case.

I had never heard a pig squeal at one pitch and, simultaneously, another an octave higher — two distinct bleats. The light fixture vibrated. Limbs cracked on trees next to the house. A Stellar's jay, bullying his reflection in my window, lit out, fleeing a possible volcanic eruption.

There was no violent eruption. Deputy Pig's manicured hooves didn't move. She stood where she landed, great roles of flesh undulated and quivering. Waves of rancid coconut shampoo fragrance curdled my nostrils. A steam cloud, rising from pig's own sweat and shock, surrounded her and within that mist little yellow and black bombers dived and stung. There were dozens of them. They seemed to know the nose was the most choice chop and attacked that pink appendage with no forgiveness.

The red bow that was tied on pig's tail, lay rumpled on the floor, a few feet from the melee, fluttering from invisible ripples of pain generated current. Barbie Jane's deputy badge leaped and jiggled, like a run-amuck yo-yo, making metallic clicking sounds as the chain and badge and rhinestone collar collided.

The escape window invited me. Be just a few seconds and the hornets would be after me. I had to skedaddle out of there and slam the window or door shut behind me. Safe and unstung. I should've left while the leaving was good and not looked one more time at Barbie Jane; chubby legs splayed out, high-centered on her belly, she resembled a beached killer whale. Eeriest thing was, the pig had quit squealing and gave off a steady keening noise, almost human-like. Like a wounded child. Her overripe squash of a nose pointed, pockmarked with insects, in my direction, huffing and puffing great gusts of foam-flecked breath. Her little porcine black eyes like fading buzzards on the horizon. Barbie Jane was going into shock, as a prelude, I suspected, to dying. Having been that route recently, I knew how helpless she felt.

I couldn't stand it. I tore the blanket with the purple and gold leaping fish pattern off the bed and cast it over Deputy Pig. Then climbed on top of the quivering flesh and, starting with her tender snout, began systematically rubbing her thick hide backwards, bunching and rolling the blanket as I went, in the hopes of trapping the attack hornets.

It felt like I was astride a mammoth banana slug. "Ride 'em cowboy. Yes, Mama, I left the big, safe city for this last, best place on earth, in search of the elusive geographic cure and here I am riding bareback, off into the sunset on a two hundred pound porker. No doubt my luck has changed, not to mention my poise and personality."

The utility room door slammed against the wall. I looked up through a vaporous shield and faced a maniacal man, in uniform, with a gun pointing at my naked chest. I was beginning to suspect that I might be in one of those pockets of America wherein it was required by law that every person of self-proclaimed authority, at the drop of a hat, brandish a weapon about. Part of a grand design to keep the presumed rabble cowed. I hoped he didn't also have a shoot now and ask questions later mentality.

"You filthy pervert," the uniformed man hollered. "What the hell are you doing to my little girl, my Barbie Jane?" It was, I presumed, the much mentioned, Sheriff Gloeckler. His face had a veiny redness to it, and his eyes, minus the sunglasses hanging around his neck, looked like chemical spills in the Columbia River sloughs.

I flashed that it didn't look good for my immediate future. I was riding the sheriff's pet pig and me without a stitch on. My intent, I surmised, could've been misconstrued.

I dared not let go of the blanket.

I needed some magic words. I pointed at the pulverized poultice nest.
"Yellow jackets in the nest"
are safe at rest,
yellow jackets a swarming,
better take warning."

What the hell had come over me? I was riding a pig, rolling a blanket full of hornets, a gun pointed at my naked chest and I tossed out incantations on demand.

"Get the hell off of her you pervert," the sheriff said, "and get your hands up or I'll blow you away . . . ah did you say yellow jackets?"

Barbie Jane, upon hearing her boss, quit keening and started sobbing like a grown-up human, almost bucking me backwards off her convulsing body. I knew if I let go of the rolled blanket, which had trapped hard little insect pellets rolled inside, it would throw a room with a gun into chaos.

"If I let go of this blanket we're going to have hornets up the whazoo. We don't need bullets flying." My voice sounded high pitched and stringy.

The sheriff's oversized gun hand shook and his eyes, shaded by a broad-brimmed hat, were twice their previous size. The magic words yellow jackets, had penetrated his lawman's mental armor, melting it down. He began to jerk, first pointing his weapon in one direction then another, at imaginary targets about the room. Oh, oh, I thought, he begins pulling that trigger we're all in a world of hurt. "Your pig is dying. Put that damn gun away and give me a hand."

Sheriff Gloeckler closed his eyes, took a deep breath, holstered his gun and knelt beside me, grabbed one end of the blanket and began rolling.

His walrus mustache close enough for me to see bits of corn flakes caught in it and his quick breath lapping me with waves of spearmint and stale cigarettes. He voice hoarse. "She's not a pig," he said, "she's my partner."

The sheriff and I scrunched live yellow jackets in purple and gold leaping salmons as if our lives depended upon it. Which, in my case, it did. The blanket grew thick and heavy with captive droners. Ugly, scarlet welts popped up on Barbie Jane's thick hide and her tender nose swelled in purple disproportionate knobs. An odor of lard and burnt beets, mingled with a vinegary mustard plaster, steamed around her.

I was afraid Barbie-Jane was going to die; her shock was going to go into some kind of swine heart attack, and I did a fast assessment of the physical limitations of administering mouth-to-mouth resuscitation to a hog.

Hey, if Qo-oo-la could do it to a dog, then surely I could do it to a hog.

Suddenly, a stray yellow jacket lit on my lower lip. I couldn't take my hands off the blanket to slap it. A hundred hornets in a blanket are worth more than one on the mouth. I shut my eyes tight, steeled myself for the nasty sting. I steeled and I steeled. I could feel the little fellow dancing on my lip; hear his macabre humming; dancing to his own drumming: The torture power dance.

It tickled. Its tap dancer's paws tickled my lip and the brushing breeze from its wings itched my nostrils. I fiffed it with my breath but it clung on. Why didn't it sting me and get it over with?

The hornet lifted off my lip, circled my head a couple times, then landed on my scar tissue; its birthplace so to speak, still wet and smelly with boiled skunk cabbage root and sow thistle seed from the nest. The hornet commenced to drum louder, tickle more intense. Other stray insects homed in on the sound and all converged on the top of my head; there to cavort with glee and abandonment.

"You got company," the Sheriff said, stretching to see the top of my head. "Makes an interesting hat."

"Good Lord, it feels like they're having a powwow up there," I said. "And where the hell's April? She'd know what to do."

"When I came to the door I sent her out to Mrs. Macomber's farm to rescue a barn owl out of her chimney.'

"As for the yellow jackets," the Sheriff said, "count your blessings. I think they like you."

Barbie Jane's curly tail sprang up, signaling the end of our blanket scouring and the Sheriff and I picked the rolled blanket up, nodded in unspoken agreement, and carried it to the open window and tossed it. I slammed the window shut. Safe from the hordes, but what was I to do about my hornet hat?

"I'll get a towel," The sheriff said. He opened the passway door and rushed out. I could do nothing about my head for the moment so I hastened to the next most important feature on a male's checklist of body parts: I examined my genitals. See if there were any yellow jackets boogying on my boys. Thank God for small favors. Upon closer inspection, perhaps I should've said, small shriveled favors. Embarrassed, more than usual, to show those things in public. When was I ever at ease traipsing around in my altogether? What if April stormed in?

I found my jeans again and climbed into them, careful not to disturb the hornets powwowing on my head.

The fish mask lay over my banjo case, an unapologetic grin on its face. Barbie Jane stared at me, her vulture eyes flying back from far over the horizon.

The sheriff returned with a towel. "Lean over," he said.

I did and heard a gasp from the sheriff. "God a mighty that's the weirdest thing I've ever seen. Why aren't they stinging? I almost hate to do this. They seem to be doing some kind of ritual dance."

"I can feel it. Do it."

"You sure you want to disturb them?"

"Feels like a regular old time hootenanny up there. Do it."

"I could get a mirror and show — "

"Give me that damn towel. If you're not going to do it, I am."

Sheriff Gloeckler relented. "Might upset them. Prepare to get stung."

I closed my eyes, felt a wiping and rubbing sensation and then the yellow jackets were gone. Not one sting.

Goosebumps earth-quaked throughout my scalp, traveled across my shoulders, down my arms, standing hairs rigid, all the way to broken fingernails, much too long and lonesome for a performing picker. I reached a shaky hand for the bedpost; the lighting in the totem storeroom flickered from bright to darkness as if someone was playing with the switch. The darkness won and I sat down on the edge of the sheet, hugged the bed-frame. Barbie Jane waddled over, rubbed pig slobber on my clean jeans, and stared up at me with newly focused adoring eyes.

I felt a stab in my neck. My hand jerked up in a slap, and I pulled away clutching a stunned hornet, the last soldier just had to get in a lick to uphold the nasty reputation of the species.

A big hand appeared in front of my face. "Let me have it."

I placed it upsidedown in the big palm and noticed the hornets little legs churned, wings fluttered. I leaned in for a closer look. In its death throes, it's streamlined body and yellow and black markings were quite beautiful. Not so sad, I had the idle thought, to be killed by one of nature's deadly beauties.

What had April said, "The nearest doctor is thirty miles either way."

32

Luna Moths and Loon Power

Stay cool. My legs pinned to the bed by an appreciative pig, I lay down backwards on the bed. Stared at a watermark on the ceiling that looked like a luna moth. My head felt detached from the rest of my body, separated by neck pain. How to spend my last five minutes? Clear my name? Or at least absolve my guilt. Proclaim my innocence to the sheriff, if not in fact, then at least in intention?

Make love to April?

I glanced up. The sheriff was gone. No doubt not wanting to witness death by anaphylactic fit. Who could blame him? It was a messy business.

I remember like yesterday the time in junior high, while going deep after a long fly ball in center field, a wasp nailed me on the elbow. First, I broke out in red blotches, then my chest constricted, followed by a rapid heart beat, throat closure, violent coughs, skin eruptions, fever, convulsions, collapse and finally my lungs went into bronchial spasms and I nearly died before the school nurse reached me with an antidote.

There was one more thing that happened. What was it? My skin suddenly felt wet from the inside-out and hot, as if I'd been dipped in a sauna and I remembered what it was: severe anxiety, indescribable panic.

I clutched the quilt with fingers that felt like fat sausages. My chest squeezed like an anaconda straightjacket, breath sounding like a train squeezing through a small tunnel. Barbie Jane, perhaps in sympathetic communication, was doing that keening thing again and lathering up my legs with pig slobber.

Where was everybody? Abandoned in life, was I to be abandoned in death? My Mama's words came to me, "One of these days you're gonna need somebody mister and they won't be there cause you done cut all ties behind you." I tried to sit up, felt nauseous. I tried calling out but it was no use; came out like a frog croak.

Maybe not? I heard a tinny voice reply. It came from up above. The luna moth hovered above me, leaning over my face. *"Harp ol' podna, you're as transparent as tic spit on a cat turd. Trying every trick in the book to get rid of me. Well it ain't going to work."*

It was Elpenor. I said, "I'm dying you twit. Show a little sympathy."

"It ever occur to you, I'm dying too and you don't see me whining like a whipped pup. You trying to kill me. Malcomb with that poultice first, and now not fighting a simple hornet sting."

"That's because you're too dense to know what's happening." I felt a liquid presence enter my lungs. Heavy as mercury.

"Not a good time to overly flatter yourself podna. Bad karma. You listen to me and you might pull through this. Quit panicking. Let yourself go. Float."

"What do you know?"

"I know plenty. Just relax. Poor self-pitying, recovering drunk. The sheriff hasn't run out on you. He's gone for help. We have to stay alive 'til he comes back. Think. What would that loon do, the one you getting attached to. Bet he wouldn't let a little hornet sting bother him." Elpenor lit on the bed post folded his green wings around him and stared at me. His black tentacles twitching.

I hate it when Elpenor's right. What, in fact, did I have to lose? Elpenor was onto something. It came to me: it's not so much what loon would do; it's what loon would be. Qo-oo-la would be immune from hornet stings. Malcomb had said, "This transformation business works both ways."

Time to try the mother of all deathbed conversions.

I closed my eyes as a prelude to gathering mental medicine. Summoned, what Malcomb called my loon power. I focused on an image of Qo-oo-la in his glorious loonness. Immersed myself in visions of water, loon's element of survival.

From faraway, I heard Elpenor say, *"That's it. Keep going. Deeper."*

I felt it first on my back. Each rabbit scratch itched, then burgeoned into tiny pinfeathers. The feathers pierced through flesh and muscle and massaged my heart. Slowed that rapid-beating organ to the rhythm of a Tennessee Cotillion. Allemande left, allemande right. Swing your partner and do-se-do. My constricted chest loosened. Allowed lungs to drain of liquid. Air passages opened in my throat. I inhaled sweet, unrestricted air. Tasted like honeysuckle blooms. My skin began to fit my body.

A cold wind hit the moisture on my face. Elpenor gone. Heard the Sheriff's out-of-breath voice. "Goddamnit Barbie Jane, they make packaging in this emergency kit so tough by the time I get it open he'll be gone."

Barbie Jane gumped and rubbed harder against my legs.

I sat up. "If that's epinephrine, don't bother. I'm okay."

Sheriff Gloeckler dropped the emergency kit. "Jesus! How did that happen? You had red blotches all over your chest. Your eyes were swollen shut, couldn't breath. I — "

"I'm a quick healer. If I was you I'd check out your deputy here. She got the worst of the deal." My legs were going to sleep. I shoved at Barbie Jane. Like trying to move a railroad freight car.

"BJ, back up. Let's have a look at you." He meant me. He took my chin in his hand and tilted my head sideways and up and down. "Damn! No swelling or blotches. I never seen anything like that." He shook his head, let go of me and Sheriff Gloeckler kneeled down, glancing back and forth between us, and ran his hands over BJ's hide. Examined her lumpy nose. Picked up her red ribbon and refastened it around her tail. Through the whole process, the pig arched her head around to stare at me with a lovesick grin on her blotchy lips. BJ must have understood that I tried to save her from the hornets. Didn't I tell you pigs were smart?

While Sheriff Gloeckler checked out his pet pig, I wobbled over to the chair I left my clothes on and finished dressing. As I was buttoning my denim shirt I had a flash: my dream where I was trapped in a video game and being pursued by pigs and hornets had come to pass. What a coincidence. Would I also become a blacksmith as a possible future?

Malcomb entered through the outside door and saw the yellow jacket nest trashed. "Did my hornet power work, Harp? You look much stronger."

"Yes," I said, "But not exactly in the way you imagined it working."

"I'll take it any way I can get it," Malcomb said. "This shaman business is not an exact science."

33

Flat Stones and Bird Feathers

"BJ is fine," Sheriff Gloeckler said, glancing back and forth between me and Malcomb. He settled on me. "I have to thank you for saving her life Mr. Harp P. Gravey." He reached in a breast pocket and pulled out a notebook. Switched into lawman mode. "But sorry to say, that's a name I'm not likely to forget." Thumbed through the notebook, read a notation and said, "Now that you're out of the woods so to speak, I'd like to ask you a few questions. You've saved me having to contact the authorities down in Portland. I want to talk to you in connection with the death of Molly Jenkins."

My feet took a step back. So April did call him and, what's the phrase, fingered me. But . . . which me. Harp, the human or Qo-oo-la, the bird? I brushed my scalp with my fingers, it felt tight. I looked at Malcomb and he shook his head indicating he hadn't revealed anything to the sheriff in their interview. I would go into victim mode. Just answer the questions. Offer nothing.

Sheriff Gloeckler continued, "Where were you on the night of sat April 12th?"

"I was in Portland," I said, "but wait a minute here sheriff. Why are you questioning me, a total stranger to these parts until a few days ago?" Only possible way he could associate me with Molly's death was through April. I felt betrayed.

"Anybody to verify that?"

"Well, Malcomb here."

"You can verify Mr. Gravey was in Portland, Oregon on the 12th?" He looked at Malcomb.

"I was only in Portland once in my life right after World War II," Malcomb said. "I was attacked and beaten and caught a case of the clap. Although if you could've seen the lady I caught it from you'd understand why I maintain it was worth it." Malcomb rubbed his cheek, remembering.

"Then how can you verify Mr. Gravey's being in Portland the night of April 12th."

"I can't."

Back to me. "Why did you say he could?" he asked, his thick sandy eyebrows arched and walrus mustache twitched in the manner of the clever investigator. Not two minutes into an interrogation, already ferreting out a telltale lie from a hostile suspect.

"I didn't," I said. "I meant Malcomb can verify I'm a stranger in these parts."

Back to Malcomb. "Is that true Mr. Old Wolf? Is Mr. Gravey a stranger to these parts?"

"Depends on the way you look at it. On the one hand I'd say Harp hadn't set foot around here in his life until last Thursday morning. But on the other hand, looking at it a different way, he could very well have been around here for a long time."

"How long?" The trail of deception widened. The Sheriff poised his pencil.

"Oh, possibly thirty to sixty million years."

Sheriff Gloeckler stopped writing. Looked back and forth between Malcomb and me. Scratched his belly. Rubbed his finger across the bridge of his nose. Barbie Jane edged over to me and rubbed her blubberous jowls against my shins.

The uniformed man didn't care for such a blatant display of affection from his deputy. "Are you two putting me on?" he said. "How about some straight answers here? Molly Jenkins, a woman of your . . .

ah . . . persuasion," he indicated Malcomb, "was murdered. I intend to find out who did it. Now, I'm asking you one more time — I'd hate to have to drag you down to headquarters, Mr. Gravey in your condition. Anybody down in Portland verify your presence on the night of April 12th?"

I put both hands on top of my matted hair. "I don't know," I said. "It all seems like a long time ago and kinda fuzzy right now. Maybe if you'd tell me why I'm being questioned my memory would sharpen."

The sheriff made a calculated decision. Flipped to another page in his notebook. "Are you the owner of Dosanomish River Tract S10, 1/4th of section 82?"

"Partially. A couple weeks ago I inherited twenty five per cent ownership of it when Josh Whittier died of a brain tumor. His ex-wife owns half interest and another twenty five per cent to someone else who Josh never told me about."

"You sure about that, eh?"

"Just telling what Josh told me."

"I don't suppose he told you it was very valuable land?"

"No he didn't. And I don't understand what this has got to do with Molly Jenkins?"

"That stretch of the Dosanomish River, the logjam she was found in, the bluff up river we think she went over, and an old lodge, with a hemlock dicing it, that we know Molly used for her liaisons, is on your property." He worried the right bar of his fluffy walrus mustache.

"So what?" I said. "That's about as circumstantial as you can get." I suspected the sheriff had an ace in the hole. April probably told him about Qo-oo-la too.

"The so what is, Molly Jenkins was the other one quarter inheritor of the Dosanomish property. According to estate lawyer William Hutchison, this Josh Lawrence set up his will so that if either you or Molly Jenkins died the other would inherit the deceased's part of the property." The Sheriff paused, his pale eyes watching me.

"I don't understand," I said, "I knew nothing about this."

His eyes didn't blink. More twirling of his mustache tips. "This lawyer also said he gave you all this information in a sealed envelope same time he gave you the deceased's ashes."

"I never opened the envelope," I said. "It's still sealed in the glove compartment of my VW."

"Well, somebody opened it," he said. "The seal was broken when I examined it and this lawyer was dead on; you now own one half of a piece of choice real estate. How convenient for you Molly Jenkins is dead."

Malcomb turned aside, shoulders hanging low, picked the fish mask off my banjo case and rehung it. Stood staring at it with his back to me. "That lodge and the immediate land around it is cursed," said Malcomb. "Best you get rid of it Harp. You don't need anymore bad luck."

"Hold on," I said to the Sheriff. "Are you telling me Josh left Molly Jenkins one fourth of the Dosanomish property?"

"I'm telling you, you got a good motive for killing Molly Jenkins."

I'll be damned. Josh left out a hell of a lot. Brain tumors, like head wounds, leave gaps. He'd told me there was a little cabin he'd built himself in lieu of building a log house, on his end of the property. Also some river frontage. I remember him saying something about some buildings on his ex-wife's section. Didn't pay much attention to that part.

The property Josh intended for me to "be steward of," in his words, and wanted his ashes scattered on, was a rocky outcropping near his little cabin. The little cabin he'd built from recycled lumber he'd salvaged from a scraped garage. Made me swear to keep it in its natural state; no trees cut for commercial use, no basalt mines allowed, not to be broken up into housing tracts. Insisted the moss not be disturbed. I humored him; the moss not be disturbed for Christ sake.

Nothing about Molly Jenkins, not a word. How the hell did Josh know her?

It was easy for me to promise Josh anything at the time, considering I couldn't tell whether he was talking or the brain tumor was raving. Toward the end of his life a very peculiar thing happened; Josh ceased raving and began enunciating an important message in a clear voice, his thin, pain-wracked lips pronouncing each word with precision, his sunken eyes imploring me to pay attention. The only problem being, he spoke in tongues. I never understood a word of it.

I miss him. Alive, he saved my life. Dead, he managed to get me into a hell of a mess. I wondered, did he have any idea of the trouble he was getting me in?

Now there were three suspects.

"I didn't know about Molly being the other inheritor, Sheriff, " I said, "But I do know this, I've never set foot on that property. It's one of those things I'm going to do as soon as I get up from here. That is, if I'm not arrested. Are you saying I'm a suspect just because I inherited the victims property?" I was a little relieved. At least he didn't know I had also discovered and tampered with the body.

He took off his hat, swiped sweat from his forehead. It was not hot. "I'm saying everyone connected with Molly or that property is a suspect. Loren Old Wolf, Malcomb's son here is top on the list. You don't happen to know where he is do you?" He looked at both of us.

Barbie Jane had worked her way to the wall where the fish mask hung, her not-so-long-ago gorer. I suspected she was a pig that harbored resentments. Most pigs do. They say elephants never forget. Pigs never forget either and they never forget with extreme prejudice.

"No," I said, "I'm new to these parts, consequently I've never seen Loren Old Wolf before." Malcomb and I exchanged a liar's compact look.

"Last I heard he's in Seattle doing research," said Malcomb.

"Yeah research. We've got the Seattle police checking the bowery. We're also monitoring all the ferries to the mainland. We'll get him."

In the honored tradition of saving your own ass I sacrificed another lamb. "Have you checked any Vietnam Vets survivalists upriver? I understand there's at least one gold-claim homesteaded up there."

"If you never been here before," the Sheriff said, "how do you know about him?"

"Josh, my benefactor, mentioned him."

"You let me do the investigating here. When you climb out of that bed don't get antsy and leave the area." He put the notebook in his pocket and addressed Malcomb. "You find out where Loren is I'll expect you to let me know. Suppressing evidence or harboring a fugitive is a crime. And if he resists arrest, he might get shot. You won't be helping him by sheltering him."

"I'm aware of that sheriff," Malcomb said. "But speaking of missing persons, I understand Billy Moody's also disappeared. Is he a suspect too?"

"We're looking for him because his brother Gabe asked us to. I hardly think a member of one of the most prominent families in the area is a suspect."

"I thought you said everyone was a suspect," Malcomb said. "Letting Billy slide couldn't be because you're a member of Gabe's militia battalion, could it?"

Sheriff Gloeckler gave Malcomb what he no doubt considered a hard look but there was no steam behind it. He glanced at Barbie Jane who had given up on the staring the fish mask down and was contently mauling and slobbering all over my banjo case. "Get away from those instruments," he ordered the pig without conviction. Barbie Jane snorted and ignored him. I wasn't too worried, that hard-shell case, with banjo inside, was scarred and battered to beat hell. Had survived a fall from a four story building, run over by a Fiat Spitfire, trampled by a team of percheron plow horses and, in general, two decades of hard use by me. Reckoned it could outlast a fatso porker.

Sheriff Gloecker took off his spiffy hat and polished his medals with his left elbow. Hesitated, not satisfied he blew on the medals and rubbed some more. It wasn't so much a nervous gesture as a stall for time to think. "Samantha, that's my ex-wife, and I came up here to escape the craziness of L. A. Wanted a quieter, less stressful life, place where we could enjoy each other without all the crime and traffic and pollution. Raise a few horses, practice the horse shoeing work myself, maybe even enter some barrel-racing competition. Samantha could have her performing arts interests." He sniffed, his mustache drooped, lopsided. "Now all that's gone. I joined the Port Gambol Militia Unit right after she ran off with the Albertson's produce manager. Didn't realize it was anti-law enforcement at first. I've since come to my senses and quit." He put his spiffed-up hat back on and patted it down. "You hear about anything connected to the homicide, you let me know. Come on Barbie Jane, let's go, we've got work to do. I've got a nice snack for you in the car. Help you forget those nasty old yellow jackets." He hooked a finger around the pig collar and tugged.

"Oh, one more thing," he directed at Malcomb, "Do you know of any Indians that practice covering up the corpse's eyes with flat stones?"

Malcomb glanced at me. "No, that is a strange ritual to me, but I can ask around. Is that how you found Molly?"

"Oh, I almost forgot, have April check on this too." He reached in a shirt pocket and brought out a white and black feather. "See what kind of bird it belongs to."

My hand jumped up to my neck. I couldn't breath. I wanted to reach out, grab the feather and stick it back on.

Malcomb took the feather. Sniffed it. "Why do you want this identified?"

"It's one of many found near the murder scene. Let's just say it might have something to do with Molly's murder. It could be some kind of ritual murder having to do with birds. You be sure and let me know about the feather. Better yet have April give me a call. I want to find out what kind of birds are attracted to bright objects." He marched toward the door.

Barbie Jane waddled after him, the long, slim arm of the law and the short, fat butt of a baby hippo, squeezed through the doorway.

"That's one big cob-roller," I said.

"And one lonely man," added Malcomb, "But don't underestimate him. He's already figured out a bird messed with the murder scene. He was a top notch LPD detective before he took this job. Right after he got here there was a homicide on one of the sailing yachts at Pleasant Harbor.

He solved it in two days. Got in a shoot-out with the suspect. Sheriff Gloeckler won. Now that he's out of that racist militia we can all breathe easier." He thought about that a minute. "Or can we?"

Malcomb handed me the feather. "I believe this is yours. Here take it. I just remembered something I should tell Sheriff Gloeckler before he leaves."

I watched my hands float up, palms cupped, to receive the feather. It was black with a white, square dot on the big end. Malcomb dropped it and left through the back door, walking faster than usual. The tiny feather drifted to fit weightless into my hand. I too sniffed it, smelled a rich mix of avian oils and mysterious flavor of Qo-oo-la's musk. I felt humbled by it. It was like finding a lock of your hair you'd thought lost. Though prettier I imagine. The feather caught an undetectable air current and tumbled over and over in my palm, catching light in its white coloring. I couldn't seem to stop staring at it.

The divers who found the body must have retrieved Qo-oo-la's neck feathers from the vine maple limb-vice guarding Molly's hand. The autopsy no doubt found an imprint of the pin in Molly's death grip. The autopsy probably also revealed the eye stones were put in long after death. Bet that threw the sheriff for a loop. Murderer visiting the crime scene underwater after the deed was done and tampering with the body. He wouldn't attribute eye stones to a bird. Would he? Pretty smart of me, I thought, confusing the trail. Well, not really. I wasn't thinking of anything but closing Molly's crying eyes. Been better off it I'd left her body alone period. Too late now though. But not too late to find Qo-oo-la before the sheriff or one of his deputies does.

Malcomb came back in and said, "I think it's time we started looking for this murderer ourselves."

"I think you're right," I said. "I want to start with a short visit to this property that's caused me to be a murder suspect. From there we can hunt for Medusa and Qo-oo-la. Ah, what did you need to talk to the sheriff about?"

Malcomb reached in his pocket and pulled out a crumpled bill. Handed it to me. "Here's the one hundred dollars Loren took from you."

"How did you get it?"

"I saw you and my son talking. I met him coming around the shop waving that pistol. I gave him a fifth of wine and we talked in the tack room until he passed out. I don't think he killed Molly. I told the sheriff where he was."

"You turned in your own son? Ah, where's the gun?"

"Yes. As crazed as Loren was he might have caused a shootout. Got himself or someone else killed. This way he'll be safe in jail until we find the real killer. I also hid the twenty-two pistol from Loren and told the sheriff where it was."

I wondered if my fingerprints were still on the pistol. "Aren't you worried about what will happen to Loren in jail? If he finds out you turned him in he'll never forgive you."

"I'm inclined to be more worried about the other prisoners. Loren's a holy terror when he sobers up. He'll just add it to the list of other things he's never forgiven me for.

I will go now and prepare myself for a journey." Once again, he left.

34

Riches and Subtler Temptations

I opened a window. Fresh air. Golden rays of sunlight — reminding me of cougar ghosts — sifted through the branches of Douglas fir and western red cedar trees adjacent to my window. The Stellar's jay was back. How did I know it was the same one? I don't know, I just knew. I was in a heated dispute with a Douglas squirrel over what looked like a cache of fir nuts in the hollow of a branch. Last year's stash. The jay swooped in, feigned and, in mid-flight, deftly plucked a nut from the squirrel's horde. The squirrel barked and scolded and bounced about in a brown rage from trunk to limb.

Sympathy for the squirrel was overshadowed by my admiration for the jay's talented bill. Remembering Qo-oo-la's joust with the raccoon family, I viewed those beak-spearing tools in a different light.

While I waited I prepared by cleaning up the room; straightening the carved animals, sweeping the hornet's nest, wiping pig slobber off my banjo case.

Suddenly the pair of outside adversaries squawked and barked and fell silent. A gray Volvo rolled into the parking lot just as the sheriff's patrol car was leaving. Didn't take Sheriff Gloeckler long to corral Loren. We, the jay, the squirrel and I, watched the Volvo. A man and a woman, partially obscured by the native vegetation, got out. Jay, not caring for crowds, flew to sparser spoils. Squirrel barked and zipped around the tree trunk.

I had never seen the pair before but sensed I ought to know them. Particularly the woman.

As they disappeared around the front of the house, I stepped outside by a side door into a full sea breeze. Freshness sucked into my confined lungs and held for a second, savoring green, salty sweetness. Qo-ool-a's senses bleeding through.

There was a dewdrop glistening on a budding nootka rose leaf and I bent down and touched it with my tongue. Tasted cool, pure and nectarous. Juice of the gods. I lapped the remaining moisture off the raspy leaf. Shot revivifying tremors through my invalid body. Chewed on a pale pink bud. Fibrous and bitter. Mouth enjoying the texture.

I strolled further into Malcomb's totem junk yard. Much more alert than last time. Everywhere stood or laid, parts and pieces of animal carvings. Bears, whales, frogs, fish and birds. A wooden wild animal farm. Spicy aroma of cedar overpowering. Malcomb's work yard and, I suspected, sanctuary.

Lots of new reddish brown carvings and some old and gray, weather worn ones. Some of the old ones had restoration work done. I came upon one restoration in progress, a full sized totem pole, very old, propped up horizontally on wooden bolts. I stood at the base, cocked my head to study the first animal. It was so pocked and pitted and charred and chipped I couldn't immediately put a name to it. At first I thought it was a skinny, or possible skinned bear, but then, on closer inspection, I recognized the naked body of a small human. Encapsulating the human was a much larger humanoid body, sitting, knees curved around the human's hips, hands clasped around the human's chest. Huge face, wide mouth full of big blocky teeth, nose chipped, eyes open large, chin resting on the head of the human. Eager yet watchful. Also melancholy. Neither animal nor beast. Both. Neither male nor female. Both. Something within me recognized it, but couldn't quite place it.

I caressed the ancient face with one hand, scratched my head, careful of recent scabbing, with the other. The carving, its rough grain gapped from weathering, skewered my stereotype of totem poles. Supposed to be animals only. I ambled along the pole, studying, touching individual carvings. There was a cat, coyote, wolf or possibly a dog, an eagle, I think, or a thunderbird, then a three-foot stretch of smooth pole and on top of everything perched my old partner, Qo-oo-la, the common loon. Head high. Solitary. Enduring.

It was recently brought out of storage, probably from the spacious workshop. Beyond the red metal roof of the shop, I could see the smooth blue surface of the Salish Sea. White sailboats cruised between dark green Islands. Squawking gulls flocked after the boats.

I traced the bodyline of the loon with my finger. The detail was remarkable. Person who carved that totem knew loons and held them in high regard. I felt a certain attraction to the totem, like I was looking at a replica of Qo-oo-la's ancestors. How old was the totem pole?

"My great grandfather carved that about one hundred years ago." Malcomb, reading my mind, padded up behind me. I jumped in spite of knowing his voice. "I've had it in storage for forty years. Waiting for a sign from the spirits to haul it out and pay it its proper respect." He was shadowed.

"I have some people came here looking for you," he said.

"You're kidding," I said. "I severed all ties behind me. Who could possibly be looking for me here?"

Trailing behind the old Indian was the Volvo couple, woman in front, long-legged assertive strides, round blue eyes straight ahead. Her blonde hair was cropped short but she still flicked her chiseled face and long neck as if she was flipping hair out of her face. She had on a cream colored blouse, matching slacks and black loafers. The woman reached out a long, shapely forearm to shake. "Hello, I'm Inge Endicott, Josh's ex. Oh, and this is my husband Dylan Endicott." Her handshake was light and quick, his brusque and quicker, as if he touched only out of civility. The back of his hand was tanned and smooth. His mouth winced as if shaking hurt. He let go quick and stepped back.

Dylan Endicott had a spiny, desert smell, as if he had just stepped on a cactus.

He wore a yellow Alpine Meadow brand knitted shirt with a tiny, black swimming logo stitched over the left breast, gray corduroy slacks with matching belt, fanny pack and a Leatherman knife sheath without so much as a smudge on it. An Australian Outback hat sat on his head and he wore L.L. Bean high-top outdoor boots. The in attire for the fashionable wilderness roughneck.

His eyes were covered with gold-rimmed sunglasses. Probably read the Wall Street Journal over a poached egg breakfast and interspersed his conversation throughout the day with pithy quotes from it, dazzling people with his white, even teeth.

Whenever I meet someone like Dylan Endicott I wonder what kind of a childhood he didn't have. You got the idea that, like me and my adolescent friends, he never got bit playing with lizards nor peed on when handling toads, never got his privates sunburned while skinny-dipping on a skipped school day, never told crude dirty jokes or cheated on a fractions test.

I said, "Nice to meet — "

"You have no right to Josh's land," Inge interrupted. She planted her hands on high hips, flipped non-existent hair out of her bright blue eyes. "Josh promised to leave it to me if I paid his share of the land payment which I did for the last two years." Her voice clear and musical. Surprising. Josh never mentioned that but then, there was a whole hell of a lot of things he didn't mention. With a voice like that, I could begin to see why Josh fell in love with her. Josh never mentioned the promise to her about leaving her the land. Did he not tell me that on purpose or was she lying?

I said, "Nice to meet you too. I hoped to see you at the memorial service."

Inge flicked her wrist. "That couldn't be helped. We were back east visiting Dylan's parents. However, I think, as the closest thing to family Josh has — he was, after all, the children's Godfather — I should take over the distribution of his ashes. I have just the place for them, a mausoleum down in Portland."

Dylan, from behind Inge, said, "We're taking you to court. Josh was out of his mind to leave anything to you, a schizoid, nut case." His voice, while baritone, had the self-righteous whine of the deeply wronged, upper middle class, suggesting he, Dylan Endicott, was sane by the self-evident acclamation of privilege and affluence.

"You want his ashes that bad?" I said.

"You can toss them in the drink for all I care." Dylan said and moved, with a self-assured athleticism, beside Inge, next to the ancient totem pole. Above the swimming logo on his yellow knitted shirt, were the words, Mike's Diving. I remembered Josh telling me that this area of Puget Sound, between Shelton and Port Townsend, was a favorite scuba diving area. If Endicott was a diver, why did he smell so dry?

Inge flipped her right wrist in the general direction of the canal. "Don't be silly. I want my land . . . our land back and we're willing to break the will to do it. With Josh having a brain tumor we'll prove that my ex-husband was definitely not of sound mind and body when he made out his last Will and Testament."

"You undoubtedly tricked or coerced him in some way," Dylan said.

"Josh didn't want to die in a hospital or nursing home." I said, "I took care of him while he was dying. Nobody else seemed to want to."

Inge's chiseled face cracked. She averted her blue eyes out to the bluer sea. "I have two children now. I didn't want to subject them to the trauma of watching someone die a slow and agonizing death. Josh, when lucid, understood my concern."

"You're right about that," I said. "He did understand. Still, he loved you dearly. He asked about you up until the very last and wondered why you never came to see him or returned his calls." It was a partial lie but what the hell. Josh did talk about Inge up until the last two weeks. After that, he was either incoherent or speaking in tongues.

Inge turned her face away from me and swallowed. Dylan stepped around her. He had one hand in a pocket and the other patted his flat stomach. "My wife didn't return her ex-husband's calls because he made no sense on the message machine. He was incoherent. You took advantage of his malady to cheat us out of our rightful inheritance." He cocked a leg up and sat on the neither man nor beast face in the loon pole. It groaned. "We need that money to invest in my latest computer game. It's a sure hit if we can just get enough exposure. Without it, I'll have to lay off eighty people. Those eighty workers have been with me since my start up. I have a responsibility to keep them working."

"Which computer game is yours?" I said. I never got into computer games until after the head injury. "At the VA recovery clinic, they had dozens of computer games donated and I played them all incessantly. Helped me to focus."

Dylan's hand went to his throat. His chest swelled under his knit shirt. "It's called Smithy Man," he said. "Have you tried it? Of all the games I've come up with this one is closest to my heart. We put it in at a few test outlets in Portland. The VA hospital was one of them."

"Smithy Man?" I said. "I think I might've tried it."

Dylan bounced up on his toes, made him appear lighter. His eyes filmed over. "It's my baby," he said. "I spent years developing it, put my heart and soul into it. I've dedicated it to the memory of Great Granddad who spent his whole life slaving over a hot forge so his kids could have a better life."

Well, well. Maybe I had misjudged Dylan Endicott. He had poorfolks roots just like me. And, by the tone of his voice, he loved his great granddad as much as I loved mine. It is always a little unsettling to misjudge someone you've just met, and, in fact, find out you have a very personal memory in common with them.

"Yeah," I said, "you know I had a great granddad I loved very much, too." Perhaps Dylan and I could have a cup of coffee together some day after we'd settled the property dispute; talk about granddads and shape changing. Aren't video games a form of shape changing?

I suddenly remembered how Grandfather Two-loons always started his shape changing story. We sit on the ground facing each other and he'd say, *I'm going to tell you a story about a man who became a bird to become a man."*

Dylan's pale eyes blinked at me several times. He shook his head and swiped at his forehead with delicate fingers as if an insect had invaded his space. "I didn't say I loved him," he said. "I just said I dedicated my computer game to him."

He unsnapped his Leatherman knife, whipped out the blade and started to carve in the old, horizontal totem pole.

Malcomb interrupted our conversation, an unusual thing for him to do. "That's a very old and fragile artifact. I'd rather you not cut on it. Or sit on it for that matter."

"Seems sturdy to me, Chief," Dylan said, jabbed it with the knife blade and bounced with his butt up and down a couple times. The pole creaked and yawned.

Malcomb, in a swift move, grabbed Dylan's knife wrist and jerked him off the pole. The pole groaned again. Dylan yipped. "Hey.... Hey! Don't get your feathers in an uproar, Chief."

Malcomb released him, straightened his rumpled knit shirt. "I must insist. I'm sure you don't want to do irreparable damage to the loon tree."

Dylan's eyes focused, locked on Malcomb, his mouth puckered in a semi-tough frown. "Course not," he said, stepping away from those bronze fingers and massaging his rump, "I wouldn't want to damage such a valuable artifact. You're kidding right? A *loon* tree? No wonder you people were conquered so easily, wasting time on *loon* totem poles. Hey, I think you caused me to get a splinter in my — "

"Wasn't a splinter," Malcomb said. "The loon tree bit you."

We all examined the big teeth of the Protector image. Was the gap between its upper and lower jaw wider than before? Teeth sharper?

"Don't be ridiculous, Chief," Dylan said. "Feels like a splinter to me. And a big one, too."

He shouldn't have called Malcomb Chief. Maybe I had misjudged my initial misjudgement. I made up my mind. "You and your husband," I said to Inge, "can't have Joshes ashes."

Inge walked past me, toward the sea; toward the aquamarine sea reflecting jagged shadows from tree covered islands across the placid waters, and indicated with her blue eyes for me to follow. When I caught up Inge said, "What do you propose to do with his ashes?"

Out of earshot of Malcomb and Dylan, I answered, "He wanted them scattered at a place he called Spirit Knoll. He left me a map of where it is."

Inge said, "Don't need a map, it's obvious. It's the highest place on our property, at the other end of it away from the lodge. Probably the highest place in the whole valley 'til you get to the mountain foothills. I suspected as much. Josh loved that place. He used to spend hours up there. At first, he took his sleeping bag and spent the night. Then he built a little cabin and after he built that little cabin at its base I hardly saw him the whole time we were up here." She peered off in the distance as if she were observing a faraway object. Out on the canal, a feeding tundra swan, its head and long neck under water, looked like a large bobbing pillow. Something to rest one's head on, perhaps to dream of cool water.

I wondered, my mouth salivating, how the fishing was.

Inge continued, "I can't exactly put my finger on it but I think that damn place had something to do with our divorce. The more time he spent on that rock the less time he spent with me. It's like it entranced him. He became a driven man. He called it home. He drifted away from me long before he got that brain tumor. Now that he's completely gone I don't exactly want to be reminded that I'm walking on his ashes every time I go up there."

"How often did you go up there? "

Inge shrugged. She was a different person away from her husband. The hard ridges around her mouth softened. She jiggled her hips as if they had just been released from restraint. Her voice grew more melodious. "Not much. It was Josh's meditation place. I found it spooky and, of course, after I remarried and the kids came, dangerous. Those sheer bluffs. Josh didn't like me up there anyway. He put a padlock on that funky little cabin he built out of used garage lumber and wouldn't give me a key. I'm surprised elk hunters haven't broken into it. They break into the lodge all the time. Which is another reason we're up here. A Sheriff Gloeckler called us up in Portland and requested we come up for questioning about the murder of that Indian woman and now we find out another body, a man, has been found buried on the property near the lodge."

"A what! Whose? I mean, who was it? Maybe Malcomb is right, he says the property is cursed."

"Maybe it is. I don't know who the murder victim is. I, unlike Josh, never associated with the locals. But I can tell you; it's not the first murder on the property. Josh and I got the place because there was a murder in the family of the former owners. Son killed his father during the son's wedding ceremony right on top of Spirit Knoll. The bride feinted and her wedding veil fell over the bluff never to be found. A few days later a tree fell on the lodge. Demoralized the mother to say the least and, after letting it stand open to the elements for seven years, she put it up for sale. Josh and I cut the tree off and repaired the damage. Wouldn't you know it, ten years later another tree falls on it. Yeah, I'd say it's cursed all right.

Anyway, a Sheriff Gloeckler called to talk to us about the recent killings on the place. He even wanted to know where we were a week ago Saturday. The gall of the man. Thank God we both were on the East Coast during the whole murder time span. The kids and I were visiting Dylan's parents in Wilmington and Dylan was at a sales convention in Philadelphia." She perspired, wiped a wisp of sweat off her upper lip. "When we first got the property I used to love it. Now I'm afraid to let my kids get near it."

I began to get a feeling. The more I was warned about it, the more the property was purported to be cursed and the more murders happened on it, the more I felt drawn to it. Which seemed strange, considering I'd never set foot on the property. Well, unless you counted a webbed foot in the Dosanomish River running through it. Could a place that, by everyone else's account be cursed, be the home I was looking for?

I never felt at home anyplace before. Not as a swaddling babe in my mother's utilitarian arms, not as a kid growing up in Missouri, not as an adult drifter canvassing the country. No place ever felt like I belonged. I'd no sooner get there than I'd be packing to leave — hit the ground running. The closest I ever felt to being home was with Grandpa Two-Loons on his one hundred sixty acre Ozark farm. That was a long, long time ago, and a fairy-tale away.

Inge and I walked out on an old pier spotted with black 'n' white gull poop, planks slick with dark green lichen. A sharp smell of fish guts hung in a Salish Sea breeze. The two-person crew of a fishing boat was pulling up nets a couple hundred yards out. I said, "I'm thinking of staying in that cabin for awhile. Gimme a chance to get on my feet. And . . . well, Josh asked me to live there. Made me promise to carry out his instructions that he said I'd find once I got in there. Said it'd be obvious what to do."

Inge glanced backwards at her husband and fidgeted with the sleeve of her cream-colored blouse. I watched Dylan intercept April and a companion, a tall man, as they emerged from the house. Dylan leaned over April close, from the neck, like a raptor taking its time over a particularly juicy morsel. He rubbed his buttock with one hand and held the index finger of the other hand alongside his cheek. April swept a non-existent lock of hair from her forehead, appeared flustered with the attention. The two men shook hands, bending at the waist, standing as far away from each other as possible.

Inge said, "Dylan and I could never allow you to stay on the property. We're going into Port Townsend now to file a court order to try and keep you from living on the property until the estate is settled."

It occurred to me, they didn't know about Molly being the other owner. Surely the lawyer or the sheriff told them. Or did they? Maybe, they thought I didn't know.

Inge paused while a jet skier *booroomed* by. The skier was covered from head to foot with a black wet suit. Some salt-water spray sprinkled us.

I caught the odor of singed rubber. It left a sour taste in my mouth, as did watching April flirt with Dylan and the other man.

I detested that jet skier. What did that insensitive clod think he was doing to my habitat, my winter feeding ground?

Whoa here! A week ago, I would not have cared about the impact a power machine like the jet ski has on the wildlife in the Salish Sea. But, I had undergone a shift in consciousness. Realized that the sea was Qo-oo-la's winter home. And that jet ski was a threat to my livelihood and, in some way I didn't understand, to my manhood; a topic that hadn't come up in a few, fallow years. Was I, Harp P. Gravey, through some avian osmosis, becoming jealous of an unattainable love.

Animal transformation, I began to suspect, had subtle ramifications as well as the obvious ones.

"Look, Josh really wanted me to have Spirit Knoll," I said, "wanted me to practice good land stewardship, whatever that is, on the property. Josh anticipated a legal battle with you and, I might add, built in fail-safe legal safeguards. In other words, you can file all the court orders you want and sue me 'til the fifty pound salmon swim up the Columbia River again but I'm going to stick to Josh's spirit bluff like mushrooms cling to mulch." I looked straight in her clear blue eyes and didn't blink. Hey, maybe I still had some of the old hustler in me yet; for I had no idea what the hell I was talking about. Or what I was going to do with my life, let alone provide good stewardship to a huge rocky bluff in the middle of a semi-rain forest. Been a hell of a lot more likely to be kept in its pristine state if Josh'd left it to some non-profit like the Audubon Society with a track record of stability.

And, it occurred to me, how could I, if by some remote chance, settle down on the Dosanomish, make a living? The area didn't exactly look like it lent itself to banjo picking or pool hustling. No marketable skills and dead broke, how else could I support myself?

Inge reached in her briefcase-sized purse and pulled out some papers and a fat brown envelope. She stuck her long, slender fingers with pale blue nails, in the brown envelope and produced a wad of one hundred dollar greenbacks. "This is for you. There's five thousand dollars in here. It will allow you to get on your feet and get established somewhere else right away. All you have to do is sign this quick claim deed and we won't have to have a lengthy, nasty and expensive court battle."

I'm afraid I stared at the money. My plan of five minutes worked perfectly. I'm rich. Take me a long time to get that kind of stake. Would give me a chance to get my pool-shooting eye back; sharpen my stroke, hone the ol' hustle. I fidgeted, felt like I already, in the past few days, regained some function and faculty. The color of money always did make me silly and I did one of those space/time continuums: saw myself in Las Vegas at the National Nine Ball Tournament, stuffed immaculately in a blue tuxedo (Minnesota Fats claimed that dressing a pool player in a tux was like putting whipped cream on a hot dog); smooth, confident, in control, making those hard buttermilk balls go *plop* in soft leather pockets — a sound that's pure ecstasy to me.

I was in the final match, last shot, looking at a straight-in on the yellow striped nine ball in the side pocket. All eyes were on me. The television cameras rolled. Nothing to it. I bent over, took aim, and noticed two liquid black spots on the white cue ball. Very distracting. Couldn't have that. Probably rolled over a pair of fat fruit flies. I heard canned banjo picking over the casino's PA system, heartless and soulless. The black spots grew bigger, watery, I drew closer; a tear rolled out of one spot and I realized the spots were eyes. Molly Jenkins's eyes. Molly's ruined eyes telling me, *"I didn't want to die, didn't deserve to die."* Molly's ruined eyes beseeching me, *"Old one, find my killer, avenge me."*

At that moment I felt my age, or, rather Qo-oo-la's age, sixty million years old.

I stroked and missed the easy shot.

"Take the money and skedaddle out of this god forsaken wilderness rat hole," Elpenor said. *"Forget Molly's ghost. You're a has-been banjo picker and pool hustler. There's no work for you around here and you're sure no detective. There's better pickin's over the next ridge. Take the damn money and run you bone-headed birdbrain."* A plump worm crawled across my heart.

I reached for the green. Beyond my extended hand, I saw the black raven and gray gull playing leapfrog on the apex of the machine shed's red roof. A celebratory game. Suddenly, above those two feathered clowns, Thunderbird hovered for an instant then dive-bombed the duo so close they tumbled down the slope a second before catching themselves and flying for cover.

I glanced around to see if anyone else had seen the aerial acrobatics. Malcomb made a hand gesture toward me. April, occasionally doing a light-footed skip, stood in between the two men, who seemed to be in earnest conversation. April was too entranced by her companions to see the aerial exchange on the shop roof.

I drew my hand back empty. "I've got some unsolved . . . unsettled business here. I'll stick around awhile."

Inge's lips pressed together so hard they turned burgundy. She put the stack of hundreds back in the brown envelope. Her long fingers trembled. "Dylan said you'd probably hold out for more; a real bloodsucking opportunist. We're prepared to double this offer, or see you in court. If you change your mind I will be staying at Portia's Bed & Breakfast in Port Townsend."

The tide retreated, sloshing at the sand. The raven and gull took off out to sea. Thunderbird flew inland. Shore birds appeared in the sand, seemingly from out of nowhere, long flowering currant blooms cleared my congested nostrils. A bald eagle cruised down from its lofty flight arc to alight on a beach log. Never feel the same about eagles again. It was far enough away I couldn't see its unforgiving eyes but it faced toward me and spread its wings — Dracula style — a half dozen times. Looked to be missing a few feathers. Good. Slow him down. Give us clumsy fliers a chance.

"Inge! Inge!" I heard Dylan shouting. A muscle in Inge's cheek flinched. "I'm coming," she hollered back, her voice strained and atonal.

Inge adjusted her hair, licked her lips slowly with the tip of her wet, pink tongue, reached out with her long sensuous forearm and thin blue fingernails and gave my cloven-hoof-by-comparison hand an unexpected squeeze. "You look like a lonely man. And, although, slight and abrasive, you have a certain animal magnetism which I find strangely attractive. Dylan has to go back to the East Coast tonight but I could stay here a couple of days. Perhaps we could get together again and I could interest you in other — things. I've been told I'm very good at the subtler arts." She fondled my stubby thumb in a downright obscene manner. It — my thumb — as if having a mind of its own, stuck out rigid, hitchhiking once again, on the road to any oblivion that's handy.

I was aghast. I rejoiced in my revivified sexuality; yet abhorred the unfamiliar animal intensity of it, like puberty striking. I recaptured, with more inner struggle than without, my errant appendage. "Bribery of the sordid sort," I said, "will get you nowhere."

"I've heard that before." Inge said, Irish fiddle tunes playing in her voice. She turned, brushing me ever so slightly with her hip, and repeated, "Portia's Bed & Breakfast in Port Townsend."

I watched her hips swinging back to the totem yard. My mind raced; what the hell am I doing? What's come over me? Refusing easy money? Refusing easy sex with a beautiful woman? Refusing a chance to cut and run? Having severe lapses of judgement? Had my whole life before the Dosanomish valley been a lie? That clout on the head had done more damage than first imagined. First, my long lost spirituality erupts out of a mud bog, then my personality does a flip flop. An ocean breeze bit my neck. Rubbing the soreness out of the hornet sting, I let the soft wind catch under my arms and lighten my step back to the totem yard.

35

Professionals and Pissants

As I approached, April stepped away from an animated conversation with Dylan Endicott and the other man. She intercepted me. "The sheriff hailed me down on 101. Showed me some more of the feathers like he gave you. I couldn't stall. He now knows they're loon feathers. He wants me to send the feathers down to the animal forensics lab in Medford, Oregon."

When she spoke forensics tiny droplets of spittle spattered my lower lip and chin. Excitement caused her to talk fast and lean close. I inhaled deeply and licked my lower lip. Her clean amber smell mingled with the faint scent of Qo-oo-la's subtle natural oil tang. "The sheriff's talked to Nat Buntler too. He knows about the loon Nat captured and about the gold in its . . . his beak."

Sheriff Gloeckler came around from behind a big leaf maple tree. "Those feathers and information about Nat Buntler are confidential police information Ms Ol' Wolf," he said. You shouldn't be telling Mr. Gravey." He had his cell phone still glued to his ear, walking slow to allow Barbie Jane to stay in step. The pig sniffed the air and made a waddling beeline for me, stomach scraping a trail in the dirt path. The sheriff grunted into the phone, folded it and stuck it in his belt.

April looked at me. "I suppose the Nat-Buntler-finding-a-loon-that-lays-a-golden-egg is confidential information too?" she said.

"Yes, It is," Sheriff Gloeckler said. "There you go giving up more confidential evidence. Didn't expect you to announce it all over creation."

While telling me, Dylan and Inge Endicott, Malcomb and the new man had also overheard. The new man was giving me the once over with liquid blue eyes. He stuck out his hand. "Hi I'm Dr. David Brandt," he said. "You must be Harp. April has told me about your ah . . . condition." We shook. His handshake felt practiced, like he'd scored a C in Elementary Handshake 101. A damp C.

"David!" said April. "What are you doing repeating what I told you in confidence?"

"My condition is in pretty good condition for the condition it's in," I said, elevating my language to the level an educated man could relate to. I released his hand and the disconnection thwocked, like a suction tipped dart off a mildewed shower wall. I wiped my palm off on my pants leg. So this was one of April's past lovers. At least she claimed he was past. I despaired. He could've been a brother to Inge. He was like a photograph out of a New Man magazine, depicting "the professional man who combines an adventurous, healthy lifestyle with a new-age sensitivity." A massive blonde beard, tipped with artificial sunshine, dominated his face. The growth obscured all facial details except for the blue eyes that looked past you and an ivory white smile stiff as a cedar plank on a smuggler's wharf. He was thin-waisted, narrow-hipped and long legged. He wore a WSU green sweatshirt, dark perspiration marks under the arms, and matching sweat pants. He carried a water bottle, half full and took a generous gulp after letting my hand go. If April liked sweaty guys that's another mark against me.

"Ha! Seems like everyone is breaching confidences around here," the sheriff said.

David snapped the nipple shut on his water bottle and indicated to me with a nod of his blond head to follow him. He strolled past the work yard to stand looking out to sea and waited with his back turned. I was curious. I followed. Drew even with him. "You look like you could use some meds," he said to the ocean.

Oh no! Not another one. "No, I don't need any meds." I said. His soft voice exuded sweet reasonableness. Sounded, in fact, just like the VA shrink, Dr. Rothenberg.

"Dr. Rothenberg, your psychiatrist, said without medication you are a danger to yourself and others." He coughed. Covered his face with a hand, but I noticed he also put something into his mouth. His neck tightened, covering a concealed swallow.

"How the hell do you know about Dr. Rothenberg?"

"April of course. She's taken a scientific interest in you. She asked me to take a look at your case. Naturally, to help you, I had to gather what records I could. Neither Dr. Rothenberg nor myself can understand, how, with the massive head trauma you sustained, you can be walking around without medication. And, more to the point, should you be walking around without medication?" He hooked a thumb behind the waistband of his sweats and stretched them out to look at his crotch. Satisfied with what he saw there, he turned a liquid eye to me.

I'd seen that liquid look before on too many good musicians. "Looks to me." I said, "like you're taking too much of your own medication there, Dr. David."

He liquid eyes turned to blue ice. "I could have you put away," he said, "you little pissant. Institutionalized where you couldn't hurt anyone ever again. It's low-life like you that were the downfall of my beautiful Molly, trusting spirit that she was."

His quiet voice cracked. Hissing his s'es in pissant. Behind his brushed golden beard, his lips were stretched so tight, if I would have flicked them with my forefinger, they would've dinged like clay chimes.

"Pissant? Pissant?" I sounded the word, remembering the devastating authority my Mama had when she pronounced the word. Higher education does not lend itself to the forceful use of words like pissant. But wait. What was that about Molly Jenkins?

"So you too knew Molly?"

"Yes, I knew her in a professional capacity. She came to me for help with her sex addiction."

"I'll bet you were a big help with that, Dr. Drug Addict," I said, "in more ways than one." I figured to get my own professional opinion into the conversation. It's a cinch, although skimpy on the sex, I knew a hell of a lot more about addiction than he did about pissants.

"Don't you besmirch Molly's name," he said. "And I'll have you know I'm in perfect control of my faculties. April said you were clever. One word from me and the sheriff will have to arrest you." His words ran together and pitched higher causing a seal laying on a rock to rise up and bark. Dr. David checked his crotch again. I noticed a strap around his waist. He looked worried this time. A cloud blotted the sun and the bronze luster of his beard faded into a shoe-polish tan. What kind of person dyes his facial hair?

"April said I was clever?" I said. "And here I thought she thought I was just another pretty banjo picker. Listen, Dr. Drug Addict, you say one word about my condition to the sheriff and I'll mention the little stash of drugs you got hanging between your legs. Couldn't even go for a jog without them. And, Dr. Lover Boy, what do you think April's going to think when I tell her you were schlonging Molly — hey maybe that's why April didn't care for Molly, she stole all her boy friends — probably while you were involved with April. I don't think you really want to mention my ailment to the sheriff." I saw the black clad jet skier buzzing some seals down the shore a ways. Heard a clunk, engine drone revved and shut off and skier went head over heels into the drink. Dr. David never even looked that way. His eyes were fixed on a distant island, face drained of color.

I turned and walked toward the group.

Dr. David hissed, "Don't underestimate me you white trash mother-fucker. I'll find a way to bring you down. Molly was too good for the likes of you. . . ." His fast voice faded out.

Once again, I spread my arms and let the soothing wind from off ocean waters lighten my step.

Learned conversations with trained professionals are so uplifting.

36

Evidence Tampering and Cult Rituals

I joined the totem yard conversation in time to hear Dylan say, "Wait a minute here, are you saying that a loon had something to do with the dead woman found in the Dosanomish?" He massaged his bitten hip.

"Could be *Kaalpekci*, the river dragon." Malcomb said.

"That's about as preposterous as Nat Buntler's loon story," the sheriff said.

"What loon story is that?" Inge asked. Both her and Dylan moved closer. Out of the corner of my eye I saw Dr. David with his hand to his mouth. April saw him too.

Barbie Jane had found me and commenced to happily drool on my Converse tennies and make affectionate grunting belches. The sting knots on her pink nose had shrunk. She had a new pink ribbon in her colic to match hot pink nail polish and her coconut shampoo was overpowering. I scratched her sow's ear. She keened.

"What's with that gaudy pig?" Dylan said, ever the sophisticated man of tact.

Sheriff Gloeckler tipped his brown trooper's hat back on his head and gave Dylan a level look. The sheriff adjusted his gun. "That pig's got an IQ higher than most people and ... ah shit, I might as well tell you about Nat Buntler's loon tale. It's all over the county by now. We've got Nat up at Chimicum in the county drunk tank. Picked him up at the Whistling

Pelican Tavern babbling on about a seeing a wounded loon swallow a nugget of gold in the Dosanomish."

Nobody laughed.

"I'm sorry Sheriff Gloeckler," Inge said, "but I don't see what some drunk's delusions has got to do with the dead body."

"Bear with me," the sheriff said, "I might as well tell you the rest too; can't keep a secret in this community. I suspect this loon of Nat's of . . . ah, tampering with the body."

"That's absurd," Inge said.

"That's delightful," Malcomb said.

"Nature is unpredictable," April said and pinched my butt. Hard.

"Do tell," Dylan said. I noticed his ear lobes sticking out from under his Aussie hat were blush red.

"I think it's time you paid me another visit, Sheriff," David said, floating back from the beach. He petted his white forehead. "Get you back into therapy."

Sheriff Gloeckler's eyebrows squeezed together, ignored all comments. "I think Molly grabbed something from off the murderer's clothes. The divers found the pin half of a gold vest or tie pin stuck in her hand. The top half is missing. The half with the logo or symbol. I want that pin. And loon feathers were caught in tight roots right above there. Combine that with Nat Buntler's gold nugget story and, as absurd as it sounds, we've got a loon that swallowed a major clue to a murder. I get that pin and I got me a murderer."

"What's the problem?" Inge asked. "Just get the injured loon from this Nat Buntler, cut it open and retrieve the clue."

My chest felt like someone took a meat hook to it. Who the hell did Inge think she was, blithely slicing up my Qo-oo-la? Barbie Jane had plopped down on my fresh slobbered feet with a thick squish. They were already numbing up to my calves. No quick get-a-ways for me. My side, where a gizzard might be, made false grinding noises.

"It's not as simple as that," the sheriff said. "Nat claims that a huge, ugly, feral dog rescued the loon from his compound and — look I'm just reporting what Nat told me — they escaped into the upper Dosy. Nat thinks he shot the dog but there's a lot of white water rapids shooting through steep canyons in that area and he gave up searching for them. I know it sounds pretty far-fetched but I'm taking some tracking dogs and deputies and going up there after that loon. They have instructions to shoot the feral dog too. Might be rabid."

"What makes you think that loon hasn't flown the coop, halfway to British Columbia by now?" Dylan said.

"Nat would've never caught it in the first place if it didn't have a head injury and couldn't fly. I suspect the loon will be floating down river to the sea." He looked at his watch. "Well, I'm supposed to meet some men up the Dosanomish Road a ways. I better get going. Come on Barbie Jane."

Barbie Jane twitched her tail and farted. The pungent odor bent my bristly nose hairs. My feet felt as flat as a train track penny, legs now numb to the knees. "What are you going to do to the loon when you get it?" I asked.

"Send it too the lab of course. Oh and one more — "

"Dead?"

" — thing, -of course dead, how else? That loon is evidence. If any of you see it I'll expect you to report it or capture it and give it to me. Remember that April, if you get one in your wildlife hospital. Your brother Loren may be the prime suspect, but he's certainly not the only one. Your boy friend here is too. That loon could clear one or both of them." Sheriff Gloeckler grabbed Barbie Jane by the ear and tugged until she huffed and puffed up on her painted hooves. They waddled away, Barbie Jane casting affectionate glances over her pudgy shoulder at me.

"He's not my boyfriend," April said, to a fading sheriff. "And the loon could also convict one or the other," she muttered under her breath. She looked at me then at David and shook her head, long black hair catching natural light and glinting blue.

I had finally cleaned myself up enough to be lovable and look where it got me; a possible coercion fuck from long-legged Inge and puppy love from a two hundred pound porker stub. April was untouchable. Heart hardened to musicians. Prefers civilized professional men. Security and consistency. Hardly my history. Dr. David, now that Molly was gone, was obviously lusting after her, jealous of me. Not good to have a druggy after you, professional or pissant.

My feet felt like they were just hammered out of a cement cast.

"So, the sheriff suspects your son of being the killer?" Dylan said. "How does that make you feel, Chief?"

Malcomb caressed his black ponytail with his thumb and index finger. "I wouldn't worry about Loren, if I was you. I'd get home and put something on that bite. Keep it from getting infected. And don't call me Chief."

"Ouch!" said Dylan, grabbing his butt. "That's got to be a splinter."

April reached out and pulled me out of earshot of the others, then touched my flat chest with callused fingertips. "Billy Moody has been found buried on your property. More bad news for my brother. Billy and Loren had a long-standing grudge against each other. However, either Sheriff Gloeckler is not convinced of Loren's guilt or he needs more evidence to convict him. Whatever, he told me he's deputized Lt. Leroy and his militia to get Qo-oo-la. And I don't think they would have capturing in mind."

My stomach lurched. They would kill Qo-oo-la as easily as stepping on a luna moth. He couldn't fly. He couldn't think. Not like a human anyway. He couldn't know of the danger he's in from the sheriff and the marauding militia. Maybe the clever Lt. LeRoy found a way to get his bloodhounds on the trail. Qo-oo-la didn't have a chance. Unless we found him first.

And what would they do to Medusa if she — assuming she's able to motate — tries to protect Qo-oo-la? Finish her off. Shoot her down like a dog . . . well, she was a dog.

The ocean breeze had changed directions and a whiff of sewer gas drifted by. "Where's that helicopter you talked about?"

April's nose twitched and she looked at her watch. We were stand-ing by the horizontal top of the loon tree and she reached out and stroked the imaginary feathers on its neck. "We're going to meet it at coordi-nates up the river a ways. I think you'll appreciate the place. I need to say good-bye to David and thank him for coming, then throw some things in a backpack." She turned to go, hollered over her shoulder, "Bring along your friend."

"My friend?"

"The ashes of your dead friend. We'll spread them." April darted over to the angry psychologist and together they disappeared into the house.

Blood began circulating in my feet, a thousand needle pricks in my calves signaling returned sensation. I latched onto the loon totem to keep from toppling over. Touch it and it will tingle. There was that telltale buzz tickling my fingertips whenever I touched anything having to do with loons. According to Malcomb the totem pole was at least a hun-dred years old and the ancient cedar grain felt rough and ready for another hundred years. It needed mending though. Maybe I could help fix it up? I may be a failure with humans but I had a feel for wood. My hands and fingers loved to squeeze it, stroke it, touch it. Loved the easy glide and feather soft swish of a well-balanced cue stick as it pistoned through my finger bridge, delighted in touching the wooden spacers in a harmon-ica with the tip of my tongue, but most of all loved caressing the cur-vaceous bodies and sensuous necks of acoustic instruments. Banjo being the most sensuous of all.

I found myself entertaining the fanciful notion that I could help Malcomb restore the loon tree and maybe, just maybe, more fanciful yet, if I ever did settle down in the area, someday buy it and put it at the entrance to my home. Let all who entered know who they were deal-ing with. I embarrassed myself. What rubbish. Three days ago I was a homeless nomad with a dog, a few musical instruments, a pool cue, a spoiled rabbit, a twenty nine year old vehicle and twenty bucks to my name. Whatever possessed me to imagine a home let alone a lone, loon totem to adorn its entrance? Wilderness air warping my senses. Senses I never knew I had before. Senses that I needed to fine tune, if I was going to keep someone from killing a common loon.

37

Gum wads and Greenbacks

Though not driving off to the big city with ten thousand dollars lining my pockets, I looked forward to driving down the road.

On the way to my bus, I passed by Merle, newly installed in a sturdy, three by six cage. Carving inlays, such as the ones on the cougar cage, graced the rabbit's door. Malcomb's brand of sacred protection. He sure took a liking to that rabbit. I too had a new admiration for Merle's strong hind legs. Escape power.

Merle hippity-hopped to the front of the cage, stood on his strong hind legs and wiggled his pink nose in a greeting to me. "Okay, I suppose we're in this together," I said and reached a finger through the wire mesh to tickle its whiffer. It sniffed me, backed off. Still held resentments about the car crash.

I slid the side door of my bus open and found Josh's ashes. "Come on old friend," I said, "I'm taking you home before you cause any more trouble." I caught myself. Home? What's with this *home* business? Beside Josh's plastic ash box lay my traveling harmonica, key of A. I picked up the harp and blew a quick spurt of summery breath in all the reeds to limber them up. I have always loved the solid feel of the music on my mouth. Pushing and pulling air through space to make music is a tradition as old as man and I felt privileged to have been able to do it at one time.

I pursed my lips and OOO, Ooo, Oee, Eee; I tooted. Spicy texture, a bashful kiss from an old flame. And just as awkward. Unnecessary torment. Too soon, if ever.

I tucked the harmonica in my pocket out of habit and thought about going to my inherited property. Did Inge and Dylan know I'd inherited the other twenty five percent from Molly, now was an equal partner with them? Surely they did. But did they know I knew? Did Inge offer me ten thousand dollars for a fourth or half of the property? If it was for only a fourth then would they offer twenty thousand dollars for half. For no hassle or fuss. Drop the lawsuit? Pretty clever of me. If I was so clever then why didn't I take the money and run?

I got in the driver's seat. I might reconsider Inge's offer later on, but for right now I wanted to see the inside of my cabin, spread Josh's ashes and catch a helicopter to find Medusa. Maybe Qo-oo-la too.

April came running up carrying a large tote bag. Malcomb followed behind her, hurrying too, carrying his transformation bag. April laid her bag in the side door opening of my bus. It clunked against the metal floor. "Father says this drives like a four wheeler. You think you can ram it up an old logging road? Might get a few scratches from limbs." She smiled. Her dark eyes danced.

"Let's go, my bus can go anywhere," I said. With April beside me, I really believed it could. April waited for Malcomb to crawl in then slammed the side door shut and hopped in. Malcomb had left the keys in the ignition. Just gun-happy militiamen, spear throwing drunks and double murderers in the region, but not car thieves. After sitting for days, my trusty bus started up. The exterior might not look like much but I kept the motor fine-tuned. We both were rearing to go, the road being familiar territory.

"Go left out of the driveway," April said. "We've got about an hour before we meet the helicopter at a clearing near this Spirit Knoll of your dead friend's. Thought we could spread his ashes and get a look at your cabin. Probably way too small."

"Way too small for what?" I said. My cabin. How about that? Made my chest heavy just to think of it. A place to settle, put down some roots? Belong. A home? A community? A watershed? How many empty years had I run screaming from that responsibility and commitment? My favorite blues song refrain was "I ain't got no home in this world anymore." My head spun, Highway 101 blurred and I had to slow down and wait for the spinning to stop.

We came to a long steep hill pointing south; the water of the Salish Sea lay smooth and light blue to my left. I rolled down my window and inhaled the moist marine air. April pointed to a brown National Park sign with yellow lettering that said, Dosanomish Recreation Area, and I realized that I was right back — from the opposite direction — where I started from three days earlier. I turned on the river road and slowed. Saw the tear in the blackberry canes but no trace of mud angels in the mud bog. Skunk cabbage smell whipped through the bus. The redwing blackbirds ignored us, had already rebuilt another nest in the cattails. Right beside the one Lt. Leroy blew apart. Tenacious nature doesn't let a lethal blast from a hate-monger stop her for long.

Up in a branch of an orange madrone tree, perched my old friend raven and behind him hovered the gray gull. Waiting for humans to supply them with another easy meal? Those guys apparently don't understand that imprinting has doomed them. In fact they seemed to be thriving and having a good time to boot. Not only feeding off man's refuse but mimicking and making fun of him while doing it. Or maybe not making fun of mankind, just making fun of me.

April asked, "What happened, did you fall asleep? I mean when you ran off the road into the river?"

"No, I don't think so. I was really tired, yes, and excited to be close to ah . . . Josh's . . . my land. But I swerved to miss a shape in the middle of the road."

"An animal?"

"I have no idea. A shape, that's all. No, that's not entirely right. It wasn't an animal, a real animal anyway. Maybe it was Elpenor."

Malcomb said, "Could have been Coyote or Loki."

Some other time I resolved to revisit the scene. Sort out my feelings. "Coyote, eh? Last sighting I had of Elpenor he was part coyote."

"Could be they've teamed up," said Malcomb.

I shifted gears, road started the foothills upgrade. Elpenor adapting so quickly to wilderness life was not very comforting. Like me, he seemed to be changing forms.

We rode in relative silence for several miles, listening to the bus's engine put-put in third gear. I missed Medusa riding shotgun, barking at objects whizzing by at fifty five mph. However, April's presence beside me felt natural.

The sun pitched shafts of light piercing through gaps in the second growth forest we sped through. The sky was a clear blue but on the mountaintop ahead, a fierce northern wind blew the snow in a southern sheet, resembling a zephyr style hat.

We came upon an abandoned cedar shake mill lot. The golden steam-shrouded sunrays nailed rusted heavy machinery. There was no pattern to the array of machinery corpses unless you consider abandonment as a kind of wacky order. Sort of a derivative of chaos theory. Massive shocks of dirty white old man's beard lichen dangling from the overhang rafters, glowed flaxen and supple in the early light. Spider webs bejeweled with pinhead dewdrops beckoned unsuspecting flying travelers. Traps everywhere for unsuspecting prey.

A horn blasted behind me. With the rising sun shining in the rear view mirror all I could make out was three men in a red vehicle pulling a trailer. I was doing the speed limit on a curvy uphill grade, but people hate to be behind a VW bus. People associate VW buses with being slow. More horn, long blasts, insistent, jarring me. I pulled over to let them pass, recognized too late it was the Jeep Cherokee, Lt. LeRoy driving, Big Steve in the back and an annoyed-looking stranger in the front passenger seat. By the enraged expression on Lt. LeRoy's face as they passed us, he knew who we were.

As the trailer drew even with us it barked and bugled, full of hound and fury. Hunt dogs on their way to sniff out Qo-oo-la and snuff out his existence. All I could see through slats in the trailer was lots of salivating mouths and sopping teeth, they knew blood and guts hovered over the horizon. They were, after all, trained by Ol' Blood 'n' Guts himself, Lt. LeRoy.

The Jeep Cherokee skidded to a stop, jackknifed, blocking the road. Lt. LeRoy leaped out, still in camouflage garb and polished snakeskin boots, a new gun sparkling in his holster, a new hat too, this one camouflaged and no self-serving slogan — as if he appreciated the perils of advertising. The whereabouts of his *"Legend in my own Mind"* hat known only to Clancy the cougar. Big Steve squeezed out from the back seat, no holster, no pistol. The stranger emerged. He wore a holster and pistol. They conferred, then, with Lt. LeRoy swaggering in front, marched toward us. The stranger marched in the middle and Big Steve lumbered in the rear.

Those guys had trouble written all over them.

Trouble takes time. I did a fast calculation and figured the best way to deal with their kind of trouble was make like a rabbit and run. I grabbed the gear stick and shoved it in reverse. April watched me, a frown on her face. I could've executed a quick turnaround easily; instead I rammed the stick up to first and shut off the engine.

Elpenor spoke in my head, *"You're gettin' bout as stupid as a June bug in a standoff with a barbed-wire fence. Can't you see there's three of them and they got guns. Fool! Escape while you can. Running like a whipped pup has always been your best feature."*

April squeezed my thigh. Her fiddler's fingers a fine and warm inspiration. "You've got that look in your eyes like Elpenor's talking to you. Don't listen to him. Hang tough. They can't eat us." She leaped out of the bus and stomped around the snub-nose front end to meet the terrible trio. Her Anglo jaw set and kissable lower lip slightly protruding, high cheekbones like folded wings.

Malcomb leaned over my shoulder. "That's Gabe Moody in the middle. Billy's . . . the murdered man's older brother. Gabe's considered to be the money and driving force behind the right wing militia movement in this area. He also owns the biggest commercial shellfish company in the area. And he fancies himself a terrific pool shot. Not, however, as good as me."

"He looks more pissed than sad about his brother's death," I said.

"They did not get along. They inherited a lot of money; Gabe made more of it, Billy spent more of it. I have heard that they also fought over Molly's affections."

"Could Gabe have killed his own brother? And Molly Jenkins?"

Malcomb uncoiled himself and slide the side door open without fumbling, which is unusual. Most people never get it because you have to bend the latch handle forward while sliding the door backward. "A frustrated pool player is capable of anything," Malcomb said. "In our younger days, Gabe Moody killed a man with his fists in a fight. He was tried for manslaughter but acquitted. So yes, he could kill, and has killed."

Lt. LeRoy stopped as April approached him, not sure of himself around an unpredictable woman, affected a menacing slouch, hand resting on new weapon, lower jaw working viciously on a large wad of something chewable.

Gabe Moody stepped around and in front of the lieutenant. Gabe was a big man, big gut, big ego. He was Malcomb's age and carried himself well; used to being in charge. Silvery mane flowed out from under a gray cowboy hat. He had fierce dark eyes, heavy jowls and so many red chins they resembled a turkey's waddle. His hands were clenched in fists.

Gabe hollered with a cigarette smoker's croak, "Malcomb Ol' Wolf get your coon dog ass out here and talk to me." He started to go past April and she stepped in front of him. He raised his arm to push her aside.

Malcomb rounded the front of my bus. "It would not be wise to lay a hand on my daughter, Gabe Moody, or pool shooting won't be the only thing you'd lose at."

Gabe stopped, put his fists down by his side. "Mal, what the hell's going on here? You and that pissant over there in that wreck of a vehicle, sicing a cougar on the commander of my militia. Are you out of your mind? Could've killed someone."

Malcomb scratched his big ear. "Didn't sic that coug on anybody Gabe. Sold 'em fair and square. Ain't my fault your man didn't know how to handle him." Malcomb broke a dry twig off a vine maple and stuck it in his mouth. "And in case you hadn't bothered to notice someone has been killed. Two someones and one was your brother, and the other was your occasional sweetheart, neither of which you seem all that upset about. Wonder why?"

"Yeah well, Billy probably had it coming. Always knew somebody was going to put a bullet in his thick skull someday; felt like it myself sometimes," he said. He took off his broad rimmed cowboy hat revealing silvery hat-hair. His big hands, pink and fleshy, held the hat over his heart. "And Molly, aahh my pretty Miss Molly, the life she was leading bound to catch up with her sooner or later. Looks like sooner. And no one is sorrier than me a delicate flower like her has left this world. Don't think I don't know that drunken son of yours is the prime suspect."

"With Billy gone," Malcomb said, "you'll inherit all the timber holdings, mining claims and shellfish operations, won't you?" Malcomb clicked a bite off the dry twig and spit it out between Gabe's outspread boots.

"I wanted to do away with Billy I'd a put him in a gunny sack full of rocks and tossed him overboard a long time ago," Gabe said, and broke off a bigger twig.

With those two in a twig-pissing match, seemed like a good time to step out of the bus. The hounds, quiet since stopping, set up a chorus. I walked over to them and the closer I got the more they howled. There were four of them and the biggest and meanest gnawed at the wire mesh to get at me.

I heard Big Steve's size thirteen boots crunch behind me. "I don't think Hondo likes you."

Hondo, a large red-bone hound, was throwing himself against the cage wall, working his way up to a feverish pitch, scaring even his cell mates with slavering ferocity.

It came to me: Hondo had my scent. Could smell Qo-oo-la on me. Lt. LeRoy probably already teased the big red-bone with Qo-oo-la's feathers from the sheriff's stash. Made me a little proud, it did. Also a little scared, if I persisted in this transformational madness, where would it end? Would I sprout feathers and grow webbing between my toes? Grow wings? Become a Loon Angel?

Ignoring the obvious, I said, "What about you? What do you think of me?"

"I don't know. Don't know you much. You're kinda weird but April likes you. You're okay, I guess." Big Steve put his ham-sized hand through the cage slats and pawed Hondo's nape. The hound calmed down and licked Big Steve's rhododendron & tomahawk tattoo. Reminded me of Molly and caused me to wonder just how good a friends Big Steve and Molly were.

"Then do me a favor?" I said. "Slow them guys down a bit. My dog, Medusa, is laying up there wounded, if these hounds get to her before we do, they may tear her apart." If they picked up Clancy's scent, it would lead them right to Medusa. We had to get there first.

Big Steve hung his handsome head. "Aaahh, I couldn't do that. Mr. Moody and Lt. LeRoy'd have my hide if they found out. And besides we're not after a dog. The sheriff deputized us to get a loon."

"You're a clever fellow, don't let 'em find out. And here's another thing. I understand that loon is wounded and can't fly. You can capture it without killing it and give it to April to — "

"Hey, what's going on over here, Sergeant? Are you consorting with the enemy?" Lt. LeRoy strutted up behind us. Big Steve withdrew his hand from Hondo's neck. The red-bone hound cocked his head and glowered at me, a cross between a whimper and a growl rumbling in his powerful chest. Confused canine, his nose and eyes telling two differ-ent tales; which one to believe?

Big Steve said, "Wasn't consorting, we was talking dogs." He looked down at me; light from the metal siding on the trailer reflected deep in his pale blue eyes.

Lt. LeRoy adjusted his belt, his thin upper lip curled, revealing his tight, crowded teeth grinding pink goo. "If I was you, mud man, I wouldn't look so satisfied. Anytime now you should be served notice I'm suing your sorry ass, along with that Injun vet'nary and that crazy Indian Malcomb for sicing that mountain lion on me and shredding my ear." At the mention of mountain lion, Lt. LeRoy's head gave a jerk and his body shuddered. Sweat beaded under his fishhook of a nose.

"Get in line buddy," I said. I found it ironic; I hadn't been a man of property but a few days and already had two lawsuits against me. Next thing you know, people trying to kill me for my money. "I admire your bravery," I continued. "Takes a special kind of courage to not give a damn if you're the laughing stock of the peninsula; broadcasting how stupid you were by buying a dangerous animal and not buying the cage too. I'm sure your militia troop will be inspired to follow you anywhere."

"That's a true god damned lie," said the lieutenant. "No matter though, I got my men trained so they'll follow me into the jaws of hell." The closer he approached the further Hondo backed, teeth bared, away.

I should've let it drop right there. "Not when they hear about that big cat wearing your *'Legend in My Own Mind,'* cap all over creation. Damndest thing. Already been spotted by Shug Norman" — I pulled a name out of the sky — "up near Sequim. A court case would let every-one know that hat is yours and how it was got."

The lieutenant paled. A right-winger and his tough reputation at odds. "That true sergeant, you hear anything about that?" He darted looks around, his glittery eyes lingering long on a big stand of Douglas fir across the road big enough to hide a big cat. A pair of robins in the fir stand trilled a spring mating song.

"Haven't heard that story but I do recollect hearing of a Shug Norman up that ways. Heard he likes to spread rumors." Big Steve coughed into his bent elbow, politely turning away.

Lt. LeRoy took off his new cap and whacked the hound cage. The hounds whimpered. The robins fell silent. "God I hate cats. Sneaky, clawing, watching things. I kill that coug I'm gonna cut off his head and use it as a hat rack."

"I expect that cougar's too smart for you or you'd have him already," I said. Maybe you need some new hounds; some that can deal with an imprinted cougar." I liked the sound of the word imprinted although I still didn't know exactly what it meant.

Lt LeRoy kicked the trailer so hard the Texas license plate rattled. Hondo cringed and dripped slobber. The other hounds huddled for comfort in the far corner. "I've had about enough of you, mud boy. I may not be able to use your head as a hat rack, but I can sure as hell put some lumps on it." He squared off in a karate stance.

Big Steve strolled in between us.

"Get the hell out of the line of fire, sergeant." The officer shifted.

"What the hell's got into you, Lieutenant?" Gabe Moody shouted. "Don't be scaring those hounds before the hunt." He eased around Malcomb and bustled over to us, his chin waddle waddling.

"They're my dogs and I'll do what I damn well . . . with your permission sir, please, with them."

"Damn straight you'll do what you please with your own dogs, as long's it's what I tell you."

"Yes Sir." Lt. LeRoy straightened up; spit a phlegm bullet at my feet.

Gabe wheezed to a stop in front of me. "I owe you an apology Mr. Gravey. Malcomb tells me you're one of us. A local property owner. Got that forty acres of prime timber near the national forest got bugs in it. Needs harvesting bad. I got just the logging outfit can do it. Got an Japanese investment company too, looking for a perfect spot for a basalt rock mine." Gabe stuck out his meaty, liver-spotted hand to me. I took it and immediately regretted it. His hand dwarfed mine and Gabe was a squeezer. Would've like to of been a crusher. Thing is, musicians, even ex-musicians, have strong hands. All those years of rigorous attention to picking and pressing while our peers saunter forth in the world and make something respectable of themselves.

I crushed back at Gabe. "I only own a half of the property and that's tied up in court." Felt like only my lips moved cause my jaws were clinched. Could feel the bones in my hand starting to gnash each other. Nevertheless, Gabe's fierce eyes squinted. A blue vein in his forehead popped up. He reeked of posh cigars, premium booze and cheap clam sauce.

"That's what I heard. You know court cases can take years and the out-of-pocket cost can be exorbitant." Gabe released my hand. It felt stepped on by a rogue rhino.

April said, "Rock mines have been studied already in this valley and been determined that they would drive away the resident elk herd."

"There's six million acres in the Olympic forest," Gabe said. "Let the elk go up there where they damn well belong."

"Right," Lt. LeRoy said. "We were here first. Let them get their own valley."

"I like seeing the elk when I'm fishing on the Dosanomish in the morning," Big Steve said.

"Many of my people rely on the elk for a winter supply of food," Malcomb said.

"That's bullshit Mal," Gabe said. "They can get their meat at the supermarket like the rest of us."

Gabe grabbed my biceps — I clinched — and steered me away from the group. When we got out of hearing range, Gabe said, "Look here Gravey, it's obvious you don't have the stakes for a good lawyer. Why don't you give it up? Make like that herd of elk's got to do. Find another valley. There's plenty of places with a lot more room for you to settle down in besides this little valley."

"I'm beginning to like it here."

"I figured you'd say that," Gabe brought out a fat billfold. He licked his pudgy thumb and extracted a bill from a wad a half-inch thick. Thrust it at me. "This here's a deposit. There's nine more of them if you sign a quick claim deed giving me your timber and mining rights. With that kind of money you can crawl back in the hole you crawled out of."

It was a thousand dollar bill. The outer rim of my synthetic plate flared with a damp heat. "There's some good folks here I'm getting to know," I said, "I'd hate to leave."

Gabe leaned into my face. His breath stank of diseased lungs and mint mouthwash. "If you won't do it for yourself, do it for Miss Molly. After I cut the trees and take the rock out, I'll dedicate a one-acre memorial park to her memory. Make it real pretty and authentic, too, with statues of deers and squirrels and birds; all things Miss Molly loved. Be nothing like it on the peninsula. The poor girl deserves a break in death, she sure didn't get many while she was alive."

A plump tear hung up in a bag of flesh below his left eye. His meaty hand pushed the money against my bony chest.

Altogether, with Inge's ten thousand or twenty thousand, I could have maybe thirty thousand dollars in my pocket and I'm driving down that lonesome highway over the next ridge and down into the next valley not a care in the world. I took my eyes off the green money and looked up at a snow-capped mountain. Clouds circled the tip and a fierce east wind was blowing the snow straight out behind the mountain giving the appearance of white feathers on a ceremonial headdress. I shifted down to the group by the dog trailer. The ditch behind the trailer was overgrown with salmonberry and ocean spray but shallow. Hondo followed me with his eyes. Reminded me of Medusa laying up there on the river, gunshot. Robins in the dark Douglas fir grove set up another spring mating chorus. Hard to keep a good songbird down. Molly Jenkins would never hear another bird song. And Qo-oo-la, all alone out there on the river, injured and confused, while other birds were busy finding nesting mates. My fault he was in the predicament he was in.

Malcomb and Big Steve were standing in between Lt. LeRoy and April. Ahh, April, long, smokey hair bobbing in time with her finger stabbing Big Steve in the chest, giving him holy hell, beautiful. Big Steve with a coon dog grin on his face, probably never set foot off the peninsula and was as lost in his own way as I was.

The raven and gray gull dropped out of a bright sky and landed on an alder branch hanging over the hounds. The raven spotted me and gronked. "Dare you," the gronk sounded like to me.

I smiled at the big money bags and took the greenback. It was light as a loon feather.

Gabe gave a chuckle. "I figured you'd take the money and run. Your kind's got no staying power, no stomach for the long haul."

"Here, what's going on!" he said. "What the hell are you doing?"

I crunched the thousand-dollar bill up in my hand and popped it in my mouth. Yuck! It smelled like crotch sweat and copier fluid; tasted astringent. Even so, I soaked it through with my good traveling saliva.

Gabe's thick eyebrows bunched like a bluff about to break off in an earthquake. "That's my money you crazy bastard." He reached for me.

I ducked, sidestepped and *PETOUEY* spit the gooey mess out in my hand. Had some weight now. "Heads up troops!" I shouted and, all eyes on me, wound up major league style — theory being, if you're going to toss a thousand dollars away do it with panache — and pitched it in the thick Doug fir forest amongst the mating robins. All humans studied the arc and trajectory of the upscale gumball. The robins continued their courtship.

The raven and gull, spotting a reward for vigilance, gave hot pursuit.

Gabe's mouth hung open, showing gold-capped molars. "I'll be damned. That's the damndest thing I ever seen. Well don't just stand there Lieutenant, you and the sergeant go find that thousand-dollar bill before those damn jaybirds get it. It went right through those two biggest trees. And as for you, you ingrate son-of. . . ."

Too late. I ran out of hearing range, hopped into my bus. Fired 'er up and pulled alongside of April and Malcomb. Malcomb as usual, way ahead of me, slid the side door open and stepped in. "I ain't seen a look like that on Gabe Moody's face since I ran the table on him to take first prize in the winter pool tournament."

April, a perplexed look on her face, climbed in the front. "What are you going to do now; turn around and run?"

Lt. LeRoy jumped in front of the bus and held up his hands to stop us.

"Hang on!" I said. I shoved it in first, eased into the shallow ditch, aimed it for the narrow space between a Doug fir and the Jeep Cherokee and tromped it. "Oh crimeny!" April said, grabbed the dash handhold and squeezed her dark lashes shut.

Lt. LeRoy leaped aside into some thimbleberry brambles.

Woody Oregon grape and elderberry canes scraped the metal undercarriage. A stout vine maple limb grated against my window. Malcomb commenced an impromptu chant, designed, I presumed, to lubricate a neck quill through the eye of a needle. We hit the opening, tilted away from the immaculate Jeep Cherokee, my outside mirror thumped the big fir, knocking the mirror flat against the bus's body, bark chips flew, the sweet smell of squeezed pulp flashed by, and, the front part of the bus was heading out the other side when metal caught on metal, twisted us crossways in the ditch — I kept it tromped — I heard a tinny groan, something gave, my bus overcompensated and flipped the other way, out into the road, tilted on two wheels, I turned into the tilt and there was that split-second when it could've either flipped or righted itself. Malcomb lunged to the other side, overbalanced the bus to slam back on four wheels. I let up on the gas and pointed down the road. Looked in the rearview mirror and saw Gabe Moody straddling a polished bumper on the roadway, a nasty gash in the Cherokee's grill, and shaking a fist at me. Lt. LeRoy, hat missing, had his weapon out but sticker vines clung to his arms, thwarting his aim. Big Steve, behind his companions, waved. Hondo, head up, howled the hymn of the hunt. We turned a bend in the road.

Malcomb propped himself up between our front seats, gave my shoulder a pat. "I may be wrong, but I got the impression Gabe Moody took a distinct dislike to you."

April stared straight ahead but I could see a ghost smile on her lovely lips.

38

Old Pictures and Botched Burials

"Stop!" April said, "Back up." We'd turned off the blacktop onto a narrow gravel road, and, after a couple miles passed a driveway blocked with yellow police tape. "You can see the lodge with the big hemlock splitting it down the middle, on the right, through the trees. Beyond that, toward the river, is Kaalpekci Peak. On beyond there, further to the northwest, is where they must have found Billy Moody's body. We need to find a logging road to the left to get up to this cabin. I told the helicopter operator we'd meet him in a clearing, near there, I noticed last summer when flying on a bear cub rescue mission up river."

Once we started looking, it didn't take us long to discover a camouflaged, little used logging road winding into the deep woods. I eased into it, cruising at five mph. The road had been cut four feet deep in places back in the twenties, and sword ferns grew on the banks, their huge fronds lapping over the road, making it seem even more narrow than it was. Low hanging limbs, fat with new buds, slapped the front windshield. The rich, invigorating fragrance of last year's decomposing leaves seeped up through rust holes in the floorboard. I breathed deeply, filling my lungs with composted air. My head cleared. A squirrel barked a warning. Or, was it a greeting?

Suddenly the logging road ended in a grove of alders and maples. I switched off the motor and listened to the forest. Western fly-catchers, mountain chickadees, and spotted towhees in spring mating voice, set-up a syncopated beat. A canyon breeze rubbed the stems of licorice ferns against each other growing up the trunk of a big-leaf maple tree, sounding like soft snare drums, and, underlining it all, faint but unmistakable, was the eternal rhythm of the river.

My legs trembled; afraid to set foot on the soil. Silly I know. Josh's ashes warmed in my hands. I felt a driving need to see how Josh had lived on Kaalpekci Peak and to give his ashes back to the earth. Release him from plastic purgatory. The forest floor felt firm under my feet.

"There's the cabin over there," said April. "Find the key and take a fast look. We're running late. The helicopter is supposed to be at the clearing in fifteen minutes. It's probably through the woods that way a couple hundred feet."

Malcomb climbed out of the bus, looked around and said, "I haven't been in this place since I was a boy. There is something different about it but a can't tell yet whether it's good or evil. I need to summon my spirit power on Kaalpekci Peak. You two have to find Medusa without me. I will stay here and guard the mask and headdress. Remember, the clock is running, the ultimate goal is to find Qo-oo-la before his gizzard grinds up the clue or the sheriff and his posse shoot him. So don't dally." Malcomb marched up a narrow trail toward Kaalpekci Peak and the sound of the Dosanomish.

Josh's cabin looked to be around twelve by twelve, with an upstairs sleeping loft. Old, weathered, barn board 'n' batting siding covered the exterior. The cabin roof was rough-cut, hand-tooled cedar shakes. Last fall's alder and maple leaves cloaked the roof, chimney and window ledges. Wolf lichen, yellow and stringy, hung down from the exposed rafter butts. There was no pigmented paint anywhere. The cabin blended with the forest. You could have walked twenty feet on either side of it and not seen it.

I found the outhouse — also camouflaged with last year's leaves — and looked behind it for the twin-trunk maple tree Josh told me contained the key. Felt around in the knothole and, sure enough, there was a little square box rusted shut. April produced a knife and took the key-box from me. While she pried on the box I moseyed around, getting the feel of the place.

The place was trying to speak to me.

I've been in dozens of towns, houses and barrooms — and bedrooms — where I didn't feel welcome; felt wrong for me. Places, like people, have subtle ways of telling you you're not wanted. I learned to look and listen for the signals and, avoiding prolonged misery, split while still smiling. The message I was getting from Josh's place was troubling. Strange. Unfamiliar. Alien. I couldn't identify it. It was neither unwelcome or indifferent.

The little trail I meandered down skirted a massive old-growth cedar. Dark green boughs hung down like a bad hairdo on a behemoth scale. Limbs, the size of hundred-year second growth, sprouted out of its trunk, then, at ninety degree angles, shot upwards — tree chairs with high backs. A solid, future place to climb-up out of harm's way and rest your weary body and soul. In fact, it appeared some creature had done just that; about seven or eight feet up, in the lap of three parallel limbs, there was a large nest of sorts. Sticks and boughs created a landing. I spotted a patch of dark cloth hanging over the edge. *What was that,* I wondered, *had I found Josh's makeshift tree house?*

I hadn't heard a call from April, so I climbed up the limbs, like stair steps. Each notch revealed deep, ragged rips in the bark. A cloying smell hit me. I hesitated. Inhaled a big whiff. I recognized that tangy fragrance.

I had discovered the lair of the golden ghost; Clancy the cougar's hideout.

I stepped back, considered getting the hell out of there. But no, my nose also told me that Clancy wasn't there at the moment. Wouldn't hurt to take a fast look-see. I stepped up, peeked over the side and saw, clustered in the shadowy light, lots of cloth. Rapid blinked, focusing, and realized I was seeing a clutch of caps and hats; a small pile of headpieces. The big cat had a hat fetish. Imprinting, at its most bizarre.

Lt. LeRoy's, "*Legend In My Own Mind,*" camouflaged cap was on top of the pile, plain as day, not a teeth or claw mark in it.

"I've got the key free," April yelled, "come on, we're running late."

I hopped out of the old-growth cedar and ran to where April had the cabin door open. We peered into the musty damp room. April said, "I once smelled a black bear's den. This stinks just like it."

I sniffed mice piss. I entered and the centerpiece of the small enclosure was a homemade, box-like wood stove, with the name Bunnswarmer bead-welded on the door. The stove had a black cast-iron skillet and a stainless steel teakettle sitting on top of it. Cobwebs connected the two.

There was a cot, a wicker rocking chair and a card table covered with the Sunday Seattle Times newspaper from a year ago. Mouse turds tracked across the front-page cover story of a boating disaster in Puget Sound. Josh cooked with a two-burner Coleman stove and lit the small room with two kerosene lamps hanging on exposed two-by-four studs, reflective tinfoil tacked on the wall behind them. Plain, off-white curtains covered the windows and April pulled them aside. Dust motes filled the stagnant air. The first direct light in almost a year soaked the spartan room. "Man, does this place ever need airing out," said April.

In the fresh light I saw shelves along one wall. There was a stack of bird magazines, a half dozen mystery novels and several thick books on how to build log homes. One titled *The Hand-Built Log Home*, looked well handled and had a tablet-sized notebook stuffed in it. I opened it to a blueprint of a modest log house. On the page, in Josh's handwriting, were the words, "This is the one I'm going to build!"

The notebook fell open and was chock-full of Josh's scribbling and doodlings. Most of the doodlings were of birds. One was a loon. My legs felt weak and I sat down in the wicker rocker. Watched, in a daze as April climb two-by-four steps nailed to the studs, up into a tiny loft. I felt Josh's presence. I held his diary in my hands and was reluctant to read it. He'd last written in the diary months before he met me. A wind rattled the rusted chimney to the cold, Bunnswarmer stove.

I opened the diary to Josh's last entry in a small, unsteady script:

I had another one of those headaches this morning. They're getting worse. Something very strange is happening to my mind. I lose track of time; I opened my eyes a while ago and I was up on the sacred knoll, not knowing how I got there. I'm afraid of getting lost in these woods, which would be okay if I wasn't so worried about the future of this land I've grown to love. While I'm still able to drive, I must get back to Portland and settle my affairs. I've decided to change my will, give the sacred knoll back to. . . .

A ragged scribble raked down the page.

"Oh my God," April called from the sleeping loft. She climbed down the ladder backwards with a framed picture in her hand. "Look at this."

It was Josh sitting on the front steps of the cabin with an Indian woman on his lap. Josh's mouth was open and I could see the tip of his tongue. The woman had an energetic smile and dancing eyes. Festive eyes, full of life and love. Very different than the last time I had seen those eyes. "Jesus, it's Molly Jenkins with Josh," I said.

"I've never seen her look that happy," April said. "Didn't this Josh mention her at all?"

"No, but then he was pretty sick by the time I met him. He did ramble on about me having to share the property with someone else besides his ex-wife."

April cocked an ear. "Listen, here comes the helicopter. We have to go."

I sat the framed photo on the card table and followed April. Stopped. Turned around. Molly Jenkins's eyes followed me. They were no longer dancing. Was it a trick of lighting or did I see moisture on her cheeks?

Malcomb, coming back from Kaalpekci Peak, met us. "Harp, you can't go in the chopper. You have to stay here and put on the mask. Before the chopper drowned them out, I heard Lt. LeRoy's hounds up the valley. They're not after Medusa, they're after Qo-oo-la and he's coming down the river."

"But, Medusa needs me."

"My daughter is a gifted veterinarian, if Medusa can be saved, she will do it."

April studied her father's face. "Since when have you started giving me credit for healing expertise? But, Father's right. You must save the loon. I'm getting as crazy as you two but we need more of a plan than just playing it by ear. Father you do the transformation with Harp in the bus and then take the bus back to the clinic. I'll have the hel . . . chopper take me and Medusa there after I pick her up. I'll do what I can for Medusa and then take the bus to the mud-bog on the Dosanomish where we first met and wait for Qo-oo-la. I'll wait on the river bank 'til dark."

The chopper vibrated overhead. Tree limbs shook and dry leaves swirled around us. April's lips continued to move but I couldn't hear her. April got her brown medical bag out of the bus, gave me a peck on the cheek and took off running after the chopper. I stuck my tongue against the inside of the kiss and felt warmth spread though out my mouth. My fingertips tingled, wanting to press pliant strings against sensuous necks again. April's black bag had been sitting on Josh's ashes. I picked up the plastic container. Josh shifted inside. The box had warmed from April's bag sitting on top of it. "Something tells me I need to put these ashes on Kaalpekci Peak now," I said. "I'll only take a minute. Who knows when I'll get another chance?"

Being so close, I wanted to see the river. No, more than that; I felt pulled to the sound of the rhythmic running water. Merely a few days ago I felt repelled by it. My legs headed up the narrow path to Kaalpekci Peak. Malcomb followed.

We rounded a boulder the size of a tugboat and climbed out of the dark forest onto a naturally lighted rock landing. Lemon yellow clouds dotted the blue sky. The clearing was about forty feet in diameter and the surface of the rock was soft with a thick green moss, like walking on a quality carpet. Growing right out of the moss carpet, a spreading manzanita shrub, with dozens of reddish brown twisting trunks, covered a third of the clearing. The evergreen branches of the manzanita were woven together with budding wild honeysuckle. The moss squished as we navigated a narrow path through the shrubs and skirted the steep landslide area — the missing tooth as seen from Qo-oo-la's eyes from the middle of the river, that deposited the big boulders in the river — to the bluff's edge. On the edge of the bluff, the roar of the river hit me.

Most of the deafening noise projecting upward from the river came from the massive, twisted logjam where Qo-oo-la had found Molly Jenkins.

Malcomb laid a hand on my shoulder. "Hurry," he said, "allow your friend to join the other ghosts in this place. You must take care of the living."

I couldn't seem to work the hasp on the plastic box. The chopper, heading upriver, buzzed us, I flinched and the box jumped out of my hands. I grabbed for it, Malcomb grabbed me. Josh, still imprisoned in plastic, hit a stone protuberance, arced away from the cliff and tumbled down, down, down to splash beside a boulder sticking out of the water.

Malcomb dragged me back from the bluff's edge. He threw his head back, closed his eyes and commenced to chant a burial dirge. The chopper, winding its way up the valley following the river channel, looked like a dragonfly silhouetted against the snowcapped Olympic Mountains. Suddenly, the chopper dropped, disappeared from view. My heart leaped; had they already found Medusa?

A thunderbird, from way across the canyon perched on her stick nest high atop a fir tree, looked up from feeding her young; see who was invading her territory. Malcomb's dirge lasted about half a minute. "Well," said Malcomb, "your friend almost got his wish. At least he's close to Kaalpekci Peak. Come let us conjure spirits."

"I promised Josh I'd spread his ashes," I said. "I'm not done with him yet." Without another word, we loped back to the bus and I donned the hair hat and mask. I lay down on the foam rubber mattress and closed my eyes.

I heard Malcomb say, "I'm going to take the bus back to the animal hospital to meet April and. . . ." I stopped listening. Well, true to form, I had botched Josh's burial. He now lay squeezed in a plastic box amongst the landslide boulders with scary faces etched on them. Josh's spirit would not rest like that. Neither would mine. Someday I would find the box and either retrieve it or open it.

I needed to forget about Josh for now. Prepare for another journey into the great unknown. Physically I was stronger than the other three times, but still my mind and body resisted the change. Abnormal fears clutched my chest. Where the hell was Qo-oo-la? What if he was already in the jaws of some animal or shot by Gabe's Goons? This time there was no pain, only darkness, the sound of water falls, the smell of skillet-fried onions and something moving at an incredible speed. It was me. I was gone.

I was there.

39

Liquid Sunshine and Loon Love

Discombobulated. Punchy. Those transmigration passages bumpy as a ride on a hand truck. Scary part anymore is not the trip but arriving. Never can tell what'll be waiting for me.

I felt the secure feel of deep water underneath me. I bobbed on the river facing east. But where on the river exactly was I? Location! Location! Location! The lemon yellow clouds were way down the valley and the sky had a bleached-washed blueness to it. Errant gray clouds, out of place in that blue skyscape, hung low, clogging the tops of firs on flanking hills.

I was starting to get the lay of the land, could tell by the pattern of tree scalping on the nearest mountain I was down river from where I had last left my loon body, upriver from where I last left my human body. Cool, spring cadis flies glided above the surface of the Dosanomish, pure feel of water underneath me. I swept into a grade two rapids. Whoa! Powerful current dragged me past small sandy islands, into a deeper pool shaded by tall cottonwoods. Settled under vine maples reaching over the water, their twisted limbs tipped with dozens of miniature pale green parachute leaves. Just a few days ago the vine maple leaves were still in bud form. Spring tromping on in spite of cold damp weather, marching to nature's irresistible drummer.

By some intuitive communication between man spirit and bird spirit, I understood I'd left Medusa that morning. Alive. The imprinted cougar looking after her. And me, Qo-oo-la, unfilleted by the cougar's claws.

My mouth . . . ah, bill tasted of fresh fish, been feeding, stomach full. Gizzard functioning full tilt, grinding away, busy erasing murder clue. My efficient body rejecting man made foreign object. Not compatible with wildlife. I don't get that pop metal pin identified pretty soon all traces of logo will be gone.

Nothing could be simpler now. Point down river, stay to the shadows or underwater all the way. Rendezvous with April. Piece of cake.

Did a quick three hundred sixty degree turn. Just me and my loon shadow. Alone again, with each other. Trying to balance emotion and intellect. Harp frightened senseless, Qo-oo-la confused but stalwart, as long as he's got plenty of water to roam and poke and play around in, he's as secure as any bird can be. Unworried about not being able to fly, doing what he can with what he's got.

Over the rhythmic pulse of the Dosanomish I heard, way in the distance, the syncopated bay of Lt. LeRoy's walker hounds, that bugling male, Hondo, in the lead. Hard to tell what direction the sound came from because of the echo in the small valley surrounded by mountains. Also, off in the distance I heard the helicopter. It was getting closer. It passed over at full speed heading in the direction of April's Clinic. I prayed Medusa was on board.

Thunderbird gave chase until the chopper disappeared behind a clump of cottonwoods.

I had a moment of peace and quiet and decided to check out my basic body parts. By swiveling my head and crossing my red eyes I could see reflected in the water a thin scarlet scab line where the eagle's talons had torn my scalp. Unlike Harp, I did not have a receding hairline. Might as well get it over with, couldn't resist sneaking a peek at the old loon profile too. Eyes red as Chanticleer's crown, beak black and sharp. I stretched my long dusky neck, admired my natural necklace, alabaster pearls on a satin black format. Flapped wings, okay but chest muscles too tight to fly. Might try in a pinch but why bother? My compact little bird body was mending fast. Water's my element. My raccoon smacking athletic legs, while ugly as two cast iron pokers in a petunia patch, were in fine physical shape, kicking, pumping, revved and ready to roll down that long liquid highway. Got a rendezvous with a beautiful veterinarian underneath a bridge of Jefferson county. Too bad romance, thanks to Elpenor, will not be in the offing.

Must concentrate on task at hand. How do I get from here to there avoiding hunters and hounds, oh and let's not forget hungry natural predators. Still midday, get there by nightfall. What's to stop me now?

Before I had a chance to get out of the starting gate, I noticed a black speck in the sky flying overhead. I swam out from under my little vine maple blind to get a better look. High clouds, thin and off-white, like waves, as a backdrop, caused the speck to appear to rise and fall, up and down, in and out, a syncopated rhythm. The speck veered, angled down, growing, pulsating, heading toward me. From the distance I could tell it wasn't that scurvy eagle, not an elegant or arrogant enough flyer. I slunk under the roots of a western red cedar, more protection than vine maples. Peek-a-boo, I see you. Could be a red-tailed hawk. Definitely coming my way. Concluded, I'd been spotted. Couldn't wait around for recognition. I hit the deep. No feathered predator could out maneuver me in water. They don't call me Diver for nothing. Water's clearer and less runoff sediment. Except for slight waviness I could see as good as on the surface. Scaly larvae of cadis flies clinging to round river rock on bottom. Curious, unlike Harp who clenched his eyes shut tight, I keep my eyes wide open under water. That Harp, laughable almost, his preternatural fear of deep water. So unlike me.

But wait! What was that splash up river? Too far to get a good look. My injured prey instincts counseled me to run or hide. My curiosity got the better of me. Underwater, I sliced toward the intruder.

Strange feet dangling, pedaling leisurely, almost languidly, not a care in the world. No hungry predator here. Some damn duck doesn't have enough sense to be afraid. Hips too far back from the middle of an avian body. Awkward damn arrangement, impossible to walk on land. Get overbalanced. Another belly skidder. Felt sorry for the poor mutated creature. Destined to be condemned forever to water. Hold on here! I've seen those stick stumps and webbed, waddly toes before. And not too long ago either. It hit me! They're mine! Or rather just like mine. Another loon had landed.

I ejected out of the water to greet my brother. Let out a loon hoot of recognition. My brother rode out the wake of my eruption then turned his head away from me and started to sail by as if I didn't exist. Close enough though to brush slightly against me and darned if he didn't nip me on the neck. Such effrontery! Pretty rude manner in which to greet a brethren. That's when I made a significant discovery; he wasn't a brethren at all, but a sistern. Well, not exactly a sister either. In fact, anything but a sister.

Kinda cute too, in a red-eyed, slink-necked, black & white, shoebox kinda way. If you happen to be attracted to the type. Which had never exactly gotten my testosterone attention before. She stopped a few feet in front of me, bobbed up and down, rocked to and fro, her little tail dipping in water and flicking warm spray on me. Must be an underground hot spring up river, water sure heated up all of a sudden.

She pivoted, threw me a demure glance, stuck a shapely leg out of the water and stroked it with her beak, slow and suggestive. I was flabbergasted. Didn't know better I'd say she was flirting with me. Pesky insects buzzing furiously around my head, muddling my mind. Sunrays bursting through rifts in the forest canopy, thick, steamy shafts of cage-like surreality.

Pretty preposterous situation here. Quite amusing too. She was adorable and yes kinda sexy but she was way out of her element. Hadn't a clue to just what sorta man of the world kinda loon she was dealing with. Quaint really, to think I was going to fall for the old webbed foot behind the neck come-on. Come on. Brazen as it was. Maddening.

I decided to nip this game in the bud before it got out of hand and twirled around to face down river away from licentious entreaties and, felt so lightweight buoyant that I spun half a dozen times in rapid succession, the shore line a green blur, my ears clattering and booming, before I was able to wind to a halt. Whew! What was that all about?

Get control of yourself Harp P. Gravey, you're wasting valuable time, must keep ultimate mission uppermost in mind, whatever it is. This Lady Loon could be a dangerous distraction. End up forgetting just who and how important you are and what you're about. No time for cheap fling, I had an important rendezvous with destiny. Let's see now, who the hell was I supposed to meet at the bridge? What was her name? This sweltering heat let up I could think. Sunlight bars, opaque as huckleberry jelly, imprisoned me in a rainbow-barred cage. Oh yes, her name was April, April damnit, the beautiful captivating April, April with whom I have vowed to remain most pure, chaste and faithful to, for the rest of my born days.

Why then was my heart thumping like a rabbit in a hollow stump, as if it desired to rupture my rib cage? My beak moist and sticky like I'd swallowed a plump slug. Gizzard gnashed mercilessly, granulating to shapeless dust the pop-metal murder clue, as loud as the midnight shift at a ten mule and pestle flour mill, drumming out the rhythm of river rapids pointing downstream to April.

My body was on fire but I felt like I was drowning, drowning, drowning.

The sun burst through a laundered cloud and drenched me with heavy light, capturing colors — red, blue and green — of insect bodies swirling around me, all droning in time with my thundering heart. Confusing, dizzying, sweltering.

Suspected I'd had an evil spell cast on me and had to break free. With all the will I could summon, I recoiled, ready to dive and get the hell out of there while I was still in control, when, behind me, she uttered a soft yodel, just a little yodel, a yodel that would hardly flutter a feather, a yodel that would've fallen flat on the Grand Ol' Opry. That voice froze me. Locked my muscles in liquid sunshine. I couldn't move, couldn't think, couldn't hear anything else. Could no more resist that subterranean call of the wild than a twelve year old could resist puberty. It was the call of Juliet to Romeo, of Cleopatra to Anthony; it was the irresistible call to perpetuate the species. And boy, was I listening down to my smallest pinfeather. My perpetuator, of its own device, poised and ready for service. Doing my unrewarding yet faithful duty to dispel the curse of extinction.

Only sensible thing to do at a time like this: Skip out of the water and propel about the pool like some throttle-stuck, everglades hydroplane. Ululating dementedly, recklessly abandoning all sentinel caution. Now, even before my knock on the head, I'd never been much of a supporter of sanity but this business of acting like a damn fool loon in front of a pretty feather stretched the limits of my tolerance.

Remembered as a kid showing off for Dixie Lee Rayfield by standing on my head on bicycle handlebars. Hit the bridge abutment over Coon Creek and tumbled onto the rock infested dry creek bed below. Broke my collarbone as well as my concentration. Humiliated and injured and to no avail; Dixie Lee went downstream and played sticky fingers with Alvin Bell Hazeykamp. Vowed never to expose my intentions with such daredevilry again.

Alas, chalk that one up as another unkept commitment. I, Qo-oola, unable to stop myself, had lost all shame. I burned with the urge to convince this female I was the best dancer and singer ever to serenade and pirouette down the pike. I hopped, I leaped, I curtseyed and flipped; cantillated, crooned, warbled and dipped. Now I know where rock musicians get their inspiration. And If I ever get back on stage gonna change my technique. There was no stopping, a genetic button had been flicked and I was on my way, out of my ever-loving fucking gourd.

A part of me, obviously a very subservient part, heard that big walker hound's baying closer, but hey, what did I care? Clumsy landlubber. My mind shoved the sound in a corner and slammed shut an insulated door. Stuff that noise! Don't tell me about it and don't open 'til fall. Right then the survival song drumming in my head had a bottom-end base line overpowering the thin high-end running-scared melody. Only thing remotely interested in run, run, running away was my pulsating heart.

For the moment the female loon, Gavia — how I knew her name I don't know — ignored me; nay, disdained and scorned me is more like it. Now that she had my full attention, had set the hook, had my quirky chromosomes impaled, she could've cared less. Satin black beak in the air, tail, so recently dousing hot spray on me with a fetching flick, tilted down as if never a thought of temptation, and sailing away upriver from me. I, without the slightest reservation, in hot pursuit. Thinks she can toy with me does she? Two can play this game. Check out these moves honey; ever see such a virtual monsoon of motion? Slow down. Come back here.

Gavia dodged. I over shot. Zigzagged. I plowed a wet, dry furrow. It seemed to be some kind of elaborate foreplay ritual. Of course, from my enlightened vantagepoint, I could see right through it. I am, after all, a loon of some distinction, a loon who has been around the flock a few times, a sophisticated loon with humanoid credentials. I didn't just fall off a fish wagon. If she really wanted to be quit of me she could take flight. Fact was she was crazy about me. And why shouldn't she be? Embarrassment aside, I admit in all modesty, I had developed some pretty righteous moves.

Gavia too, had some subtle but undeniably raunchy moves. Her silken neck never stopped rotating from side to side, a blues rhythm, always keeping one ribald red eyeball on me. Those eyes, those sultry scarlet orbs, those beacons from beyond the pale, hypnotized and magnetized me. Inviting me to participate in pleasures untold. Her sculpted back and sybaritic tail bobbing and dipping, leading me on a lavish chase. During one dodge I caught a glimpse of the bright flesh on the inside of her lovely gray flanks. I stuck to her like glue. No pull-toy, with a connecting string, ever followed so faithfully.

But, at the risk of sounding new-age, it was her mind I most admired, that most captivated me. Such a mind! Such a mind! Gavia's mind had somehow locked onto mine. No, that's not quite it. Her mind and my mind had become joined, engulfed in the same fire, intertwined in a mental mating dance, as our bodies were boogying to a physical beat. Her cooing voice, husky and steamy, the flame that mentally melted us together.

Suddenly, as if from a mutual signal, we both leaped out of the water and commenced racing, with tiny fast steps, side by side, across the top of the Dosanomish. I'm not making any comparisons or, heaven forbid calling forth any religious significance, but I know now, if you have powerful piston legs, and heated hormones, it is possible to walk on water.

Suddenly Gavia stopped. Run aground on an island sandbar. I was on top of her before I knew it. Clumsy, confused, what was happening? Could be hurting her, started to back off, ran into resistance from her upturned tush. I took one look at that curvaceous posterior and gave up any humanoid semi-intellectual hesitation. Species survival took over. Good by safe sex.

Hello innocence. I, Qo-oo-la, was at a loss at how to consummate. How embarrassing for Harp, an ingrate recipient of groupie love since age nineteen. Qo-oo-la was, I blush, a virgin. Spent the last three years in the ocean gaining strength and maturity enough for this moment and now at a total loss as to . . . ahem . . . how the damn thing fit. Where the hell do I plug in this throbbing perpetuator?

Gavia too was pure as the driven snow. Her first time as well. Here we were, on the sandy banks of a rushing river, spring sunshine warming our backs, naked; it was the stuff — discounting the loon angle — of epic romance and lust and neither of us had a clue of what to do. Oh we had the wooing and the courting down, it was this last little detail that confounded and perplexed us.

I labored mindlessly, ramming her exposed bottom. Gavia turned an unfocused red eye on me, sexy neck bob, bob, bobbing to the beat of some inner gland; and I swear Gavia was humming some primordial melody for mine ears only. Suddenly my body fused with hers. And ignited. Gavia yodeled. I hooted with exaltation, trumpeting hallelujah to the heavens.

After a quarter hour of bodacious aquatic foreplay the actual landed mating took . . . oh . . . hmmm . . . maybe all of ten seconds. But what a ten seconds! Ten seconds of ecstasy, ten seconds of experiencing the ultimate connection with nature, ten seconds in which I almost understood the origin of the universe. Almost.

And ten seconds in which I had no response from Elpenor. Not in the foreplay either. I had discovered the secret of getting my human emotional and sexual needs met without interference from a belittling dragon, avian love. It was a sensuous breakthrough.

Consummated, I ejected backwards, plunged in cool water, snuffed the flame, and the flamethrower.

When I emerged, the lovely Gavia only had eyes for me. What can I say, must have been as good for her as it was for me. Gavia rubbed her long neck against mine, stroked my legs underwater with her exquisite webbed foot and waddly toes. My body tingled, I ate it up. Ritualistic after play.

We floated aimlessly, petting and snuggling. Oblivious to the world around us. Mentally we shared a vision of a happy home, a little mountain lake nest, nothing fancy you know; some red alder sticks for color and ballast, vine maple for elasticity and bounce, eel-grass for strength and just a touch of security nastiness, and old man's beard lichen for comfort and warmth. Frogs and crickets croaking and chirping, singing us a song of domesticity, in stereo. Thunderbird fishing off our front porch, close friends in a friendly neighborhood.

Perhaps some of Gavia's precious breast feathers woven in for that indefinable personal touch. Frivolous, you say? *Tres Chic?* A bit too decorative? Well maybe the feathers are going too far, unnecessary, but who amongst you has not adorned your abode with bright trinkets?

Reflected a moment on those quickie Reno marriages. Performed by an imitation Elvis. How I had scoffed at them. Ridiculous and impulsive. Testosterone overload. Never last. Doomed to failure. And yet, there I was contemplating eternal fidelity to a female I had met thirty minutes before. If my old cronies in Portland could see me now probably wouldn't recognize the former ardent bachelor. Worse yet, visions of shiny brown-speckled eggs danced in my head. Witnessing, camcorder cocked and ready, the blessed event, a hatching. Picking sticky eggshells off helpless, darling chicks. Perfect in every way. I longed to hear the ululation of little yodelers.

Gavia, my love, my mate, my pastime, by a subtle signal involving body movements known only to us loons, (if it must be known, she stuck her tail feathers in my ear, drove me nuts) wanted to mate again. My body responded, burned instantly. I found myself to be in a totally cooperative frame of mind; a male doing his obliging duty to please a demanding oversexed female. Way I felt, with snuggle pauses, this could go on all day. Ten seconds ain't no quickie if you multiply it by twenty or so.

Gavia sashayed around to face me, fixed me with one bright, red eye and cast a come-hither look that I could only interpret in human terms as, "I'll race you to the hot tub." Oh well, if you insist. We lit out like train cars on a three mile downhill grade sans brakes.

With only a few yards to go to connubial bliss, Gavia yipped and dived. More foreplay games eh? And what kind of kinky love-yip was that? Signaling underwater sex? Sounded more like an alarm horn. "You'll never get away from me my little checkerboard beauty," I said, and dived after her.

40

Hell Hounds and Lost Heaven

Something lunged over top of me. I didn't at first recognize it but it was huge and it was fast and it had teeth like porch supports. It smacked the water above me. Gavia up ahead, churning for all she's worth for other side of the pool. I did a loop-de-loop, recognized underbelly of a hound dog. That big, red-bone beast, Hondo, pedaling awkwardly in my turf, unaware that he'd committed a bad case of *coitus interruptus*. Fear passed, chafe arrived. There is a time and place — apologies to the spirit of the song "Ya Gotta Quit Kicking My Dog Around" — to kick some dog butt.

I stared at the soft underbelly of the great macho landlubber Hondo (I had only been a water animal for a few days and I already disdained landlubbers), choosing my target. Teach that sucker a lesson; stay in your own territory. Surprising the power surge I felt. I relished it. Hondo's throat exposed, easiest thing in the world to pierce it and severe his jugular. Or how about a straight to the heart shot? Pop that organ like toothpick to an ear tic. Naw, too much blood. The gonads now, hanging helplessly, would be a fitting touch. But then again that rank briny aftertaste lingers in the beak a long time.

So clever and hormone driven was I, I missed the connection between hound and hunter.

Though bursting with testosterone, who was I kidding. Neither Harp nor Qo-oo-la had a bloodlust let alone a killer's instinct. A hound does what a hound does. Can't blame a dog for being a dog. Even if the said dog would think nothing of severing your spine. Nothing to stop me from having a little fun. Shun vital organs. Slow em down. See how he likes the tables turned. I attacked. Latched onto the pad of his hind paw and ripped a piece of meat out of it. He howled like a monkey and dived, fangs bared, for me. I dodged out of range — I knew exactly how far that was — then floated a couple inches in front of his face so he could get a good look at me. This easy prey turned into his worse nightmare, probably hadn't seen too many attack loons before. I tweaked his spongy black nose. His eyes nearly crossed with rage. "Oh, that pisses you off does it? How aggravating of me. So very sorry oh great baying beast of the hunt. Perhaps I've misinterpreted your intentions, why don't we take a little swim together and you can explain them in detail." This time I grabbed his tender snooze and locked jaws. Infuriated him so, I thought he was going to have an apoplectic fit, forgot he was underwater. The prey has got me by the nose boys, hurry and send in backup. Ol' Hondo jerked and jacked and lunged for me and got nothing for his troubles but a mouthful of river water. His distemper didn't last long. Animated into panic, lungs sucking water, he propelled toward the surface. And didn't get nowhere without his nose. His ass paddled upwards, hysteria in his eyes, I held onto his churning body a couple more seconds just to give him something more to dream about when he retires to the back porch, then released, with one more for-the-road righteous tweak of his bruised whiffer. See how good a tracker he is sporting the equivalent of an organic muzzle.

He limped to the surface; head broke water sputtering, feet pedaling weakly. Perhaps I was too hard on him. The shore was only a few feet away but it didn't look like he could make it. Could barely keep his head above water. Drowning. I sympathized with him. Been there. Harp P. Gravey's a lousy swimmer too. I darted underneath him and gave him a boost to where his paws reached river rock. I was getting pretty good at preventing dogs from drowning. Start my own canine rescue unit.

Hondo stumbled ashore, coughing and hacking. Collapsed. He rolled over on his side, glassy mucus streaming out of his nose, which had already swelled to the size of a Townsend chipmunk. The pack of hounds burst out of the forest and surrounded their fallen leader, whimpering, confused. Their snouts sniffing and peering into the murky depths of water for some hint of an answer. Landlubbers. Hardly a threat.

I stayed deep though, just out of eyesight. I'd done all I could there, time to locate Gavia, sooth her downy brow, allay her feathery fears. Guide her through the treacherous rapids to find another secluded romantic spot for amour. All that nose tweaking activates the juices.

How long had I been underwater? Three . . . four minutes? I ducked between some vine maple branches hanging over the water and surfaced for a deep breath. New pale green leaves hid me but I felt exposed and vulnerable. Took a fast peek at the dog pack, still milling about the bank on the other side. Their leader down, they waited for directions. Needed some frail human to tell them what to do. Humans? Back there somewhere. Gabe Moody and Lt. LeRoy.

A dry wind blew across the shallow waters, causing the new parachute leaves of the vine maple to temporarily close, trapping an unsuspecting gnat. Dust, from underneath a rocky overhang, coated the pale green moist leaves, turning them gray and droopy. A kingfisher chattered maniacally, dipped a frantic wing at me and disappeared in the branches of a cottonwood upriver. The dry wind quit and the leaves opened revealing the crushed gnat stuck to a petal. An insect's life more ephemeral than a loon's. I dived again.

I found Gavia cringing beneath some red cedar roots, long neck extended to give me a quick utility caress with no nonsense to it and no foreplay hinted at. Shook-up but solid lady. Red eye to red eye, an inch apart, her communication wasn't hard at all to decipher: "Something there is lurking about trying to kill us. Let's vacate this death trap."

Couldn't of anticipated my sentiments any better if we'd been together fifty years instead of fifty minutes. At long last a mate that has the good sense to agree with me. I faced down river, "Follow me my love and I'll guide you through the wilderness," I shot out under water like a straight arrow, Galahad breaking trail. Beeline for the bridge but if a convenient little hide-a-way shows itself, well then we can stop for some afternoon delight. Way I felt could perform all night. All that dog fighting making me horny.

Sensed I had no follower. I circled back to where Gavia waited, a stubborn tilt to her black beak; a look in her eye would topple one of *The Standing People,* feathers hunched, tight with dissension. I flipped my head indicating to follow me. She flipped back negative. She wanted to take wing, fly out. Our first argument. Sweet, the way her long neck cocked to one side when angry. And over such a self-evident thing. I had a couple of good reasons for not wanting to fly, I just couldn't think of them. Brain addled with easy sex.

Oh yes, I needed some healing time. I probably could fly but why take a chance of causing permanent damage to my chest. Gavia not accepting. There was another reason too. More important but it wouldn't come to me, flitting about the transformational debris in my brain. The reason stayed buried but of a sudden my body quailed with apprehension. Some hideous reflexive knowledge about the above world permeated my heart and made it thump like a washtub base. All that water and my mouth felt dry and tinny, chewing on sardine cans. My non-existent arms wanted (needed) to grab Gavia and hold her fast, stroke her glorious back with phantom hands, keep her forever from evil.

Gavia made up her mind, clicked my beak with hers, stroked my neck, then, to her the course of action settled, torpedoed, at a forty five degree angle toward the surface. I hesitated, her wake rushing over me, washing away resistance, I couldn't deny her, I had to follow, the survival of the species was at stake.

By the time I'd made up my mind to follow Gavia to the end of the earth, she was high-stepping it across the surface runway, on her long take-off process. Underneath, I admired her supple flanks and powerful hips. My, what a wonderful strong mother she was going to be. No doubt in my mind that our offspring would be the most beautiful and healthy chicks in the known galaxy. And what a lucky bloke I was that she chose me as her lover.

Without another minute to lose, I shot after the galvanizing Gavia, testosterone level high enough to pressure cook cracked corn.

Gavia lifted off; off to that lakeside nest, off to lay dappled eggs and nurture inquisitive chicks, off to perpetuate sixty millions years of living in harmony with the universe.

A sound . . . three of them, underwater, came to me as an explosion muffled, distorted and disjointed, not of this world. I instinctively aborted inches before I reached the surface and raced in Gavia's direction under water, praying she was okay. Her body, seconds before, so perfect in every way, slammed into the water, a broken and bloody, misshapen heap. She flopped and fluttered, a hint of life left.

A sea of red engulfed me as I approached my love, one wing blown to smithereens, the other flopping out of sync, shapely legs shattered and twisted, a mangled hole in her magnificent checkerboard breast. She had taken several shotgun blasts dead center. Gavia's sculpted head hung down, she recognized me, greeted me, glad to see me, signaled, what happened to me? Am I home yet? Will you love me always? Watch out for coyote, don't let him get my babies. Did I implode from too much love?

I cradled her head with my neck; one red eyeball was leaking color into the water.

I babbled too: "Please forgive me my sweet love. I should never of gotten you into this mess, should have ignored you, sent you on your way." Gavia gasped, her wing quit flopping, shattered legs relaxed, the sinew of skin holding onto one webbed foot let loose and the current grabbed the part and carried waddly toes down river like an autumn leaf.

I only had seconds. A great calm came over me. A voice from deep inside me transmitted, "I promise to live the rest of my life in such a way so as to honor your memory. I will honor also your People, the Bird People and play my part in the scheme of things to the best of my ability. I will no longer deny and will, in fact, embrace Loondomness, never be ashamed of it and never dishonor it and always protect and defend my fellow creatures right to live in harmony with Mother Nature."

Gavia gave my neck necklace a love bite. Held it for a second. With the last of her strength, she tensed. Shuddered.

And died.

Something, an energy, a soul, a wondrous gift, lifted out of her body and passed into mine. A foreign invader, unfamiliar, alien, then acceptance. It was the gift of pure love, untainted and uncomplicated; I felt the ghost of my mother and GrandFather Two-Loons saturate me. I bathed in it, held it for only seconds. It washed me clean, then faded.

Stunned, I stroked Gavia's limp neck with mine. The knowledge of her death came back to me and, although the sting had been taken out, sadness seeped in.

Splashing noises also penetrated my mourning. Underwater, I saw a strange sight paddling toward us. Three sets of four legs apiece. Dogs! It dawned on me. Going to rip and tear what's left of her. I tried to drag Gavia's bloody body out of harms way but one of the scurvy hounds locked jaws on her hip; and circled, carrying her body back to their masters, a good retriever.

I needed air. And quick. I darted to the far bank, and again surfaced under cover from a branch of a vine maple. Didn't completely surface, but did catch the sound of human voices shouting encouragement to hounds from the other bank. Taking a real chance by staying above water for any length of time but I wanted a look at Gavia's executioners. There were four of them; I made out Big Steve, Lt. LeRoy, Gabe Moody and Sheriff Gloeckler. All had guns at rest, which meant they weren't looking for another target. Hadn't seen me. Attention focused on hounds.

I surveyed the opposite bank, spotted some log debris caught in an eddy about twenty feet from the killers. Dived, hugged the river bottom and emerged behind the debris, just my head, within earshot.

The lead hound waded ashore and dropped Gavia's body at Lt. LeRoy's feet. The militia officer picked it up by one shattered leg and, holding it at arms length, snapped his fish knife open. Sheriff Gloeckler grabbed

Gavia's body away from Lt. LeRoy. "There'll be no messing with evidence in the field. I'm taking this carcass to the lab." He did a quick inspection and snorted with disgust. "Jesus! Which one of you isn't using birdshot? Half its body is blown away." The sheriff drew a plastic sack out of his knapsack and dropped Gavia's body in.

"Why don't you just operate on its gizzard here, slice it open," Gabe Moody said. "See if that Viet Vet knew what he was talking about. Clear this up once and for all. Probably some Indian trinket belonged to Loren Old Wolf. Put another nail in his coffin."

Lt. LeRoy said, "What if it was a nugget of gold? We could all stake claims and — "

"Don't be stupid," Gabe said, "there's never been an ounce of gold hauled out of the Dosanomish."

Sheriff Gloeckler said, "This might be a close trial. We really don't have much evidence against Loren other than twenty people heard him say he was going to kill Billy and he doesn't have an alibi. We can't prove the twenty-two pistol found with him is the murder weapon. I once lost a verdict down in L.A. because of improper police procedure with evidence. That won't happen here. I'll put a rush on it at forensics. Won't hurt to wait 'til tomorrow to see if this bird's got a clue in its craw." Sheriff Gloeckler had a red bandanna wiping the blood and feathers off his hands.

Big Steve stooped down to sooth Hondo. "We need to get Hondo to a vet. He's hurt and confused. Thinks there's still something out there." He stared out over the water. "I've fished this river dozens of times and it's not the same river it used to be. Something's different. Something's out there."

Gabe snorted, his red chins flopping. "Whatever got a hold of his nose and paw could still be out there. Maybe it's the Dosanomish river dragon old Malcomb Old Wolf blabbers about when I whip his ass at pool. Thinks one of his ancestors was killed by it."

Sheriff Gloeckler put his red handkerchief in his back pocket. "Let's get out of here, get this evidence back to the lab while it's still warm," he said. "I've got to see how my Barbie Jane is doing. She hates being alone."

Big Steve handed his gun to Lt. LeRoy and threw the sixty five pound injured dog over his shoulders like a winter shawl. The four hunters headed back to civilization. From his elevated position, Hondo, though hurting, scanned the Dosanomish, pure hate in his hard eyes projecting around a bulbous nose.

Blame it on revenge, blame it on cantankerousness, or you can call it devilment if you've a mind to, but I couldn't resist allowing ol' Hondo — the indirect cause of Gavia's murder — a peek at me.

I surfaced in plain view and shot Hondo the equivalent of sticking your tongue out and hollering "Nay, nay, na nah naa," or, if you prefer, flipping him the bird. Took some doing but who better to approximate that anatomically complicated feat than a common loon.

Hondo was one outraged hound. Howled his head off as he disappeared into the forest.

I was alone. Danger gone, I absorbed the full impact of Gavia's murder. She — her body — was headed to be dissected on a surgeon's table. Alone with my guilt. It was all my fault. How, in only a few short days, did I go from barely being responsible for my own existence, to having the power of life and death over other beings? It wasn't fair. Self-pity set in like a swamp mosquito swarm.

I allowed my body to become an anvil, sink to the bottom and settle on a round river rock. The current down there weighty and insistent, rough against my raw feathers, sandpaper. Little green, blue and red colored trout, sensing I wasn't in the mood for lunch, swam around me with impunity. Simple creatures; what did they know of lost love? Perhaps, I reasoned, if I held my breath long enough my lungs would burst and I would be quit of this awesome pain. That gnawing in my gizzard a reminder I/we still had a murder clue to deliver. And only two and a half more days to do it. Maybe I could stop the process. Challenge my gizzard to stop grinding.

Grinding gizzard stop! No go. Gizzard had a mind of its own, erasing murder clue even as I lay dying in self-pity.

I didn't much care about anything any more. Let the humans solve the murders. But wait. If I died, what would happen to Mr. Harp P. Gravey laying all safe and secure behind his magic mask, two-loon sweatshirt, and silly hat? Would he too cease to exist? Or would he be better off, remember me as only a blank spot or a bad dream.

Hard enough thinking for one, too much of a burden thinking for two entities.

That damn voice spoke to me again, *"You have a need to mourn Gavia. Quit thinking and quit avoiding it. Let it out and let it go. The sooner you mourn, the sooner you can end this journey and keep anyone else from getting killed."* I don't much care for edicts on high but this one triggered a sympathetic response. No loon was ever so alone. My body jerked and convulsed.

I cried. I cried 'til my eyes clouded over, leaked blood. And when I couldn't stay submerged any longer, I charged to the surface and wailed; wailed to the ancient Changer God, wailed to the Spirit Lord of Sorrow, be damned hounds and hunters. The sounds that came out of me were neither loon nor human but some half-breed hybrid voice, some mongrel mutt moan, some bastard dirge.

I had created a voice never before heard, at least in this century, on this earth, my beak a mighty trumpet blaring to all the composition of a new species (a species that might indeed — like the sweatshirt says — if not speak for the wilderness, at least give ample voice to its torment and agony).

I paddled around the pool, oblivious, nay, impervious to danger, proclaiming first to the red cedars, then the mountain blueberry, and finally the river rocks themselves, my newfound mantle of transcendent preeminence.

What rubbish.

Loon emotions skip from one extreme to the other. Going from abject melancholy to recessive egomania in the space of five minutes.

Further, if you don't watch it, conceit can get you caught.

41

River Imps and Mad Chases

I tried to ignore the nudge from behind. "Get out of here! Don't bother me while I'm pontificating." My attitude.

There it was again, the nudge. Harder. And again. Insistent. Silent assailant. Couldn't be a hound, as noisy in water as a locomotive. An alligator turtle? No way, not in these frigid waters. Sensed though, whatever it was, by not going for a quick kill, had something else in mind. Such as slow torture; a cat playing with a mouse.

I about-faced. "You want me buddy you're gonna have to wade through a stiletto beak." I stabbed. Hit empty air. Nudged again from behind. I circled. Nothing! Water spirits playing tricks on me. Fool you. I played like I was going to turn then ducked my head underwater to look behind me. Came face to face with a bewhiskered imp. Upside-down. The imp swiveled, churning water, white bubbles frothing, and we stared at each other, underwater, rightside-up. Or was it upside-down? No matter, the imp's hide 'n' seek game busted, he grinned a Cheshire Cat grin and darted away. Dark brown mammal body, size of a large house cat.

I knew that cheeky fellow. It was the river otter that led me to Molly's body. Nudge me out of my self-indulgent, time-wasting antics! How dare him! I gave chase down river. My domain, thinks he can out swim me got another think coming.

We dashed through tree root mazes, leaped over logs, zinged in & out of underwater caverns, and loop de looped in upon ourselves so many times I got dizzy. What a swimmer, and what a chase. For a mammal type, and to be such an ornery cuss, Otter wasn't a half bad diver either.

We must of raced two miles. Self-pity peeled off in layers like Walla Walla onions. Feathers scoured to a glassy brightness, steel wool sleek and frictionless.

Suddenly Otter stopped chasing down river, spun around me a few times, chattering in a foreign dialect, stopped and touched my beak with his nose, rubbed the back of his head against my long neck, slithered over my back and lit out up river. I watched him disappear around a bend and the sun dipped out of sight behind the Olympics. How much day-light left?

What's the nightlife prospects of a flightless loon? Nocturnal preda-tors hungry and invisible. Already a coolness in the air. Fluffs of cot-tonwood seeds floating on hesitant drafts, randomly seeking that one special spot on earth that they are able to land, take root and grow.

My gizzard was grinding a message of deliverance. Deliver me to April. Get this Goddamned golden egg laid. Don't let anyone else get killed.

What's that April said to Harp, "I'll take your loon mask off at dusk." April! My God! How did I feel about April now? After my brief but torrid love affair with Gavia. Gavia of the sculpted back and lavish flanks. Flanks blown to smithereens by twelve gauge shotguns.

A double murderer was out there and he, or she, had caused the death of my innocent Gavia. How many more deaths would happen until the murderer was identified? Until I found the killer, for in some supernat-ural way I now understood that I, Qo-oo-la, and I, Harp P. Gravey, had been summoned to avenge Molly Jenkins's death. The sooner I found out who killed her the sooner I could follow my own destiny.

Seattle no longer had a grimy, neon appeal.

42

Petroglyphs and Tight Burials

I would never know how I felt about April if I didn't skeedaddle. If I didn't make rendezvous, no telling where Qo-oo-la would be by the time I, Harp, woke up too weak for another immediate metamorphosis.

If I could only communicate between my spirit animal and human animal. What would I say?

A clamor coming through the forest toward the Dosanomish caught my attention. Louder and louder, hell of a racket, making me jumpy but, for some reason, not fearful. Huge brown blurry shapes burst out of the forest for a one hundred yards down the south bank and plunged in the river. Elk. Mothers with smaller calves bring up the rear. A whole herd. The lead bull with a new rack heading right at me. Not carnivorous, of course, but I'd hate to get tangled in those hooves. Sank to the bottom again and watched as the lead bull paddled overhead. Must of weighed close to one thousand pounds, yet graceful in water, long legs churning the water to bubbly froth. All around me giant hooves sloshed and gurgled and the last one to pass over me, a yearling calf, pooped black licorice pellets. The pellets, spaced evenly at around two inches, were caught by the current and squiggled down to plop gently all around me. Some glanced off me and I detected the tang of digested salaal berries.

Something spooked them and I didn't care to wait around and see what it was so I uncoiled and sprinted. Quick as a sea serpent I swerved around the bend, going all out, a mad dash, seeing what that little loon body could do revved up, a torpedo with a homing device targeting the heat in April's body.

April's body? Sorry, not interested anymore.

I developed a traveling system. I'd find a sheltered spot and come up for air about every minute or so. Making good time until I came to the logjam where I had found Molly Jenkins's body. Skirted it, determined not to let dark memories detain me, surfaced and looked up. Sure enough, there to the west was the rocky outcropping with the tooth missing, where Molly Jenkins had taken a bullet in the back before falling to her death. And where Malcomb and Harp P. Gravey had stood that very morning, and where clumsy Harp had dropped the plastic box with Josh's ashes and it bounced over the edge into the Dosanomish. Oh Josh, dead three weeks and still causing aggravation.

I felt a pull to the underwater boulders. Might as well do a quick search for the box, locate it for later salvage. How hard could it be to find? Famous last words. It was a much bigger rockslide than first noticed. Avoiding the area where I'd seen the river devil etching, I darted in and out and around and over and through and finally saw Josh snuggled up, tucked-in by the current, in a cave-like crevice where no human diver could get to, had never in fact been visited by or seen by humans since the boulders, via landslide, plunged into the Dosanomish.

I made a decision.

I squeezed through the slit, found the cheap hasp on the plastic box. "It's time you got out of there old friend. I'm giving you your freedom. This is not your Spirit Knoll but it used to be and the winter rains would wash you down here into the Dosanomish anyways. Go, become one with the creatures you adored and the land you loved best." I lifted the lid. Stuck my beak in and stirred up the ashes. Lighter particles drifted up, caught a current and rode it downstream.

While twisting around to escape the tight-quarters crevice, I encountered more etchings and realized, the boulders had been visited by human hands while part of the bluff and had, in fact, if my infrared red eyes weren't betraying me, been etched upon with ancient tools by artisan hands. I flipped over, stood on my head so to speak, to interpret the nearest drawing. Near as I could figure the image depicted a person sitting down playing a drum-like instrument. Hey, what-do-ya-know, musicians were at least important enough back in ancient times to merit sculpting.

A word came to me from Josh describing Native American etchings in the Columbia Gorge. Petroglyphs. I realized I was seeing petroglyphs. There were other petroglyphs, or pieces of petroglyphs, partially hidden beneath the huge boulder. A visual story possibly, the plot, or punch line at least, buried for centuries under ten tons of truculent rock. Small wonder the River God was pissed.

Oh my, I had lapsed, effortlessly, into pagan god worship.

My feathers ruffed, flesh chilled, the longer I stayed there the eerier I felt. Some unfinished supernatural business skulking about. Gizzard grinding like some insistent alarm, sending a frosty tentacle down my spine, feathers feeling like inverted porcupine quills. Must tell Malcomb about etching done by his ancestors if I ever get out of this haunted hole. Does the drum player have a name? Malcomb would know what it all means.

Had I found Malcomb's ancient sacred ground, an underwater artistic museum?

For the first time since being a loon, I felt oppressed underwater. I surfaced out in the open for a breath of fresh air, took one, then slipped underwater and, hugging the north bank, darted down river.

43

Journey's End and Snagged Again

On with my grinding odyssey. Did I detect a subtle difference in the feel and sound coming from my gizzard? A less abrasive touch, a softer granulating sound, as if the material being ground to passable poop dust had changed texture. Was I already too late? If the gold pin was worn smooth, why was I risking my life heading toward civilization and more people?

If you're not already, metamophosizing makes you nuts.

A pattern was beginning to emerge, the more people I encountered as either bird or human, the more uncertain and fragile my life became. Josh's last wild place was a myth, more deadly and more dangerous because it wasn't that wild anymore.

Numbing my mind to extraneous diversions, I plunged ahead.

I'd come this far, and if I didn't get x-rayed tonight and see if the clue was still detectable, the real killer might never be caught, and Loren, or Harp, might take the rap.

At every turn in the river, I encountered billowy shadows and overhanging pockets of dank darkness so numerous it was useless to try and avoid them. Songbird calls became louder and insistent; as if they were shouting a last ditch roosting warning to the day prey to find safe sanctuary against nocturnal predators. A winter wren flitted above me from alder branch-to-branch, cheeky and rambunctious, filling the cool river air with a tune chesty and melodic, a far bigger sound than its body size indicated. The little wren was easy to hear, hard to see. My mouth, though submerged in cold water most of the trip, felt hot and itchy, swallowing difficult, throat still sore from gulping that accursed pin, which was only three to four days ago.

Seemed like a lifetime.

Suddenly, when I surfaced, I could no longer hear the little brown wren's emphatic call. Songbirds were silent, roosting. Forest sounds ceased. A dog barked, small and yippy. I tasted on my tongue the acrid scent of meat sizzling and briquettes burning. I had rounded a bend and come upon cabins and trailers on either side of the river; the little blue-collar vacation tracts near Highway 101. In fact I could hear the zoom and swish of cars on the road up ahead and the intermittent harsh sucking sound as the autos passed under the individual Dosanomish river bridge stanchions.

According to our agreement, April waited for me just around the bend, no doubt with open arms. Total darkness was only a few minutes away.

Nightlights flickered on through the cottonwood leaves. Except for a couple of kids playing grab-ass with a stick on the beach up ahead I didn't see any people, smooth sailing and not a pirate ship in sight. I had made it to a safe port.

"Cawack! Cawack!" blasted in my ear as I passed under a cottonwood branch. In the shadows, the gray gull monitored my progress and right beside him perched the resolute raven. They stretched their necks, peering at me as I passed under their perch. Those guys made my pinfeathers curdle. Why were they harassing me? Didn't know better I'd say they were on Elpenor's or maybe Coyote's payroll. I shot past them, turned and gave a hoot of triumph.

The hoot clipped as I felt a prick and then a stab in my lower neck. I gagged and jerked backwards, impaled and panicky. Then I felt an invisible line crease my beak. What the hell was happening! It came to me, a fishhook! A steel-barbed, Goddamned fishhook!

The line jerked and electrical jolts erupted from my neck and shot out through the webbing on my feet fusing my toes together. The hook was set, deep, intractable and excruciating. There was no escaping the nasty impaler. I knew 'cause I had set my own hooks hundreds of times fishing in my misspent youth.

I grabbed the line with my beak to ease the tension on my neck and swam a few strokes toward its source, weak and nauseous from sudden fierce pain. Trees lining the bank swayed with swarthy intensity. The river water swelled and hissed around me like a punctured air balloon. The fishing line in my mouth twitched like an oily viper. My gizzard kept grinding, grinding, grinding away at the murder clue, my throat filled with blood.

I fought the onset of shock. The blinding pain let up and I was able to follow the direction of the line and there was the silhouette of two kids I had observed from upriver a distance fighting over a stick. I now knew the stick was a fishing pole. There was never a loon that was any match for a fishing pole connected to two tenacious kids. Rather than fight the hook and risk breaking my neck or severing my trachea I swam toward the kids, now emitting bloodthirsty shouts and cavorting like mad night demons on the inky beach. Wondered, in the dingy light, if they had any idea what they'd snagged. Wished to God I'd never read *Lord of the Flies*, or watched the first scene in the movie "The Wild Bunch." Totally dark, I felt an inner wrenching of my body balancing the exterior wrenching, could April be removing the mask from Harp's face? Can't say I was disappointed to be shifting back to human control. Out of this condemned body, a loon's life — first my lovely Gavia and now me — being insignificant in the grand scheme of things. Civilization is merciless. If the hunters don't get you the fishermen will. Pain making me light-headed and spacey: maybe I'm taking this whole thing the wrong way; since I'm captured — possibly killed — by sportsmen shouldn't I be a sport about it? What's going to happen to the murder clue? And my spirit brother Harp P. Gravey.

Oh Lord, something firm and unyielding clutched my mortal heart with a grip like catfish jaws. I convulsed. My body, regardless of the shape shift and hellish fishhook seemed to be ripping apart from some other source, some inner torment, some ineluctable sorrow. I, Harp P. Gravey, had become so spiritually joined and psychically linked with Qo-oo-la I could not bear to float away like some cowardly incorporeal phantom and leave him to be brutally murdered.

And yet, and yet, every survival cell in my body trumpeted high across the outer edge of delirium that I had to go, had to leave Qo-oo-la and wake Harp from his coma. Then and only then might Harp be able to rescue Qo-oo-la.

In the meantime have to throw Qo-oo-la upon the mercy of little monsters. That is if I did not go completely schizoid bonkers with fear first.

I knew Harp was just around the bend and across the river. Across the river, across the river, echoed in my mind as I quit fighting the shape shift and, gave myself up to my captors. I could see, by the reflection of synthetic night lights, the yellow brittleness of their crooked teeth and glimpse in the hand of the biggest one reaching for my neck, one of those foreign knives, steel blade gleaming, a handle the color of blood.

44

Drowned Hopes and Cold Reality

I awoke to darkness and blind panic, blinked grit out of my eyes and shook my head. It clunked against metal. No feeling and still blind. I reached for my eyes and encountered a protuberance. I still had on the loon mask. Like water out of a fire hose, Qo-oo-la's plight flooded me. I managed a weak cry.

Where was April?

I flung off the mask and attempted to leap up. No such luck. My head spun, dizzy and faint. Patches of manufactured light glittered through the opening of the VW's sliding side door. I rolled out on roadside gravel. It bit my elbows and knees. I cried out again. "April!" Grabbed hold of the VW floorboard and hoisted myself up on my knees, chin clinging to the cold metal. I heard highway noise, the rustle of the Dosanomish, and running footsteps.

April's voice, "What the hell are you doing? How did you get the mask off without my help?" She knelt down beside me, put her arms around me, her warm breath on my neck, smelling like seaweed and salt.

"Qo-oo-la's got a fishhook in his neck, just around the bend on the other side," I said. "Two little monsters . . . a knife, I must get to him." I pushed up, stood on legs like hollow tubing. April hung on, arose with me, grabbed around my waist.

"You're rambling and your skin is freezing. Get back in the bus and lie back down." She pulled me toward the rectangular side door opening.

I shoved her inside the opening and slide the door closed, metal grating on metal.

"No," she wailed. She began fiddling with the door latch with her left hand and banging on the window with her right. Her lips, by reflected nightlights, dry as a wilted flower.

The sliding door was hard to open from the inside but she could crawl out of the broken back hatch or the front door in seconds. I stumbled toward the river, my feet in blackberry vines, I fell, pricking my hands and face, got up, waded through bog mud, heavy with shore bird excrement and rotted fish odor and dove head-first into the Dosanomish. The river waters, so comfortable and inviting to Qo-oo-la, collided with me like liquid ice. My arms and legs seized-up, eyelids refused to part, my nose felt like it had been flattened by concrete shingles and my ears stuffed with sherbet.

I skimmed rocks with my forehead and nose on the river bottom; I was an unguided torpedo, dead in the water. I had forgotten that Harp P. Gravey was a gutless swimmer. I had a few seconds of breath left.

My mind ...? spirit ...?, soared out of my body and connected with Qo-oo-la. I caught images of grimy fingers and long teeth and grunts and silver blades and red something ... and fear ... but life; Qo-oo-la was still alive.

So near and yet so far.

I had to get to him. My arms and legs couldn't move.

My catatonic body mysteriously relaxed. The river carried me to its surface where a hand grasped my hair and began jerking me toward the bank I'd dived off of. No! No! It was the other side I had to get to; can't you understand that my brother was on the other side around the bend! Might as well have been across the continent for all I was able to help. I struggled but the hand, who else but April's, was too strong. My chin and lips felt as if they'd been ironed with an anvil. My eyelids cranked open and I saw stars weaving in and out of elliptical paths in the night sky, heard a truck rumble over the Highway 101 bridge.

We crawled out on the mud bog a few feet down from where I'd entered. April dragged me ashore, clasped my numb nose and numb-er chin and French kissed me. Well, not exactly a French kiss, no tongue action at all, lots of huffing and puffing and pushing on my chest. "Don't die on me you stupid banjo picker," she said between breaths.

Her voice like butterfly wings fanning my ears.

Feeling from the mud seeped into my fingertips first, up my arms and washed down through my cold body. As much as I liked the feel of April's warm lips on mine, if she kept up her huffing and puffing I was as much likely to suffocate as I had been to drown. I threw my arms across my face. "I'm freezing, not drowning. We've got to get to the other side of the river. A couple kids snagged Qo-oo-la in the neck with a fishhook." My lips vibrated, slung spit in April's face and the heels of my feet dug quavering trenches in the mud.

Was I back to the mud bog beach where I started from a mere three days ago?

Could feel that shore mud, still thermal from recent sunlight, cradling my back and cupping my heart. My heels stopped drumming. April's face quit spinning. My stomach warmed as if a pilot light lit up.

April began hoisting me up with one arm while unbelting my pants with the other. "Don't get ideas," she said, "we've got to get out of these clothes. I've got a change in my pack and you've got that filthy doggy blanket in the back. At least it's dry." April ripped my pants and shorts down to my ankles. "Step up." I stepped with first one leg and then another. Pants off, frigid testicles hiding if not disappeared forever, we staggered over to the bus, the mud squishy and sunny between my toes, strength flowing upwards from the black gum, stirring smells of moist, earthy cavities. The flow reached my gonads and caused the boys to peek out from their hiding place.

The high hills, humped and ponderous like dreaming dinosaurs, framing the entrance to the Dosanomish river valley, appeared closer, pressing in, than in daylight. Black clouds, rimmed with an outer glow of moonlight, gobbled the tiny stars in their path. Gulls, their wings radiant with silver reflections, called their off-center CAWK! CAWK!, a celebration of darkness. Out in the channel a freighter, its booms like burnt toothpicks, cruised toward the Juan De Fuca Straights. A right-of-way horn moaned.

I took off my soaked two-loons sweatshirt and April toweled me down with a shirt from her pack and wrapped me in my navy doggy blanket. April then stripped down, with nary a concern for me watching her, toweled down and dressed from a backpack. It was dark and I didn't peek. Much.

I said through chattering teeth. "I sense Qo-oo-la is still alive. How do we get to the other side of the river?"

"Jump in," April said.

"I already tried that."

"In the car, you thick-headed banjo picker." April ground the gears, cussed, and we spun gravel out of there, turned right on Highway 101, crossed the Dosanomish River Bridge and about a quarter of a mile turned right again into a maze of roadways. April took several turns on two wheels, forcing me to break out of my snug blanket cocoon and hold on to the dashboard handle. We almost smacked a pick-up coming the opposite way around a bend, our headlights creasing shacks and trailers of every shape and variety on narrow woody lots. Few of them had night-lights; working-class vacation homes.

We sped down a sharp grade with a hairpin turn at the bottom and I saw red alder and cottonwood trees. We were at the river. April hit the brakes. We jumped out and ran through someone's yard, past a trailer yellowed and greenish with algae, with an American flag mounted on top, down a narrow path to a gravelly delta. Nobody there.

I glanced around. Reality is a matter of perspective; things look different from one species to another. I said, "I think this is the place."

April, with a flashlight, far ahead of me, playing her light along the water's edge. "Here's fresh blood."

I ran to her, took my finger and touched a drop of the dark liquid on a round river rock and placed my finger on my tongue. The blood was sticky and tepid, tasted feral. I thumped my chest, heart stopped for an instant. "It's Qo-oo-la's."

I pulled my blanket tighter around my neck, squeezed my eyelids shut tight and rubbed them with the palms of my hands. A coyote yipped up-river and the sound echoed through the valley. A foreign car horn answered on the highway and the two noises glanced back and forth between the valley walls then finally rolled into each other and disappeared.

April put her arm around my waist, guided me toward shore. My feet walking as if on snowshoes.

"Well he's not here now," April said. "There's a light in that trailer across the road. I'll see if they know anything about the two boys. You stay in the car out of sight."

I huddled in my blanket, saw April knock on the door, a porch light came on and April talked through a crack in the door. Could hear a television racket coming from inside. Mud hardened between my toes. I was too sick of soul to wiggle it away.

April ran to my bus, hopped in, "They heard a car peel out of here a few minutes ago. Probably that pickup that almost hit us driving in." We were off. Backtracking, once again we raced through twisty roads, me holding on with both hands, my blanket slipping off my shoulders, and came to Highway 101.

"Which way?" April said.

My feet pulled me out of the bus. I walked in front and sniffed the air. All my senses seemed to be more alert since leaving the city. But nothing came to me. I opened my blanket to concentrate the wind toward me. I caught odors of stewed cabbage and seal excretion. A car swished by, slowed, then continued on, faster. The car brought a whiff of Qo-oo-la. I ran to the bus and pointed. April never hesitated, turned right and, by the sound of my little four-banger engine, pressed the foot pedal to the floorboard. One of the few times since I had the bus, I wished for more speed and power.

We climbed a long hill and were starting to pick up speed when April abruptly slowed and turned off the highway. "What . . . ?"

"I'm playing a hunch. Trust me." I recognized the road leading into her clinic. Suddenly I knew Qo-oo-la was near. We pulled into the clinic's parking lot, up beside a blue pick-up with its lights shining on the entrance to the building. The headlights nailed two kids holding a big cardboard box.

A tall man, wearing a straw hat, in a cloud of cigarette smoke, got out of the truck to greet us. "Thank God it's Arlan Coats." April said. "Probably his grand kids fishing." April intercepted Arlan and I hustled to the box. The boys guarding the box had frightened eyes as I charged toward them; a wild-eyed man, matted hair, wrapped in a Navy blanket. "How is he . . . the loon?" I said.

The littlest kid was an Indian. He had straight black hair under a Mariner's baseball cap, dark eyes scared but defiant, skin, under the night-light, the color of scorched copper. He stepped between me and the box. "We didn't mean to hook it. We were fishing for cutthroat."

I reached around the boy. "Let me have a look."

"It was really weird," he said. "It didn't struggle. It swam right up to us, right into my arms. I grabbed it and then it died. Or at least we thought it did at first. But it was still breathing. Can birds faint?" The boy talked fast, his flat voice intonations echoless against the beige enclosure.

The other boy was Caucasian, bigger, and also wore a Mariner's baseball cap. He had sandy hair, and, not saying a word, set his end of the box down and loped to the passenger side of the pick-up. Something thumped against the side of the box. My heart pounded against my rib cage, mouth and tongue parched like an amateur blues harmonica player. I lifted the lid and wondered; how many people throughout history have been lucky enough to know and then meet, face to face, their spirit animal?

Qo-oo-la was heaped in a lower corner, not moving. A dark crimson stain had soaked the bottom of the brown box under him and a vinegary reek of cardboard, confined blood and wet feathers washed over me. His neck crooked crazily underneath him and I couldn't see his head. I held my breath.

I laid my hand lightly on his black and white checkerboard back and felt warmth and a slight up and down breathing motion. My fingers tingled and then a current moved up my arm, across my shoulders and into my chest, filling my heart with an ancient ache. "Oh Lord, let this innocent animal live," I whispered. Qo-oo-la stirred, bobbed his head up and looked at me with one glassy red eye.

Common loon and ordinary man meet. Common loon is not much impressed. Ordinary man feels extraordinary.

Common loon, by way of accentuating the cosmic significance of the encounter, speared my thumb with his rapier beak. I took it as an honest though primitive attempt at communication. I held fast and my blood dripped down and mingled with his. The two bloods swirled together like nest mates.

Qo-oo-la then uttered a feeble hoot; splayed feet scratched cardboard, bony gray reverse knees tangling each other. I hooted recognition back, put some strength and encouragement in it. Qo-oo-la's webbed toes couldn't snag a hold on the cardboard, struggled to rise toward me and it was then I saw, reflected in the glint of the overhead light, the fishhook in his neck. It had torn a quarter inch gash and was embedded well past the barb a couple inches above his alabaster necklace. Blood oozed from the wound. The dark red color had spread down his necklace to his chest, leaving a crooked trail like a serpentine birthmark.

I surged and ebbed back and forth between fainting and flying. Qo-oo-la, my brother was alive but so near death and only one thing I could do to help him. I hollered at April.

Only then did I realize she'd been standing right behind me the whole time.

45

Sons and Anvils

"Let's get him onto the x-ray table," April said over my shoulder and pushed through the entrance door. The inside of the building exploded with squawking. Squawking strange and foreign, not of the Olympic Peninsula or North America for that matter. Jungle squawking.

My legs wobbled as I picked up the dropped end of the box. The Indian boy had squatted down to level the box, still had hold of the other end. He looked at me with slate-black eyes no longer frightened, waiting for direction. We carried Qo-oo-la after April. April switched on lights as she glided through the building of many rooms and chambers, past cages and cages of colorful, rung-rattling birds. We entered a spacious room with a polished silver sink, cabinets stocked with white sterile boxes and bottles and three glass sliding doors, tables and state of the art somber-colored medical monitoring equipment.

Noise cacophonated throughout the building. Birdcalls, of every ear-piercing pitch and peal, vibrated the medical containers in the glass cabinets. In the next room I spotted a large white tropical bird stretching its neck above a box of gauze to make unapologetic eye contact with me.

"That's Roger," April said. "He's got an intestinal problem which he's sore about. His owner feeds him too much junk, people food."

Faint but unmistakable, a dog barked. My breath caught but it was not Medusa's bark.

"How is my dog?" I said, feeling guilty for not having thought of her since morning.

"Medusa's in the back," April said. "She's alive. In a coma right now. She's lost a lot of blood. Her right front leg is in a cast. I don't know whether I can save it. Or her."

April pointed at a stainless steel table in the far corner. The table had a brown rectangular machine hanging over it and a foot square lead plaque about three quarters of an inch thick directly under it on the table. "Pick the bird up and put him under that machine. Carefully."

I reached in the box, put one hand under Qo-oo-la's limp neck, my other hand under his breast and, as gently as possible, lifted him out and under the x-ray machine. I was surprised at how heavy he was. He was conscious but lay still in my arms, his red eye following my face. I leaned down and kiss-pecked him on the space between beak and eyeball. His beak clicked open and shut as if he was trying to kiss me back or, more likely, bite my lip. I got him into this mess. His red eye blinked and stayed open, a taffy colored mucus rimming the lower edge.

April appeared beside me in a drab blue, lead apron. "Stand over there. Better yet look in the drawer under that table and put on some surgical clothes. I don't need a partially nude assistant. I can handle the x-rays by myself." April began adjusting the overhead machine and, not looking, spoke to the Indian boy, "Emerson, you and Arlan and Benny can either wait out in the lobby or go on home. Thanks for bringing him in. I'll let you know what happens."

I got the light green surgical clothes out of the drawer, dropped my blanket in a pile around pale, blue-veined feet, dried black mud between my toes, and stepped into the airy pants. My calves began thawing.

The Indian kid, Emerson, had not moved. "It was my fault," he said. I looked up; his chin was tucked down, resting on his bony chest. "Benny wanted to go home because of the dark and I wouldn't quit. I hooked the loon. If it dies it's my fault." His flat voice, talking to the scrubbed burnt-tile floor, wavered.

I cinched the waist string on my green pants. "You did right by bringing him here as quickly as you did. He's not going to die. April won't let him."

He peeked up at me. "I'm pretty good at bird calls," he said. "I can imitate a chickadee and a royal kinglet but I've never heard anyone do a loon before. It must hurt your throat. Can you show me how?"

April clicked the machine with a foot pedal under the table. Only did a couple x-rays of Qo-oo-la's neck, then switched to further back in his body, turned Qo-oo-la every which way and did half a dozen more. She seemed a mite rough. "Okay," she said, "you can hold him while I develop these. It'll take about ten minutes." April handed Qo-oo-la to me.

I cradled Qo-oo-la in my arms. It was like holding my own flesh and blood. I suddenly felt a dull ache in my neck. Emerson reached up a grimy little hand and softly petted Qo-oo-la's back. "Is this your pet loon or something? Is that how you know it's a male?"

"No," I said. "Qo-oo-la's . . . he's not anyone's pet. Intuition; I know he's a male by intuition."

"If he's not a pet how come he's got a name?" Emerson said. "And what kind of name is Qo-oo-la? Sounds like my grandfather's tongue when he'd been drinking too much; Qo-oo-la." He rolled the name over in his mouth, experimenting.

Qo-oo-la raised his head, turned to Emerson and crooned. The sound came out tight and constricted. Emerson's face paled and his onyx eyes widened and flashed. "Hey, that's pretty cool, he knows his name, a loon that knows his name."

April charged out of the dark little closet and took two flexible film sheets, stuck them on a wall-mounted viewing case and flicked on the hot light. They were Qo-oo-la's neck shots and the first image I saw, solid and bright, lit up like a fluorescent scimitar sword, was the barbed hook. It was imbedded between the spinal cord and a pale clear tube. April pointed and said, "This line here is the trachea. It looks like the hook nicked it . . . and . . . it might have nicked the spinal cord too."

I didn't like the sound of that. "What does that mean. Paralysis? What?"

"It means your loon — "

"Qo-oo-la, his name is Qo-oo-la." I said it slow, drawing it out.

She squinted at me. "Alright Mr. Wiseguy, it means Qo-oo-la, if the trachea is too damaged and vital nerves in the spinal column are severed, hasn't a ghost of a chance." She headed for the glass cabinets. "Put him on the operating table. Emerson, I thought I told you to go home?"

"Mr. Coats and Benny already left," Emerson said, "I can walk home from here. Can't I stay and help? It's my fault."

"Go call your Aunt Lucille and tell her you're here helping me with an emergency operation." April stood on tiptoes to reach a tray of tools. Her light green pants pulled up past her ankles and muscular lower calves.

Emerson ran out of the operating room.

"Why are you letting the kid stay?" I said. "He asks a lot of questions. I mean, he seems like an okay kid and he kinda reminds me of somebody, but won't he be in the way?"

"He knows his way around here," April said. "Be better help than you I suspect, and besides, he has a vested interest in Qo-oo-la. Strange how things work out."

"So he hooked Qo-oo-la," I said. "how does that give him a vested interest?"

April retrieved a tray of plain old carpenter pliers with handles of every color and tips of every kind. "It doesn't. I just so happens that Emerson is Molly Jenkins's son. Her sister, Lucille, raised him since a baby, but he's Molly's all right."

April handed me the tray of tools. It shifted and rattled. I held it at arms length. "Does he know it? He doesn't seem broken up about her death."

"I'm sure he does. But Indian kids, 'specially boys, don't show their emotion very much. They stuff a lot."

"So he was abandoned at an early age. I've heard tell that leaves emotional scars. What about his papa? Emerson looks like a mixed blood to me. Does he know who his papa is?"

"Not likely. He's definitely a mixed blood like me." April slammed the tool tray on the operating table, causing a yellow-handled pair of pliers to bounce out, twirl on its needle-nose like an ice-skater, and plop on the padded surface.

"No more non-relevant talking," she said. "If you want to save your loon get that tubing protruding from that orange canister and hold his head in it."

Emerson slipped back in the room. His breath fast, black eyes wide and watching. I could see it now; those were Molly's eyes. Alive and curious. Come back from the grave to check up on me. See how I was doing at figuring out who killed her.

Oh-my-gosh! What about my property? Upon her death, did Emerson inherit his mother's one-fourth? If not legally, then morally? Did I now have another unforeseen partner?

I shut-up my mind and placed Qo-oo-la's beak in a oxygen-type mask while April twisted some dials on top of the canister and read some gauges. "That ought to do it," she said.

I could hear a faraway hissing and smelled methane and ammonia. Nasty unnatural chemicalized odors. Qo-oo-la eyelids drooped. "How long before he's under?" I said.

"I'm guessing at least two minutes."

"What the hell do you mean guessing?"

"Sorry, my anesthesiologist is off getting his Cadillac waxed. He'd probably be back by now except he's got a bunch of banjo pickers getting their Mercedes detailed ahead of him. Look around you white eyes, this is a one person operation. I'm the nurse, doctor, respirator and janitor and I've never anesthetized a loon before. Avian surgery is not an exact science. This is a tricky and dangerous business. There's a high mortality rate. Fifteen per cent survive. If the anesthesia doesn't get them the shock will. Two minutes at this setting is all I dare do and that's probably enough to knock out a Brahma bull."

Qo-oo-la's eyelids were locked shut and his body limp. "I'm sorry," I said, "It's like having your own kid under the knife."

"Yeah, Mr. Domesticity, how would you know?" April said. "Do you have a reaction to blood? You're not going to pass out on me are you?" Without waiting for a reply April put on a head ornament, flicked a switch and an intense beam of light hit the table. She took out a red handled pair of wire cutting dikes. "This light magnifies as well as illuminates — you can ease up on your bear hug. He ain't going anywhere."

The white macaw, Roger, blared ear-splitting constipated jungle calls at us. Liked attention. Called to mind Elpenor.

I heard that faint dog bark again. My skin felt prickly and sweat congealed in my armpits. My throat was parched like I'd inhaled a gust of torched air. Lungs inflated, full, like I'd swallowed a basketball and it lodged in my chest. Light danced back and forth between the stainless steel fixtures. I wandered over and leaned against the wall. Emerson took my place, thin arms holding Qo-oo-la.

April, the optic light focused on Qo-oo-la's neck, carefully nabbed the hook below the butt-eye with a pair of yellow-handled needle-nose pliers in one hand and took the red handled dikes and, with a resounding hard snap, severed it. The butt-eye flew across the room and pinged against the glass cabinet, dinged to the tile floor. Roger squawked and beat his wings against the cage like a condemned man rakes his prison bars.

Suddenly, Qo-oo-la exhaled, a noise like wind releasing from some broken-sealed tomb, and then pitched and bucked and would've fallen off the table had not Emerson moved faster than a mother hen protecting her chicks, and caught the convulsing bird.

I rushed over too and steadied Qo-oo-la's neck from flopping against the table. "What the hell's going on?" I said, "I thought you said there was enough anesthesia in him to knock out a Brahma bull. Are you trying to kill him?"

"Your bird held his breath for the whole two minutes. He didn't take in but a tiny bit of anesthesia. He almost outfoxed himself. He's probably choking and in a lot of pain. Put him up here, we'll have to try again."

Emerson and I put Qo-oo-la down and I held the mask over his wild-eyed head. "Hurry and give him more," I said, "I can feel his pain."

"No," April said. "I'll have to give him less volume. More would kill him. But, you hold him and I'll keep it steady, and we'll give it more time."

This time, I pressed Qo-oo-la firm against the white table cover. He didn't struggle but his unfocused red eye rolled around in its socket. He click-clicked his bill. Pink mucus dribbled on the white operating cloth.

Emerson and I rubbed hips. I could smell the meaty odor of worms from his hands.

Five minutes later, April grabbed the point of the embedded hook and slowly worked it to where it punched through skin and feathers and peeked out of the other side of Qo-oo-la's neck. April clicked onto the bloody point with the needle-nose pliers and pushed and pulled, firm and steady. Qo-oo-la's mildly anesthetized body jerked and his glazed red eye closed as the barb emerged. I felt a tiny stab in my neck in the same area as Qo-oo-la. April held the gore-smeared hook up to the light for my viewing. "There it is. Pretty isn't it?"

The thorned grapple was slathered with flesh and blood. Tiny red-stained feathers clung to it. I'd never seen anything so gruesome.

"Awesome," Emerson said, "can I have the hook. I'll never use it again. I'll put in my medicine bag."

The whole operation took maybe fifteen minutes. Drops of dark red flowed and spread on the white tablecloth. My neck no longer ached. My stomach felt like it'd been punched though. I eased my grip on Qo-oo-la. April picked up one gray leg and let it drop; limp as a thread.

"What now?" I said.

"Can't tell yet. Except you might pray. All I can do now is clean him up and watch him closely. He's a tough fellow but he's got to survive both the anesthesia and the operation. While I swab him you can get those other radiographs from the dark room and hang them up. Let's finally take a look at that gizzard."

"Fuck the gizzard and the gold pin," I said. "Look where it's got my brother. I don't care about the damned gold pin anymore." I was reluctant to take my hands off Qo-oo-la, as if my hands kept him alive or, at least, helped his healing.

46

Pale Popcorn and New Partners

"If he lives he'll be out for a while," April said, wiping her hands on a white towel. "We've done as much as we can for now. You and Emerson hang the film on the hot light." April cradled Qo-oo-la's languid, docile body, wrapping the wound.

I inched my arm out of April's way, hating to break the physical connection with my spirit self. As Qo-oo-la's feathers filtered through my fingertips, I gave a parting light caress. April pushed in front of me. I turned toward the dark room and met Emerson with his hands full of films. He handed the twelve by eight inch rectangular films to me one at a time as I clipped all six on the display case hot light.

From the first radiograph the gizzard would have been recognizable even without the pin. It was the size of an egg and had white puffs of flack dotting it, like pale popcorn. The pin however was a dead giveaway: It lit up like a radioactive rat. The first two shots were sideways and revealed nothing. The remaining four blurred. I could make out some lines and shadows but nothing concrete. "Damn, all that agony for nothing," I said.

April joined us with a professional eye, Qo-oo-la wrapped up in a mauve towel in her arms, holding him like he was a newborn child. "Not so fast, we're in luck. There's two different substances — probably hard plastic and pop metal — and there's definitely an image there." We three stared hard at each of the remaining radiographs, a science about as exact as reading clouds. Emerson said, "Looks to me like an Aladdin's lamp."

"It's not a banjo, thank God," I said. My body shuddered.

"You were worried?" April studied me.

I lied. "Only for a little while."

"Those things above it are feathers," Emerson said.

"No," April said, "You're wrong. It's an anvil. Actually before Qo-oo-la's gizzard chewed it up there was probably an arm, a hammer and a piece of pounding iron too." She traced a finger over the images. "It's the logo of a blacksmith league." She seemed disappointed.

As soon as April said it, both Emerson and I said in unison, "I see it."

I said, "But who in this day and age belongs to a blacksmith's union. Not many I'd bet. That narrows our suspects." I remembered Purple Nat's metal pounding in the background. Hey wait a minute; didn't the sheriff say something about shoeing his own horses? Sheriff Gloeckler a suspect? His adulterous wife making him hate all women?

April rubbed the back of her neck, sniffed three times, one end of her mouth curled down. "That's not true. Father belongs to the local black smith's league and, unfortunately so does Loren."

"But so does my Uncle Danny," said Emerson. "Lot's of people do. They all take turns on the weekends during tourist season giving demonstrations at the reservation."

"Is the league all Indian?" My mind was struggling to remember something.

"No, it's mixed," said April. "Or at least it was when it started up some years ago as sort of a joint celebration of pioneer and Native American days. Seems to me, Big Steve and Gabe Moody had something to do with it too. Looks like we're right back where we started from." She clutched Qo-oo-la to her breast and cooed to him like a baby. Took him to a small table with an incubator square unit on it, put him in the unit and turned on an in-line switch. Pulled a syringe out of a drawer and gave him in injection. "Vitamins," she said over her shoulder.

The hairs on my arm felt heavy. "I remember that Purple Nat, the Vietnam Vet, made clanging sounds when Qo-oo-la was captured at his place. Shit, that's all the suspects. Except me of course. I never used an anvil in my life." I took small pleasure from that. But some other tidbit of information was lacing through the dead booze cells in my brain.

I studied the radiograph again. Something peculiar about the angle of the anvil dangle. I reached up and moved the images around, pieces of a puzzle. I tried to adjust it, as it would fit on a person's shirt. It had one straight line then an oval, like a tiny coat-of-arms. If I was right, the anvil image was not sitting, it was falling. And, those blurs around it were not an arm and hammer. What did a falling anvil need of a blacksmith? What did anybody need of a falling anvil? I drew a blank.

April came up behind me and her arm wound around my waist. "Forget it," she said. "You'll not find Molly's killer in a those radiograms."

We had forgotten about little boys with big ears. "Are you all talking about my mother and Billy Moody being killed?" Emerson said. "I don't understand. What's that anvil got to do with my mother and how did it get in Qo-oo-la's belly? How did he swallow it?"

"Emerson, I'm sorry you had to hear us talking about your mother," April said. "I hope you didn't take it the wrong way." She stroked Emerson's hair.

"That's okay," he said. "She never cared much for me anyway." He turned away and looked at the white macaw, his black eyes like round ink drops.

"That's not true, Emerson," April said. "Molly loved you very much. She told me so many times." She stretched her tired neck. Something popped. Her shoulders sagged. "Go home now, Emerson, and I want you to promise me something: don't mention any of this to your Aunt Lucille. Just tell her you were helping me clean up around the clinic like you usually do. I don't want the natural rumor pipeline around here to speed up."

Emerson hung his head. "When I called Aunt Lucille like you told me to, I told her about you getting ready to operate on the loon I hooked and she told me something pretty strange. She said she's lived here all her life and never heard of a common loon on the upper Dosnomish and, in one day, there's two of them. I'm sorry if I did wrong."

"No, no you didn't do wrong. You couldn't know. Ahh . . . what do you mean two of them? Where's the other one?" She looked at me.

My heart suddenly felt on fire, like an ignited damp match. "I can answer that," I said. "The sheriff and his posse gunned her . . . Gavia, a common loon, down, up river. They took the body to forensics to get it dissected." I wrapped my arms around my rib cage and squeezed, kept it from blowing apart.

April eyed me, scanning below the surface. She had tired furrows above her eyebrows and her shoulders slumped. I hadn't noticed before but an opaque mustache of sweat had formed on her upper lip.

Roger grumbled and complained and banged his cage with magnificent white wings. The glass medicine cabinet rattled. That dog barked faintly again in the back of the building. Still not my Medusa.

"Gunned *her* down eh?" April said. "Curious use of words. I suppose you were there, saw the whole thing? No matter. We've got to get out of here and turn off the light, let Qo-oo-la get some rest. Emerson, go on home. You can tell your aunt about the fishhook, just don't tell her about the anvil. Might save us a little time."

My mental strings were not in tune. "Time, time for what? We know now that the murderer belonged to a blacksmith organization. Can't we just feed the sheriff that information and take a breather? You look beat and I'm suffering from . . . from . . . post-transmigration-stress syndrome."

Beyond which, I felt wretched for Emerson. We had probably traumatized him by talking out of turn about his mother.

"Can't I stay?" Emerson said, taking off his Mariner's cap and slicking back his jet-black hair. Looked at me with dark eyes that danced. "This is way too much fun."

April kicked the operating table. "Fun, fun. The fun's over, Emerson. Get out of here. Go home." April's voice had edged toward hysteria. She rubbed her wrists together as though starting a fire, her silver leaping salmon earrings leaped and twitched, reflected light played against the walls.

"Okay," he said. "But I'll be back tomorrow for early morning feeding. Do you want me to do anything special with Qo-oo-la?"

April pointed toward the door as if she had a fiddle bow in her hand. "I'll take care of Qo-oo-la. You get."

I followed Emerson to the door. "Hey Emerson," I said, "thanks again for bringing Qo-oo-la to the wildlife clinic." I put my hand on his shoulder, collar bone sharper than mine.

"That's okay," he said, "that's what my dad would've wanted me to do."

"Oh, your dad is around?"

"No, not really," he said. "It's just pretend. I only know he's white." He squinted his dark eyes at me. "Hey, maybe you're my dad."

"No, I'm nobody's dad." I said. "I don't know anything about having a family." I looked into Emerson's eyes. Molly's eyes. "But I've always wanted to have a partner like you," I said, "someone to teach bird calls to."

"Okay," Emerson said. "It'd be really cool to have a partner that could speak the language of the birds." He went out the door.

Back in the operating room, April pointed the fiddle bow at me. "As for you . . . no, we can't take a breather. What do you think will happen when they don't find a pin in that other loon's — "

"Gavia. Her name was Gavia," I said.

"In Gavia's — how'd you know her name? Never mind I don't want to know — gizzard. They're going to start looking for another goose with a golden gizzard. And when they, the sheriff, hears about me having a loon here at the clinic, captured on the Dosanomish, he's going to want to confiscate Qo-oo-la for evidence." She paused, slumped against the operating table.

"So what. We won't let the sheriff have him. Show him the radiographs of the anvil. That should be enough."

"No, the radiographs are subject to interpretation. And why just use the radiographs when you've got the real thing in hand. All the sheriff has to do is cut open Qo-oo-la's belly. They'll want forensics to analyze that pin. I imagine the prosecuting attorney will insist on it."

My facial skin squeezed the bone in my forehead. My eyebrows scratched each other. "I'll explain to the sheriff about me and Qo-oo-la being spiritually connected."

"Ha. Ha. Yeah I want to hear that. Explain to a sheriff from L.A. that you're linked cosmically with a loon. That'll go over like clam cake. He's liable to eviscerate you too. Ha. Ha. Just kidding." Her laughter set off another peel of birdcalls throughout the building.

I glanced at Qo-oo-la, checkered black & white chest moving slightly, fluorescent lights making his head feathers green-black, gray legs stretched out flat and motionless against the mauve surface of the incubator. Would he ever sing again?

47

Peg legs and Demons

I hadn't noticed before but ever since stepping into her clinic, April had taken even more control of the known universe than when she was outside. Her rich copper skin generated a red-orange glow of authority. April shook her head, tossing her waist-length blue-black hair, still damp from the recent river dip, and every strand fell back in its proper place, good soldiers keeping in step with the master drummer.

April took my hand and, switching off lights, led me past rows and rows of raucous caged jungle birds into the back of the building. The further we went through dark hallways and rooms the more hesitant her steps became, a chink in the control freaks armor. She was leading me toward a destination she wasn't sure of.

Her hand was balmy and moist. It pulsed. I held onto it with very little pressure.

Years ago, in one of my hundreds of temporary homes, a humming bird got in my house and flew behind the refrigerator and got stuck in cobwebs, its thrumming wings stilled. I had to grab it with great tenderness and take it back outside for release. It weighed less than ounce. Before I let it go all I could feel was its heart beating rapidly in my hand, a chimera heart in gossamer clay. Slow the beat down some and that's the way April's hand felt. If I squeezed I might crush it.

We left the commercial aviary and entered a room that reeked of bleach and offal and small things scurried in small metal places. Two exit lights lobbed spectral green light around the chamber, reflecting movement through barred windows. One wall was stacked with built-in cages. Wing tips scratched against aluminum walls. April whispered, "This is the Wildlife Care Center. Normally Qo-oo-la would be in here. The injured animals need rest. So be quiet. I'll show you around tomorrow."

We passed through another hallway and out into nearly empty dog kennels. A malamute that had one gray eye, one pale blue and a bandaged ear, greeted us with a fence-rattling *woof.* "That's Kodiak, he had an ear chewed up by a Rottweiler. The same Rottweiler that your cougar killed."

"He's not my cougar. You're the one that rescued him. Lt. LeRoy is suing all of us over his chewed up ear." The words jumped out of my mouth before I could stop them.

"Whatever. Been better off if we'd let Fish & Wildlife put Clancy down on the spot. The level of human imprinting that cougar's been subjected to, he'll never adapt to the wild. Just a matter of time before he gets into more trouble with humans." April had her hand on the door-knob, stopped, and bowed her head. Her shoulders hunched against the door. "What am I saying? I could no more have let Clancy be put down than I could've left you stranded on the Dosanomish mud flat . . . what was it . . . a mere three-four days ago . . . seems like an eternity. So what if I lose my clinic over the cougar and. . . ." April's sable eyes flared at me, "my sanity over you." Tears ran off her cheeks and dripped on her light green surgical smock, making stains like dark green skid marks.

I touched her shoulder and she came into my arms. She was soft and weightless, like a humming bird. She spoke, her breath smelling like spring cherries and flushed my neck. "I spent two hours operating on Medusa. If it were anyone else's dog I would have recommended putting her down. Then I rushed over to wait on the banks of the Dosanomish for a god-damn common loon to float by and then you almost drowned yourself and then operating on . . . on . . . what's that goddamn loon's name again?"

"Qo-oo-la."

"Qo-oo-la. What kind of name is Qo-oo-la? Sounds like. . . ." April babbled a couple more minutes then abruptly stopped, pushed away from me, blew her nose on a scarlet handkerchief from her pocket and, back in control, said, "What I'm trying to say is I don't know if Medusa survived the operation this afternoon or not. I couldn't find anyone to stay with her. I left her here in the recovery room by herself. Brace yourself, she may be dead."

April twisted the knob and shoved the door open.

Medusa lay on a multi-colored, loomed, rag rug in the corner of a small room, empty of furniture. The walls were the color of Clancy's eyes and the room smelled of antiseptic, humus and cheap glue. Medusa's whole upper body was encased in a cross between a cast and a yoke-like apparatus around her neck usually reserved for skittish oxen. Her bone-crunching mouth was muzzled tight.

My legs turned to threads and gave out from under me. I lay down beside her and hugged her broken body as gently as I could, laying my cheek against her muzzle. My nose came in contact with a pink bristly spot spilling out from the cast where April must have shaved her fur. Medusa's eyes were sealed tight. Her natural canine musky smell seeped through the dried blood and ether odor of the cast. I listened for the sound of breathing. I could detect nothing through the black leather encircling her mouth.

Then Medusa's dry black nose quivered. From somewhere I heard a weak thump. Then another thump. Thump, thump, thump and thump, getting stronger. I had been listening to the wrong end. Medusa inhaled so strongly I thought her nose might collapse in on itself. She whined and her tail beat a steady rhythm on her loomed-rug bed. Her eyelids, sticky with death-stealth mucus, struggled open, cleared and focused on me. Her dry tongue slapped against the muzzle.

April knelt down beside us. "We can take the muzzle off as long as we're here. I didn't want her chewing off her cast." April, brown face soft as silk curtains, undid the muzzle and slid it out of the way. Medusa's parched, pink tongue went lapping wildly and she tried to rise. April slipped an arm around the dog and the other around my neck. I encircled April's waist with an arm and inserted my other one under Medusa. Together we stood the injured dog on her three good legs and one peg leg. We then all three engaged in a cluster lick. Medusa, emitting chesty grunts of pleasure and clearly having the edge in tongue action. Me, with erratic sobbing sounds erupting from my solar plexus, and coming in a close licking second. And April, sobbing too, content to be the major lickee from both of us.

Before you knew it, I was kissing away April's tears and our lips touched together and we were into some serious mutual tongue action of our own. Medusa continued to lick my neck and ear. Ear lick. Tongue lick. Soul lick. We three swayed in perfect sync, like a well-balanced old-growth cedar, with three trunks, in an east wind.

I could've swayed like that forever had not Elpenor whispered in my inner ear, *"I'm back."*

My body jerked. Medusa uttered a pained whine. April groaned. We unclinched. April and I fell back, propped up by our arms, her mouth open as if shocked, a trickle of saliva hanging off her lower lip.

Good-bye soul mates, hello torment. *"Ol' Podna',"* Elpenor said, *"thought you could get away with some hanky-panky while I was gone, eh? I tell ya, you're no better than a hot guitar picker with the morals of an ally cat. Taking advantage of the poor exhausted Vet while your spirit animal — Quacko-oo-moo-la, isn't it — is lying dead not two rooms away."*

"Qo-oo-la damnit! You ass. He's not dead."

"Oh I forget I can't fool you anymore since you proclaimed yourself a shameen. You're much too clever now. Ha. He. Ho. Just kidding. I tell ya Harpy; you got the brains of a Brahma bull. Not to worry though, your one true pal Elpenor's gonna help you out. I've come to the conclusion that the only way we're ever gonna escape this wilderness hell hole is to catch this murderer. I've got some information on the murderer you might be interested in."

I screamed at Elpenor, "Keep your misinformation to yourself. It's confusing enough as it is."

Medusa, unsupported, barked and fell over with a clunk.

April licked her bottom lip, looked at me shaking her head, her silver and purple earrings cutting a half-moon ellipse, and ran her expert hand over the dog who lay panting, tongue lolling. April glared at me. "Well, well, Elpenor's back," she said. "I'm getting pretty sick of some phantom apparition coming between us every time we get close." She thought a minute. "This is absurd, you've convinced me that your spiritual connection to Qo-oo-la is real and now, I, a respected member of the scientific community, am beginning to the talk about your deranged hallucinations as if they were real. The longer I hang out with you, the more I feel like every thing I've built my reputation on and believe in, is false. I'm losing my ever-fucking-loving mind." April paused, stroked her comely neck where it dovetailed into her shoulder. She pushed up. "I'll get some fresh water and food for Medusa."

She opened the door to the Wildlife Care Center. The patients, sick and sedate when we had walked through minutes before, were shuffling, squawking and stirring.

While April was gone to get dog food and water, I sat with Medusa's head in my lap, looked for the knobby tic bite to scratch but it was covered by her cast. I petted her knotted fur on her lower back. She snorted and sighed. Weak but happy to be back in her pack. No malice at all at me for having almost gotten her killed. Forgiveness came natural to her. I could stop beating myself up over her. But what about Qo-oo-la? I had forever skewed his life. Would he forgive me too? Must I cause hurt in everything I loved? And who would be next? April? Malcomb? I had to flush out the killer. Stop the madness. But how?

Sometimes it takes madness to catch madness. Hadn't Elpenor said, *I've got some information might help you catch the murderer?* Did he know who the killer was? I did something I've never done before; concentrated very hard, went into a hypnotic trance, not to get rid of Elpenor but to summon him.

I'd decided to make a bargain in hell. If you cannot kill your demons then you must join them. Or, rather, trick them into joining you.

Medusa growled and scratched her peg leg with a back paw. Dog musk, plaster and antiseptic smelled like deep-fried turnips.

48

Catfish Tears and Coyote Tales

I reached way back in my mind and unlocked a door. Surprised Elpenor trying on masks. Tables turned. Me jumping out at him. He had on a catfish mask but his body was almost all coyote. One ugly combination.

"I've decided this place is my home," I said, "and I won't be needing you anymore. You can go of your own accord or I have the power now to get rid of you."

Catfish cried. Big slimy tears out of gooey eyes. Tail between legs. *"You wouldn't do that Harp ol' Podna. You and me are old drinking buddies. We had some splendiferous times together."*

"You had a good time. I was wretched. No, you have to go."

"No! You can't disappear me. I may not be human but I have a right to live." His big whiskers shook. Back paws jittering.

I found myself feeling sorry for him. "Okay, I'll give you a reprieve. You have to do two things and I'll let you live."

His catfish mouth smacked together like cloth covered band symbols. *"You name them."*

"Tell me what you think you know more than I do about the murderer."

His tail popped out from between his legs. He came at me jaws agape. I thought at first he was going to bite me. But no, he wanted to whisper in my ear. One of his spiny whiskers jabbed me in the neck. It hurt but I stood my ground. My skepticism out weighted by desperation. I listened.

Elpenor finished, back peddled and grinned. *"What do you think of that ol' Podna? Pretty clever eh?"*

Elpenor had made some associations I never would've considered. The connections were, of course, in my subconscious all the time but without ol' catfish breath I doubt if I would have discovered them. "I'll give it some thought," I said.

"You must keep your bargain. I get to live."

"Not so fast, there's one more pledge. You have to let me make love to April without interference."

"Done! That's too easy Podna. She done soured on you. That's never gonna happen."

"Then it's agreed."

"Agreed." His tail stood straight up and twitched. Where had I seen such a tail before?

I came out of the trance and saw Malcomb's nose ring jiggling. He was pouring dry dog food in a ceramic pot. A woody smell clung to his clothes and his big ears looked wrinkled in the fluorescent lighting. "You were making some good moans," he said. "Did a ghost *Tamánamis* come to you for a visit? Bring you healing powers?"

"In a way, yes, a *Tamánamis* came to me. If I can figure out how to make it work for me, it may be my best vision yet."

Malcomb reached in his shirt pocket and got some beef jerky. He gave a strip to Medusa. She stood on three good legs and a peg leg and wolfed it down. Her healing powers at an accelerated pace.

Malcomb's hand came out of his pants pocket. He had a B-flat harmonica and a gold pin, handed them to me. "Here," he said, "I was doing some laundry and these dropped out of Loren's shirt pocket. They must be yours. Who else would have a banjo pin?"

"Probably thousands of people," I said, "but thanks. This one is mine, alright." I was more gladdened to see that pin in my palm than when I first won it. Belated proof, beyond all doubt, I hadn't lost it in a blackout. I threw my arms around Malcomb in a bear hug. Surprising me, he returned the embrace. Two mature men hugging each other for the hell of it. For the love of it.

Medusa leaned against our legs. Whined. I released Malcomb and reached down and petted my dog with one hand, wiped the wetness out of my eyes with the other.

"I've got something of yours, too," I said. "I think I know where this sacred ground is you've been hunting for. It was hidden right under your eyes. I think you know it too, but won't admit it.

When I, as Qo-oo-la, was swimming down river I stopped to find Joshes ashes. I saw many rock carvings amongst the boulders of the fallen bluff, a drummer, water demon, animals. Kaalpekci Peak, or at least the waters below it, is your ancestral grounds."

Malcomb shook his head back and forth, up and down. Neck muscles popped. "Yes, I have suspected it for a few days now. I have been in denial because I will have to challenge the river demon, *Kaalpekci*. I am an old man. Century old stories say many young men tried and failed to kill him.

Time to prepare myself. And time to quit of this nose ring for good." He reached a hooked finger up to rip his nose ring out.

I stopped his hand. "Maybe *Kaalpekci* has forgotten about you. Or, maybe the proper ritual to summon him has been lost forever. Anyway, I don't think I want to see this nose ring thing again," I said. "I'm getting out of here. I need to make some phone calls anyway. Please sit with Medusa until I get back."

49

Threatening Calls and Midnight Escape

It took the community information pipeline three days to catch up with Sheriff Gloeckler. Three merciful days for my loon brother, faithful pooch and, yes, me too, to recuperate. I spent part of that time making phone calls. Among others, I talked to my VA shrink, Dr. Rothenberg, who told me Dr. David called him and wanted authorization to have me institutionalized. Dr. Rothenberg refused. He also warned me, in his non-aerated tenor voice, that I was flirting with hallucinatory trouble by not taking my medication. I told him not to worry. So far I had experienced no problems at all.

Speaking of calls, the morning of the third day, the clinic started getting concerned inquiries about the loon. By the afternoon, inquiries about Qo-oo-la quickly changed to anonymous threats against my life. Not a week gone by and already sued and threatened. I'd certainly made a big splash on the Olympic Peninsula.

I spent the time helping April muck out cages and tend shot, mashed, maimed and mutilated animals. I seemed to have a talent for it, especially the birds. Every chance I got though I spent with Qo-oo-la and Medusa. As soon as Qo-oo-la had strength enough we filled a plastic washtub full of water and put canine and loon in the same room. Those two took to each other like littermates. They seemed to help each other heal. Their energy and enthusiasm certainly helped me to heal. The healing fast track was a good thing because our time was up.

April did some research and found out loons don't do well in captivity. It was time to put Qo-oo-la back out in the wild.

Late the afternoon of the third day Sheriff Gloeckler showed up and wanted to take possession of the loon. April wouldn't let him, and told him that whatever clue was in the loon's gizzard was probably ground to metal dust by now. He said he'd be back early the next morning with a search warrant.

At midnight, I dressed in the dark, leaving my shoes off 'til last so as not to wake April in the next room and involve her as a tampering-with-evidence accomplice. Medusa awoke too, her eyes red flames from the reflected green exit light. She licked my offered hand, with a familiar wet and velvety tongue. In three days she had regained some of her health and vigor. Although probably still too injured to travel, Medusa would never forgive me if I left her and, I feared, protest vociferously. Wake every bird in the building; send a signal all the way to Seattle.

Sensing my exit plan Medusa leaped up and started her circle "go" dance, her peg leg clunking the tile. I grabbed her, picked her up and crept out to the back parking lot to my VW Bus, deposited her in the shotgun seat. She took up her post with canine authority.

Off to the northeast there was a glow on the horizon which I took to be the night-lights of Seattle. An east wind blew and I got a faint whiff of sewer gas and gull shit. I hesitated, unconsciously attracted to the luminous horizon. It beckoned with a rarefied radiance. Even in the wild, the call of civilized oblivion is not far. Were I a luna moth, crazed with incandescent lust, I would take off for the synthetic light immediately. As a human, I could be there in two hours, money in my pocket but not one song in my heart. Without a song in my heart where would I be? No matter where I was.

A bat arced through the phantom glow, a silent hunter of the night, deadly to graceful and elegant flying luna moths, yet the bat itself, an awkward and stumbling flyer. From the inland sea, I smelled the egg and sperm-bloated, spring, silver salmon that were amassing for their last heroic swim up the Dosanomish, their epic journey ending up river, if they make it that far, in a perilous final fuck.

The east wind picked up, whistled across the black sea, churning the pregnant waters and sneaking under my clothes causing my body hair to fluff, like feathers, insulating me and adding a buoyancy to my step.

I bounded back into the clinic for Qo-oo-la and couldn't resist taking a moment to admire his comely features. His body upright in the water, rocking back on smart splayed feet, elegant neck practically healed and regal head held high, expecting me, ready to rock and ready to roll. In the eerie green light, Qo-oo-la's collar shined and shimmered like polished jade. He arched his neck, spread his serviceable wings and tilted his head, poised as a prelude to voice.

I, feeling self-conscious, with a finger to my lips, closed the fingers of my other hand over his beak, shushing him. Qo-oo-la immediately sat back down on his haunches. I ran my fingertips over the scabbing on his neck. I had no time to revel at the ease in our communication. I picked up Qo-oo-la and carried him to my bus, put him on the floorboard between me and the dog, whereupon Medusa began licking his proffered head. Those two, the domestic dog and wild loon, were pals. I jumped in the driver seat. No keys. April took them. I went around back, opened up the motor hatch, felt behind the light panel for my extra set of keys. I may have been a flake in the old days — The old days? Can it be that was only six days ago? Can so much happen and change in six short days? — But I always had backup keys.

An extra set of keys was rule number one of a road nomad.

I started the engine and eased out of the parking lot. I could have released Qo-oo-la in the Salish Sea, his winter home, but Malcomb convinced me that, because of ancient ceremonial significance, I had to do a spirit dance and sing a spirit song on Kaalpekci Peak. Qo-oo-la was the key to making the healing ceremony work.

Still, I would never trap my beautiful Qo-oo-la in the river again, at the mercy of hounds and hunters. I knew, by some subtle communication between bird and human, if I did the spirit healing ceremony right, Qo-oo-la, in spite of his fishhook wounds, would no longer be flightless. Give him an ample take off strip of water and he could fly away to a high mountain lake, perhaps to find one of Gavia's sisters and start a family.

And, once airborne, of course, elude all the folks trying to gut him for the treasure in his gizzard.

So I couldn't dance and I couldn't sing. A small clunker in my plan.

I had one more stop to make. I pulled over next to a telephone booth I'd seen in front of a realtor's office adjacent to Highway 101. The booth was lit and anyone traveling 101 could see me, but who would be up at twelve fifteen in the morning?

I looked up the phone number and dialed the Jefferson County Sheriff's office. It took several minutes — in which I was buffeted by the draft of eighteen wheelers speeding along 101 — of negotiating with a recording before I was down to two options: leave a message for Sheriff Gloeckler or punch star to have the privilege to wait another eon to talk to a real person. I left a carefully composed message for the sheriff, condensing everything I had learned in the last three days.

I threw in an urgent plea for him, in spite of what he thinks of me, to follow-up on the leads I suggested, then hung up, jumped in my bus and threw gravel taking off for the Dosanomish. It was five miles of curvy road from April's clinic to the river and I drove it with the foot pedal to the floorboard. My bus, unaccustomed to such harsh treatment, screamed in protest and vibrated like a dyspeptic helicopter.

A great horned owl hooted up the valley. I could smell the snappy freshness of forest vegetation putting out new growth after a long dormant winter, mingling with the wet oil odor of the highway. My headlights caught the wind gusting the tops of roadside trees, giving the sky a ghost-dancing feel.

I headed for my property. My property? "Myyyyyy property." There, I said it out loud, drawing it out. "Myyyy home." Did it mean I was getting territorial; that I might have a place to set my feet squarely on the ground, dig in and stay put? My hands felt clammy. A hunger of unknown origin filled my chest cavity and soaked my brains. I thought of fireflies blinking in Grandpa Two-loons' palm, grits and pan-fried bread, obscure banjo tunes played on a homemade instrument.

I turned onto the logging road and stopped, blinded by an intense unfamiliar longing. I could feel blood bulging behind my eyelids. Medusa whined, nudged me with her nose. I opened my eyes and shook my head. Strange desires scattered.

I started again and drove until I came to the end of my road, could drive no more.

50

Failed Intimacy and "Faded Love"

As soon as I opened the shotgun door, Medusa's nose started twitching in the direction of the old growth cedar on the other side of my cabin. "No," I said, "You stay with me. I need you for the ceremony." Medusa hopped down, her peg leg thumping the ground, pointed her busy nose at the cabin and whined. I recognized that whine. It was her recognition of a familiar, an acknowledgement of a pack member. "So you smell Clancy, your ol' gravel-bar buddy, eh? I don't know what happened between you two but, with every trigger-happy cracker in the country looking for that cougar, he's probably long gone up in the mountains by now. At least I hope he is."

I picked up Qo-oo-la. He strained in the direction of the river and Kaalpekci Peak. I opened the sliding door with my free hand, undid the hasps on my banjo case and got my pick bag out. I massaged the soft leather. Could feel the individual picks, thumb, middle finger, index, with my fingers. A banjo picker's fingerpicks, like a fiddler's bow, are an extension of his body, more valuable spiritually than the banjo itself. I'd had those same picks for twenty years; slept with them on, ate with them on, made love with them on.

They were worthy of sacrifice.

The sky had a half-moon casting wedges of light through the trees.

We trudged toward Kaalpekci Peak. Carrying a loon uphill for several minutes made me gasp for breath. I paused several times. My lungs ached from the exertion, dreading the task at hand.

Walking out of the forest onto Kaalpekci Peak, I was struck again at the environmental contrast, like a different climate, dry, desert-like. I sat Qo-oo-la down, took off my shoes and felt yesterday's stored sunshine radiate up through the moss, from the stone. My toes wiggled with the wonder of it. Why had I ever worn shoes?

There was a hollow the size of a hubcap in the rock, and someone recently, probably Malcomb, had built a fire. The ashes were fresh enough they had not been rained on. I broke some dead twigs and limbs off the creeping manzanita shrub and built a fire.

I stripped off my clothes. Brrrrr! Reached next to the fire and grabbed a piece of charcoal. Made some black stripes across my forehead, down my nose and on my chilly cheeks and bony chest. I reached in my shirt pocket pulled out my fingerpick pouch.

I was struck by the heady aroma of twenty years of sweat and stale leather.

I took the pouch to the fire and tossed it in. Blue flames leaped up.

I danced a step. Another. The moss hurt my feet. A hint? Dancing was not my path. I plopped down between Medusa and Qo-oo-la. Both the dog and the loon nudged me. They wanted more; wanted to become part of the ritual. But what could I do? I picked up my pants to get a handkerchief to wipe the sweat off my face and felt the B-flat harmonica in my pocket.

I took it out. Its silver casing gleamed in the fireside shadows. Its wooden innards wanted kissing. I gave it a dry smack. Then a brisk toot. Qo-oo-la and Medusa jerked to attention. My lungs throbbed; my lips and tongue hungered to devour that little ten-hole tool.

Dare I do it? Take a chance? Flirt with failure so soon after botching "Faded Love," the song, looking back to a mere week ago, that got me into this fix? Dr. Rothenberg said I would never be able to play music again.

I clinked the harmonica between my teeth and clamped down. I started out doing some blues chops and riffs, basic stuff, nothing fancy. My lips, though hesitant, liked the long-time-absent feel of the hard metal. My dehydrated tongue fattened with diffused blood. It touched the keyboard, a humming bird probing for wild nectar.

Medusa began to get that glazed look in her eyes, which signaled she was searching for the groove. Qo-oo-la bobbed his long neck, uttering a near-purring sound. Without further ceremony, I put the harmonica to my lips, closed my eyes and blew. "OOO-WAA-WA-WA, OOO-WA-Wa-Wa-WAAAAAA." It came to me: harmonica, with its harsh descant and nasty bend notes, was the perfect instrument medium with which to speak to the gods. And to the dead.

You must also listen to the living. Medusa blasted me with a baritone howl to my left and Qo-oo-la, in my other ear, trilled a low tenor. Dog snout and loon beak pointed straight up to the heavens. Ready to do choral service for home and heaven and compadre.

The fire jumped up as if a bright wind had billowed under it.

My lips loved the solid feel of music clamped between them.

Enough warm up, I took the plunge. I began wailing. So did Medusa and Qo-oo-la.

Qo-oo-la's sweet tenor soared out over the bluff and down to the river, skimming the surface, penetrating its depths to saturate migrating salmon, compelling them to leap out of the water; then the loon voice followed the murky water up to its source, doubled back and came jetting down river, gaining strength.

Medusa's rich baritone stirred the needles on the fir and cedar trees surrounding the Peak, resonated down to their roots, sending ground waves along the valley floor to the great herd of elk foraging for swamp grass in a sheltered peat bog, causing the lead cow to snort and stomp the earth and move the herd to higher ground. One young bull, confused, bugled a mating call.

I pulled out all the stops. Didn't play any known tunes. Let the instrument choose the path. Follow an interesting riff in infinite variations.

My lungs had never felt so full of bellowness. Could bend a note a whole step and hold it for ages. I had never, never known such wondrous breath before. Where did it come from?

My chops echoed off the nearest mountain, reverberated throughout the valley, mingled with Medusa's and Qo-oo-la's and blanketed the land with such discordant, raucous sounds, the likes of which have never been heard in the Dosanomish valley before or since.

Clancy, the golden ghost of the mountain, flitted his tiny ears and twitched his magnificent black-tipped tail. Left off stalking the elk herd and headed at an easy gait for the source of the sound.

The sound was brassy; the sound was nasty; the sound was shameless. The sound became an aural tsunami of torment and ecstasy, rushing down river to the Salish Sea and stunning moon-basking seals, inspiring them to roll sausage-plump bodies into the water and dive deep. Shrimp fishermen hauled up their nets and faced their boats west into the ghostly gale. The harbormaster in Port Townsend sent out a distress call and got on the Bigfoot web site to report an audio sighting. A trolley conductor in Seattle punched his forehead with the palm of his hand thinking maybe he should get that new hearing aid after all.

We chortled and giggled, yodeled and growled, and howled and hallelujahed until I thought my lungs would burst. Oh, that cursed Kaalpekci Peak did sore ring with wild music that new-dawning morning.

I can't say how long my little but loud trio played together: could've been two minutes or two hours. Sore-throated Qo-oo-la gave out first, laid his long neck across my legs. Then Medusa did the same across my other leg — beak and snout lapped like littermates.

A pale morning light made the moss glow lavender.

My charged lungs could've gone on forever, but I had to pause to give my lips and tongue a chance to catch-up. The feeling had gone out of them like they'd been slapped with a frozen fish. My upper lip felt as thin as a banjo string. But I wasn't done yet. I'd been too long fallow. I was onto the first good musical French kiss since the wrecking bar unstrung my strings, and I wasn't going to let it pass without going all the way.

My flattened lips fleshed up and I cupped the harmonica against them. Reached out with the raw tip of my tongue and touched the tangible speech of my tortured soul.

Only the first note was painful or doubtful; then I floated into that unbearable lightness of being vouchsafed for fallen nincompoops that have renewed faith — however fumbling — with the gods. However untraditional those gods may be. I could've done an easy, light version of "Faded Love," no fuss, just the simple melody, but that's not what I needed to do or where I had to go. I risked all and reached deep inside myself, exploring psychic scars, opening subconscious wounds and exposing a lifetime of abysmal failures: failure at family, failure at career, failure at friendship, failure at compassion, failure at courage, and finally failure at love and intimacy.

I drew out all past moral ruptures and emotional bungles, like a hollow needle sucks puss out of a boil, and filtered ethical flops through the thin brass reeds of the ten-hole harmonica. I wailed and cried. Oh I was hot with confession. My toenails were molten steel. I went into a euphonious trance. Toxins and poisons rushed through my arteries to fill my lungs and gush out of my mouth. I saw hideous, gaseous images hovering in the hot air above the flames and then burn, damnit, burn.

My consciousness switched back to "Faded Love." I was done with simple melody and light, surface touch. I climbed right into the musical stirrups of "Faded Love." I used every bluesy technique I knew and then some, to grub for its backbone. I became ecstatic with inflections, intoxicated with infinite tonality. Lips and tongue and lungs functioned as one. I tasted a sanguine core. Finally, I owned that tune and, in turn, that tune owned me.

"Faded Love" wasn't faded no more.

I hit one last, long resolution note and stopped. An eerie brown mist blanketed the Peak, making a whispering sound. The forest was silent. I was played out. Perspiration oozed from my pores and soaked a substance covering my body. My eyes too, were dripping with sweat and at first I thought my skin had changed colors, that my Native

American ancestry, biding its time, had grown through. I was a reddish brown color. Medusa and Qo-oo-la's fir and feathers were the same rich rust color. We were anointed with, what I thought in my mystical state of mind was consecrated dust. It smelled dry and musty, like dust from an enclosed closet.

I touched the back of Qo-oo-la's neck and bestirred last year's dead cedar needles. Gnashing sound waves must have dislodged them, en mass, from the big trees' boughs. They made tiny hissing sounds hitting the fire.

51

Sober Sex and Virgin Territory

A voice from the edge of the forest knifed the sacred stillness of the moment. "A big wind must of come up. Blew all those dead cedar needles down." It was April. She emerged from the trees, skirted the fire and knelt beside me. "Look, " April shoved her short graceful forearm against mine; "our skin is the same color. "

Medusa raised her head and licked April's hand. Qo-oo-la yabbered.

"I was attempting a power song and haven't got on any clothes." I wasn't modest or ashamed; I was still in a semi-trance. I did make a half-hearted attempt to cover my kachubies with my little harmonica. Sad to say, it worked.

"Don't bother," said April. "I've been watching you for ten minutes. Heard the yodeling, howling and harmonica way down the valley. This valley is like a giant resonance cavinator funneling sound down to the sea. Quite a painful cacophony. I can't decide whether it was exalted or just plain awful. Then when you played "Faded Love," like I've never heard it played before, I knew you were the real thing."

My forearm, where we touched, smoldered and smelled like cedar pitch. April's long black hair fell over my naked brown thighs. I could feel each individual strand caress my skin, a thousand infinitesimal kisses. I leaned over and put my cheek against hers. My nose in her honey-suckle-scented hair.

"Wait. Let's get some of those dead needles off you." April unbuttoned and removed her green plaid shirt. She didn't have on an undershirt or a bra. I swallowed half a dozen times to control my breath. "Close your eyes," she said. I reluctantly obeyed. I felt my eyelids and face being scrubbed down. Made a rustling sound, like barnyard straw. April moved down to my scorched chest with practiced efficiency; her medical hands sure and professional.

Was I no more to her than an oil-tainted shore bird, needing cleaning?

A song sparrow, deep in the forest, broadcast a mating lullaby. Other songbirds took courage and began spring territorial calls. Warmth flowed from Kaalpekci Peak into my rear and spread through my loins up toward April's competent fingers.

I felt my sex stir, scattering rust-colored needles. April skirted my lap and moved down my legs, scrubbing a tad more vigorously. Now I could see her naked back, curving over my feet, hair tickling between my toes. Suddenly she straightened and looked up at my face with those misty sable eyes. The pupils were ebony and wet and inviting in the caressing yellow-red firelight. A coyote gave a spirited yip-yip-yip across the canyon. Medusa growled and moved away from me a few yards, lay back down, facing toward the big cedar. The Dosanomish hummed in my ear. April stood up and unbuckled her belt and slid out of her jeans and light blue panties. All she had on was her purple and gold leaping-salmon earrings, which caught a ray of light from the fire and seemed to jingle and jump up a phantom waterfall launched by spawning fever. She straddled my lap, bit my ear and whispered, "If you're going to be visited by Elpenor, tell me now, before this madness goes any further and I make a complete fool of myself again."

I placed one hand around April's supple waist and the other under her firm butt. Her skin was moist and warm. I lifted her off me. Set her buns down on the moss. "Forget Elpenor. I'm worried about everyone else, namely the sheriff and possibly the killer. If you heard our song from way down the valley so could they." I turned my eyes away. Tried not to look at her nakedness. My penis was having none of it. It had eyes in the back of my head. What I couldn't see my penis could sense. And it had a wicked sensor.

April slithered around behind me. Began massaging my neck. Felt something warm and wet touching my back.

"What are you doing?" I said.

"I'm tracing your rabbit scratches with my tongue. You know. . . ." Lick, lick, lick.

"Stop it," I said.

"Stop what? Whoever heard your noise probably mistook it for coyotes and loons caterwauling. Hey, your ear is pierced."

"A girl friend did it years ago while I was passed out. Don't do that to my earlobe. We have to go." I attempted to rise.

"I don't think so," April said. She hooked her arms around my neck and pulled me over backwards. For a five foot, ninety-six pound veterinarian she was strong as a sumo wrestler.

A long time later, we lay sticky and sweaty beside each other. My mouth, after intense harmonica playing and then, fierce, prolonged kissing, felt like it'd been slapped with a hot, iron poker. I was not technically — like Qo-oo-la had been before the beautiful Gavia — a virgin, but spiritually I certainly was. Not only was it the first time in two years I'd had sex, it was possibly the first time ever, as an adult, I'd made love sober, without some drug in my system. Further, it was definitely the first time I'd ever had sober sex with someone I loved.

Didn't seem possible, but there it was. I'd never experienced such deep sensations before. As a human anyway. You'd think I'd at least had a clue. Something — or someone — would've said to me, "Hey, clod-brain, the reason you have watered-down and insipid orgasms is because you've desensitized yourself with drugs." Sober orgasms: is that why clean and sober people saunter around with that self-satisfied look on their faces?

I could feel the incessant rhythm of the Dosanomish pounding far below as I lay on my back in a mossy bed — no finer bed for making love existed — atop Kaalpekci Peak and watched Thunderbird circling above us. How could I have missed it all those years? Sober sex. Sober love. Sober music. Sober living. Living life physically, mentally and spiritually sober. What a unique concept. The possibilities seemed endless.

What a place to conceive my newfound knowledge.

"Where's Qo-oo-la?" April propped up on her elbow and looked around.

Medusa, bored with our lovemaking, had slept and, hearing April's raised voice, roused.

I too scanned the Peak. No Qo-oo-la. I saw awkward skid marks on the moss, marks a water animal makes trying to move on land. Medusa clamored up, whimpered, her leg probably still sore as hell — and followed the spoor to where it led between two Douglas firs. There was a low-canopied animal trail that led toward the old growth cedar. Medusa sniffed the ground, then sniffed the air, turned to me and barked. Her, "Okay-it's-time-for-action," bark.

April pushed up, turned her backside to me, and began dressing. "We'd better go after him. I heard a coyote yip and that cougar — even though you say it's friendly — is out there and all cats are unpredictable."

I watched, from the rear, April squirm into her tight jeans. From every angle, her body was sensuous. I was reluctant to vacate the mood. "Qo-oo-la's headed to the water," I said, "his home. That's where I was taking him anyway." I circled her ankle with my needy fingers.

April blushed and pulled away. "No, not again, not now anyway. I think we should go after Qo-oo-la. Something's not right. Don't you feel it?"

Medusa barked again. Insistent. At me. She trembled for a command.

I struggled to my feet. My legs shook. I wobbled over to my canine pal. Stooped down and hugged and petted her. Her body was aquiver with suppressed movement. "Okay, you go after Qo-oo-la. Look after him 'til we get there. Now git." Medusa lunged to go and then stopped. Her black nose sniffed the air all around. She looked up at me with confused eyes and whined. "Go on now, git to Qo-oo-la," I said, and patted her rump. She plunged down the low-canopied trail, her peg leg scraping and banging against tree trunks.

"You think she understood?" April said. She shook her shirt full of fir needles, raised her arms to put it on. Her small breasts jiggled.

Songbirds had stopped singing. The air turned dry and hot. A brown creeper — a wren-sized bird that feeds by flying to the base of a tree and creeping to the top — mid-way on a Douglas Fir, suddenly panicked and flew into the deep forest. A white haze had covered the morning sun and a dim alabaster light spilled over the clearing. The clearing shrunk, low hanging limbs, lower and denser, closed in. My senses had gone to red alert. A branch swished downwind.

April said, "I think we should get out of here with all possible haste. That cougar's still around and there's still a killer on the loose. This place is a trap with only one way out."

"Two, if you count jumping off the bluff."

April gave me what is known as a withering look. Happy to see that prolonged intimacy hadn't dampened her field marshal attitude. "That is not an option Mr. Harp Pearl Gravey. Besides, you'd drown in ten seconds."

I thought an explanation was called for. "I wasn't prepared for the icy cold the last time I — "

"Well, well, ain't this the intimate little scene." Lt. LeRoy stepped out from the forest opposite from where Medusa had entered. His nine mm Sig Saur, silencer attached, pointing at my heart. Low hanging branches blackened and spun. The lieutenant had flushed a swirl of tiny, black, no-see-'em gnats which clouded around his camouflaged head.

"Haven't you learned anything, you clown?" April said. "You can't go pointing a gun at people when ever you feel like it." She was ever on point to make a rotten situation worse. She pulled at her leaping salmon earrings. Hey, one of them was missing. Maybe she didn't see that fat serious silencer.

"Thank you Pocahontas," he said. "When I first saw you here, I thought, 'Darn, it's a down right pity but I'm going to have to kill her too.' But then you just reminded me; I've got a big score — two slaps if I recollect right — to settle with you." The Lieutenant grinned. His facial skin was stretched taunt over his lean jawbone, which worked incessantly, yet the wad of gum was gone. He chewed on emptiness. For some reason that worried me more than his officer-sized chaw.

The word "kill" hung in the air. April hands fluttered to the sky, nipples outlined against her shirt.

I had managed to get my jeans on. Still, my penis tried to hide from the gun. One ear felt heavier than the other. I tugged on April's other leaping salmon earring. She had slipped it on me while I snoozed. Going to my death and wearing an earring. I felt courage radiate through my fingers from the earring. "Nice hat," I said, "looks familiar too. Isn't it just like the other one, the *Legend in My Own Mind*,' one the mountain lion snatched off your head." My voice was the only weapon I had.

"Sing! Damnit! Sing your way home!" said Elpenor.

Lt. LeRoy's face turned to stone. His pool hall-yellow, facial pallor became waxen, two eyes, ovals of glittery white, glancing around the clearing. A twitch traveled up the rigid set of his jaw to where his ear was still bandaged. He touched the brown bandage with his left hand, leaving his right hand to clutch the nine mm, drooping so it now pointed at my crotch, which clutched and felt as exposed and heavy as a bowling pin and a pair of bowling balls.

52

Cougar Fetishes and Canine Courage

"Son-of-a-bitch lion chewed off my ear," Lt. LeRoy said.

"You're lucky it wasn't your head," I said. "That killer cat took a distinct dislike to you."

"Never you mind about that son-of-a-bitch lion, mud-boy." The distended, swollen gun barrel flicked up to my forehead. "My hounds will get him eventually and I'll make me a throw rug with his pelt where I can walk over it and wipe my pillow-stompers on it every day. Then I'll mount his head in my den, hang my cap on it every night." He flicked his cap off and snagged it on the imaginary head of a mountain lion. His military-cut hair was like tarnished brass. A vein in Lt. LeRoy's neck, right under his damaged ear, popped up, pulsed and turned purple. His skinny forehead broke out with sweat.

He reached around behind him and produced some twine, threw it at me. "Take that piece of twine and tie your gal friend's hands behind her back. Keep her out of trouble 'til we get down to the river and I can take care of . . . hey where's your ugly dog and that stupid duck? I need to get the stupid bird. Killing you two is just icing on the cake."

"What do you mean, kill me?" April said. "Oh my God, you're the killer; you killed Molly and Billy, and you're planning to kill. . . . " April's shoulders heaved. I could hear her breath coming in short gasps.

Lt. LeRoy was at least twenty feet away — too far to try a rush and tackle. Only chance we had was bullshit. Across the canyon, the osprey's nest was silent and still. Abandoned or gone fishing. No help from the sky. Just as well, get herself killed too. The air on Kaalpekci Peak felt stale and stagnant. The tops of the trees, way out of reach, swayed with an unsteady breeze.

I caught the roll of twine.

"That's it mud-boy," Lt. LeRoy said, "now tie your girl friend's hands behind her back. And don't try anything, I've been in four campaigns, and know every trick in the book. I asked you a question; where's that damn dog and duck? I heard all three of you while ago making the worst racket I ever heard and I'm a man of the world — heard it all."

"They've gone down to the river," I said, "and he's not a duck. That racket you heard is called music." Stalling for time. I circled behind April and guided her trembling hands behind her back, her fingertips fluttering like the wings of a captured humming bird. She'd got the message that we were in some serious shit. Good. Best thing for us is if she keeps quiet. I gave her slim wrist a squeeze of reassurance. April squeezed back, whispered, "The second escape route."

Lt. LeRoy cackled. "Hey, no talking. Yeah right, if that was music, I'm Snow White. Make that binding tight. I'll check it. The three of us are going to take a little walk down to the river too; visit your worthless mutt — be a pleasure to put it out of its misery too — and the duck. I know your duck can't fly and can't stay under water forever so I'll just have to wait 'til it surfaces. Easier'n shooting clay pigeons. If you're lucky I'll let you live long enough to watch me slice it open and jerk out its gizzard. Just for drill. Ha, ha, get it mud-boy. Just for *drill*, I might rip out its bloody heart and eat it raw. All the trouble it's caused. Now get away from your gal friend and let me check your knot." Lt. LeRoy's guzzle, in his buzzard throat, galloped and galumped.

I stepped aside, as close to the trees as possible. "No need to kill the loon," I said. "Your pin in his gizzard has been ground to dust by now. So no one can tie you to the murders. Just your word against ours and we ain't talking, right April? We can't be sure what was on that pin when we x-rayed it. Could've been an Aladdin's lamp for all we could tell."

Maybe I could talk the military man out of killing us. Far off, down by the river, Medusa barked.

"Don't plead to this creep," said April, "it was an anvil. I'm certain of it. Tin Soldier here is a blacksmith, or better yet maybe a gunsmith." She turned her body and looked at me. Her oval eyes reflected the orange-red glow of the fire. I pinched the flesh around her armpit. Get her to shut the fuck up. She yelped. The fire glow, mirrored in her eyes, burned a hole in my forehead.

"I wouldn't know one end of an anvil from another," he said. "You're not as smart as you think you are Pocahontas."

I said, "If you don't have anything to do with black smithing or gun smithing then you don't have to kill the loon . . . or us either." Thing was, I was certain he wasn't *the* killer; yet, I was just as certain he was *a* killer.

"Nice try but sorry; the three of you have to go. That damn duck 'specially. Four, counting the dog."

"At least tell us why?" I said.

"I don't have to tell you shit. Move away from your gal friend. Over there on the other side of the fire."

"I know you didn't kill Molly or Billy," I said.

"Don't be a blockhead Harp," April said, "of course he killed them. Why would he be doing this if he didn't?"

"Yeah Harp — what a dumb name — why would I be doing this if it wasn't me?"

"Because you're a mercenary, soldier of fortune, hired gun, that's why. You're getting paid to do it."

"Well ring one up for lover boy. He's not a dumb as he looks."

"If this nincompoop didn't do it, then who did?"

I regretted I didn't duct tape April's mouth shut. Every stalling step I took forward, she took two steps back. If the soldier of fortune was innocent then I might be able to reason him out of killing us. "Doesn't matter. The good Lieutenant doesn't have any blood on his hands yet. He could pack up and leave and — "

"It's Gabe Moody isn't it?" April said. "That's who's paying this red-neck, cracker — "

" — And we wouldn't say a word. Would we April? In fact, we'd pay you an equal amount to let us go — "

" — Of course; it's Inge Endicott, murdering jezebel, while her poor hard working husband is off selling kiddy games. Just like her to send some hair-trigger, half-wit to do her dirty work. And I wouldn't pay one red cent to — "

" — That way you could leave this peninsula with a clear conscious. And, you know you'd never get away with killing us anyway, so why don't we just forget the whole thing?"

Lt. LeRoy said, "I could retreat I suppose, except for a couple of things smart-ass: For one thing, I wouldn't leave your bodies where they'd be found. I've killed dozens of people on three different continents and haven't spent a day in jail yet." Lt. LeRoy stopped talking as he walked behind April. He grabbed her bindings and gave a stout tug. April's chin jerked up and she let out a little cry. An air pocket in the fire fizzled and popped. The treetops swayed and twirled in random patterns. The swirls of no-see-'em gnats, in frenzied motion, followed Lt. LeRoy, and swirled around April. I tasted lead on the end of my tongue and smelled the odd sweetness of gun oil soaking into honeysuckle. A dull ache started around my acrylic plate and spread to the back of my neck.

Medusa's baying sounded down by the river.

Over April's and Lt. LeRoy's shoulder, I thought I caught movement in the ancient cedar. Probably a squirrel going about its business of mating and procreating while we humans off each other.

"You said a 'couple of things?'" I said. Keep him talking was my only strategy.

"Oh yeah: the second is — killing is what I do for a living. It's the only good skill I ever got from this lousy gov'ment. I'm good at it, I like the hours and I get a lot of satisfaction out of it."

"Only a low-life pervert would live like that," said the ever bad-timing April, through clinched teeth.

My love, I thought, *if I had a sock I'd stuff it in your pretty mouth. As kissable as it is, it's gonna get us killed.*

Lt. LeRoy grabbed a fistful of April's long thick hair, forced her head back as far as it would go. His thin upper lip recoiled as if he'd touched a catfish corpse, but he didn't let go. Jerked her off-balance. Small glittery eyes, sunk back in a teakettle skull, focused on me. "Payback time mud-boy." He stiff-armed the nine mm's fat, unblinking muzzle at my face. Taking dead aim. My back, where the rabbit had scratched, felt as if pins were sticking me in the wounds and my head had the ethereal thought that I could escape that black metal hole by diving into the great rock that was Kaalpekci Peak and swim to safety. Me, swimming in stone.

I was twenty feet from the trees — seemed like a thousand — there was no escape.

"No!" shouted April and leaped up and back just as Lt. LeRoy squeezed the trigger. The silencer made a phlegm-choked spitting noise and I felt the bullet's breath as it parted my hair.

"Fucking bitch," said Lt. LeRoy as they stumbled backwards. Lt. LeRoy regained his balance and slung April down backwards, clubbing her with the barrel of the gun. She groaned and rolled over . . . and over . . . and over . . . picking up momentum, toward the edge of the bluff, mouthing broken sentences so that what we heard was, "Pervert . . . maniac . . . and pea brain."

"Stop," shouted Lt. Leroy, leveled his gun at the tumbling body.

I realized what April was doing. "Over here soldier." I screamed and made a leap for the forest. Bark stung my back before I heard the muffled silencer sound.

April's down-spiraling shriek cut through the pain in my back like a razor. I heard a splash and silence. She had gotten away clean. Except for being in deep water with her hands tied behind her back. I figured I had three minutes to get to April.

Medusa's muffled bark sounded. Sharp ears heard the gun report. She was in the trees and coming up the bluff as fast as her three legs would carry her. A bullet awaited her unless I thought of something.

What was I saying: a bullet awaited me unless I moved. I heard Lt. LeRoy's running footsteps close behind. I pushed straight back through the thick forest, using the big silver fir for cover. Another bullet kicked a low hanging limb inches away from me. I dodged through thickets of tall mountain blueberries, around springy vine maple, under clumps of greenish-gold wolf lichen. My legs had wings, bare feet unflinching, sure and certain of every step. I wondered at the perfect fit of my footprint in the forest, like I was a deer, born to run through these woods.

I had a calm pervasive sense of destiny. If I had to die, it was a good day for it and I would die on hollowed ground, ground on which my bones would find peace and ground on which my spirit could rest.

Someday, but preferably not today. Not without one last ditch effort.

Lt. LeRoy crashed through the forest close behind me.

How long ago had April rolled over the cliff? Thirty seconds? I summoned all the telepathic energy I could muster and sent Qo-oo-la a message, *"Save April, as she saved you, 'til I can get there."* I almost broke running rhythm. For the first time one of my animal *communiqués* felt like it might have been received. I shook my head; was it merely the delusions of a demented man?

In the distance, Medusa clumped up the bluff.

Not consciously aware of it, I had circled around to the old growth cedar. A faint but unmistakable aroma had come to me. A wind blew up a trail from the river swirling around the ancient cedar, bringing with it the scent of decayed mushrooms, decomposing tree bark, and, ah yes, the subtle essence of supine feline. Could it be that Clancy, the golden ghost, heard my power song call and was couched in the big cedar with his trophy caps? A compulsive trophy hunter could always use one more. Ask Lt. LeRoy.

I thought I'd do just that. I stopped, hollered in the general direction of his footsteps, "Who's your boss?" He stopped running.

Started walking. "Show yourself and I'll tell you."

I stepped backwards. Except for the in-step sounds of our feet, the near woods were silent, no spring bird song or morning squirrel mating chatter. A crooked hemlock, in a sudden gust of wind, rubbed against the trunk of another, grating like heavy wheezing.

Above the tree-top canopy, Thunderbird called, *"Cheeerkee, cheeerkee!"* Looking for us. Her shadow crept across the hazy sunlight that eased through the tops of the tallest Doug firs, casting the lower canopy in deeper shadows.

Thick low-hanging limbs hid us from above.

I hid behind a limb of the old growth cedar and would never have seen Clancy were it not for his magnificent curly-tipped tail. It hung down in shadows amongst some cedar boughs. I said a prayer to the cougar god to keep him invisible. Then the pungent tanginess of giant predator enveloped me like an invisible net and I was amazed Lt. LeRoy couldn't smell him. *Please, oh cougar god, also make him odorless. Give Clancy all the feline skills necessary to survive, 'cause in the next few seconds we have to surprise attack a highly skilled killer with a powerful weapon in his hands. And us with only our teeth and claws and hands. Oh yeah, what about voice? What was I missing about voice?*

Strangely enough, I felt no stirrings from Elpenor. My legs quit wobbling.

I figured I had about thirty seconds and April was history.

What was there about voice I couldn't see.

"Even primitive societies give a dying man his last request," I said. "I just want to know who hired you, that's. . . ."

"What are you up to mud-boy? As I said before, I'm an expert in real jungle warfare and this dinky, little rain forest ain't nothing by comparison. Piece of cake. There's nothing you can do I ain't already seen, trained and prepared for. You can't get away."

Medusa was now sounding like a buffalo herd and down and over to the side of the steep cliff, I could see a green wave of underbrush swaying with her onrushing body. As if she wasn't already a dead giveaway, she gave voice to a howl of the hunt.

I became fused with the sap of the tree and an image of Grandfather Two-Loons flashed beneath my closed eyelids, reminding me, "The best pool players play defense as well as offense. And the best pool hustlers do not have to out shoot their opponent. They have to out maneuver their opponent. The overzealous players will beat themselves."

It came to me; why not do the opposite of what he expected? Shun defense, play offense.

I hollered. "So what happened in boot camp when your mates found out you were a teenage bed wetter?" I said. I took a step backwards. And another.

"What? What? Who . . . who told. . . . That's a goddamn lie. I spilled some water in bed and they accused me. Hey, mud boy I've got the gun here, You better shut your mouth." I saw him through the tree coming straight for me, matching me step for step.

I talked and walked my talk backwards. "And what about all those letters you wrote home to your mama, begging, nay, pleading with her to rescue you from the cruel company commander cause he was persecuting you to death."

"Shut-up you som'bitch or I'll drop you here and now." The gun sneezed and a limb of vine maple snapped next to my throat, slivers stung my skin. I kept moving backwards. Wondering among wonders that my mental meanderings were striking a discord with the tough-as-nails Lieutenant. I was merely taking a clue from Gormley Longdoffer, the poorest, most pitiful soldier in my boot camp outfit. Gormley hadn't lasted two weeks.

Medusa howled louder and bashed the underbrush. She plowed up the trail with all the stealth and subtlety of a three wheel lawn mower with a stuck throttle.

The expert marksman matched me step for step but swiveled the weapon to point where the attacking canine would emerge from the thick foliage.

"What'd they give you — a dishonorable discharge? That's it isn't it? Ol' LeRoy couldn't cut the mustard in the real army and got a dishonorable discharge." We had gone about ten steps. I remembered what it was about voice. I sent a telepathic message to the golden ghost. *Sing!*

Sing to the good soldier! Sing your song of blood-boiling terror and mind-blinding torment. Sing damnit!

Lt. LeRoy refocused the weapon on me. His chinless chin bobbed for shameful memories. "Weren't no dishonorable. A medical. The bastards gave me a medical discharge. You don't understand, I loved the army and they mistreated.... You're just like them. Smartass know-it-all. Well looky here who's going to get a medical discharge; a discharge from life." He leveled the nine mm at my chest.

Medusa broke out of the underbrush pissed and frothing. Took a second for a look and a breath and then bore down on the Lieutenant, bugling like she'd just stepped off the boat from hell.

Clancy leaned his wide, nail-cutter, mouth down and, right in the bad ear of the armed-to-the-teeth lieutenant, canaried the primordial scream of the hunt. Even as I charged the gun-wielding mercenary, I saw the bedwetter's body leap in a spasm of terror, and he began firing the nine mm at Medusa, bullets bucking up the trail all around her. The lion's scream and Medusa's erratic locomotion saved her life.

Lt. LeRoy, his trigger finger frozen, sprayed the forest with bullets as he swept around toward me running at him. A semi-automatic weapon is a sprinter's inspiration. My feet flew. Nevertheless, there was no way I could tackle him in time. In the split second before the exploding gun aligned with me, a tawny cats paw, the size of a Pentecostal collection plate, swung down from the cedar limb and bopped the para-military man on his good ear and clawed upwards, making a noise like a brush stroke on a snare drum. The contact between paw and skull came in the split second interlude between gunshots, and resonated off-key and flat. Lt. LeRoy gave a toneless howl and somersaulted into a nootka rose bush. His cap and part of an ear, snagged on a cougar claw. The trained military man still hung on to automatic weapon, albeit silent. Undaunted, Medusa clamored over him and chomped down on Lt. LeRoy's trigger wrist. He yelped again as I pounced on him and wrestled the weapon away. It was hot, heavy and stank of scorched powder and cordite. It had an evil handgrip. Too evil to hold. I tossed it deep in the woods.

I grabbed Medusa's collar, and barked a release command at her. I was afraid the Lieutenant was going to have a ruptured wrist artery along with another missing ear. Medusa's jaws had only dented the flesh. Medusa took a second to lick my hand and then took up sentinel duty, growling from deep in her chest, at Lt. LeRoy's throat. The mercenary man, so cock-sure of himself was undone. He clapped his hands over his ears, and squeezed his eyes shut tight and curled in upon himself. He said, "Keep 'em away from me. keep 'em away from me, keep 'em away from me."

"Stay back Medusa." I said.

"No, no not the dog, the lion. Keep that killer lion away from me. Don't let him get me. Please! Please! Don't let him get me. Every night since I first saw that cat, I dream I wake up in its belly with all the other things its killed half rotted away. Don't let him eat me." His little tight teeth looked littler and drool dropped from his mouth.

Clancy, on a limb above Lt. LeRoy, chewed on his trophy hat. Oblivious of anything else. "That killer cat's right above you, Lieutenant. Make a move and he'll rip you apart." For all I knew, it was the truth but I didn't wait around.

My three minutes were used up.

I took off at a dead run. Fastest way from one point to another was as the crow flies. I sprinted across Kaalpekci Peak and did a flying leap into the unknown, shouting a prayer to the God "Ho-had-hun," "Teach me to swim."

I almost collided with a cruising raven. *"Gronk,"* spoke the raven. So close did I come that I caught a whiff of road-kill.

I hit water with a butt-flop splat.

The frigid water shocked my lungs. They stopped for an instant. But my heart still beat. My head called for panic. I refused to obey. April's life depended on me getting control of my fear of water. Besides, what's a little death by drowning when you've just survived a death by nine mm Sig Saur execution? Everything in perspective; once dead, the fear of death is greatly reduced.

For oneself. But not for the love of your life.

53

Pecked Eyes and Petulant Lips

The God, Ho-had-hun had failed me though; my prayer went unanswered. I still couldn't swim. My feet hit gravel bottom, surprising a six-inch cuttroat trout who thought himself hidden from predators. I flexed my legs and bounced — in slow motion — up. I needed air but oddly enough, my lungs weren't bursting. Nor, when I hit the surface, did I gasp for breath. I did a quick scan for April; in the fog I could see that there must have been an overnight storm in the mountains with mudslides from clear cuts in the watershed. The water level had risen and was the color of raw rabbit liver, reflecting a sky covered with a low-level lavender cloud.

No April.

A raven cruising for an early morning meal began nipping and cawing at something hidden in the logjam out of my sight. The raven hopped over to the petroglyph boulder where the force of the rushing waters spilling over the dam made hissing and slamming sounds. Pulverized water crab-clawed over the fossil-pitted rock, coating the raven's coral feet in yellow rabid slaver. A trick of light from the twisted trunks of madrone trees — reposing jazz dancers — in the dam, gave the raven's black coat orange blotches, as if it had some kind of diseased bird pox.

Still no April on the surface.

I went under again. Totally submerged, this time with eyes wide open, searching the bottom for my tethered love.

I felt the vibration of something in the current coming toward me. Fast. I flapped my arms in the swift waters and managed to turn around and face the speeding object. On land, facing the likes of Lt. LeRoy, I had some purchase, some maneuverability; but in water I was an amoebae in a drop of alcohol, I couldn't even control my floundering enough to grab a rock from the bottom as a battering tool.

I saw a pair of eyes so red and round they looked like blood marbles. Thank the river god, it was Qo-oo-la. He swam a few quick circles around me, slapping my chest and shoulders with his tail and then nudged my hand. I got the idea and grabbed the base of his neck, right around his pearly necklace. I put myself totally in his aquatic charge. My feet came alive, started pumping. Qo-oo-la piloted me to the surface. Commenced tugging me — my feet pistoning like a well-oiled engine — toward the logjam where I'd discovered Molly Jenkins's body a week ago.

We cut around a stump and there was April, head barely above water, hanging onto a bobbing branch, with her chin. The wary gray gull, with a red tipped yellow beak, stabbing at her eyes. My mind flashed crazily on the poster of the kitten suspended by paws and chin from a trapeze bar; the poster caption read, *"hang in there baby."*

Then I heard April's sweet voice. "You fucking bitch, peck at my eyes. I ever get out of this I'll cut off your god damned pecker." I let go of Qo-oo-la, grabbed the branch, unwittingly dunking April, and swatted at the disgruntled gull, who seemed more than happy to have an excuse to relinquish a lunch that sassed back. I scooped under April's arms when she bobbed back up — eyes okay, cheek gouged and bleeding, probably from Lt. LeRoy's gun-barrel swat — and worked my way along the branch to where it joined the main logjam. April spit a mouthful of water on me and coughed and choked and tried to speak, "Watch . . ." cough hack, "watch . . . out." . . . hack hack. I braced my legs against an underwater log and heaved April, on her breast, half out of the water. I moved around behind her and pushed on her buns and thighs. Could see her hands still tied by the twine. There were red welts around her wrists where the rope had cut into her flesh. Face stuck in a fistful of twigs and brush, April still jabbered at me. Pure gobbledygook.

Suddenly I heard an alarm tremolo from Qo-oo-la coming from the logjam, then the *"Kee! Kee! Kee!"* of Thunderbird, the *"gronk"* of the raven followed quickly by a *"gaack"* of the gull. The thick, damp air filled with bird sound, four species trying to out shout each other.

There was a percussive rhythm to it. My ear-ringed ear, in spite of good sense to the contrary, paused to listen, purely for the pleasure of hearing nature's impromptu symphony. I should have paid more attention to melody rather than meter.

A demon exploded out of the deep pool. Monster hands grabbed me from behind by the throat, then pushed off from the logjam with powerful flippered legs and catapulted me head first into the raging water.

Underwater, stiffened with fright, I grabbed feebly for the beast. His skin was slick and leathery. My grip slid off him like fingers off an oily eight ball. My nose caught a whiff of rotten eggs. The monster pulled me through an opening in the dam and crashed my head against the petroglyph boulder, causing jolts of pain to spasm my body; again and again the monster banged my head on the rocks, missing a direct blow to my acrylic plate but mangling the scar tissue around it and the thick brown water turned a thin seashell pink color. Smoke-coated fluorescence lights lit up the murkiness. The incessant banging knocked some sense into my head. My vision sharpened, I could see clearly.

It was *Kaalpekci*, Malcomb's invincible river monster emerged from the petroglyph rock to wreak vengeance on me the pretender shaman/god. I was a fraud, a false prophet, and deserved to be vanquished. Drowned like a sewer rat.

I had no breath left.

I could not fight it. There was no escape. I was a goner. I choked. I opened my eyes, tried to see death coming. Lights flickered off. I saw only black water. Black water. Black demon. Black death.

"This is a part-human monster, you disgusting quitter, you can fight back." Elpenor's voice rang in my cranium like a warped gong. My acrylic plate palpitated, a belfry on Easter morning.

I squeezed an answer out. "I don't care if he is part human, I have no way to combat the demon part."

"You are as thick-headed as a three-eared possum. You have no right to die and kill me too. We have a bargain and I expect you to stick to it. You too have an animal part you nincompoop, use it! Follow your own recent advice. Sing! Damnit! Sing!" Just like Elpenor, selfish to the end. Only interested in saving himself.

But I didn't die and my eyes adjusted to the turbid water. I faced a beetle-nosed, frog-eyed, humpback whose truculent claws were clasped around my throat. A gray flex protuberance snaked out of the monster's mouth and angled backwards over his head — a tubed hat — anchored by red mandibles.

My head sparked, short-circuiting, my body savaged by cold. My lungs were bursting. How long had we been underwater? Fifteen, twenty seconds. Thirty seconds was my limit and that had been years ago in a silly breath-holding contest in a tavern dive.

Suddenly, a black & white checkerboard projectile streaked out of the murky gloom and speared the gray flex tube. The momentum ripped it out of the mouth of the monster. Qo-oo-la, Deep Diver, Breath Holder, understood the source of the monster's air.

Behold! The beast had a human mouth. A petulant human mouth. A petulant mouth that, I swear, mouthed a modern cuss word. Aha! Ageless monsters wouldn't cuss. Would they?

One powerful hand released my throat and grabbed for the tubing which had disgorged a cascade of air bubbles bustling toward the surface. The other intractable hand held me fast. My eyes feasted on the air bubbles wasting away overhead.

The pretend-monster with the petulant mouth missed the flex tubing and grabbed Qo-oo-la's leg instead. Held it for a second. A second that resonated, and made some grounded, electrical connection.

Qo-oo-la and I, using the beast as a conduit, fused minds. In that brief time, my aquatic brother Qo-oo-la sang to me a birth song of awakening, a melody originated from the river. The song leaped to the sky, circled the pale, new moon and streaked back to earth, found a solitary penny whistle player standing on a beach boulder in Port Townsend, Washington, rode the crest of music waves back to me. So pure a rhythm, so simple a beat, so eternal a song that I forgot all about breathing, relaxed and felt my body take on ballast, become leaden and started sinking to the bottom; brimful of bird song, water song, earth song.

I settled in with my back resting against the boulder sporting the Warning Devil petroglyph. The rock shifted and emitted a sound like a whole chicken factory of eggshells cracking at once.

The man monster let go of Qo-oo-la, kept ahold of me, and followed me down, probably thinking I was done for. It had been at least a minute since I'd drawn a breath, maybe longer. I encircled both hands around the monster's rubbery wrist and intertwined my fingers into a vice grip. I looked him in his amphibian eyes and I mouthed the words, "Molly Jenkins told me to give you this message."

> "Fill your lungs with air my friend
> and this watery game you'll win,
> but suck a drought of H 2 O,
> and down the tube to hell you'll go."

Bubbles flitted in metered burst out of my mouth. Their popping sounded to my ears like distant tunnel drums. I threw in a smile as a downbeat. His lips returned a downright unfriendly frown. To me, with my new-found underwater vision, his frog eyes behind the mask, refocused into, first, an awareness that he had ahold of a singing dead man and second, that he was in deep trouble himself. He grabbed the fidgety air tube, stuck the end in his mouth and covered up Qo-oo-la's speared beak hole with his free hand. An imperfect fit.

He sucked a draught of H 2 O.

I heard the sound of a drain clogged with pasta come from his throat, he spit out the tubing along with a wad of purple phlegm, released my throat and jerked to free his hand from my unflinching grip. Flailed me with his free fist, kicked at me with flippered feet. My chin and shins absorbed the blows like a hot fire eats dry twigs. The beating sputtered and stopped and the monster went into a frenzy of convulsions. Random bubbles poured out of his mouth and nose. I held to his wrist, made myself into an inextricable weight, anchored fast to the rocky river bottom. Knew I had to hang on.

Knew also, in some deep-breathing giddy sort of phantasmagoric way, something hallucinogenic this way comes.

Even as the diver's rubbery body slipped into unconsciousness an ancient power gathered in from the shapes etched into the surrounding spheres, the great boulder I sat against cracked and split, tumbling me and my twitching prisoner along the river bottom. I let go of the diver, who floated face down toward the surface, and righted myself. Then beheld, emerging from a black, hellhole chasm, an amorphous voltaic river wraith.

54

Ancient Demons and
Modern Dragons

Kaalpekci lived. *Kaalpekci* was disturbed. By the looks of his chiseled teeth, *Kaalpekci* was a meat eater and bloodsucker.

My spirit power song and the hallucinogenic effect of three minutes of breath holding had summoned Malcomb's ancient river dragon. How long had the superannuated hellion slept, waiting for a human vessel dumb enough to call forth its corporal form? The succubus stank of centuries of slow digesting rotting corpses and blood sacrifice. Large-bowel tubing with dripping human body parts hung around the scaly folds of his trunk-like neck. One foot-long fang wore a human skull like a diamond ring; the other fang gnawed through river rock like a gizzard through grit. His headgear consisted of a derby hat, under which a bloodstained wedding veil flowed behind him winking with imbedded broken mirror glass. Buffalo horns, covered with owl skins protruded through the derby. His breast had the broken shafts of dozens of arrows sticking out, some buried up to the fletching. They resembled toothpicks in a voodoo doll. On each of his four legs he wore different stockings; one wrapped in a red-white-and-blue American flag, another an orange silk shawl, another in pale blue spider webbing and the last hind leg, was covered in black & white loon feathers.

"By the gods," I said.

Kaalpekci was a magnificent machine of death. *"Malcomb, ol' friend,"* I thought, *"I wish you were here to see this. All your ancient stories and superstitions are validated. Somehow I've blundered and blotched my way into another dimension. And you know what Malcomb? I'm so stoned I don't give a fat rat's ass."*

Kaalpekci spoke, "I heard your summons and challenge. I have been waiting. For thousands of years foolish shamans of your clan have tried to destroy me. I have heard your drugged and drunken songs. I have absorbed your puny weapons. I have killed and eaten you all."

"I don't have a clan or family and, look, no weapon. So eat me," I said.

"You must be even more addled with ritual song and dance and under the influence of drugs than your predecessors, to face *Kaalpekci* without a weapon," *Kaalpekci* said.

"Accuse me of song, accuse me of sin, accuse me of loving the lady April and I'm guilty as hell, but no drugs fat boy. I don't do drugs. I don't have to do drugs to destroy you." I put up my fists like a boxer. Did a couple jabs. "Yeah I can take you apart with my bare fists or my name isn't Harp P. Gravey." Qo-oo-la grabbed my good ear lobe and tugged.

"You dare to mock *Kaalpekci* with such a ridiculous name." The great beast roared like a train through a tunnel. Jagged sound waves cleared my clogged passages.

Shocked me out of my stupor. I needed some company. Time for my secret weapon. I summoned my own dragon. "Here you are Elpenor," I said. "Here's a chance to show your stuff. Have at him."

"Bullshit!" Elpenor said. *"Would you look at that thing? It's not human."* Elpenor, in his present shape was no match for a mouse. He was a sluggish cringing catfish, the size of Qo-oo-la.

"I hate to tell you this Ol' Podna," I said, "but you're not human either."

"Yeah well, your Papa peed on the courthouse lawn in broad daylight in front of nuns," Elpenor needled me and slunk around behind Qo-oo-la, who had taken up post on my right. Left red eye engorged with fighting blood.

Kaalpekci paused. "Ah I see you brought me a loon for dinner. And some strange little ugly fish."

"Who you calling ugly you under water garbage dump."

I said to Elpenor. "You can't run and there's no rock to hide under. I die you die."

"I'll need my full dragon power. And our other deal is off too."

My head was so airy, I couldn't remember what the other deal was anymore. "You got it," I said. "Go get em Podna."

A swirl of transformation sediment clouded the area out of which came Elpenor's voice. *"Harp, I told you the first morning there be dragons in this river. But no, you wouldn't listen. You were too damn stubborn to pay attention to your ol' Podna. Now look what you've got us into."*

Elpenor's baseline voice beat a steady rhythm in my ear. First time ever he never dropped a beat. *"I reckon you'd better get on out of here, out of my way. We gonna live here in the god-for-fucking-saken wilderness I'm gonna set some boundaries, define some territory. But I want you to know, you may never see me again."*

"That's a chance," I said, not without some sadness, "I'll just have to take."

A stout, gray, bushy tail swatted me in the face and a paw the size of a plow horses hoof, kick-shoved me backwards. The raging river gathered greater force, muddy water eddies swirled up from every footstep Elpenor, now a hybrid cross between the head of a raven and body of a coyote, made toward *Kaalpekci*. The petroglyph boulders rocked on their axis, spawning salmon stopped their relentless suicidal journey and hid their sex-crazed eyes. The two behemoths clashed, amidst grunts and growls and bones snapping and flesh tearing freeway sounds. I saw Elpenor and *Kaalpekci* carried, in a tidal wave of water displacement, back toward the dark pit *Kaalpekci* emerged from.

I saw them through the muddy swirl and if I looked real hard, also saw right through them, like some flattened aqueous mirages. Qo-oo-la and I watched them fade from sight. It took another few seconds for the stink of decay to follow. Then my feathered brother swam under my arm and buoyed me up from the bottom.

I was getting altogether too comfortable under the warm healing water.

> "Oh give me air,
> give me air,
> on the riverbank above,
> Don't give me fins."

I warbled. Even in my deep-breathing euphoric state, I needed a breath of air bad. Bird and I jetted to the surface.

55

Warm Tongues and Loon Hearts

Powerful hands waited to latch on to me. I, giddier still from the first fresh gasp of oxygen, was plucked out of the water like a hushpuppy from a hot-fat pot. What now, thought I, too weak and intoxicated to fight anymore? Was there still another conspirator waiting to deliver the *coup de gras*? And if so, did I care? Give me a bluegrass band to hang on my hearse wagon to raise hell as we stroll alone and El Dorado here I come. Hallelujah I'm a bird. Hallelujah, I'm a loon. Hallelujah, loon again.

Medusa barked in my ear and smooched my face. She had competition from another smoocher. I sniffed April's clean fragrance and felt her warm tongue and breath on my lips before my watery eyes cleared enough to see her. I clutched both April and Medusa in a cluster hug. Water squirted and squished, washing away some of the dreamlike film that cloaked my eyes.

Turgidity in the river slackened and spring salmon began to stir, relentlessly pursuing their date with destiny. I rubbed my eyes; perhaps the river demon had been but a Zen-like deep breathing vision. And Elpenor, was he gone forever?

I squinted from around April, who began dabbing at my banged head with a handkerchief, and saw Big Steve and Sheriff Gloeckler. Big Steve administered mouth-to-mouth resuscitation to the monster, who, of course, wasn't a supernatural monster at all, just your ordinary run-of-the-mill human variety of mass murderer/bottom-feeder. And Molly

Jenkins's and Billy Moody's killer. I still couldn't make out the identity of the drowned man. But I was pretty sure who it was.

Malcomb stood with his feet firmly in the river, in a trance. He waved his arms and proclaimed, "Here there be dragons no more. *Kaalpekci* is gone." Malcomb peered into the water — which had cleared somewhat — at the huge boulder that lay in two halves, like some mighty meat cleaver had struck it. Hmmm, I didn't hallucinate that earthquake.

I had to take a better look at my attacker. I released April and Medusa and crawled around an oxygen tank, gray tubing flat and flaccid, to the figure clad in a black wet suit.

Big Steve, fish knife lying alongside the body, had cut the head of the wet suit off, the better to gain easy access to the man's mouth and nose. By the way Big Steve took control, you could tell he knew what he was doing.

I stared into the face of the man/monster with the pale, petulant lips. It was Dylan Endicott. Dylan Endicott, the Olympic swimmer and computer genius. Dylan Endicott who, if I died, stood to inherit, through his wife, forty acres of mature second growth timber, a potential rock mine worth a fortune and several thousand feet of river frontage.

Endicott's slack lips had turned blue and his face, the charcoal color of kiln-burned ashes. Endicott no longer looked like a monster but like a frail human being overdressed for a party in ridiculous synthetic black skin.

I sat back on my haunches. Medusa plopped herself down in my lap staring up at me with a what-next-boss look, and April, began rubbing my blue feet.

"Aren't you freezing?" she said.

I clasped her wrist with a hand that, like my enlarged lungs, felt light and expansive. "I'm fine. Water's invigorating. In fact it's like a sauna. You should try it sometime when you're not all tied up."

Malcomb stopped chanting and stooped down to give me a close scrutiny. Placed a big rough hand on my forehead. "Sheriff Gloeckler and me have been on this river bank for over five minutes. No human could hold their breath that long. You have completed the metamorphosis. You are one with Qo-oo-la. The ancient legends that spoke of the return of the Changer God have come to pass."

Now April, maybe I can get a little more respect from you for your ancestors?"

"Yes Father, but it's over. No more persuading Harp to transform. He's fulfilled his destiny. He needs to stay a man now."

"Yes Daughter, I will respect your wishes." The old man looked at me. "I have been waiting for April to say 'Yes Father' in that tone of voice since she came back from Delaware."

I heard gurgling and hacking and spitting coming from Endicott. Good. I hadn't drowned him. Big Steve helped the scooped scuba diver to a sitting position. One fin and part of his wet suit had scraped off and his naked foot was crisscrossed with pale blue veins. Endicott's head swiveled, eyes blinking rapidly, lips quivering. Pink coloring flushed his cheeks. He saw me, eyes quit blinking, pupils opened wide, clutched Big Steve's massive shoulder. "That man . . . that man . . . is a freak. Save me!" Endicott also recognized Sheriff Gloeckler. "Arrest him! He's not human. He tried to drown me."

Gotta give him credit: one minute he's dead, the next he's accusing me of having killed him. All the studies indicate computer games give you quick wits.

Sheriff Gloeckler produced a pair of handcuffs. Endicott looked at me and managed a ghost of a smile.

Sheriff Gloeckler said, "American Airlines Flight 181."

"AA Flight 181?" said Endicott. "What are you talking. . . ? The pink fled from his cheeks. His breath came in small gasps.

Big Steve took Endicott's long slender hand from his bulky shoulder and held it out to Sheriff Gloeckler. The sheriff put the cuffs on. "Mr. Gravey here left me a message late last night. Flight records show you flew into Seattle the day before the murders and flew out the day after. You told me you were on the East Coast during those times."

"So what? Big deal. I forgot I visited some clients in the Northwest. I fly so much sometimes I don't remember what city I'm in or have been to. A lot of people in high tech do that."

"How about clients in the little logging town of Quilcene? A man of your description stayed in the only motel there during those time frames. And we already got a search warrant and searched your house down in Portland. Portland police found a twenty-two pistol your wife says you use at the target range quite a lot. It's at the lab. Arrogant bastard. Didn't even get rid of the murder weapon." The sheriff checked the cuffs for tightness.

"But how did you find out abo. . . ." And shut up.

Sheriff Gloeckler tipped his hat at me.

I said, "When we x-rayed Qo-oo-la we found an anvil image on the pin in his gizzard. A canted anvil image. I remembered playing your new computer game at the rehab center. Your hero was a blacksmith who was harassed by falling anvils and pigs and wasps. Hadn't a been for those pigs and wasps I never would have figured it out."

"Why did he kill Billy Moody, too?" said April.

The sheriff said, "We figure he arrived just as Molly took off running with the pin in her hand. Bad timing on Billy's part."

"I want a lawyer," said Endicott.

I said, "You should hire another programmer, your new game is a rip-off. It'll never fly "

"You have the right to remain silent. . . . "

From high on Kaalpekci Peak came a high pitched squealing. I could barely make out Barbie Jane's red tuft bow and pink pudgy snout peeking over the bluff. Stuck up there, by reason of morbid bulk. Also, beside the squealing pig, stood a boy. Emerson waved at me.

I waved back.

"I know my rights," Endicott said, "I refuse to ride in a vehicle with that overweight pig."

Sheriff Gloeckler cinched the cuffs a couple notches on Endicott's elegant wrists and jerked him to his feet. Eyeball to eyeball, he said, "Not

to worry. I wouldn't let my little girl ride in a vehicle with scum like you."
He shoved Endicott back a step. "Maybe I can get Mr. Harp P. Gravey,
a law-abiding citizen, to ferry my Barbie Jane and Emerson home?"

"I'd be most happy to oblige," I said.

Out on the Dosanomish, Qo-oo-la tested his damaged wings, taking off, running high on the water's surface, his athletic legs pumping
in an all out sprint. Wings flapping and feet slapping, Qo-oo-la took
flight and skimmed the top of the logjam, scattering raven and gull, who
auwked and *gronked* in protest, squabbling between themselves.

Qo-oo-la circled, climbing higher and higher, above the cottonwood
trees heading upriver in a high sky of unbroken blue, in the same direction he headed days ago when I so abruptly captured his consciousness.
There, waiting way up, Thunderbird called *"Cheeerkeee, cheeerkeee."*

I let go of April and Medusa, leaped up and shouted, "Don't forget
me!" No response. Without hesitation, I tried the song of the loon: I
wailed an ancient keep-in-contact melody reaching falsetto pitch. An
answering wail filled the river gorge and Qo-oo-la and Thunderbird braked
and turned, Qo-oo-la in the lead, dive-bombing toward me. He averted
and glided over my head, twisted his long necklaced throat, fixed me
with one bright red eye and transmitted a message. . . . *"You and I are
brothers under the skin. We are divers and singers together. There is no discord between us. This river and the Salish Sea are now our home. You must
never, never stray far from our home.*

*I have to leave you for the summer. I may already be too late. Gavia's sis-
ter calls me. She has so much power I cannot deny her."* Qo-oo-la and
Thunderbird flashed over us, flapped their wings out of the dive and
once again, headed toward the western Olympic Mountains.

I felt the sympathetic pull of Qo-oo-la's call to fulfill his mating urge.
My eyes, on the same level, were drawn to April's cheek where the gull
had pecked her. I wanted to kiss it and make it better.

The group stared at me. April said, "Your voice, my god, that's the
strangest sound I've ever heard."

Malcomb said, "It is the song of the loon-hearted one."

While everyone watched me, I watched the river. And saw, for mine eyes only, a giant catfish swim between the spilt boulder, with a derby hat in its mouth and the upright twitching tail of a coyote as a rudder.

Later, driving home, April rode shotgun. Barbie Jane was stuffed between the seats slobbering on my knee. Emerson was in the back seat with Medusa's head in his lap. Only a few cars were on Highway 101. It was a perfect time to put on my harmonica holder and play a soulful, summation tune like "Will The Circle Be Unbroken."

What could be more appropriate? No worries about dropping a beat. I could pick the heart out of that tune. My rhythm was back, melody truer than ever, soul primed to make music.

I reached in the glove compartment for my metal harmonica holder. Medusa lifted her head and barked. Barbie Jane gaacked. Emerson cleared his throat.

April looked at me over the bandage on her cheek. She looked at the harmonica holder. The middle of the bandage had a pink spot on it the size of a quarter.

"Right," I said. I put the holder back.

The last time I played music while driving I crashed into the Dosanomish. Could've hurt myself or Medusa. Worse yet, I could've hurt some other innocent party.

My picking and driving days were over.

The End

The text of TO KILL A COMMON LOON is
set in the Adobe Caslon typeface family.

Original chapter art illustration
Copyright © 2001 Barbara Macomber, Portland, Ore.

Photo by Sue Bronson

Mitch Luckett is an avid birder and claims to at least partially understand the "language of the birds." Although, when challenged on this claim, he will frequently go into a high-pitched yodel that will float your eyeballs.

Mitch has been a free-lance writer for twenty-five years with dozens of articles and several short stories published in regional magazines and newspapers. For over a decade he's written a monthly Naturalist column for the Audubon Society of Portland. Two naturalist pieces are in the anthology and guidebook to Portland, Oregon's natural areas, "Wild in the City." Also a bluegrass and old-time musician, Mitch combines two art forms, music and storytelling, into humorous and sometimes poignant stage performances.

Whether Ozark Mountain tall tales, narrative songs, Olympic Mountain parables, Native American myths or a book-length yarn, Mitch has a gift for the ancient art of storytelling.

TO KILL A COMMON LOON is his first novel.

To order or to
request a catalog:

Media Weavers, L.L.C.
P.O. Box 86190
Portland, OR 97286-0190

telephone: 503-771-0428